W9-BDC-314

THE PROPHECY'S CHILD

The Unseen

A novel by
W. E. D. Wilson

iUniverse, Inc.
New York Bloomington

This is a work of fiction. All of the characters, names, incidents, organizations, and dialogue in this novel are either the products of the author's imagination or are used fictitiously.

iUniverse books may be ordered through booksellers or by contacting:

iUniverse
1663 Liberty Drive
Bloomington, IN 47403
www.iuniverse.com
1-800-Authors (1-800-288-4677)

ISBN: 978-0-595-50447-3 (pbk)
ISBN: 978-0-595-49932-8 (dj)
ISBN: 978-0-595-61515-5 (ebk)

Printed in the United States of America

iUniverse rev. date: 1/19/09

This book is dedicated to the three people who have touched my life the most with their incredible gifts.

1. To Corporal Danny Davoit, Royal Army. You gave my life direction at an early age and taught me that reading opens a whole new world.
2. To Commander James Higginson, World War II Navy fighter pilot and uncle extraordinaire. You taught me the meaning of honor, loyalty, and duty.
3. And finally, to the anonymous mother who donated the kidney of her deceased son so that my youngest boy could have life. May God comfort you in your loss and pour out his blessings upon you.

"It is an abomination for Kings to commit wickedness: for a throne is established for righteousness."

Proverbs 16:12

It was a time of wonder, a time of conflict and growth; it was a time when one man had the power of life and death over his people with the wave of his hand—it was the time of kings. Israel was such a kingdom. No other kingdom in history has been conquered as much, divided, and had its people scattered throughout the earth, and yet still remained a nation. In almost every conflict, they were outnumbered, yet they emerged victorious. How could such a promised and powerful people lose such favor? The very kings who offered such promise failed at every level, and yet there was always hope with each ruler—hope that would ultimately disappoint. Kingship in the northern kingdom was plagued with instability and violence. Twenty rulers represented nine different dynasties during the approximately 210 years from the division of the kingdom in 930 BC to the fall of Samaria in 721 BC. In the southern kingdom, Judah, there were also twenty rulers, but these were all descendants of David (except Athaliah), and spanned a period of about 345 years from the division of the kingdom until the fall of Jerusalem in 586 BC. Why had the north failed so miserably over its southern counterpart? The answer lay in its loyalties, loyalties to another god—the God of Ba-al.

CHAPTER 1

THE DECEIT OF KINGS

807 BC

DAYLIGHT WAS SLIPPING AWAY in northern Israel, which promised a cooler existence for the wildlife inhabitants on the road to the mountains west of the Jordan River. Summer in the desert makes no promises, other than death for those unprepared for its wrath.

The peace of the late afternoon was shattered by the two chariots running at full speed on the valley road. The driver of the lead chariot looked ahead and saw the small encampment where fresh horses awaited them. The team of men at the camp looked up to see the approaching chariots and readied themselves to assist the travelers. The two-horse teams were almost spent as they came to a halt at the site. Men in the camp rushed to the chariots to change the teams. Once the horses were secured, the drivers and passengers stepped down onto the hot desert sand.The relief station had been chosen for its strategic value and remote location to avoid detection. The passenger of the lead chariot nervously looked back toward the west at the winding canyon road for any signs that they had been followed.

The tall dark-haired passenger of the lead chariot was clearly a man of authority. The deep blue tunic and cape, leather helmet, and breastplate were the uniform of the palace guard at Jezreel. As captain of the guard, Noam commanded respect from all who were in his presence, with the exception of the priest who accompanied him.

Noam stepped next to the trailing chariot and looked at the bundle lying on the floor. He looked up and addressed the priest standing to his left. "How is she?"

Isaac lowered the bladder of water after taking a long drink. "She is fine," he said, without looking at the girl.

The unconscious seven-year-old girl on the floor in the front of the chariot was dressed in peasant clothing and bound at the feet and hands with rope. Noam cringed as he looked at the dirt on her face. "At least clean the dirt from her," he ordered.

"There will be time for that at the camp," Isaac replied.

Disgusted at the sight, Noam took the bladder of water from Isaac and turned, walking back toward the west, looking for dust plumes in the distance. He took a long drink from the vessel, sighed, and thought, *"What have I gotten myself into?"* Only now was he beginning to understand the brutality of his mission. He couldn't pursue the matter any further; his loyalty and his oath precluded any intervention at this point. He had gone too far to stop the events of this day.

Isaac shouted at Noam with that irritating and demeaning voice Noam had grown to hate. "Let's go, Captain. We're ready!"

Noam walked back toward his chariot. He handed the bladder of water to one of the men and stepped up and into the chariot. Grabbing the reins to the horses, he glanced back to the west one last time before departing. With a crack of the whip and shouts from the drivers, the two fresh chariots sped off for the final leg of their journey. After negotiating the valley road, the lead chariot set the grueling pace as they climbed the thirteen percent grade of the mountain with their precious cargo. The driver's eyes were riveted to the narrow road as the outboard wheel came within inches of going over the edge at every curve. The four horses labored against the grade, maintaining the grueling pace at the lashes of the whips.

Noam had been the captain of the guard at the palace in Jezreel for eight years. His dedication to the security of the palace and the royal family was only exceeded by his loyalty to the man he was now rushing to meet. Noam's aide rode next to him, his bow knocked with an arrow at his side. From the trailing chariot, Isaac looked up and noted the position of the sun in the western sky. He shouted to the driver, "Faster … I tell you go faster or I will have the skin torn from your body with your own whip!"

"Yes, Lord," answered the frightened driver. He said nothing further as he knew it would only further anger his passenger; besides, they were only minutes away from the campsite.

The last two miles of the road made a long arcing right turn as it moved northward up the mountain to the campsite. The chariots' wheels slid on the hard surface of the road as they sped around the long curve. Their occupants leaned to the right, fighting the forces of gravity as the drivers continuously cracked the whips urging the horses on. Reaching the plateau, both chariots slid to a halt outside the largest of the tents, the horses stomping at the ground with saliva foaming from their mouths and sweat from around their harnesses. Isaac picked up the still unconscious little girl and rushed her into the tent, shouting to the women inside, "Prepare her, and be quick about it." Without responding, the four women took the girl and placed her on the table. They removed the bindings, undressed her, and began washing the girl in preparation for her new clothing.

The campsite was on the western side of the tallest peak in the area, and just two hundred feet from its jagged summit. On the eastern side of the mountain, over 1,500 feet below, lay the green and peaceful valley where the Jordan and Jabbok Rivers merged. The green valley was in sharp contrast to the arid and desolate location of the campsite. Far away from any traveled roads and forty miles from the nearest settlement, the secluded spot was perfect for someone avoiding travelers, and also perfect for this day's pending ceremony. The almost perfectly flat campsite was devoid of vegetation, and offered no protection from the blistering desert sun save the tents that had been erected for this day. The natural plateau with its twenty-five acre area was more than adequate for the 150 occupants. One hundred and fifty-three tents, two hundred and ten horses, seventy-five sheep, and fifty-eight carts dotted the landscape. The site had swollen to its current size over the last week for this day's ritual.

The 150 occupants had swollen from their original four members just eighteen years earlier. Four sons of priests—four children whose fathers and mothers were worshipers of Ba-al, and who had been executed by the Jewish King Jehu, just thirty-eight years earlier. Their crimes had been heresy of the highest order, fulfilling the orders of their pagan Queen Jezebel by killing the prophets of the God of Abraham. Once the four had learned of the murder of their parents, they vowed revenge.

They had waited decades for this day, to lead their converts to the sacrifice that would defy the God of Abraham and avenge their parents' and their queen's deaths. Thrown from the palace wall in Jezreel at the commands of King Jehu, Jezebel's body had been torn apart by dogs, leaving only her head, hands, and feet. Her priests and prophets had fared no better. They had all been killed either at Mount Carmel or inside the temple of Ba-al in Samaria. Once the children had learned of the horrific deaths, they began plotting the revenge that would lead them to this day. Over the years, the four became the self-appointed priests and high priest of Ba-al and the leaders of the resurrected followers of Jezebel.

Their following had grown slowly over the years and was comprised mostly of the descendants of the children of other Ba-al worshipers that had been killed by King Jehu. Exploiting the anger of the descendants, the four men slowly began rebuilding the following to its current size. The fear that they may suffer the same fate as their parents had driven the followers into seclusion. For almost two decades, the organization had avoided detection by conducting all of their services in secret. All communication within the order was conducted verbally. Only the high priest, Aaron, was allowed to possess any written material, which included their holiest of writings, the Sacred Scrolls. Recovered by Aaron from his father's possessions after his death, the scrolls had provided invaluable guidance to the followers for their worship and the events of this day. The scrolls were considered so valuable that they never left the house where he resided. Aaron naturally assumed the role of high priest, based solely on his father having previously had the same position. While Aaron placed complete confidence in his three priests—Ethan, Isaac, and Uriel—his very life was entrusted to the one man that had been at his side for ten years—Noam. He had secured

Noam's loyalty through the oldest of sins—greed. Noam's enormous wealth was due solely to the gifts of Aaron.

Noam stepped from the chariot and ordered the two men holding the horses to attend to the animals. He removed his leather helmet and walked to the bladder of water hanging from the tent pole. He bent down and poured a large portion of the contents over his head, and then opened his mouth and drank intensely.

Uriel approached Noam from the main tent. "Were you followed?" he asked.

"No. We were met outside the town with the child and then came directly here."

"Where is the girl's mother?"

"She escaped from my men at their house."

Uriel snarled at Noam. "You fool! You know she was to be killed here at the temple. They will discover us now."

Noam bristled at yet another outburst from one of this group of priests he had come to despise. He held back his disgust for yet another time. "Do not worry, Lord, my men will find her and kill her."

"And what of the father?"

"He was killed at the house, by your orders."

"Excellent. Our secret must be kept or we will suffer the fate of our ancestors and prophets."

"Do not worry. She will be dead before the sun sets."

Uriel nodded his acceptance and entered the tent. He approached the table and stood next to his assistants. He watched as the final preparations were being made to the girl lying on the table. The unconscious child was dressed in beautiful linens while two women painted her lips, cheeks, and eyes. The shallow breathing made her appear almost lifeless. Isaac turned toward Uriel. "Tell the Lord we will be ready soon."

Uriel bowed and exited the tent, walking toward the side of the mountain. He stopped and raised his head, looking at the sky. Small black clouds were forming over the campsite. How unusual, he thought; there was no wind accompanying the dark, fast-moving clouds. They were spinning in a large circle only fifty feet above the mountaintop. He continued walking toward the mountain as he looked up. A feeling of unease came over him as he stepped through the entrance.

The only indication of any access into the mountain was the six-foot-tall carved facade of the doorway, which was covered by stones when the site was vacant. The cave that would be transformed into the makeshift temple of Ba-al had been discovered by the worshipers eleven years earlier in their quest for a secluded spot to worship where they would not be discovered. Uriel entered through the doorway and walked through the carved hallway toward the cavern. The cooler temperatures inside the cave brought relief to Uriel as he breathed in deeply, enjoying the cooler air. The cave had proven to be suited to their purpose, once the work on the interior had been completed. The entrance sat at the midway section of the 150-foot-high cavern and provided an opening for the setting sun to enter. The descent to the cavern floor was made from the circular steps carved into the southern side of the cave. Dirt and rock had been carried in to form an almost perfectly flat floor. The western wall had been carved flat, ten feet high, to display the writings of the priests in worship to their god. A four-foot-high altar, six feet long and three feet wide, was carved from a naturally placed stone on the cavern floor and was fifteen feet from the western wall. A three-foot-square bronze box with its heavy bronze lid sat near the western wall behind the altar. Halfway up the eastern wall of the cavern, the workers had carved out a five-foot concave section that was inlaid with polished blue and white stones, surrounded by a ten-pointed star.

The cavern paled by comparison to the temple of Ba-al built by King Ahab in Samaria some sixty years earlier, but would serve its intended purpose on this day. This day—the seventh hour, of the seventh day, of the seventh month, of the seventh year, an innocent girl would be sacrificed on her seventh birthday—sacrificed to the God of Ba-al.

Uriel entered the temple and walked down the steps to the altar. The altar was illuminated by ten oil lamps placed in a circle around it. The lamps provided minimal light and gave an eerie amber colored tone to the cavern. Only shadows could be seen outside of the circle of lamps. The High Priest Aaron and his assistant Ethan were dressed in hooded robes of white linen that revealed little of the features of their faces. The full sleeves covered their hands, and the full-length robes touched the floor. Aaron's robe was adorned with blue linen bands around the cuffs and the opening to the hood. Gold thread was ornately stitched on the blue linen at the cuffs and the front edge of the hood. He wore a gold necklace, with the six-inch medallion of Ba-al attached at the chest level. Without looking up, he acknowledged Uriel's presence. "Yes?"

"Lord, the child is ready for you."

"I will be up for her soon," Aaron responded.

Aaron placed a leather pouch on the altar and unrolled it, revealing a ten-inch dagger. He bent at the waist and kissed the weapon, and then slowly stood, looking upward. "Lord, we have waited many years for this day. Your justice will be swift, your vengeance complete. We praise you for the honor of fulfilling your prophecy. Your daughter will be avenged. Accept this sacrifice from your servants in defiance of the God of Abraham."

Aaron bent over and kissed the dagger again, and then looked at the eastern wall and saw the beam of sunlight below the concave star. He calculated they had thirty minutes remaining. "*More than enough time,"* he thought. He and Ethan bowed at the waist facing the altar and slowly backed away with their hands out in front, palms up. Walking backward, they turned and proceeded toward the stairs.

The shadows of the camp from the evening sun were longer now, and the temperature had dropped ten degrees. Normal activities in the camp had ceased as preparation for the ceremony was underway. The rest of the inhabitants of the camp were now outside their tents and dressed in white linen robes. They stood silently, waiting for the ceremony to begin. Outside the main tent, Noam watched with a sense of unease as the black clouds continued to grow above the camp. He had never seen storm clouds such as these, black ominous clouds that were spinning in a large circle above the camp. The rest of the sky, all the way to the horizons, was clear and a beautiful deep blue color. *Could they be rain clouds?* he wondered.

Aaron and Ethan emerged from the cavern and walked toward the main tent. Aaron stopped in front of Noam.

"You are to stand guard over the temple. No one is allowed to enter once the ceremony begins, Noam," the high priest ordered.

"Yes, Lord," Noam responded, bowing at the waist.

Aaron and Ethan turned and walked toward the main tent. They stopped at the entrance and bowed their heads in preparation for witnessing the sacrifice that had been delivered to them. As they slowly entered, they watched the preparations that were nearing completion. The women bowed toward Aaron. He slid the hood of his robe back on his shoulders and looked at the girl lying on the table.

"We are truly blessed. The Lord has given us the sacrifice that will fulfill his prophecy. Praise be to Ba-al, the one true God," Aaron said, smiling as he looked upward.

He gently placed his hand on the girl's head. "Let us begin."

Uriel and Isaac stepped forward and lifted the girl from the table, placing her on a wooden-framed litter strung with strips of animal hide. She bore little resemblance to the innocent child who had arrived at the camp earlier. Her black hair was now in long curls that framed a heavily made-up face. The scent of perfume and oil surrounded her as she was dressed in a white linen robe, with blue and gold stitching. Her eyes had heavy black lines around them, and her cheeks and lips were rose colored. Gold jewelry adorned her neck and wrists, and a bejeweled crown of gold rested on her head.

The worshipers outside the tent bowed reverently as the priests exited the structure. Led by Aaron, the other three priests carried the litter and were greeted by the entire camp, assembled in a semicircle around the entrance. All of the worshipers, dressed in their hooded white linen robes, bowed when their high priest stopped in front of them. Aaron held out his hands at the waist, palms up.

"We have all waited a long time for this day … a day on which we honor our queen and her father. This day will be remembered as the date that the God of Abraham was defied and forever defeated." He pulled the hood back over his head and walked slowly, with a bowed head toward the temple.

An eerie howl came from the clouds above the camp and echoed throughout the entire site. The wind suddenly picked up and began to moan loudly as it sped through the camp. The clouds above grew larger and darker as a funnel appeared in the center and boiled with intensity, pulsing up and down toward them.

The startled Aaron jerked his head toward the sky and fixed his eyes on the growing funnel that circled above them. The wind began to pummel the worshipers with sand and pebbles as the tents swayed with the power of the wind. Even the animals looked for shelter—shelter that was not to be found.

The entire camp was now looking up at the ominous sky that was increasing in intensity. The funnel grew rapidly and extended its opening toward the camp. Spinning, whirling, growing larger and larger, it generated winds that hurled sand at them from all sides. Disoriented, they fell to their knees, covering their heads with their arms to avoid the onslaught.

The funnel boiled above them, howling, screaming, and increasing in power as it came closer to the ground. The moaning and growling from the clouds became ear splitting as the worshipers tried to get lower and lower to the ground. Aaron and his priests raised their heads in time to see the funnel cloud touch down in front of them, pulling the girl from the litter, vaulting her into the sky above them. They watched as she disappeared into the clouds. The wind and dust continued as the funnel pulsed up and down toward the camp from above.

Aaron and his assistants raised their heads and stared at the empty litter in amazement. The funnel withdrew, but the spinning black clouds remained. The worshipers appeared frozen to the ground, staring in awe at what had occurred.

Lightning flashed in the clouds, as the ear-shattering thunder became so unbearable the worshipers fell to the ground covering their ears, screaming and writhing in pain. Aaron, covering his ears, ran toward the cavern entrance screaming, unable to stop the pain. Before he could reach the opening, a bolt of lightning shot down from the clouds, engulfing him in flames. The crowd watched in horror as the flesh was burned from his body. None of the worshipers moved to help him as he cried out in agony. The intense flames burned his body completely, leaving only a pile of ash where he once stood.

Bolts of lightning began striking others in the group, burning them completely and leaving the same small pile of ashes. Ethan, Isaac, and Uriel knelt together in fear, watching the people around them burst into flames after lightning had struck them. The bolt of lightning shot down into the three men. They screamed in agony as they watched the skin melt from each other's bodies.

Gripped with fear, Noam ran toward his chariot. The horrible stench of burning flesh filled his nostrils as people were struck by bolts of fire all around him. He dodged and weaved his way through the crowd of people, watching them burst into flames as the bolts of lightning hit them. He jumped to the safety of his chariot, grabbing the reins and slapping them to the backs of the horses, speeding off toward the road leading to safety. Claps of thunder exploded above him as he turned and looked up, just in time to see the bolt of lightning that engulfed him in fire. His shrill screams of pain fell silent as the charred skin fell from his body.

Bolts of lightning continued to strike the camp until the screams of the worshipers had been silenced. Nothing was spared—animals, tents, carts, all were burned to ash. Nothing remained, not even a stick of wood. The approaching wind howled as it entered the camp, blowing the ashes into the air, scattering them for miles.

The bolts of lightning focused on the mountaintop above the site. One after another, they created explosions of rock falling on the barren plateau until the cavern entrance and the entire site were completely covered in rock and dirt. As quickly as they had started, the winds subsided and the clouds slowly dissipated. The vortex of black clouds evaporated, leaving the calm of another summer night in the desert. The entire site had been destroyed and covered for all time, never to be seen again. Only the peace of a starlit night remained.

CHAPTER 2

DISCOVERY

January 2000 AD

NOONDAY SUN BORE DOWN on the construction site in Northern Israel. Located on a mountaintop just sixty miles north of Jerusalem, the site was selected for its strategic importance. Sixth in a series of fifteen, the site had proven to be the most desirable for a missile defense battery once the construction was complete. The site proved to be ideal because the eastern side of the peak offered an unobstructed view from 1,500 feet above the Jordan River Valley, just eighty miles due west of Amman, Jordan. Even more desirable, the team had discovered during excavation that the western side had a natural plateau for the missile batteries. Of greater importance, the mountain had the potential to house a command bunker that would control six of the surrounding sites.

The completed project promised a level of missile defense unlike anything in the past. A lesson the Israeli military had learned in the first Gulf War of 1991. In spite of the accuracy of the Americans' Patriot missile batteries, the warheads had fallen on Jerusalem even after the Scud missiles had been intercepted. The entire eastern border would now be manned with the upgraded systems, denying the enemy access to any part of Israel from an eastern threat.

The United States construction company Smith, Harrison & Reed (SH&R) had been selected for the project because of their experience in military hardened facilities and the Top Secret clearance the company held. SH&R had chosen five teams of engineers to work on the project; each team would be assigned to three separate sites. Each team had been given ten months to complete their projects. At six months into the assignment, team two was on the final site, already ahead of schedule and, to the delight of the Israeli government, on budget.

Team two was headed by thirty-two-year-old Garrett Carter and his wife, twenty-nine-year-old Elizabeth. This would be the final assignment for Beth Carter, as she was three months pregnant. They had decided not to have children until their careers were established, but the surprise pregnancy had changed all of that. Beth had given notice to SH&R that she would be leaving the company once the project was completed to be a full-time mother. The Southern California native had grown up in an athletic and competitive family. Being the only girl in a family of four brothers had taught her to be aggressive in both her opinions and her sports. Her trim and fit body had turned a golden brown from the months she had spent in the Israeli sun. Beth's natural beauty afforded her the luxury of never needing makeup. The only flaw the natural beauty possessed was a tiny scar on her upper lip from a racquetball injury in college.

Gary and Beth had met and fallen in love while attending Northwestern University in Chicago eight years earlier. Gary had been the pursuer in the courtship. He had met her in a study group and was smitten with her from the beginning. Gary often commented that had she not ultimately succumbed to his charms, he would have gone bankrupt buying all the pizza he had purchased for the study group trying to impress her. The truth was Beth had noticed him from the beginning. It was a case of him chasing her until she caught him.

Upon graduating, they were married and began their careers with SH&R. The husband and wife team had the blessings of the company, and over the years had proven to be a beneficial asset to all parties. They were generally considered to be the brightest of the engineers on staff. Gary was the more cautious of the two, and his mannerisms more resembled a schoolteacher than an engineer. Hardly athletic, Gary's six-foot-three, 175-pound frame was always in a permanent slouch, a condition he attributed to being self-consciousness because of his height, which was almost a foot higher than his petite wife. His hair was usually in disarray and longer than he liked it, a condition of always being too busy to get to the barber. Of average looks, he often wondered how he had been able to catch such a prize as Beth. Beth, however, knew exactly what had piqued her interest; his soft-spoken manner and those light blue eyes that could stop her cold in her tracks. His rumpled clothing and carefully thought-out speech were the opposite of his wife. At five-foot-four, the blond-haired blue-eyed beauty tackled her job in the same manner she played racquetball, aggressively. The two different personalities made for a very successful team, both professionally and socially.

The Carters had been assigned construction at three of the sites—numbers four, five, and six. Six had been the most promising because of the plateau, the proximity to Jerusalem, and the old road that led to the site. Everyone involved was excited about the possibility of an early finish, especially Beth.

On the western side of the mountain, two D-10 Caterpillars were clearing what remained of the rubble from what they surmised had been a landslide that had occurred centuries earlier. A large construction trailer sat on the western edge of the plateau, surrounded by temporary living quarters and a fenced yard for construction equipment. The site was occupied by eight SH&R employees and one Israeli military liaison officer, Colonel Adar Stern.

Gary and Beth poured over the plans for the hardened facility inside the trailer. The plans were spread out over the four-by-six-foot table. Preparations were being made for tunneling into the mountain for the military installation. Colonel Stern reviewed the progress from the doorway.

"The Caterpillars will be done soon. We can start first thing in the morning," Stern announced.

Beth and Gary looked up from the table and decided to take a break from their task. They all walked outside the trailer into the noonday sun.

Clad in her usual cargo pants and tank top shirt, Beth pulled the sunglasses from the top of her head and covered her eyes as she looked at the Cats moving back and forth next to the mountain. Her long blond hair was pulled back in a ponytail and blew in the breeze as she wiped the sweat from her head and neck with her hand. "Can it possibly get any hotter in this place?" she asked.

"Yes, it can," Colonel Stern answered with a smile.

"I have never seen it so hot in January." She looked at Stern. "How do you people live in this oven?"

Gary chimed in. "Now, honey, this is the Promised Land. Be a little more tolerant." Stern smiled at the two Americans. This would be Stern's last assignment. At the young age of forty-eight, he was retiring after this job and devoting himself full time to his second love after the military—working on his farm.

"Well, I don't see much promise here … I miss green," Beth commented.

Gary took off his glasses and wiped them with his handkerchief. "Only three more months, honey. You can hold on for three months, can't you?"

"Okay, but if you see the turkey timer pop out of my stomach, just send me home in a doggy bag."

"Actually, I like you with a good tan," he replied, "and quit complaining. It'll give you wrinkles."

"Quit trying to suck up. It'll give you a black eye," she responded, trying not to laugh.

The three walked to the surveyor's tripod where Matt Hardesty was busy scribbling in his record book. Matt Hardesty had been on three jobs with the Carters, and not only appreciated their professionalism, but their humor as well. The forty-year-old surveyor routinely requested to work with the team.

"What does it look like?" Gary asked Matt.

"We're there. This could not have been better. I don't know what happened here, but a landslide covered an almost perfectly level plateau," Matt replied.

"Guess we just got lucky, Matt." Gary smiled back. "Can we start boring the tunnel in the morning?"

"Sure thing. We'll be done today. Jeff and Dave are clearing the last of the rubble against the hill with the Cats now. I'd say about three hours should see it done. Do the guys have the boring equipment ready?"

"Yeah, it's been checked and rechecked a dozen times. It'll be ready to rock and roll as soon as they're done," Beth replied.

Matt queried the pair. "How long do you think it will take to finish this up?"

Gary responded. "We think eight weeks should finish it."

"Good, I can't handle this heat anymore."

"You and Beth sound like a recording. Pete and Repeat," Gary said with a grin.

"No, Matt's not pregnant," Beth responded with a smile.

The four people watched from thirty yards away as Jeff Harper and Dave Puller chewed away at the dirt with their D-10 Caterpillars. Dave was concentrating on the mountain to his right as he slowly moved the Cat northward. His focus was so intense, his cigar had gone out. He unconsciously sucked on the smoke, trying to revive the fire. At twenty-five years old, the former Navy Sea Bee was the youngest member of the team though still very experienced. Called a "Jock" by the rest of the group, the tan and muscular six-foot man feared nothing, except his boss for this job, Elizabeth Carter.

Puller unconsciously chewed on the cigar with the right side of his mouth as he manipulated the controls. The Cat began to bog down from the weight at the blade. Dave eased in a little more throttle, but the big machine still continued to slow. The Cat was almost at a stop when he gave more power to the right-side tracks to turn from the obstruction. Dave could see the top of the boulder that was slowing him. He poured on the power as the Cat dug in with a growl from the engine. This was nothing; his machine had moved larger rocks than this. He knew what this piece of equipment was capable of, and this obstruction was not about to stop him.

Dave bit down hard on his cigar and opened the throttle all the way. The four people at the surveyor's site turned their attention toward the Cat as they heard the increased whine from the engine and saw the black smoke pour from the stack. Dave could feel the boulder beginning to move as the tracks grabbed at the ground. He smiled as the boulder pulled away from the mountain. "Atta girl, I knew you could …" The sudden explosion of dust and rock from the mountain enveloped the Cat and rendered it invisible to the onlookers. Gary instinctively grabbed Beth and pushed her to the ground, shielding her with his body to protect her from the approaching debris.

The cloud from the explosion rolled toward the four people, covering them with dust. All four of them slowly stood up, looking back toward the mountain. They looked to see the remaining people from the site running toward the Caterpillar. Jeff Harper was fifty yards from Dave's Cat when he saw the explosion. He raised the blade on his machine and opened the throttle to close the distance.

Dave's Cat finally came to rest as everyone stopped at its side. He emerged from the cab of the machine with his hands in the air. "I'm all right! I'm all right!" he shouted, with the cigar still in his mouth. He climbed down to meet everyone and survey the damage. Beth was the first to reach him. She grabbed his head and turned his cheek toward her.

"You got a nasty cut on your cheek. What happened?" She asked.

"It must be from the glass. The whole right side of the cab is gone," Dave responded with excitement and bewilderment in his voice.

"What the hell happened?" Gary asked Dave, as he brushed the glass and dust from Dave's head and shoulders.

"Don't know," he answered. "I ran into a boulder and put the hammer down to move it. Just when it broke free, the whole right side of the Cat rumbled … next thing I know, I'm covered in glass and dirt."

By this time, Jeff had brought his Cat to a halt and was running toward the others. One of the mechanics, Rudy Burton, also slid his pickup to a stop and exited with the first aid kit in hand.

"I'm okay, Rudy," Dave said, "It's just a cut."

Beth took the kit from Rudy and began cleaning and dressing the wound. "Quit fussing. I have to clean it so it doesn't get infected!" Beth said impatiently.

"Okay, Mom," Dave replied with a smirk.

As Beth continued to take care of Dave, Gary walked over to the side of the mountain and looked around. The Cat had continued to move ten yards beyond where the boulder was before Dave had been able to shut it down. Gary squinted his eyes to see through the dust around the side of the mountain.

An excited Jeff Harper looked back and forth at his colleagues. "I've never seen anything like it. It was like the whole side of the mountain exploded!"

Matt Hardesty, who had been standing near Beth and Dave, walked over to the truck and got a bottle of water that he handed to Dave. He then asked, "What could have done that?" Before Dave could answer, they all turned toward Gary as his voice rang out. "You guys need to see this!"

The dust had settled as Gary looked at the carved stone entranceway into the mountain. Dirt and stone still covered two thirds of the opening, but there was no mistaking that it was man-made. There was no writing carved into the façade to indicate its origins, but there were carvings of a bull, lightning bolts, and what looked like clouds on the edges of the opening. The darkness beyond the opening was less than inviting.

Colonel Stern was the first to break the silence. "Well, there goes the site," he said.

"What do you mean?" Dave asked.

"We just went from a construction site to an archeological dig," Stern replied.

Beth chimed in. "But we don't even know what it is yet. We should check it out."

"Ooooh, no you don't," Gary said, shaking his head, "you're not going in there!"

"Come on, Gary, just think. We may be discovering something really important. Aren't you curious?" Beth pleaded.

"Curiosity killed the cat, Beth!" Gary snapped back.

"Yeah, but satisfaction brought it back," she said, grinning with a childish smile.

Beth turned and looked at Colonel Stern questioningly.

"Okay," he replied, sighing. "I suppose we should make sure there's nothing important in there before we report it." His own curiosity aroused.

"Great!" Beth exclaimed excitedly.

Dave was already climbing back up on the Cat. "I'll have the entrance cleared in no time," he told them.

Rudy was jumping back into the pickup. "I'll get some lights from the compound!" he added.

Always the cautious one, Gary stood back quietly as he watched his wife and the others look on in childlike anticipation. He had seen this look on Beth's face before and knew he had little chance of changing her mind. They watched Dave as he removed the remaining boulders and dirt with the skill of a surgeon. Rudy pulled up in the pickup as Dave was shutting the Cat down. He exited the cab and walked to the back of the truck, lowering the tailgate. "Help yourself," he said, "There are plenty of lights for everyone."

Gary thought he would make a final plea for sanity to the group. "Come on, you guys. The thing exploded a few minutes ago. Dave could have been killed, and you want to throw caution to the wind?"

Beth came over and squeezed his hand. "It'll be okay, honey," she said. "Maybe it was just geothermic pressure … for once in your life, quit being such a stuffed shirt!" she joked.

"Okay, but I'm going in first, not you!" he ordered.

Gary walked to the cave entrance at the side of the mountain and stopped. He took a deep breath, sighed, and turned on the light. Beth nudged him in the back, and he stepped inside. The cool air coming from the cave would have been soothing had it not been for the musty odor that accompanied it. Gary cautiously moved forward into the darkness. The ceiling was just six feet high, causing him to stoop down to avoid hitting his head. He noticed that the roughly hewn tunnel had been hand cut from the tool marks on the rocks. He looked down, following the beam of the flashlight with his eyes to see that the floor they were walking on was covered in stone tiles. Always the engineer, he couldn't help but be curious as to how primitive people could place tiles together so uniformly.

"Look at this," Gary said, as he stopped to admire the work. "The tiles fit almost perfectly, and this was obviously done with primitive tools. How did they do this?"

"Come on, Indiana Jones," Beth kidded as she pushed at him from behind.

The tunnel continued for another fifty feet. Gary's light moved up and down the walls, admiring the work, as he inched his way along. His light was pointed at the ceiling when his beam disappeared into the darkness. The jerk from his belt stopped him immediately. He turned, shining his light on Beth, who was holding onto him with a frightened look. Startled, he blurted out. "What did you do that for?"

Without speaking, Beth pointed her light on the floor of the tunnel in front of Gary, revealing a ledge, and the darkness beyond. Gary felt his stomach sink as he realized what had almost happened.

"Thanks, honey," Gary said nervously. "That was a close one."

Standing on the five-foot-wide ledge, the flashlights from the group partially illuminated the cavern. Words escaped everyone as they took in the cave beyond. Even Gary had become excited to look at their discovery.

"How tall do you make this, Matt?" Gary asked the surveyor.

"A hundred and fifty feet maybe," Matt replied, "and about a hundred feet wide. It looks like a natural cavern that someone turned into a meeting place or quarters of some kind."

Dave panned the eastern wall of the cave with his light in an attempt to determine its full dimensions. As the beam passed by the midway point across from them, bright lights briefly danced around the inside of the room and then vanished. Startled, he moved the light back, stopping on the ten-pointed star on the opposite wall. With the beam pointed directly at the star, the light partially illuminated the cave. "Wow! Check that out," he exclaimed.

The team stood in awe at the sight before them. Blue and white beams of light danced off the walls of the cave. Dave set his light down on the floor of the landing and pointed the beam toward the star. They all remained silent, taking in the features of the room and feeling as if they might have stumbled into a holy place.

Gary moved back into the tunnel and kneeled down looking back into the cave. "From the looks and position of it," Gary announced, "it's supposed to capture the setting sun." But why, he thought. It makes no sense to illuminate the cave with maybe an hour's worth of light. Why would someone do that? Clearly this was constructed for a temporary purpose.

Beth looked to the right to see stairs that descended to the cave floor. "Come on, you guys. There are stairs over here. Let's go down."

Gary grabbed his wife by the shoulder, holding her back. "Honey, I've got a bad feeling about this place. None of this makes sense. Whoever built this thing didn't have permanence in mind. This whole place gives me the creeps. I don't think we should go any farther."

"Oh, Gary, you're too cautious," Beth replied.

"I'm not kidding, Beth. This is creepy. I feel like someone's watching us."

"Give it a rest, Gary. No one's watching us. Let's go."

Gary knew he couldn't stop his wife, but he felt compelled to try. He rubbed the back of his neck in a vain attempt to stop the tingling feeling that had now set in. It didn't work. He felt like someone's eyes were boring a hole in him.

The beams of light from the group danced around the cavern as they descended the stairs. At the bottom, they began to branch out to survey the cavern.

"Stay in close!" Gary barked.

Colonel Stern repeated the order. "He's right. Stay in close. We don't know if this cavern is stable."

The lead mechanic, Dick Hansen, shouted to Stern. "Hey, Colonel, what are these?" pointing his light to illuminate bronze stands placed around the cave.

"Oil lamps, I believe," Stern answered. "How many are there?"

"I count ten," Dick responded.

The group moved toward a stone table by the western wall of the cavern. Dave reached out to touch the cloth covering the table. It disintegrated in his hand.

"Don't do that!" Gary warned. "This is an archeological site. Everything in here is of extreme value and must not be disturbed."

"Sorry." Dave sheepishly replied.

Beth moved closer, shining her light on the table, illuminating the two small oil lamps on either side. Everyone was silent as they stared at the middle of the table seeing the ten-inch dagger lying on a leather skin sheath. There was no denying what the weapon was supposed to be used for.

"Okay, I am getting freaked out here!" Gary said, shakily. "Something here was supposed to die."

"It was probably for some sort of animal sacrifice. That was common in ancient times," Stern responded. His words had a calming effect on the group, easing Gary's concerns as well.

Gary called to the colonel as his light illuminated the western wall. "Hey, Colonel, there's writing on this wall. Can you tell what it says?"

Colonel Stern walked to where Gary stood, pointing his flashlight on the wall. "It looks like Aramaic."

"What does it say?" Beth asked.

"I can't tell. From what I can see, it's gibberish. It's random words all turned around."

"Wow … check this out!" Jeff shouted with excitement as his light shone on a metal box. "It looks like gold!"

Going over to where Jeff was standing, Gary bent over and brushed away the dust. "No, it looks like bronze." The group all gathered around the box.

Dave could hardly contain himself as the excitement in his voice echoed his emotions.

"There has to be gold or jewels inside! Let's take a look."

Jeff and Matt followed up with a chorus of excitement. "Yeah, let's get this lid off."

Beth came over to join the men and stood at the end of the box while Dave, Matt, and Jeff, without waiting for a response, kneeled and tugged at the lid. Suddenly, they stopped short and stood up sharply, staring at each other. Beth was standing the closest to them. They looked toward her with wide eyes as the haunting female voice entered their ears in a caressing whisper. Dave, Matt, Jeff, and Beth all looked at each other with a frightened look on their faces.

"Did you hear that?" Jeff asked in a choked whisper.

"What was that?" Dave replied.

Beth nervously turned to the others who were standing behind the stone table. "Did you guys hear that too?"

"Hear what?" Gary asked.

"It was a woman's voice!" Beth exclaimed.

"A woman's voice? You're joking," Colonel Stern replied.

"What did it say?" Gary asked.

"I don't know what language it was, but it was definitely a woman's voice." Beth turned to Jeff, Matt, and Dave. "Did you hear it too?"

"Yes." They all replied in unison.

Beth turned toward Gary with a look of concern on her face. "Suddenly, I think Gary is right. We need to leave here now." Beth smiled at her husband with an apologetic look on her face.

Ignoring Beth's pleading, Jeff and Dave leaned back down and pushed against the box's lid.

"Come on, you guys, let's get this thing open!" Dave said.

With their feet planted firmly on the ground and their hands on the lid of the box, they both grunted and pushed with all of their strength. Almost immediately, Beth's hands reached to cover her ears. The woman's voice, no longer a whisper, began screaming with rage. Beth bent over in pain.

Gary took two steps toward his wife just as the box's lid slid to the side. The resulting explosion of gas and dust coming from the box knocked everyone to the ground. Dave, Matt, and Jeff were slammed against the wall. Colonel Stern and the others were thrown down and pushed away, sliding on their backs. Beth was blown against the west wall, hitting her head and falling into unconsciousness as her body crumpled to the floor. The howling coming from the box was ear shattering. The moaning, shrieking voice filled everyone's head, forcing them to cover their ears, trying to protect themselves. The smell now permeating the air was horrific, filling everyone's nostrils with an unbearable stench.

Gary grabbed a flashlight and crawled, reeling in pain from the screams, to where his wife lay. He kneeled at her side, checking her for signs of life. He held his left index and middle fingers on her neck, the carotid artery responding with the hoped-for thumping. The pain was searing, and Gary felt his body going limp. "No!" he shouted, as he began to slump over his wife. The last thing he saw before losing consciousness were the writings appearing on his wife's forehead, writings like those on the wall of the cave.

"No ..." he defiantly moaned as he fell over Beth's body, falling into unconsciousness along with the others in the cave. The woman's screams faded, slowly falling away until gone.

CHAPTER 3

A REVELATION

June 2007

MORNING WAS JUST BEGINNING for the residents of Lake Forest, Illinois. Early June in the Chicago suburb meant that soon the neighborhoods would be filled with the voices of children enjoying their summer break. At many of the homes, the children were already sitting down to breakfast and readying themselves for the activities of the day—with the exception of one—one well-groomed, but quiet house on Maple Street.

Built in 1932, the gray and white trimmed two-story Cape Cod was home to Gary and Beth Carter and their six-year-old daughter, Allyson. The neighbors saw very little of Gary and Beth, and almost never saw them together. Not one of the neighbors had seen Allyson since her first birthday. A selected few of them had become friends to Gary and Beth, but had not enjoyed the usual invitations to dinner or the backyard barbecues most of the other neighbors enjoyed. They seemed to be satisfied by the explanations from Gary and Beth that Allyson was a "special needs" child, although they thought to themselves that even a handicapped child would come outside from time to time.

Dressed in his gym shorts and a white T-shirt, Gary opened the front door of the house and walked to the lawn where the morning paper lay. He heard his neighbor's greeting from across the street as he picked up the paper.

"Morning, Gary," Walter Dixon called out while watering his flowerbed.

"Hi, Walt," Gary replied with a smile and a wave of his hand as he walked back inside the house.

Gary walked into the kitchen, unfolding the paper and scanning the front page. Beth was at the stove making breakfast. Gary walked over to her and kissed her on the cheek. "How's Ally this morning?"

"She's fine, honey," Beth replied. "You know, I think she's really showing signs of improvement recently. She's become more active and alert over the last few months."

"Has she eaten yet?"

"Yes, she just finished and is at the table with her pads of paper."

The past seven years had aged Beth disproportionately. Her once golden hair was now streaked with gray. The thirty-five-year-old woman now looked as if she was in her mid forties. Her once long hair was now cropped short above the neckline, and age lines now adorned her face. She no longer possessed the trim and fit athletic body she had once enjoyed. With very few opportunities to play her beloved racquetball, she could feel and see the fifteen extra pounds that had magically appeared, seemingly overnight. Gary had done no better age wise over the past seven years. He now sported an extra twenty-five pounds and a lot more gray hair than he had ever wanted. The wrinkles in Gary's face came from both the worry of his daughter's condition and the increased workload he had placed on himself. After Allyson's problems began, he had taken a management position with SH&R to avoid the regular out-of-town trips a field position demanded. He helped his wife whenever he could and was always available to stay at home with Allyson when Beth wanted to enjoy some time away, albeit rarely. No matter how tired or stressful his day had been at work, he would immediately usher his wife out of the house when he got home so she could enjoy some quiet time if she needed it. The burden of raising a shut-in child was great, but the love they shared had carried them through the roughest of times. The birth had been normal, although Allyson had arrived two weeks early. The joy of her entry into the family had been short-lived however. Within months, she began to have problems. Her screaming episodes set the family on a path they could have never believed possible.

The inside of the Carters' home had been changed very little since being built. The original light oak trim surrounded the windows and doorways, and the heavy oak interior doors still retained the original cut glass knobs. The kitchen still had the original heavy wooden cabinets, painted in white with thick white tile countertops. The large and heavy antique cherry wood kitchen table and chairs had become the central meeting place for the Carters. Beth's love for antiques accentuated the home and retained the original flavor of the early thirties construction.

Gary sat at the kitchen table reading the morning paper as Beth placed a plate of bacon and eggs in front of him. "You better hurry up and eat, honey. Bill will be here soon," Beth said.

Gary turned and looked at the clock over the stove, which now read seven forty. "I will, babe," Gary replied, as he hurried through the meal.

Saturdays at the Carter house were reserved for their best friend's weekly visits. Even though he would have enjoyed relaxing for the entire weekend, Gary dedicated Saturdays to Bill Monroe, the only person who had given Allyson any hope.

Beth was standing at the sink washing the dishes when Gary set his plate on the counter next to her. He reached around and hugged her from behind. "I love you, babe," he whispered in her ear.

"I love you, too," Beth responded.

"Oh yeah, how much?" Gary said smiling.

"Two weeks," she replied with a grin.

The family joke had started years ago while Gary was still working in the field. He would give Allyson a hug and kiss before going out of town, telling her he would be back soon. When she would ask, "How long?" he would respond, "two weeks." To Allyson, two weeks seemed like forever. After a while, when she would say, "I love you" to Gary, he would smile and ask, "How much do you love me?" Her response would always be "two weeks." Despite Gary and Beth's daily interaction with Allyson, she would almost always respond with a head nod. On rare occasions she would speak, but never in sentences of more than two or three words.

Gary hurried up the stairs, skipping every other step. Beth was wiping off the table as the doorbell rang. She hurried to the front door, wiping her hands with the dishtowel. She opened the door with the usual warm smile she offered to their best friend and mentor. Bill Monroe smiled back as he stepped forward to hug Beth.

"Coffee?" she asked, as they both walked toward the kitchen.

"You bet," he responded with enthusiasm.

The fifty-eight-year-old theology professor and widower had been friends with the Carters for almost four years. Bill had a grandfatherly look, with his full head of completely gray hair and bushy gray moustache. At five-foot-eight inches and 225 pounds, Bill looked more like a football player than a theologian. His demeanor, however, was anything but that of a ball player. His gentle voice was soothing and professional. Dressed in his usual slacks and golf shirt, Bill always looked professional.

After medical reasons for Allyson's condition had proven to be unfounded, the reverend at their church had referred them to Bill. It had been the right choice, as Allyson seemed to enjoy his company. That is to say, she didn't scream when he came into her room, as she had done with all the previous visitors and caregivers. Bill had taken on the challenge of helping with Allyson's growth. Although progress was minimal, Gary and Beth were pleased with any kind of progress at all.

His weekly visits to the Carter home had become something Bill enjoyed and anticipated. A professor at Northwestern University, Bill had access to all the information and medical experts he could ever want. Allyson had initially been diagnosed by doctors as autistic, something Bill had rejected from the beginning. He had always seen something in the girl's mannerisms and character that indicated otherwise; he had just not been able to put his finger on it yet. He never gave up the hope that at some point he could bring their little girl back to Beth and Gary.

Beth had given up long ago on medical answers and theories regarding her daughter. Always reserved in her analysis, she had come to believe that Bill's grandfatherly image kept Allyson calm. His gray hair and moustache seemed to be a point of focus whenever Bill talked to her. Bill, more than any other person outside of the family, had been able to interact with Allyson. The Carters had seen more progress since he began working with Allyson. Beth truly welcomed his visits.

"How's my girl doing today?" Bill asked.

"She's fine, Bill," Beth replied. "How are you enjoying your summer break?"

"Good, although you wouldn't know it by my golf game," he responded with a sarcastic smile.

"You can't be good at everything, Bill," Beth said laughing.

"I'm not asking for good. Mediocre would be acceptable," he quipped with a smile. "Is Allyson continuing to write more?" he asked.

"Yes, she is. I don't know if it means anything, but she's drawing more of the bird pictures, too. I still can't make out the words she's writing, if they are even words at all. If I didn't know better, I'd say it looks more like a foreign language than English. Her lines run together so much, you couldn't make it out anyway, but it sure looks like some kind of words to me."

Bill smiled. "Beth, for the first time in a year, I am optimistic. Any change is good at this stage."

"Me, too," Beth replied enthusiastically. "I can't explain it, but it's almost like she's communicating more." Beth's words were more hopeful than analytical. Over the years she had seen her hopes dashed on so many occasions that she now found it hard to be optimistic. But this time seemed to be different; Allyson had been writing and drawing at a substantially greater rate.

Gary rounded the corner into the kitchen, opening the fridge door to get a bottle of water. He put his hand on Bill's shoulder, winking at his friend. "What you got for us today?" he asked as he sat down at the table with them.

Bill put on his reading glasses and opened his notebook. His notes on Allyson were extensive and increased in their volume on a weekly basis.

"Did Dr. Harris have anything to say about Ally's increased activity?" Beth asked.

Darren Harris was one of Northwestern University's professors of psychology and Bill's very good friend. Bill had involved Dr. Harris in

Allyson's condition from the beginning and kept him abreast of her progress on a weekly basis. Although he had never been to the Carters' home, Dr. Harris had proven to be invaluable to Bill's analysis.

"He's more clinical than I am," Bill replied. "But he believes it could be positive. Keep in mind though, he's never seen her. He's responding only to my notes."

"But still, increased activity is a good sign, right?" Beth asked hopefully.

"Yes, that's his analysis," Bill responded. "And mine as well. But keep in mind, I'm not a medical doctor."

"If she could only respond in kind vocally, that would be *real* progress," Gary added.

"Yes, but it may take more time. Slow growth is better than no growth at all," Bill replied.

Gary patted his friend on the shoulder. "I know, Bill. I'm sorry. We just get so hopeful at times."

Bill smiled back at his friend. "It'll be fine, Gary. God created Allyson for a purpose, and that purpose will be fulfilled … but in his timeframe, not ours." Gary nodded his head in agreement. He had felt helpless in the growth of his daughter. He constantly fought the urge to become jealous at the attention Allyson had given to others. All he ever wanted was what every other father on earth had wanted, the love of his children.

"Is she up for visitors?" Bill asked them both.

Beth smiled at Bill. "She's always available for you, Bill."

Bill sat his coffee cup on the table and followed the two upstairs to the second-floor master bedroom carrying his notebook with him. Gary and Beth had sacrificed the large master bedroom to Allyson because of its size and the adjoining bathroom. Beth opened the door slowly and entered the room, with Gary and Bill following behind. The eighteen-by-twenty-four foot room was more than suited to its purpose. The room's four windows had been blacked out with paint and heavy cotton drapes covered them completely. Outside light had no possibility of entering the room. Inside, the walls were painted powder blue with white trimmed woodwork, and bright white curtains hung over the windows to brighten up the room. A single bed sat against the inside wall, away from the windows.

Gary and Beth had everything in the room they needed to take care of their little girl, allowing for them to spend as much uninterrupted time with her as possible. Two reclining chairs sat in front of a twenty-seven-inch television; a stereo and small refrigerator lined one wall. The room even had a microwave oven on a table in the corner for small meals. The center of the room was dominated by a six-by-three-foot dinner table used for many of the family meals and doubled as a workstation for Allyson.

Sitting at the table with her back to the door was Allyson, her long dark red hair in neat pigtails, and her slight figure dressed in her favorite flower-print knee-length dress. She didn't acknowledge them entering the room, her focus entirely on the eleven-by-eighteen-inch artist pad that lay on the table. Each day, Beth bathed and dressed Allyson in clean and bright clothing. She always said it was to cheer Allyson up. The truth was it brought a sense of normalcy to Beth that was missing with Allyson. Beth kneeled down next to her daughter. Softly, so as not to startle her, Beth said, "Doctor Bill is here to see you, honey."

Bill sat down in the chair next to her. Allyson turned slowly and looked at him. The beautiful little girl had not only an innocence about her, but a sadness that could be seen in her blank stare. Allyson had been given her mother's beautiful features and the one characteristic Beth loved so much—her father's hauntingly beautiful light blue eyes. Her hand reached out and gently touched the moustache that always seemed to fascinate her.

"It's good to see you, Allyson," Bill said as he gently placed his hand on the top of her head. Her eyes looked into Bill's as she smiled softly at him, before quietly turning back to her work. Bill gently patted her on the back as he stood up from the chair. This was always the most difficult time for him. To see this sweet and gentle little girl locked in a room, a prisoner in her own house. The true sadness of it was that Allyson preferred the solitude and security of the room that had become her only world. Bill once again had to choke back the tears, thinking about how this little girl should be outside playing with friends, laughing, running, and experiencing life. Instead, she spent her days locked away in a darkened room. His only solace was in knowing she had two parents who loved her deeply.

Bill looked at the surface of the table. The usual clutter of used art paper with Allyson's drawings and writing covered the tabletop. Gary kept a supply of the pads and boxes of pens and crayons for her at all times. She only took her focus away from the pads long enough to eat and sleep. Bill looked more closely at the pieces of paper scattered on the table. He picked up one of the sheets with the bird drawings on it.

"The drawings look almost like blue jays. Split and forked tails, with wings and open mouths," he said.

"They're all the same, with the beak open like that," Beth replied.

"It doesn't make any sense," Gary chimed in. "The only bird pictures she's ever seen are in the books Beth has used for teaching her. Why she would fixate on birds specifically is beyond us."

Allyson's days were always the same. After waking up, eating, and bathing, she would sit at the table, drawing and writing. Once a page of the pad was full, she would tear it off and start on the next page. The routine was repeated throughout the day, using up a minimum of two of the 150-page art pads each day. Not bothering to look at her work, she would tear the page away from the pad and immediately begin writing and drawing on a new page. Beth, Gary, and Bill had assumed the writing was words, but could not make out the characters. Gary referred to them as *hieroglyphics*, but felt in his gut that it was writing, due to the order in which they were written. The tabletop was always full of the completed pages. The only interruptions were for meals, sleep, and the occasional preapproved visitor.

Bill began his weekly ritual of taking notes on Allyson's progress. He pulled the chair up to the table and sat next to her. After asking her if it was okay, he would take her blood pressure and temperature from the medical bag that was kept in the room and enter the results into his notebook. He would record her movements and facial expressions as she scribbled on the pad. On rare occasions, Allyson would even allow him to check her reflexes. Questions asked of her were rarely answered, but when she would speak, the sentences were of the usual three or less words. He would take the results of his findings back to his home and enter them into the computer file he painstakingly maintained. Bill began the final portion of his session by reviewing the pages of the art pads Allyson had completed.

His eyes locked onto one of the pieces of paper he had not noticed before. He focused on the word in the center, the characters looking strangely familiar. Could it be possible, he thought. He gathered several of the papers and motioned to Gary and Beth to leave the room with him. He bent over and kissed Allyson on the head. "Good-bye, honey," he said. Allyson, not replying, continued to work on the drawing in front of her as they left the room.

Beth was the last one out of the room. "What was so interesting?" she asked, as she closed the door.

"These," Bill replied. "I need to do some checking, but if I'm correct, and what I think is happening is true, this could be a major breakthrough."

"What in the world are you talking about, Bill?" Gary asked.

"Come on, let's spread these out on the table downstairs," Bill answered, as he descended the stairs. When he reached the kitchen, he began clearing off the table to make room. His excitement was clearly visible as he laid out the pieces of paper. He reverted to the role of university professor as he put on his reading glasses and began pointing to the words on the papers with his pen.

"I believe we are looking at something amazing," Bill finally explained. "It didn't hit me until I remembered Beth saying how it looked like she was writing in a foreign language. As incredible as it sounds, I believe that may be exactly what is happening."

Beth was the first to say what she and Gary were both thinking. "Are you mental?" she exclaimed. "A six-year-old special needs girl writing in a foreign language? What … in Greek?" Beth asked sarcastically.

"You're not far off," Bill responded with a serious tone in his voice.

"What?" Gary exclaimed, not believing what he was hearing.

"Look, I don't speak or write the language, but this looks like Hebrew," Bill replied.

"Okay, Bill, this isn't funny anymore," Gary said, the frustration clearly building in his voice.

"Look at this," Bill said, pointing to one of the words. "If I remember correctly from my doctoral thesis thirty years ago, this word here is Hebrew. The characters Allyson is writing aren't very good, and the lines run together a lot, but this clearly looks like Hebrew."

"Wait a minute, wait a minute!" Gary snapped back. "Can you tell me how my six-year-old daughter, with a diminished capacity no less, can write in Hebrew? This writing, as you call it, just looks like gobbledygook to me, more like Egyptian hieroglyphics, and you somehow see a foreign language?" Gary's frustration was mounting by the minute.

"Calm down, honey," Beth said as she put her hand on Gary's arm. "This can all be verified easily … right, Bill?"

"Yes. There is translation software available at Northwestern, but I have an old friend in D.C. that's a linguist. He could make sense of this in a New York second," Bill answered.

"Fine, then. Let's all calm down until we can find out for sure," Beth said as she looked at Gary, with a furrowed brow.

"Okay," Gary said, visibly calmer. "Who is this guy, Bill?"

"He's an old army buddy of mine, a retired colonel, that works part time for the Smithsonian," Bill answered.

"And he can read Hebrew?" Beth asked.

"Yes," Bill replied. "He reads writes and speaks several different languages, most of which are Middle Eastern."

"So what do you need to do?" Beth said.

"I need to get this stuff back to my house where I can scan it and email it to him," Bill said as he gathered up the papers.

"Okay, so you'll call us when you know something?" Beth asked Bill as she walked with him to the front door.

"Yes—yes I will." Bill stopped at the door, hardly able to contain his excitement. "I will call you as soon as I find out." He spun around and headed down the driveway toward his truck.

Bill was almost trembling with excitement as he entered his truck. Why hadn't he seen this before? Either Allyson was focusing more on her writing, or he had arrogantly assumed it was a poor attempt by her at the written word.

As they walked back into the house, Beth turned around and lightly punched her husband in the chest. "What's the matter with you? I've never seen you launch like that, especially on someone who is trying to help us!"

"I know, honey. I'm sorry. I guess I just felt like Ally was being made out to be a freak. Maybe I'm being too protective of her. I don't know."

"You know, if Bill is right, this could be a real breakthrough."

"But, honey, a foreign language? How could that be possible?"

"I don't know," Beth admitted. "But it's like you said—*any* progress is good."

Gary smiled at his wife. "That's why I love you so much. You keep me grounded."

"Oh, yeah, how much do you love me?" Beth replied.

"Two weeks," Gary responded as he hugged his wife.

CHAPTER 4

THE HOOK

SUMMER IN THE NATION's capital meant two things for the permanent residents: humidity and tourists, both of which are begrudgingly tolerated. Georgetown, located to the northwest of Washington, D.C., only had to tolerate the humidity, with the exception of the occasional tourist looking for the house where *The Exorcist* was filmed. A quieter version of downtown D.C., Georgetown was filled with sidewalk cafés, charming boutiques, and what residents consider the best university in the nation. To live in the area, one had to accept three conditions: very little yard, no parking, and traffic that would choke off the best-laid streets in any city of the world.

Located in the historic Cleveland Park area of Georgetown, the three-story red brick townhouse on Macomb Street was home to Clayton Harker, a retired U.S. Army Colonel. The home was not much different from the surrounding townhouses. The wood trim had been painted a bright white, with a heavy, dark-brown stained front door. The front porch, once adorned with brightly colored flowers hanging in pots, had been enjoyed by all the neighbors. The flowerpots remained, but for almost six years now, the flowers had all died, leaving brown twigs in their place.

Clay and his wife had purchased the seventy-five-year-old Brownstone in 1976 during his first assignment at the Pentagon. After an extensive remodel, they had enjoyed the fruits of their labor until his wife and daughter's deaths on September 11, 2001. Their bodies had never been recovered from the rubble of Flight 77 that hit the Pentagon. Nothing seemed to matter to Clay since their deaths. An only child, Clay had been completely alone since Mary and Jody's deaths. Mary's parents and her two sisters had vowed to keep in touch after Mary died, but distance had proven to be the enemy. Although he had not realized it, his own parents' deaths in 1980 and 1984 had sealed his fate as a recluse. His life had been completely dedicated to his family.

The once brightly lit and cheery interior of the home was now dark and dreary. All of the windows and curtains had been closed years ago, allowing the musty smell of cigars and dust to fill the house.

The fifty-seven-year-old colonel was fast asleep in one of the two spare bedrooms of his home. The folding card table next to the bed was covered with books, newspapers, an ashtray filled to overflowing with cigar butts, and an empty pint bottle of Jack Daniels. Clay had not slept in the master bedroom of his home since the death of his wife and daughter, nor had he gone a day without drinking himself to sleep. His daughter's room remained the same as the master bedroom, untouched for over six years. The alcohol had become his surrogate wife and a companion he never failed to embrace. On several occasions, he had contemplated putting a gun to his head, not wanting to endure the pain of loneliness any longer, but preferred the extended version of suicide through alcohol. For the past eight years, since his retirement, the former intelligence officer and linguist had been employed as a consultant for the Smithsonian Museum. Most of his work was performed in the den downstairs. The bedroom, however, doubled as a spare office, which was evident from the clutter on the table.

The quiet of the room was interrupted by the ringing phone next to his bed. A low groan came from under the sheets that covered his head. A hand slowly emerged from under the sheets and groped for the phone on the nightstand. The receiver was lifted and then promptly hung up. The hand disappeared back under the sheets. The phone rang for a second time. The groan was louder now. "Ooh rats!" the voice bellowed.

Clay was lying on his stomach and slowly pulled back the sheets and answered the phone, pulling the receiver to his head. "What?" he barked.

"Don't tell me you're still asleep!" Bill Monroe exclaimed.

"Monroe, you had better have a damn good reason for waking me up on a Saturday morning."

"It's ten o'clock in the morning, Clay. You sick?" Bill asked.

"No—tired. What do you want?" Clay protested sarcastically.

"Come on, Clay, get out of bed. This is important."

"I'm retired. Nothing is that important anymore."

"Come on, be all you can be. Get your butt out of bed, light a cigar, and turn on your computer."

"Okay, okay—hold on. I'll go down and get the cordless." Clay laid the phone down and slowly slid his legs off the bed. He arched his back and yawned while scratching at his stomach. He slowly stood up with a moan and walked over to the cigar humidor on top of the dresser. Pulling a cigar out, he cut the end off with the guillotine cutter and placed it in his mouth. Clay adjusted his boxer shorts and mumbled at the phone through the cigar in his mouth as he walked past the nightstand. "Hold on, be right there."

The colonel was still an intimidating figure at six-foot-one inches tall and 215 pounds. Very little of his weight had made its way to his midsection, but his gait had been changed over the years from the wounds he received in Vietnam. Large deep scars could be seen on the upper portion of the hamstring on his right leg from the wounds of his last engagement. Although the wounds had healed over the years, his steps were noticeably slowed by the slight limp. His hair was now a deep salt-and-pepper gray, but still cropped in a traditional military crew cut. Lines of age cut deeply into his face, but his gray eyes still displayed the fire of a warrior. He had become more and more of a recluse since his wife and daughter's deaths, but he never failed to make time for his lifelong friend, Bill Monroe.

Other than neglect from its lone occupant, the three-story townhouse had changed very little over the years. Mary Harker had insisted on neutral colors of beige and white for the walls and ceilings, with light oak hardwood floors. The home still retained her subtle feminine decorating touch, something that Clay had complained about as being "too girly" when she was alive, but now vowed to never change. He spent most of his time either in the home or at work, something that was clearly evident from his less than desirable cleaning skills. The vacuum cleaner was rarely turned on and sat out in the open against the wall of the living room.

Clay made his way down the stairs and into the den next to the living room, turning on the computer. He turned on the desk lamp and shuffled through the mountain of papers until finding his wireless headset. With the device on his ear, he threw the switch to the "on" position. With a yawn he made his announcement. "Okay, I'm ready. What's up?"

"How's your Hebrew?" Bill asked.

"It's still working—why?"

"I need your help with translating something."

Clay was walking to the kitchen as he spoke. "Why? That excuse of a school you work for doesn't have a language department?" Clay had always enjoyed every opportunity to take a jab at Bill's university, claiming that his alma mater of Georgetown was the better of the schools. He poured himself a cold cup of coffee from the pot and placed it in the microwave.

"Yes, it does, but I really need an expert's help, and I can't wait until Monday," Bill answered.

Clay opened the microwave to grab his coffee. He pulled open the silverware drawer to see an empty spoon slot. Turning and reaching into the sink of dirty dishes, he pulled out a spoon and stirred some milk into his coffee.

"Is the computer up yet?" Bill asked.

"Hold your horses, I'm getting a cup of coffee!" Clay said as he walked back to the den.

"So, Colonel, you still drinking your life away?" Bill asked, changing the subject.

"Yes," Clay answered sarcastically. "Are you still putting your nose in other people's business?"

Bill laughed on the other end of the phone. "How's the job at the Smithsonian going?"

Clay put the cigar back in his mouth and searched the top of his desk for the matches. "Not bad ... this contractor thing is really working out well. I set my own hours and don't have to answer to a bunch of pencil pushers. If I had known then how good it was, I would have never put thirty years in the army."

"Well, I wish I'd done thirty years. If I had, I wouldn't still be teaching," Bill replied.

Clay lit the cigar and puffed out a huge stream of smoke. "Well, you know what they say? Those who can, do—those who can't, teach." They both laughed. Bill and Clay had a history together unlike anyone else. The thirty-nine year friendship started the day they had met in Vietnam. Bill had dragged his friend to safety after Clay had been hit in the leg by an AK-47 round. Although many years had passed, Clay's limp constantly reminded him of the debt he owed his friend. The voice from the computer announced loudly, "You've got mail."

"Okay, the file is here. What am I looking for?" He asked.

"There are seven pages of papers I attached. Bring up the first page," Bill instructed.

"Got it." Clay closely reviewed the page in front of him as he took a sip of coffee. "It's a little fuzzy, but I think I can make it out."

"Sorry, the sheets were too large to scan, so I had to take digital pictures of them."

"Bill, what the hell is this?" Clay demanded. "You sent me really poor drawings of what looks like birds."

"No. Look at the words scattered around them."

Clay zoomed in on the characters in the document. He studied the writings closely, squinting through his glasses.

"Isn't that one in the center Hebrew?" Bill asked.

"Nope, it looks like Aramaic," Clay replied.

Bill took in the response he had just heard. Aramaic was not what he had expected to hear. "Aramaic? What does it say?" He asked, with curiosity.

"*Behold*."

"I couldn't tell what it said, but I didn't think it was in Aramaic! It was so poorly written, I wanted to have you look at it to make sure." Bill said.

"Bill, Aramaic is really a group of Semitic languages, which includes Hebrew. It belongs to the Afro-Asiatic language family."

"Clay, what in the world did you just say?"

"It's different but same."

Bill smiled. "Okay Colonel. Can you make out any of the other words?"

"From what I can tell, it's just *behold* repeated, except for the one at the bottom."

"What does that say?"

"It looks like *Jezebel.*"

"Like what?" Bill exclaimed, not believing what he was hearing.

"*Jezebel.* Damn, you gotten deaf in your old age?" Clay replied dryly.

"The *biblical* Jezebel?" Bill asked.

"How the hell am I supposed to know that, Monroe? You're talking to a linguist, not a magician," Clay fired back.

"Clay, it's important that you're accurate. Are you sure?"

"Yes, I'm sure, Regis … Jezebel is my final answer," he said, sarcastically. Clay had rarely heard his old friend so excited and wondered why he was being so forceful.

"What about the other pages? Anything stick out on those?"

"I can't make most of them out, but a few look familiar." Clay's focus was intense as he reviewed the pages, taking occasional puffs on his cigar. "This one on page five looks like *light*, and I think the one on page seven is *buried*. Bill, these are written so poorly, I'm going to have to do some more studying. Why is this so important?"

"It's who wrote them that makes them important," Bill answered, bewilderment evident in his voice.

"From what I can see, he's a drunk. I could do better with a full bend on," Clay replied.

"Clay, it was a little girl who wrote this."

"And that's supposed to impress me? My nine-year-old niece is fluent in German. Anyone with Internet access can do this. Every language on the planet is listed on the web."

"Clay, this is a six-year-old special needs girl who has no formal education. She's a complete shut-in and hasn't left her house in six years … and doesn't own a computer."

The silence on the other end of the phone told Bill he had sparked his friend's curiosity. After several seconds had passed, Clay inquired, "Autistic?"

"That was the initial diagnosis by the doctors about four years ago, but she doesn't display the classic symptoms. I'm almost positive she's not autistic. She has more verbal communication and interaction than the symptoms of autism. While she speaks very little, her facial expressions and speech appear normal."

"What about her parents?" Clay asked.

"No history of mental illness going back at least four generations. Two people, both with master's degrees in engineering, above average IQs, and very stable," Bill responded.

"How long has she been writing this stuff?"

"The writing since she was about two—the pictures started about six months after that."

"Can you send me more of her writings?"

"I could send you reams of it, but it would take forever. She sits at her table all day long and does nothing but write and draw. There are literally hundreds of pages."

Clay puffed on his cigar while speaking. "Why is she a shut-in?"

"When she was younger, she'd go into screaming episodes whenever her parents would take her out in public. The episodes were so violent that after a while, they decided to keep her in the home."

"And how old is she again?"

"She'll be seven next month."

Clay lifted the cup to his lips and drank the remainder of the coffee. He took in a deep breath and exhaled slowly. "Man, I would sure like to come out and observe her," he said as he leaned back in his chair. Bill had successfully exploited that characteristic that resides in all intelligence analysts—intense curiosity. He jumped at the opening Clay had just created. "Why don't you? You can stay here with me."

"Oh Bill, I can't get away from here."

"Why not? You just said you set your own hours at the Smithsonian. Besides, if they have anything that comes up, you can do most of your work on the web from right here, can't you?" Bill pleaded.

Clay had to admit to himself, he was more than just a bit curious. This was an amazing story and one that any linguist would get excited about. Besides, it had been almost nine years since he had traveled outside the Washington, D.C., area. "Okay, I suppose I can come out for a few days."

"Great, you can have the spare bedroom. It'll be good to see you," Bill said.

"Just so long as I don't have to hear any of your old lies about that two-for-nickel school you work for," Clay couldn't resist adding.

"No problem. I've got a whole bag full of new lies for you," Bill responded.

"Okay, bud, I'll call you when I get a flight. Can you pick me up?"

"Of course ... just let me know when you'll be arriving. Thank you, Clay, I really appreciate this."

"Later," Clay said, hanging up the phone.

It had been over six years since Bill had seen his friend. The last time they had been together was at the funeral for Clay's wife and daughter in Georgetown. Bill knew how difficult it had been for Clay to lose Mary and Jody; after all, they had been his entire life. Bill had routinely asked his friend to visit him, but the invitations had always been declined until now. Bill was excited to have his best friend involved in this and was hopeful he could help. He could hardly contain his excitement as he dialed the number for Gary and Beth.

Beth came into the kitchen carrying the laundry basket when the phone rang. She set the basket on the kitchen counter and picked up the handset. "Hello," she answered.

"Hi Beth, this is Bill."

"Hi, Bill," Beth said warmly, "did you find out anything?"

Gary was sitting in the living room easy chair and turned his head toward Beth when he overheard the conversation.

"Yup, sure did." Bill couldn't keep the excitement from his voice.

"Hang on, I'll get Gary on the line. He's right here and he's gonna want to hear this. Let me put it on speaker." Beth depressed the speaker button and hung up the receiver. "Okay, Bill, go ahead," Beth said as Gary stood next to her.

"Well, I was partially right—the word is *behold*, but my friend says it's in Aramaic, not Hebrew." Beth's brow furrowed as she heard the words. Gary's head snapped back as his eyes opened wide. "How can that be, Bill? She's had no exposure to that."

"I don't know, Gary, but I promise we will stick with it until we have an answer. I do have some great news though. My friend, Clay Harker, is coming in from D.C. to help. He's already translated some of the words, and he wants to help further."

Still not believing what he had heard, Gary asked the question. "What were the other words?"

"The ones he's translated so far are *light*, L-I-G-H-T; *buried*, B-U-R-I-E-D; *behold*, B-E-H-O-L-D; and *Jezebel*, J-E-Z-E-B-E-L. The rest were unreadable."

"Jezebel … what in the world could that mean?" a confused Beth asked.

"I don't know, Beth. I just don't know. But I'm confident that after Clay gets here we can translate the remainder of the words and maybe get a picture of what's happening."

"Bill, you know we'd offer for him to stay here, but I'm still concerned about Allyson," Beth went on, apologetically. Allyson's condition had meant that guests to the Carters' house would be nonexistent in the foreseeable future, a condition that Gary and Beth felt very bad about. The gregarious couple looked forward to once again being able to have guests, but not until the present situation was resolved. And that was something that no one was at all sure about.

"I know, Beth, not to worry. He's gonna stay with me. Besides, if I know Clay, he's going to be buried in research, and I'm closer to the university than you guys."

"Thanks, Bill. There is absolutely no way to repay what you have done for us," Gary went on.

"No thanks necessary. You guys have become like family to me, and Allyson is like a granddaughter. This will all work out … I promise." Bill had been hopeful regarding Allyson before, but with her increased activity and now Clay's arrival, he felt especially optimistic.

"Thanks, Bill, and I apologize for my conduct when you were here earlier. I just got too defensive about how I thought Allyson was being portrayed," Gary said.

"Apology quite unnecessary, Gary. I'll be in touch soon."

"Good-bye," Gary and Beth said in unison as Bill hung up. They looked at each other, bewildered. What could this possibly mean? While they were excited to hear the possibility of progress, a feeling of dread fell over them.

"What could possibly be happening, Gary? What could possibly be behind Allyson writing in a foreign language?" Beth queried her husband.

Gary tried to ease the fear he had seen in his wife's eyes and the fear in his own mind. "You're making too much of this, honey. I'm sure there will be a perfectly logical explanation for all of this," Gary responded, pulling Beth close to him.

"I wish I had your optimism. I can't help but feel that something really bad is around the corner waiting for us." Cold chills came over her as Gary held her close to him.

"And exactly what would that be?" Gary said as he leaned back to look into her eyes.

"I don't know. I just have a bad feeling about this."

Gary hugged his wife. "No such thing as the Boogie Man, Beth," he said teasingly.

Beth smiled at her husband and fought to rid herself of the fear that had suddenly come over her. "*He's right.*" She thought. "*No such thing as the Boogie Man.*"

CHAPTER 5

PRIDE OF THE CITY

IN THE HEART OF the city of Jerusalem on Ruppin Boulevard resides one of the most important institutions in all of Israel, the Israel Museum Jerusalem (IMJ), and it is one of the largest encyclopedic museums in the world. Nearly five hundred thousand archeological and anthropological exhibits reside in the museum, including the shrine of the book where the Dead Sea Scrolls are found.

Nearly one million people visit the museum, almost a third of which are international tourists. The twenty-acre facility is located on a terraced site and positioned in close proximity to the Israeli Parliamentary building, the Knesset. The museum features various facets of Jewish history and international art in several separate buildings. The IMJ represents the history of world culture from nearly one million years ago to today. Founded in 1965, in its short history, the IMJ has become the preeminent museum in the region and certainly one of the most beautiful structures in Jerusalem.

Saul Curwin had been the IMJ director for the past eleven years and enjoyed an unrivaled reputation in his field. A Jew from Great Britain, Curwin had immigrated to Israel in 1980 and dedicated his life since then to Judaica history. At just under six feet, Curwin was of thin build and wore his trademark suit and tie, something he was always seen in, no matter the occasion. Always clean shaven and meticulously groomed, the sixty-two-year-old man struck a professional pose.

As impeccable as his appearance, Curwin's office would make any "Type A" proud. Pictures of his wife and children adorned his desk, and his awards and decorations sat proudly on the large wall shelf to the right of his desk. The shelf housed the tools of the trade necessary for any museum director: hundreds of books and manuals for research. In front of the desk was the large conference table Curwin used for meetings with the staff. The table was equally as neat and clean as the rest of the office. Curwin was sitting at his desk poring over files when his administrative assistant called on the intercom.

"Mr. Curwin, Jacob Riesman is here to see you."

"Send him in please, Anna." Saul answered as he stood and pulled his suit coat from the back of his chair and put it on. He retrieved his pen and notebook from the desk and walked around it to the conference table.

Jacob Riesman opened the door and entered the room holding his loose-leaf binder. Curwin demanded his staff always come to any meeting with pen and paper, a practice that Jacob had learned the hard way.

"You needed to see me, sir?" Jacob asked.

"Yes, Jacob, please have a seat."

The forty-five-year-old Israeli-born archeologist was the brightest on the staff of IMJ. A complete opposite from the director, the disheveled and seemingly disorganized Riesman always displayed the classic characteristics of a workaholic. Dressed in denim shirt and jeans with his bushy hair and beard, it gave him an Indiana Jones quality, were it not for the yarmulke on his head. Riesman took a seat at the conference table in front of Curwin's desk. Curwin picked up the files from his desk and sat at the table across from Jacob. Saul extracted the pen from his suit coat and slowly opened the three files in front of him. He leaned forward looking at the folders while he put on his glasses with both hands.

"Jacob, I wanted to go over these three projects and see where we are. They're getting pretty old now, and I wanted to see what progress has been made and if we can close them out."

As director of the Research Department at IMJ, Jacob Riesman's plate was always full. His staff of eight was responsible for the research on virtually every item in the museum's inventory, a task that was truly never ending. IMJ had become the central repository for virtually every archeological discovery in Israel. The three projects were getting old, and little progress had been made on identifying the artifacts or the sites where they were found.

Jacob pulled the three files to his side of the table and reviewed them. He wrote the word "Completed" on two of the file covers with his signature below it and slid them back toward Curwin.

"I think we can close these two out, sir. They are both of small villages with redundant artifacts that we've found in many other locations. They're small settlements, probably no older than five-hundred years. Nothing significant regarding them."

"Can you have final reports on them to me by the end of the month?" Saul asked.

Jacob opened his loose-leaf notebook and began scribbling. "I certainly can, sir."

"All right, what about the last one—site 482?"

"Virtually no progress. We initially thought it was an Assyrian site, but ruled that out," Jacob informed.

Saul thumbed through the photographs of the artifacts. "What about the oil lamps? They look like the ones from King Solomon's temple."

"Yes, they're almost exact copies of the ones at the temple. If we hadn't recovered the originals, I'd have thought these were the ones from the temple," Jacob responded.

"And what about the dagger?" Saul asked Jacob, pointing to the picture in the file.

"Clearly a sacrificial dagger. We've had a hard time identifying its origin. It's like almost every other dagger we've seen. The only thing that separates it is the seven jewels on the handle. It's the first one we've seen like it."

Saul glanced at the pictures of the dagger while writing in his notebook. He set the pen down and turned the page, running his index finger down the pictures. "And what about these remains?"

"That's what really has us stumped, sir. We had all the bones checked, and they are from several different people."

"What?" Saul said as he looked across at Jacob with furrowed brow.

"Although it's a complete skeleton, they are from completely different people as far as we can tell. It looks like they would sacrifice someone, then place one of their bones into the box, then sacrifice someone else and place a different bone in the box. Male, female, old, young, it doesn't matter. It's a mix of everything. It makes no sense," Jacob went on.

"Do you have any idea how old the remains are?"

"Carbon dating places them at about two thousand years old, but that is not very accurate. If I were to guess based on the site and all the artifacts, I'd say closer to three thousand years old."

Curwin methodically thumbed through the remainder of the photographs as he pondered a decision regarding the status of the site. He looked across at Jacob, "Can we take a look at them, Jacob?"

"Yes, they're in the vault. I'll have Uri set them out," Jacob said as he reached for the phone.

Saul gathered his notes together as Jacob talked with his assistant. "Hello, Uri. Mr. Curwin and I would like to come down and look at the artifacts from site 482. Can you set them out? Very good, we'll be right down."

"They will have them out for us, sir," Jacob said.

"Good, I'd like to get this file closed out, one way or the other, Jacob."

As the two men left the office, Saul smiled at Anna as they walked by her desk. "I'll be in the vault if you need me, Anna."

"Yes, sir," Anna replied. Anna Rhoades had been with the museum since 1979 and was Saul's most loyal employee. The fifty-year-old Anna was both efficient and professional. Always attired in business suits and with short gray hair, her appearance rivaled any librarian. Her true talent was in keeping Saul's time as efficient as possible. No one got to Saul without going through her first.

The two men talked as they walked to the elevator. "You know, Jacob … we could have the Smithsonian take a look at the items," Saul said.

"Mr. Curwin, I don't want to admit defeat so soon."

Saul and Jacob entered the large open-top freight elevator, preparing for the ride to the lower level. "Jacob, I know you don't like using other museums, but the Smithsonian has always been a friend. Besides, we've used them on numerous occasions in the past."

"I know. I'm just not ready to give in yet," Jacob insisted.

"Well, let's take a look at what we have and then I'll make a decision."

"Fine, sir," Jacob said.

The two men exited the freight elevator at the basement level and walked toward the vault door at the end of the hall. The seventy-five-foot long hallway was both wide and tall to accommodate the equipment and artifacts from the vault. A guard station was placed next to the vault double door, manned by a single security officer, Michael Kazez. Michael stood up from the security podium and approached the door.

Michael greeted the two men. "Good morning, Mr. Curwin … Mr. Riesman."

"Good morning, Michael," Jacob responded.

Kazez removed the proximity card from his breast pocket and waited for Riesman to present his card. The two men passed their cards in front of the two different readers simultaneously. The bolts on the door snapped back, and Jacob pulled the right side of the large double doors open.

"Thank you, Michael," said Saul as he and Jacob entered the vault.

The twenty-two-thousand-square-foot vault room housed the bulk of IMJ's projects. Many of the items were secured in fenced off cages or in the hundreds of drawered chests and open shelving. The center of the vault was used for artifacts that were too large to be placed inside the cages around the perimeter. Statues, crates, and equipment created a maze that workers had to negotiate to get to the back of the room. Large halogen lights in the thirty-foot-high ceilings illuminated every section of the room and was enhanced by the white walls and ceiling. Placards on the floor next to each item identified them by date of discovery, location of the find, and current museum status. The vault had an unusual odor about it, a combination of the antiseptic smell of a hospital operating room and the musty smell of old age from the artifacts. At the back of the vault was the Clean Room, where items were inspected, cataloged, and distributed. The fifty-by-eighty-foot room was against the south concrete wall of the vault. The three remaining walls were made of inch-and-a-half glass, with two large glass doors. The entire room was environmentally separate from the rest of the vault.

Jacob and Saul approached the Clean Room and could see Uri Goldberg, the lead archeologist, and Gershon Cheifitz, his assistant, inside through the glass walls. Jacob opened the glass door, and he and Saul entered the room.

"Good morning, gentlemen," Saul said.

Uri and Gershon responded in unison, "Good morning, sir."

Saul and Jacob stopped next to the door and retrieved white cloaks, knit caps, and gloves from the rack. They put on the protective equipment and walked to the table.

Two desks with stand-alone computers sat against the concrete wall, along with filing cabinets and shelving for books and research material. The large wooden table in the center of the room was covered with a linen pad that had the artifacts from the site placed on it. On the floor next to the table stood one of the ten large oil lamps. A three-foot square bronze box was on a pallet and had been brought into the room by the electric forklift parked just outside the room. Spread out on the table were two smaller versions of the large oil floor lamp, a dagger, the human remains, and two clear plastic sleeves, which held a linen cloth and the sheath for the dagger. Saul and Jacob set their notebooks on the table and put on white gloves to examine the pieces.

Saul was not ready to examine all the pieces. "All right, now, what do we have?"

Uri opened a large binder containing pictures from the site and laid it in front of Saul. "These are pictures from the site, sir. As you can see, the table was cut from a large naturally placed stone. The cloth was on top of the table, and the dagger was placed in the center with the two small lamps, one at each end," Uri explained.

"It looks like a sacrifice was about to happen," Saul mused.

"That's our supposition as well," Gershon responded.

"And where were the floor lamps placed?" Saul asked.

"Around the altar in a circle," Uri replied.

"Was there any evidence of dried blood there?"

"No, sir. We checked the entire cave. Best we can tell, no sacrifices had been made," Uri went on.

"And the remains?" Saul asked.

"They were all in the box."

"In this box?" Saul asked, pointing to the bronze container.

"Yes. The lid had been moved a few inches, but not opened all the way."

Saul looked at Jacob. "What about the construction team? Did they remove anything?"

"No. We interviewed an army colonel, Adar Stern, at the site. He was the military liaison officer for the project. He said it had not been opened more than a few inches. No one at the site that day ever found out what was inside."

"And what did they say happened that day?" Saul asked.

"That's where it gets strange, sir." Jacob responded excitedly. "Adar said that a loud ear-shattering howl started, and when the box was opened, they all passed out. No one remembered anything after that. When they all woke up, they left the cave and called it in."

"And did anyone enter the cave after that?"

"No. They were pretty shaken up. They all stayed in the construction trailer until the military and IMJ staff arrived," Jacob continued.

"Who responded to the cave?" Saul asked.

"Uri and I were the ones that went out there," Jacob replied.

"And were they all interviewed?"

"Yes. All said pretty much the same thing … ear-splitting howl and then they passed out."

Saul bent down to look at the bronze box. He raised his head and looked at Gershon. "What does this inscription on the top mean?"

"It says, *The Anointed One shall return,*" Gershon read.

"*The Anointed One shall return,*" Saul thought to himself. "*What could that mean?*" "Do any of you know what *Anointed One* means?"

"Not so far. It could mean any number of things," replied Jacob.

Uri pointed to a picture in the book. "We thought it had a reference to the writings on the wall, but we couldn't find a connection."

"*Anointed One*—wish we had more data about that."

"We're completely in the dark about it, sir. There's nothing else that would be considered specific about it. The Anointed One could refer to anyone," Uri said.

"And what did the words on the wall say?" Saul asked.

"Random words in Aramaic, none of which makes sense. We believe it's a code, but so far we haven't been able to break it."

Saul rubbed his chin. "So we have a box containing bones from what we assume are sacrifices, a sacrificial chamber that from what we can tell never had a sacrifice, and a jumbled code written on a wall that we haven't been able to decipher yet. So, basically, we know nothing about this site after almost seven years of research," Saul summarized.

"Not exactly, sir. There is one thing we found out," Gershon said.

"What's that?" Saul asked.

Gershon turned the pages of the album to a picture of the ten-pointed star on the eastern wall of the cave. "This, sir ... this star is lined with polished stones to reflect sunlight."

Saul bent over and looked at the picture. "That makes no sense. The only place you can get sunlight from is the entrance. Judging from the size of the concave dish on the wall, you're going to get maybe one hour tops."

"We figure about an hour as well. At a particular time in the evening, the sun is in the right position to shine through the doorway and hit the concave star, illuminating the cave. For two weeks in late June and early July, the sun enters the cave through the entrance and illuminates the star, which reflects on the stone table and wall area of the cave," Gershon went on to explain.

"Well, that makes no sense. Why construct something like that and to what purpose? Light all the time is one thing, but for a couple of weeks a year. Also, why would they hide a facility like this out in the middle of nowhere? It would have been easier to build it in the valley. It's almost like they were hiding it from someone," Saul said, intrigued.

"Yes," Jacob said, "but why hide it?"

"Something illegal?" Uri suggested.

"That's not likely if the carbon dating is even remotely accurate. Sacrifices were common in the North then. Whether it was Ba-al, El, or Dagon, people were sacrificed to false gods for a multitude of reasons. Why hide what was considered to be a common practice? The only thing that is puzzling, however, is why they kept the bones. Usually the remains were burned, or burned and then scattered," Saul reminded them.

"That is very curious indeed. You're right—why keep them? It really makes no sense," Jacob said.

Saul picked up the skull and slowly rotated it in his hands. "Adult female … certainly not a child." He set the skull back down on the table and picked up the dagger, closely scrutinizing the weapon. "Jacob, my decision to ship the items to the Smithsonian is making more and more sense. We can get help from their forensics lab regarding both the dagger and the bones. And they also have access to agencies that can help with the words on the wall … if in fact it is a code."

"As you want, Mr. Curwin, we'll send them right away. Do you want everything sent?" Jacob asked.

"No, I don't think that's necessary. For now let's just send the remains, the dagger, the sheath, the linen cloth, the photo album, and the initial report. Can you have them sent out tomorrow?" Saul asked.

"Yes, sir, we'll have them sent out by tomorrow afternoon," Uri answered.

"Excellent. I'll contact the Smithsonian. Thank you, gentlemen."

Saul took off his gloves and set them on the table. He picked up his notebook and turned to leave the room. As Jacob reached for the handle to open the door, the lock snapped shut.

"The door just locked. What's going on?" Jacob protested with a confused voice.

With a puzzled look on his face, Uri approached the door. "Impossible," he said as he tugged down on the handle.

Gershon walked to the desk and reached for the phone. "I'll call Maintenance and see …" A bolt of electricity shot from the phone striking him in the hand. Gershon shrieked in pain as the others looked on in surprise. He raised his hand to see burn marks in his palm.

"What is going on here?" Saul shouted with a shaky voice.

Jacob dropped his notebook and shook the door handle violently. Bolts of electricity shot from the handle throwing him back and onto the floor. Saul and Uri picked up a dazed Jacob, helping him to his feet.

Still holding Jacob, Saul screamed at Uri, "What is happening?"

Gershon pounded on the thick glass walls with his fists screaming for help. The twelve ceiling lights in the room began to flicker on and off as the four men huddled together. One by one, the lights exploded, raining glass down on the men as they covered themselves with their arms. Then it came—the ear-splitting howls. They all covered their ears with their hands, dropping to their knees screaming in pain, writhing on the floor.

Bolts of bright white electricity began shooting from the broken lights in the ceiling. Growing in intensity, the electricity shot back and forth from one light to another as the group huddled together, terrified. Suddenly, the bolts merged into one large column of fire that shot down towards the skull on the table. Electricity, engulfed in flames, shot from the eyes of the skull and struck the four men in the chest.

The four men's bodies burst into flames as they screamed in agony. The flames burned white hot, incinerating everything until only four piles of ash remained. The bolts of electricity then shot toward the computers, melting the metal and plastic into two pools on the desktops.

The shrieking slowly subsided as the bolts of electricity withdrew back into the skull. The only sound that remained was the oscillating thrum of the fire alarm.

CHAPTER 6

THE REUNION

THE UNITED 737 TAXIED to its gate at O'Hare International Airport. Clay Harker readied himself to deplane. He turned his head away as the evening sun struck his eyes through the window. The aircraft came to a stop, and the tone from the seatbelt warning announced arrival at the gate. Clad in his usual Levis, tennis shoes, and Polo shirt, Clay stood and stretched away the discomfort of the flight. Flying was never a travel option for him, unless driving to his destination proved impractical. He had always hated flying, and since Mary and Jody's death, flying moved into the loathing category. It had become impossible for him to get on an airplane without reliving the horror of their deaths. The practice of numbing his senses with alcohol on the flight had become his comfort.

No matter how full the flight was, Clay habitually sat in the rear of the plane, a habit he had developed as a result of his thirty years of military experience. Survivors of airplane crashes were almost always sitting in the tail section of the aircraft. He put the two empty mini bottles of Jack Daniels into the pouch in the seat in front of him. He then pulled his computer bag from under the seat and placed it into the seat next to him, waiting for the plane to empty.

Clay turned on his cell phone and punched in the number for Bill Monroe. Bill's voice bellowed as he answered the phone.

"Hey, slacker, you on the ground?"

"Yeah, we just pulled up to the gate. I'm waiting to get off," Clay responded.

"Do you have to get baggage?"

"No, I brought everything in the carry-on."

"Okay then, I'll see you outside of the baggage claim door."

"See you in walking time."

Clay opened the overhead bin and removed his carry-on bag. With the computer bag on his shoulder, he walked to the front of the plane pulling his wheeled carry-on. He exited, smiling politely at the attendants in the front of the aircraft. It had been almost nine years since he had flown into O'Hare. He shook his head in disbelief as he dodged in and around the crowds of people. Even Dulles wasn't this bad, he thought. At one point years ago, O'Hare International had been the busiest airport in the United States. That honor had now been taken by the Atlanta airport. But to the people who travel through O'Hare, it still remains the busiest.

Clay stepped out of the baggage claim doors and into the heat and humidity of a June evening. As he put on his sunglasses, Bill pulled up in front of him. Clay hesitated as he looked at the two-tone red and white 1962 Ford pickup in front of him. He smiled as he placed his bags in the bed of the truck, opened the passenger door, and entered the vehicle. Bill extended his right hand and gave Clay a firm handshake.

"It's good to see you," Bill greeted him warmly.

"You, too, bud. I see you painted it," Clay said, as he buckled his seatbelt.

"I had a ground-up restoration done earlier this year. I've only had it back for a couple of months."

"Well, it really looks good."

"Yeah, they don't make 'em like they used to," Bill said patting the dash.

"No, they don't … they make 'em better," Clay teased.

Bill smiled sarcastically back at his friend as he pulled away from the curb to exit the airport. He pulled the truck onto Highway 190 for the short drive to I-294 North.

Since he was a little boy, Bill had been a "car nut." He and his wife Carrie always looked forward to the summer break to take their classic cars to shows and meetings throughout the Midwest. Carrie would put on her poodle skirt with black and white saddle oxfords, and Bill would roll up the sleeves of his T-shirt and take the old truck to the shows. Everyone in the car club missed the gregarious couple after Carrie's death. He continued to attend the club functions, but at a substantially reduced rate.

"How are the boys doing?" Clay asked.

"They're well. Steve is still with IBM in California, and Jerrod's business in Oregon is doing exceptionally well."

"Do you get to see them much?"

"For the most part, only on holidays. They both like the West Coast too much, and since Carrie's death they just aren't up to the trip as much. They always seem to be uneasy in the house." Bill understood his children's feelings, probably more than they knew. He had often thought of selling the house to move on, but never could take that all important first step. Besides, it was easier for him to make the journey to the West Coast than for the boys to handle the logistics of bringing the whole family back east. Bill pulled onto I-294 North. "Hey, it sounds like the Smithsonian job is going well for you."

"Yeah, it's the best thing I ever did. This whole double dipping thing has really spoiled me. Getting two paychecks and only having to work for one is the best. America … what a country, huh?"

"I wouldn't know. I still have to work for a living," Bill answered with a sigh. "Hey, this trip won't hurt your position with them, will it?"

"No, I just told them I'd be gone for a while. All my projects are done anyway. Speaking of which, what's the story with this family? Bring me up to speed."

"Like I said before, good family and very dedicated to tackling this problem. They both worked for SH&R until Allyson was born. Gary worked on the road for about three years, and then when Allyson's problems got worse, he took a desk job. Her episodes gradually increased in numbers and severity, putting him in the position of having to stay home more often. As you might imagine, the stress on Gary and Beth is enormous, especially Beth. What mother wouldn't be a mental case watching this happen to her daughter? She's extremely protective of Allyson, and spends every waking moment with her. Gary tries to get her out of the house as often as he can, but Beth prefers to stay at home with her daughter. She only leaves the house when she has to for doctors' appointments, shopping, and the like. She always wanted to be a stay-at-home mom. I don't think she ever had this in mind, though. Gary does just about everything else that's needed, going to the grocery store, dry cleaners, whatever else needs to be done. They're a real team."

"What about family? Where are the grandparents?"

"Beth's parents live in Southern California. Gary's father is deceased and his mother lives in Florida. Naturally, they're as supportive as possible, but Allyson freaks when she sees them as well. They all come to Chicago as often as they can to see Beth and Gary, but they've been carved out from seeing Allyson."

"When did the problems start with her?"

"They started noticing problems with her right after her first birthday. Prior to that she would scream and cry, but they attributed it to normal baby anomalies. They noticed that it mostly occurred when they would go out in public. She would cry and tremble so hard she would pass out at times. They just started staying at home after that."

"How do they deal with school, doctors' visits, checkups, and the like?"

"After going through about two dozen pediatricians, they finally found one that Allyson didn't freak over. He visits once every three months for checkups. As for school, Beth homeschools."

"Only one doctor? I would think they'd have a team of specialists."

"They did initially, but Allyson rejected all of them. They truly wanted to help, but just couldn't get past Allyson."

"And when did you come on the scene?"

"Beth and Gary came to me shortly after her third birthday. They had just about exhausted all their options. Their pastor, an old colleague of mine, referred them to me."

"They actually took her to church?"

"Only a few times. They stopped because of the episodes. Now, Beth or Gary go to church alone—usually Beth."

"Have you seen her during one of the episodes?"

"Yeah—the poor thing screams uncontrollably and trembles so hard you'd swear she was going to come out of her skin."

"When was that?"

Bill hesitated while he exited I-294 East onto Dempster Street toward Evanston. "She was about five years old. They brought in a behavioral specialist, and as soon as Allyson saw her, she went ballistic. I was in the room with them when it happened. Allyson started trembling when she saw her, and as she walked closer to her, she began screaming. Beth and Gary tried to calm her down, but she only got worse. Gary shouted to me to get her out of the room. I walked her to the front door, and when I went back into the room, Allyson was lying on the bed trembling with a blank stare. She had screamed so loud and long that the color had gone from her face. She was chalk white and her skin was ice cold. It's something I'll never forget."

Clay listened to Bill with his mouth open, not believing what he was hearing. "You mentioned that they were about out of options. What other options do they have?"

"Just one, but they rejected it completely. The psychologists suggested they put her in a full-blown mental facility."

"They would have just pumped her full of drugs and stuck her in a padded room," Clay mused, shaking his head.

"You're absolutely right. So we just continue to monitor her, catalog progress, if any, and look for alternatives—which brings us to you."

"What do you mean?"

"About six months ago, Allyson started writing more and her drawings increased tenfold. Prior to that, she would just scribble on the paper—circles, squares, and squiggly lines for the most part. She would draw what looked like birds—at least that was what they looked like then. Now they are clearly birds and the squiggly lines have morphed into characters. Thanks to you, we now know the characters are Aramaic. Gary and Beth were very encouraged by the news. To quote them, any progress is good, but *this* progress is phenomenal."

"But I'm still baffled about how she writes in Aramaic."

"And with your help, we hope to answer that question."

"Look, Bill, I'm no psychiatrist. I'm a linguist and a tuckered out old intel officer. All that means is I can tell you to kiss off in seven languages. Other than that, I'm pretty much useless. Besides, what's to say she won't freak when she sees me?"

"We do run that risk, but we think the risk is worth it. Clay, this is the first breakthrough we've had. Nothing that has happened before has shown any hope. She even seems to be more alert and attentive over the past six months. We have to try."

"Okay, okay, I showed up, didn't I?" The story of Allyson had intrigued him from the beginning. He had to admit that for the first time in very many years he was excited about a project.

Bill pulled into his driveway and pressed the garage door opener. The door opened and he pulled into the garage next to his blue and white 1955 Chevrolet Nomad.

A very impressed Clay whistled as he looked at the car. "Oh sure, you couldn't pick me up in the Nomad, huh?"

"That only goes out for car shows," Bill commented.

"How long have you had this one?" Clay asked as he grabbed his bags from the back of the truck, looking at the car.

"Got it four years ago and put it through a full restoration two years ago. Carrie always wanted a Nomad, but we never got around to it, what with raising the boys. I found it in North Carolina on EBay and decided to get it. It was trashed, but all the parts were there. It turned out pretty good, huh?" Completing the project had given Bill a sense of accomplishment for his wife and was a constant reminder of her for him.

"Boy, it sure did," Clay said as he followed Bill to the door. "The only car Mary ever got excited about was that damned Mercedes we bought. She always wanted one, and when we finally got it, she was too scared to drive it in the city. Finally had to trade it in on the Honda."

"But at least she fulfilled her dream," Bill interjected.

Clay smiled as he heard the words. "Yeah, she sure did."

Bill opened the door to the house, and they both walked up the stairs to the main level. The house was located in the older section of Evanston, Illinois, not far from the campus of Northwestern University. The two-story structure had been Bill's home for the past thirty years. The older brick house was quiet and had a peace about it that reminded everyone of their grandmother's house. It was decorated with early American antiques that he and Carrie had collected over their thirty-year marriage. Built in the 1930s, the house lacked a lot of the modern amenities, but was truly a work of craftsmanship. Over the years, Bill had upgraded the wiring, the heating system, the plumbing, and to the delight of his wife, added air-conditioning. They had decided to retain the beautiful hardwood floors that were visible around the large area rugs Carrie had picked out. The quiet home had a peace about it that welcomed every visitor. The only sound was the rhythmic ticking of the grandfather clock in the living room.

"The house looks good, Bill."

"Thanks. Carrie did a great job."

"She sure did." Still holding his luggage, Clay looked toward his friend. "Okay, where do you want me to sleep?"

"Just put your things in the guest room upstairs ... first one on the left."

Clay carried his bags to the top of the stairs. He entered the guest bedroom and placed them on the bed. He sighed as he looked at the pictures on the wall. Pictures of Bill, Carrie, and the two boys with their wives and children, something he knew he would never see on the walls of his house. Clay, more than anyone, had looked forward to being a grandfather.

He walked down the stairs and into the kitchen. "You got anything to drink here?"

"There should be something in the hutch in the dining room. It probably has an inch of dust on it though."

The 1,800-square-foot house was small, but comfortable. No longer used, the dining room offered little use other than a place to store unused kitchen utensils and the holiday alcohol stash. Clay walked to the cabinet and opened the door revealing a half-full bottle of Wild Turkey. "This will do just fine," he announced with a smile. "Hey bud, do you mind if I smoke cigars out on the deck while I'm here?"

"Absolutely not, knock yourself out. Mi casa es su casa," Bill replied.

Clay sat at one of the stools at the peninsula counter while Bill placed a glass with ice in it in front of him. Bill removed a can of ice tea from the fridge and placed it at the end of the counter.

"I told Gary and Beth we'd get to their house about 9:00 a.m. tomorrow, if that's okay with you?"

"Sure, that works. Where do they live?" Clay said after taking a long drink from his glass.

"Lake Forest. It's just up Green Bay Road about twenty or thirty minutes from here, so we should leave by about eight thirty."

"Okay, I'll be ready. Hey, can I take you to dinner tonight, bud?" Clay asked.

"No, that's okay. Thanks for asking. I went to the store, so the fridge is full. Besides, I made my killer lasagna. I put it in the oven before I went to get you."

"Excellent," Clay said after draining his glass. As far as Clay was concerned, Bill made the best lasagna on the planet. Clay fidgeted in his seat as he pondered the question. "Bill, do you mind if I ask you a personal question?"

Bill responded after checking on the lasagna in the oven. "Of course not—shoot."

"How do you deal with not having Carrie around? I mean you two were close, at least as close as Mary and I. How do you cope with the loss? "

Bill took a deep breath as he sat back down at the counter across from Clay. He opened the can of ice tea and took a sip. "I don't."

"What the hell do you mean you don't?" Clay inquired.

"Look, Clay, there's not a day that goes by that I don't think of her. Some nights I cry myself to sleep. Most mornings when I wake up, she's the first thing that pops into my head."

"Then how do you keep from going mad?"

"Clay, my loss was horrific, but at least I had time to say good-bye—you didn't. We had time to reflect and enjoy our children together before she died. From the time she was diagnosed with cancer to the time she passed was six months. We were all able to come to grips with it. You didn't have that opportunity. Mary and Jody were snatched from you. You didn't have a chance to say good-bye."

"But what gets you through each day? What stands you up in the morning?" Clay asked as he stared into his glass.

"Well, I have the boys and their families to be sure. And then there's the job, but the real peace comes from God."

"Oh, there you go, putting on the theological headdress," Clay fired back.

"Hey, you asked."

"Well, he wasn't much help when I needed him. He took everything in life that meant anything to me."

"Clay, you know better than that! God didn't kill them. A handful of cowardly terrorists did that."

"Hey, don't give me that. I haven't been your friend for almost forty years without listening to you. You said nobody dies but what God doesn't will it."

Bill leaned on the counter with a sarcastic smile on his face. "How is it that you avoided God for most of your life, but you remember something I said decades ago?"

"Because you're good at what you do," Clay responded softly.

"Apparently not that good, because I said, but what God doesn't *allow it*, not *will it*. And if you really listened to what I said, you'd recall that I also said that God can always turn something bad that happens into something good."

"And exactly what good can come from having Mary and Jody die?"

"I don't know, Clay, but you have to trust him, and give him a chance to show you. Besides, what we're really talking about here is guilt—right?" Bill fired back.

"What the hell is that supposed to mean?"

"Come on, Clay. You don't think I didn't go through the same thing with Carrie? It should have been me that died, not her. You're feeling guilty because you believe it should have been you instead of them."

Clay stared at his empty glass while he turned it in his fingers. He slowly raised his head looking at Bill. "Yup, it's not fair."

"What's not fair, that they should have to grieve over you and not the reverse? That's selfish, Clay."

Clay refilled his glass. "It should have been me. Besides, if I didn't die then, why not now? Life without them is pointless. I'm ready to go."

"You're not ready to go. God still has something for you to do. You know it's ironic that our lives have paralleled each other's so much. We should have died so many times, but God wasn't ready for us to go yet."

"No, I'll tell you what's ironic. It's that those gutless bastards flew a plane into the Pentagon killing my wife and daughter three offices away from where I used to sit. That's irony!" Clay said.

"And what about the other passengers on the plane? They had families too. What about them? People die from cancer every day—they have families that loved them. It's life, Clay."

Clay didn't respond; he continued to focus on his glass, swallowing against the lump in his throat. Bill leaned over toward his friend. "Look, bud, you have to get on with your life, and the best way to honor Mary and Jody is to complete what God has for you. Trying to kill yourself with alcohol isn't the way to address this. The answer you want is not in that bottle."

"You probably are a really good teacher, Bill—you certainly talk enough to be one," Clay said smiling at his friend. He certainly knew the statement was true, but it was, however, easier to shut out the pain.

"Only to those that are the closest to me," Bill answered with a smile of his own. "Now, let's get some food. We have a long day ahead of us tomorrow." Bill stood and walked to the oven. He pulled the lasagna out of the oven and placed it on the stove top. The cheese bubbled on the top as the aroma filled the kitchen. He turned the oven on broil and placed the garlic bread inside. Clay reached for the bottle of whiskey and unscrewed the top. He started to pour more of the liquid into his glass but stopped. He looked at the bottle in his hand and took a deep breath; setting the whiskey back on top of the counter, he screwed the top back on and folded his arms. "*Oh well, probably enough for today anyway,*" he thought.

Bill smiled as he looked at Clay's reflection in the glass of the oven door.

CHAPTER 7

A TURNING POINT FOR CLAY

BILL TURNED THE TRUCK into the driveway of the Carters' house and shut the engine off. He and Clay exited the truck with notebooks and Starbucks coffee in their hands. As they walked to the front door, Clay turned and looked at the surrounding area. He couldn't help but admire the manicured yards and pristine homes in the neighborhood.

"Nice neighborhood."

"Yeah, nice place to raise a family," Bill said as he rang the doorbell.

The door opened and Gary Carter greeted Bill and Clay. "Good morning … please come in." Gary extended his hand to Clay. "You must be Clay Harker? I'm so very glad to meet you."

Clay smiled back. "Yes, nice to meet you as well."

"Come on in, you guys. Beth is in the kitchen."

The three men entered the kitchen to find Beth making coffee. Both she and Gary were dressed in their usual summer attire of shorts and T-shirts.

"Honey, this is Clay Harker."

Beth dried her hands with the dish towel and shook Clay's hand. She unconsciously straightened her hair as she greeted him. "I'm so glad to finally meet you, Clay. I've heard such nice things about you. I see you both have coffee. Can I make you breakfast?"

"Thank you, no. We ate at the house," Bill said.

"Please have a seat," said Gary, motioning toward the kitchen table.

"You have a beautiful home, Mrs. Carter," Clay remarked as he looked around the inside of the house.

"Thank you, but please call me Beth." She couldn't help but be surprised by Clay. His rugged good looks and dark suntan were not what she was expecting a doctor to look like.

"Bill tells us you two met in Vietnam," Gary said as they all took seats at the table.

"Yes, we did, but that was about a million years ago. And I'll bet he didn't tell you that he saved my life over there," Clay told them with pride in his voice.

"No, he didn't," Beth said turning to look at Bill, obviously impressed. "What happened?"

"I was a brand new ninety-day wonder lieutenant, in country about three months. Bill was my sergeant and had been there about eight months. It was early in the morning on the last day of a four-day patrol. We were at the edge of a clearing, and after determining that it was clear, we pushed out. Charlie was waiting for us and the whole jungle erupted in gunfire. I was hit in the leg by an AK-47 round and went down like a load of coal. In the confusion, while everyone was running for cover, I found myself all alone and unable to move. I looked up to see Bill here bending over to pick me up. Before it was all over, Chuck had shot me three times in the same leg—twice while Bill was carrying me. He took two rounds in the arm, and still managed to get me to safety. To this day, I still think he decided to use me to shield himself just to get back to cover." He laughed, looking at his friend affectionately.

"Of course I did … you think I was stupid?" Bill responded with a smile.

"For his trouble, they gave him the Silver Star. I got lead. He gets silver. Least he could have done was share it with me for stopping those other two rounds from hitting him," Clay laughed, looking at Bill.

Clay always enjoyed bringing attention to his best friend's heroics. He knew that without that action so many years ago, he would have never gotten out of that jungle alive. Every time he rubbed his right leg, Clay was reminded of that day and the incredible debt he owed his best friend.

"Wow!" Gary said in amazement. He and Beth sat with wide eyes and open mouths as Clay told the story.

"And there's not a day goes by that I don't regret saving his miserable hide," Bill said, winking at Clay.

"Bill, all these years, and we had no idea," Beth said.

"It's no big deal. Anyone would have done the same thing," Bill responded humbly.

"Riiiight," Clay said with a smile.

"What happened after that?" Beth asked, intrigued.

"They flew me to Japan for care and then back to the states."

"And how did you become a linguist?" Beth asked.

"After Vietnam I went into intelligence and was later sent to the Defense Language Institute in Monterey, California. I studied Farsi while I was there. I guess I had an aptitude for it. I picked up a few more languages over the years."

"Don't let him kid you," Bill chimed in. "He reads, writes, and speaks seven languages. He was the best the army had." Bill wanted to shift the focus from himself to Clay.

"Hardly," Clay muttered, with a humble tone in his voice.

"Your family must be very proud, Clay," Beth said as she got up to get more coffee.

Clay shifted uncomfortably in his seat. "They died six years ago."

Beth placed the cup of coffee in front of Clay. "I'm so very sorry, Clay—I saw the wedding ring and …"

"It's okay, Beth. They died on Flight 77 that hit the Pentagon. I still wear the ring out of habit," Clay replied while looking down at the wedding ring.

"Oh, no," she went on with a furrowed brow, "your whole family?" Beth asked nervously as she shifted in her seat.

"Yes, my wife and daughter. They were on their way to see my wife's parents in California."

"I'm so very sorry." Beth felt awful for having brought up the subject. How horrific for him to have lost his entire family in one day. Bill finally broke the awkward silence. "Clay has translated the words from the pages I gave him. I think you should see this."

Eager to change the subject, Gary and Beth looked to Clay as he opened his leather bound journal. "What have you found out?" Gary asked.

"Not too much. There are only a few words I could translate. Most of her writing is unintelligible. The few I could translate repeat themselves over the seven pages. I was hoping to review more of them if I could," Clay continued.

"Sure—we started saving them after Bill asked us to. They're up in Allyson's room. Do you want to look at them now?" Beth asked.

"Not right yet. We can look at them later before we leave. "

"Do you know what the words mean?" Gary asked.

"Just repeated random words, as it appears now. At this point, it doesn't look like there's a pattern, but maybe after we've translated more of them, something will emerge," Clay explained.

"What were the words again?" Gary asked.

"*Jezebel*, *light*, *behold*, and *buried*."

Gary looked at Bill with a furrowed brow as he asked the question. "I still don't understand how a six-year-old girl can write in Aramaic. It just makes no sense."

"I don't have any idea either, Gary, but now that Clay is here, we might be able to make some progress," Bill said.

Clay turned to Beth. "Bill mentioned that you've homeschooled Allyson. Has she ever seen any books or pictures of languages?"

"No, we've seen very little progress from the homeschooling. The only progress comes from Gary and me interacting with her," Beth told him.

"Television, computers, anything else she could have gleaned information from?" Clay asked.

"No, nothing. She gets scared when the television is on. The only thing she will watch is baseball or football games Gary records and watches later and most of the Disney movies as well."

"She watches baseball and football?" Clay asked, with a grin.

"Yeah … she sometimes sits in his lap and watches until she falls asleep," Beth said. To Gary and Beth, this was one of the few times that Allyson seemed to be a normal little girl.

Clay continued to scribble entries in his journal as Gary and Beth spoke. He couldn't imagine how he and Mary would have dealt with this if Jody had been afflicted with the same condition. What must this family be going through? Clay's problems seemed to vanish as he thought of the pain that had been wrought on this family.

"We pretty much live in Allyson's room. She doesn't come out of there. We eat there, listen to music, work, and sometimes sleep in there with her. And, no, she's never been on the computer," Beth continued.

"So there's nothing you can think of that would tie her to the language?" Clay asked.

"Not that we can think of," Gary replied.

Clay made an entry into his journal regarding the homeschooling and placed an asterisk next to it. It was easy to see why everyone had made the initial diagnosis of autistic regarding Allyson. "Bill told me that the doctors initially gave you a diagnosis of autism. I can see how they could have made that supposition based on the repeated behavior," he said.

"But she would have still had to have been exposed to Aramaic to be writing it … correct?" Beth asked.

"That's right. I've always discounted autism because of the interaction she has from time to time," Bill reminded them.

Clay looked up from his journal after writing. "These screaming episodes she has, what happens exactly?" Clay asked.

Beth took a deep breath and exhaled slowly. "Terrifying—absolutely terrifying. She screams so loud and shakes so violently that she collapses in a few minutes from exhaustion. It's horrifying to witness, Clay."

"What brings them on?"

"Whenever someone gets around her—someone new, that is. We initially thought it was a physical ailment. After many examinations, she checked out physically perfect."

"I don't understand. Everyone she comes into contact with?" Clay asked.

"Everyone but Gary, me, Bill, and Doctor Peterson, her pediatrician."

"When did you first attribute it to being around people?" Clay asked while scribbling in his journal.

"We really noticed it at her first birthday party. We had some of the neighbors over, and when they came into the room, Allyson started screaming. My mother was here, and when she picked her up to try to quiet her, Allyson went into convulsions. Neither of our parents has seen her since. They don't understand, and it breaks our heart to keep Allyson from them, but we just don't have a choice," Beth sadly advised.

"And when was the last time she had an episode?" Clay asked, still writing in his journal.

"She was downstairs in the living room with us about two years ago. She was standing by the window and saw the meter man walk by outside. He froze when he heard her scream. Gary took her up to her room immediately and stayed with her until she calmed down. It scared the man half to death. We later apologized to him, but I don't think he ever understood. We've kept her in the room ever since."

"She has always cried uncontrollably whenever we would go out in public. Restaurants, the mall, it didn't matter where. We finally decided to keep her in the house … mostly because we worried that one day she wouldn't recover from one of the episodes," Gary interjected.

"And what about these pictures of birds all over the pages? Does Allyson like birds?"

"She seems to. I've shown her a lot of picture books over the years, and she seems to react more to the birds," Beth added.

Clay took his glasses off and rubbed his eyes. He leaned back in his chair and took a deep breath before asking the question. "Do you think it would be possible for me to see her?"

Gary took a deep breath. "Boy, I just don't know, Clay. Beth and I are pretty guarded about anyone getting around her. She just reacts so badly."

Beth turned toward her husband. "Honey, Clay brings us the only hope we've had in years. I think we should at least try." She certainly didn't understand what she was feeling, but somehow felt comfortable about Clay. His revelations about Allyson's writing had brought new hope to her.

"Look you guys, I think we need to try. I'll stand back by the door with Clay, and if Allyson has any negative reaction whatsoever, we'll back right out of the room," Bill assured them.

"Okay, we can try—but don't expect much, Clay. Even if she doesn't start screaming or shaking, she'll probably ignore you," Gary said.

"That's okay. Bill has been ignoring me for years. I'm used to it," Clay said jokingly.

Beth stood up. "Okay, let's try this, but Gary's right, Clay—don't expect much."

Clay set his pen on top of his journal and stood up to follow Gary and Beth. As he walked behind Gary, Beth, and Bill, he couldn't help but notice that every blind and curtain in the house had been drawn. He also noticed that the walls were void of family pictures. His personal loss seemed to fade compared to what these people were dealing with, to be confined to the room of a house out of total fear. What must this family be going through?

Beth stopped before entering Allyson's room. She turned and looked at Clay pleadingly. "Remember, if she gets scared, please leave immediately."

Bill and Clay both nodded their heads, acknowledging her request. Beth opened the door and entered the room followed by Gary. Bill and Clay stepped inside and closed the door behind them, remaining by the entrance.

Clay looked to see a little girl seated at a table with her back to them. The scene would have been that of any little girl had he not been told of her condition. He was struck by how antiseptic the room looked. It was brightly illuminated by artificial light, no wall decorations, and windows covered by black paint. The abundance of furniture and kitchen appliances confirmed to him that the family did in fact spend a lot of time here.

Allyson was drawing on a large art pad and didn't look up as Gary and Beth kneeled down next to her. Beth placed her hand on Allyson's head.

"Honey, Doctor Bill is here and he brought a friend with him to meet you."

As Allyson slowly turned her head, Clay felt his muscles tighten, ready to move out of the room in an instant should he need to.

As she looked at Clay, he was struck by how cute and innocent she looked. Her dark brown hair was done in pigtails, and she was dressed in a clean and pressed dress with white shoes and socks.

Allyson stayed frozen, her gaze totally fixed on Clay. She slowly slid off the chair and turned around, her eyes still locked on him. As she began walking toward him, Beth reached out a hand to stop her, but she was already on her way toward Clay.

Clay felt helpless; he didn't know what to do. Based on what he knew about her so far, he prepared himself for anything. Allyson reached out with her arms, stood up on her tip toes, and hugged Clay tightly around the waist. The four people in the room looked at each other in amazement. This had never happened before. Beth stood up, staring at her daughter, her mouth open, and her hands clasped against her chest. Then it happened. The silence was broken as Allyson looked up at Clay still hugging him tightly, smiling, and asked, "What's your name?"

Beth placed her hands over her mouth and began to cry. Gary sat back on his heels, his mouth open wide. Bill's eyes snapped wide open, his head tilting toward Allyson. No one could believe what had just happened.

After what seemed like an eternity, Clay smiled at her and responded, "My name is Clay Harker, Allyson. I'm very glad to meet you."

Allyson lowered her head and continued to hug him tightly. Clay remained motionless, wondering what to do. No one else in the room was talking, each wondering what the next step was.

Clay placed his hand on Allyson's shoulder and knelt down next to her. "You sure are a pretty little girl, Allyson. How old are you?"

"I'm six years old," she responded.

"Allyson, Doctor Bill brought me here to meet you, and he told me I could see your drawings. Would that be okay with you?"

Allyson nodded her head yes and took Clay's left hand leading him to the table. Clay stopped next to her table, his left hand still clasped by Allyson. Everyone gathered around the table, still awestruck watching the interaction between the two.

Clay picked up one of the pieces of paper. "Your writing is very good, honey. Do you know what these words mean?"

"No," she said in almost a whisper.

"Allyson, I would really like to take these with me and look at them some more—they sure are good. Would that be okay with you?" Clay asked.

She turned her head toward Clay looking at him when she responded. "Yes."

Gary gathered the sheets of paper on the table and handed them to Bill.

Clay then knelt down and spoke directly to Allyson, making sure he had her attention as he wanted to observe her reactions. "Allyson, Dr. Bill and I have to go now."

She looked into Clay's eyes and asked, "Will you come back and see me?"

An emotional Clay, looking into her eyes, choked the words out. "I sure will, honey. We'll come back as soon as we can."

Allyson hugged Clay around the neck. He stood up and touched her gently on the head. Allyson turned and sat back down at the table and continued to write on her pad, saying nothing further.

Clay and Bill walked to the door. Before exiting, Clay looked back to see Gary and Beth hugging their daughter with tears in their eyes.

CHAPTER 8

THE WELCOME GIFT

BACK DOWNSTAIRS IN THE kitchen, the shock of the conversation Clay had with Allyson was just now beginning to wear off for Bill. He stood staring at Clay with disbelief in his eyes. For Clay, the revelation of Allyson's conversation with him had yet to be understood. He was completely unaware of the miracle that had just occurred.

Bill stumbled for the words as they sat at the kitchen table. "Clay, what just happened?"

"I don't know, bud—I really don't know. It took me by surprise, too."

"I have never seen Allyson react like that. She's never communicated with sentences of more than two or three words."

Gary and Beth came into the kitchen. Gary was holding a large stack of Allyson's papers, and Beth was still crying. Without a word, Beth sat next to Clay and reached around his neck, giving him a huge hug. She tearfully choked the words out. "Clay, I don't know what just happened, but Allyson has spoken more words to you in ten minutes than she has to anyone in as many months. Thank you—thank you so much." Clay felt helpless as he looked at Beth's tear-stained face. He was unable to respond to anyone. A flood of emotions swept over him as he contemplated an answer. Usually quick witted and ready with a snappy response, he sat silent with a confused look on his face. All he could do was smile through pursed lips.

Gary set the papers on the table and sat across from him. "Clay, I can't thank you enough. I'm totally speechless."

Clay looked back at Gary with a furrowed brow. "Believe me, I don't know what happened either. I'm not sure I did anything."

Beth took a deep breath and attempted to control her sobbing. She started to reach toward Clay with her right hand to touch his face affectionately, but noticed the trembling in her hand. She immediately pulled her right hand tight against her stomach with her left hand trying to control the shaking. It did no good; her whole body began to tremble. The impact of what had just happened slammed into Beth's consciousness. Seven years of little or no progress with her daughter had just been violently undone by a man they had just met. What could have happened? There was no logical answer to what she and Gary had just witnessed.

Gary looked to see his wife shaking. He reached out and pulled her into him. "Are you okay, baby?" he asked as he held her tightly.

With a trembling voice, Beth responded. "Yes, I just need to sit down for a while."

Gary helped her to a chair, and then went to the refrigerator to get her a bottle of water. He quickly returned and handed the bottle to her. Beth took the water and drank intensely as her hand shook. "I'll be fine, honey. I just need some time to absorb what just happened." She turned and looked at Clay. "I certainly don't have the right to ask what I'm about to ask, but I hope you can stay long enough to help us unravel this. Allyson clearly has connected with you, and we just had the only real progress we have ever experienced," she said, trying to control her emotions.

"Beth is right, Clay. If at all possible we would like you to stay for as long as it's convenient for you," Gary continued.

"How long *can* you stay, Clay?" Bill asked.

"I'm okay, you guys. I can stay as long as you need. I wouldn't mind finding out what just happened myself. I don't know how much I'll be able to help, but I'll certainly try," Clay responded. He sat down hard in the chair as he tried to connect with what had just occurred. Just days before, he had questioned why he was still allowed to remain alive. Now he had been thrust into these people's lives by the interaction with a six-year-old little girl. Excitement poured over him as he suddenly felt a renewed purpose.

"Good," Bill said enthusiastically, slapping Clay on the back.

Clay had always felt uncomfortable about being acknowledged for his deeds. The reason for his shyness went all the way back to his childhood when his mother would dote over his accomplishments. Clay's father only seemed to notice his athletic endeavors, causing his mother to overcompensate. Clay had found it easier over the years to fold away into obscurity and lose himself in his schoolwork. When the army placed him into the intelligence community, Clay had truly found a home. Not used to accolades, *intel pukes*, as the community referred to them, were used to living a quiet life of servitude. The job was not for the self-absorbed, or the upwardly mobile. Clay had always marveled at attaining the rank of full bird colonel, but he never felt worthy of it. His superiors, however, knew the reason for his ascension, and would have placed a star on his shoulder had he not declined it in order to retire and be with his family. He had enjoyed a mere eighteen months of retirement when Mary and Jody perished in 2001. He had never regretted giving up the army. He often commented to Bill that it was the most wonderful time, though short-lived, of his life and a wonderful chance to connect with his daughter in a manner that he and his father had never achieved.

Still feeling uncomfortable about the exchange, Clay opened his journal and placed his reading glasses low on his nose. "Is it okay if we look at these papers now or are we interrupting?" he asked.

Gary shot to his feet with enthusiasm. "Absolutely not! It might be better however to spread this out in the living room," he quickly responded, leading the way. His eagerness was something they all felt.

"I agree. The living room would be better," Bill said as he followed.

"I'll get some drinks and snacks for us. Is iced tea okay with everyone?" Beth offered.

"Sure thing," Clay replied with a smile as he gathered up the papers and his journal.

As they all entered the living room, Gary and Bill began moving chairs and tables to the edge of the room, opening up a large area in the center of the floor. Bill took the stack of papers from Clay and began placing them on the floor. Clay knelt down and began numbering the papers in the upper right-hand corner, beginning with the number eight since he had previously received the first seven pages from Bill via the Internet.

Clay sat back on his heels and looked at the arrangement on the floor. "This is going to be perfect. Gary, do you have a TV tray I can write on?" Clay asked.

"Sure. I'll get one."

Beth came into the room with a pitcher of iced tea and placed it on the table behind them with four glasses filled with ice. Gary opened the TV tray and sat it next to Clay.

Clay rolled up his sleeves and sat on the edge of his seat, leaning toward the papers closest to him on the floor. The three people hovered over the papers as Clay began methodically reviewing each page. He circled each word that he had previously translated and then placed a check mark next to the word in his journal. He counted the number of times the word was repeated on the page in the classic manner, four small vertical lines with one diagonal slash through them. Once the page was done, he placed a large *X* in the upper left-hand corner and put it in the stack on the floor next to Bill. Beth and Gary knelt on the floor in the middle of the papers and waited for Clay to reach for the next page. Bill sat on the couch and transposed the highlighted words into his own notebook as he kept the completed pages separated from the others.

After almost an hour of working, Bill uttered the first words directed at Clay. "Anything new yet?"

"Not so far, just repeated words. They're pretty difficult to identify. Allyson's writing is hard to decipher." Clay removed his glasses and rubbed his eyes. He leaned back in his chair with a sigh. "Out of curiosity, why the art pads?"

Gary chuckled and looked at his wife. "She actually started by writing on the walls with a crayon. I picked up some art pads and Ally took to them. Crayons on the wall are a nonnegotiable item." They all laughed.

"My wife went through that with our daughter, too." The words came out before Clay realized what he had said. He quickly changed the subject when the room got uncomfortably quiet. "She must go through a poop load of paper."

"About twelve to fourteen art pads a week, at 150 pages to a pad," Gary said with a chuckle.

"Must keep Office Depot busy supplying you?"

"I just buy enough for the week every Saturday," Gary responded.

Clay turned around and removed one of the sandwiches from the tray. He took a bite and sipped from his glass of iced tea. "And how long has she has been scribbling on pads?"

Beth took a sip from her glass and placed it back on the coffee table. "She started shortly after her second birthday. It wasn't much to look at at first, but about six months ago we started to notice some structure to the writing, and the pictures of the birds got better as well."

Clay stood up and stretched backward. He looked at the stack of papers on the floor. "About two-thirds of the way through. Better get back to work." As he put his glasses back on, he continued to review the papers. It was about ten minutes before he struck pay dirt. "Got one," he exclaimed.

Everyone stopped what they were doing and turned to look at the page Clay was working on. They focused intensely on the word he had circled. "*Joined*," he went on as he wrote the word in his journal.

Bill entered the word in his notepad and turned toward Clay. "Any particular meaning to that?"

"Aside from the standard meaning … no. Maybe after we get more words it might make sense," Clay said, as he continued to work. He had gone through six more pages before he found another word. "*Defiance*," he muttered as he furiously wrote it in his journal, completely engrossed in what he was doing. Clay crossed through repeated words as he went through the papers with the skill of a surgeon. Bill, Gary, and Beth removed and replaced the papers as soon as Clay was finished with them. "*Sayeth*," Clay announced again as he found another word.

After fifteen minutes had passed, Clay pulled the last page in front of him. "That looks like all we're gonna find today," he said as he took off his glasses and leaned back in his chair. This day had transported Clay back to his intelligence days in the army. He remembered countless hours of reviewing documents with little to show for his efforts. His tenacity was a testament to just how good he was at this task. Clay, better than anyone, knew it took a special kind of personality to do this kind of work. He had taken to it like a duck to water. His linguistic skills in Middle Eastern languages limited him regionally, but not vocationally. The army had placed great faith in his abilities and put him in charge of his own unit at the Pentagon. In spite of his commanding officer's pleading, Clay had decided to retire. Even after his wife and daughter's deaths, the army continued to ask him to return, especially after the 9-11 attacks. Clay opted for a less stressful contractor position at the Smithsonian.

He put his glasses back on and leaned forward. "Do you think there are anymore upstairs?"

"I'm sure Ally has more up there. Do you want to look at them now?" Beth asked.

Clay stood and arched his back, trying to stretch away the discomfort. "No, that's okay. We'll just take them with us," he responded with a sigh.

"I'll go pick up what she's done. I have to take her lunch anyway," Beth said, looking at her watch.

Gary, Bill, and Clay stood and went into the kitchen as Beth went upstairs to check on Allyson.

"Any idea yet what the words mean, Clay?" Gary asked.

"Not yet. Maybe a phrase, a sentence, or a statement; it's still too few words to say right now." He opened his journal and looked at the words he had translated so far. "They just don't make sense. I can't figure out what she's trying to communicate, or if she's communicating at all."

"And you're sure the words are Aramaic?"

"Yes, positive," Clay replied.

"What's the difference between that and Hebrew?" Gary asked, curiously.

"There's very little difference in how the characters look. Small turns or twists in the characters … the real difference is in the meaning. That's what makes it so much more difficult to translate," Clay explained.

Beth came downstairs with a fresh stack of papers and placed them in front of Bill. "So what were all the words again, Clay?"

Clay opened his journal and thumbed through the pages. *"Behold, Jezebel, light, buried, joined, defiance,* and *sayeth."*

Gary sat down at the kitchen table. "Is there any particular meaning to those words?"

Bill responded as he combined the papers. "If I were to guess, it's biblical in nature. As to what they mean, I agree with Clay. It's probably too early yet to speculate as to their meaning. Separately, the words don't mean anything, so I think we should hold off on any meaningful analysis until we get more words."

"If we get any more words," Gary said.

"Well, hopefully we will," Bill replied.

"You know, the one word that keeps jumping out to me is *Jezebel.* How many times is her name repeated?" Beth asked.

Clay thumbed through his journal, stopping at the name Jezebel. "Two-hundred and forty-three times … more than any other word," he responded.

"Bill, what exactly happened with Jezebel?" Clay asked.

Bill took a deep breath before answering. "She was the most hated woman in the Bible," he began.

"Who was she? I mean, why so hated?" Beth asked.

Bill leaned forward and placed his hands together, fingertip to fingertip. "In order to understand Jezebel, you have to first understand her namesake. The name Jezebel means daughter of Ba-al."

"And who is Ba-al?" Gary asked.

"Ba-al, spelled B-A-A-L, and pronounced bail, ball, or the Middle Eastern pronunciation Bah-all, was the Phoenician god of rain and fertility. He was unquestionably the most influential and prolific false god in history. Ba-al means Lord … in fact, one of the spin-offs of Ba-al is someone everyone has heard about in Sunday school. Beelzebub, which is actually spelled B-A-A-L-Z-E-B-U-B," Bill went on to further explain.

"But that is one of the names for Satan, isn't it?" a shocked Beth asked.

"Yes. In fact, Beelzebub means 'Lord of the Flies,'" Bill replied.

"Wow!" Gary said, as he listened intensely.

"He really comes into focus because of the marriage of Jezebel to Ahab, the son of King Omri in Northern Israel. This was probably an arranged marriage for the purpose of trade, peace, or power. When Omri dies, Ahab assumes the throne and Jezebel becomes queen. Jezebel actually means 'daughter of Ba-al.'"

Beth tried to hold her emotions in check as she listened to Bill. Her daughter was somehow being linked to an ancient Samarian queen. Her thoughts traveled back to that day in Israel seven years ago as fear gripped her whole body. She had discounted any connection between the event in Israel and Allyson's condition after the doctors had given her a clean bill of health, but couldn't eliminate the connection from her thoughts. She fought the urge to become emotional in front of Clay and Bill. She decided to wait for further confirmation until revealing her thoughts. "Why would the king of Israel want to have an arranged marriage with the Phoenicians, Bill?" Beth asked.

"Phoenicia was the major seaport of the day, and some of the greatest seafarers of the time lived there. So many needed goods from around the Mediterranean were shipped by the Phoenicians," Bill explained.

"During what time period did this all happen?" she asked.

"We don't know exactly when Jezebel and Ahab were married, but he was king from 874 to 853 BC. Jezebel's influence was the greatest during that time." Bill took a drink from his glass of iced tea and continued. "She set out almost immediately to eradicate the true God from Israel. She had Ahab build a temple to Ba-al in the northern capital of Samaria," Bill continued.

"I don't get it. How was the influence of a false god able to take over a people so dedicated to their own God?" Beth couldn't contain her curiosity.

"God had told the people of Israel not to marry outside their faith because of the seduction of other religions. The common wisdom by theologians today is that the Israelites thought they could convert their spouses to Judaism. In fact, just the opposite occurred. Throughout First and Second Kings in the Bible, each time a successor to the throne in the North took over, the Bible says, 'They did evil in the eyes of the Lord, and sinned more than all those before them.' It really comes to a head during Ahab's reign. Jezebel sets out on a campaign to have all of God's prophets killed. This, however, only led to her death. A successor to the throne, King Jehu, had her thrown from the palace wall in Jezreel. Chariots ran over her, splattering her blood on the palace walls, tearing her body to pieces, and then dogs devoured her flesh," Bill said, raising his eyebrows.

"Ooh," Beth said as she scrunched her face. She felt sick to her stomach at the thought that Allyson could somehow be tied to what she was hearing. She stood and carried the tray of snacks into the kitchen to avoid an emotional outburst in front of the group. The joy of seeing unbelievable progress from Clay's interaction was overshadowed by the fear of what Bill had said. Beth composed herself before walking back into the living room.

"But what could all of this possibly have to do with Allyson?" Gary asked.

"Maybe nothing, maybe something, it's still too early to tell. But with Clay here and the progress we saw today, we certainly have reason to be hopeful," Bill remarked.

"And we are. Thanks to you and Clay, we truly have hope for the first time."

Clay smiled at the Carters. "It will all be okay. We'll find the answer to this—I promise. But for now, I need a drink and a cigar. Besides, Bill and I have a lot of work to do. Will you say good-bye to Allyson for me?" Clay said, as he and Bill stood up.

As she stood up to say good-bye, Beth assured him that she would.

"We'll keep you guys informed of anything we find," Bill said as they walked to the front door. He stopped and turned to Beth as they reached the door. He had seen the reaction Beth had experienced when he spoke about Jezebel. He wanted to calm her as he said, "It's going to be fine, Beth. I'm excited that we may be on the edge of discovery here. It's exciting to see progress. I'll call you tomorrow."

"Thanks again," Beth said, as she hugged both men before they left.

Bill and Clay exited the house and walked toward the truck. Clay couldn't help but feel excited about what had happened earlier. For the first time in years, he was truly engrossed in something. This had touched him like nothing before. Even so, he couldn't help but think that something dark and perhaps sinister was surrounding the situation.

His old intelligence instincts were kicking in and giving him that "itch" in his stomach. He had to admit to himself that it felt good.

"You know, Clay, it is exciting to maybe be on the verge of discovery here … don't you think so?" Bill said before entering the truck.

Clay nodded his head yes as he opened the passenger door and looked back at the house, to the window where he knew Allyson was busy drawing. *"But discovery of what?"* he whispered to himself.

CHAPTER 9

THE HAIFA CONNECTION

The red Toyota FJ40 Landcruiser sped along the road toward Haifa in Northern Israel. Michael Kazez listened to music from the cassette player in the dash as he negotiated the desert road. The two-hour drive from Jerusalem to Haifa was not a trip that Kazez normally took during the week. The business of this day would warrant the journey.

Kazez unconsciously shifted his focus from the road to the package resting in the front seat next to him. He could have used this sick day from the museum in countless other productive ways. This trip, however, would be the most important he would make in his entire life. Kazez entered the city from the south and slowed to maneuver through the business traffic of a weekday in Haifa.

His destination was a small business in the industrial portion of the city. Kazez had made the trip from Jerusalem to Haifa once a month for the last ten years, a little over a third of his life.

As the main seaport for Israel, Haifa is strategically located approximately forty minutes from the Lebanese border. The Haifa Bay houses not only the Israeli Navy, but is home to the United States Sixth Fleet as well. In ancient times, the city was called Sycaminum, and during the Crusades of the eleventh and twelfth centuries, it was known as Caiphas. In the twelfth century, Saladin, Sultan of Egypt and Syria, destroyed a Crusader castle on the site. The city remained relatively unimportant until the twentieth century, when a railroad from Haifa to the Syrian capital of Damascus was built. After the establishment of Israel in 1948, Haifa became a leading port. Today approximately four hundred and fifty thousand people live in metropolitan Haifa. As the third largest city in Israel, Haifa sits on and around the beautiful Mount Carmel and the Carmel Bay. Although it is lesser known than Tel Aviv or Jerusalem, to its inhabitants it is not only a city of incredible beauty, but also the site where the prophet Elijah destroyed the four hundred prophets of Ba-al.

Living in Haifa is not without its perils, however. The city has been the target of countless attacks from the north over the years, something the inhabitants have grown to accept. No one purposely decided to live so close to a foreign border with a history of violence without good reason, especially in the environment of the twenty-first century—no one except people who had a history there. Michael Kazez was one of those people. The five-foot-ten, thirty-three-year-old man had been an orphan since he was eighteen. An only child, Michael had been on his own since his parents died in an auto accident some fifteen years earlier. Of Lebanese descent on his mother's side, Kazez had claimed to have ancestry back to the days of the Phoenician Empire. The city of Haifa was at one time on the southern border of that empire.

Kazez pulled up to the office building in the northern industrial sector of the city and exited the Landcruiser with the cardboard box in hand. The modern two-story glass and concrete building was home to JDR Business Solutions, a software company that had sprung up, seemingly overnight, to become the major provider of software to the growing refinery business in the North. The front entry to the building was like most new structures in Israel. Several large four-foot-tall reinforced concrete barricades disguised as planters stood as sentinels denying vehicle access to the building's entrance. Michael walked up the three steps and onto the entry level, stepping between the planters and entering the building. His numerous trips to the software company had made him well-known to the staff. He stopped at the front desk and addressed the receptionist.

"Good afternoon, Arnona, I'm here to see Mr. Gutstein," Michael announced.

The shapely and beautiful dark-haired woman had been the object of desire for many of the male employees of JDR. Focused on her education and career, she had avoided all of the advances, including those from Michael. The twenty-five-year-old Arnona responded in her usual professional demeanor. "Do you have an appointment, Mr. Kazez?"

"No, I don't, but this is important."

"I'm sorry, Mr. Kazez, but Mr. Gutstein is very busy today and does not want to be disturbed."

"Arnona, this is extremely important, and he will definitely want to see me. Please let him know I'm here," Michael insisted.

"Very well." An obviously irritated Arnona depressed the intercom button. "Sir, Mr. Kazez is here and insists on seeing you. Yes, sir, I told him you were busy but he insisted. All right." She looked back up at Michael. "Go in. He will see you."

Michael walked to the controlled door and waited for Arnona to buzz him into the other area. The bolt slammed open, and Michael entered through the door into the main hallway. He quickly walked the seventy-five feet to the end of the long hall, passing by the pictures of employees and awards that decorated the walls. Michael stopped as he grabbed the door handle and took in a deep breath before opening the office door.

As Michael turned the handle and stepped into the large office, he noticed Shimon Gutstein sitting in his desk chair with his back to him talking on the phone. Michael sat at one of the two leather chairs across from the man and placed the small cardboard box on his lap.

Gutstein's office was very large, doubling as a conference room. At one end of the thirty-by-fifty-foot office was a moveable wall, allowing the room to open into the adjoining space, increasing the size to thirty-by-eighty-five feet. At the opposing end was a twenty-foot-wide cabinet with folding lockable doors. Gutstein's desk was at one side of the room and presented an odd arrangement in what appeared to be an incredible waste of space. Equally as eerie was the lack of wall decorations or windows. The odor of cigarette smoke flooded the dark and drab office. None of the staff enjoyed visits to the office to see the owner of the company, which included Michael's monthly visits.

Although Shimon was only in his late fifties, his hulking figure at over three hundred pounds plus his six-foot-one height made him a very imposing figure. His black and gray bushy moustache hid most of the features of his mouth, including the four-inch-long scar on his upper lip, a trophy from the Yom Kippur War. Only the top of the scar was visible through his moustache, giving him a sinister look. Completely bald, the middle-aged man was a threatening figure, and not someone who was used to having his daily schedule interrupted. He commanded complete loyalty from not only his employees, but his followers as well. Still talking on the phone, Gutstein swiveled in his chair glaring at Michael. Michael shifted uncomfortably as he looked back at his leader.

"That program should have been completed last month and now you want an extension!" Shimon barked into the phone. "Well, I don't care about your problems. I want it on my desk by the end of this week!" Shimon slammed the phone down and turned toward Michael. "I've told you before, no unannounced visits here."

"I know, sir, but this is very important," Michael nervously responded.

"Well, make it quick. I'm very busy," the big man warned.

"We had an incident at the museum, and I knew you would want to be told."

"Yes, what kind of incident?" Shimon demanded.

Michael shifted forward in his chair nervously. "Thursday afternoon, the director and three of the staff at the museum were killed in a fire."

Shimon leaned forward and opened the cigarette case on his desk. He removed a cigarette and lighted it. "And this affects me how?" he asked, obviously still irritated by the interruption.

"Four men were burned to death."

"And how can this possibly be of any interest to me?"

"They were all standing next to a desk with artifacts on it," Michael continued as he opened the cardboard box nervously.

"Kazez, you had better get to the point … and quickly," Shimon responded gruffly.

Michael stood and removed the two articles from the box. He placed the dagger and sheath on Shimon's desk.

Shimon's eyes opened wide as he reached for the dagger. He cradled the weapon in both of his big hands as he slowly exhaled. "Oh, Lord, can it be?" He looked upward reverently. "Can this be your instrument?"

"Yes, it is," Michael said excitedly.

"And how can you be sure of that?"

"Because there were bones on the table with it, sir," Michael went on.

Shimon leaned forward in his seat and excitedly asked, "Were they *the* bones?"

"Definitely! They were mixed with other bones just as the prophecy has foretold—two hands, two feet, and a skull." Michael knew this was what Shimon wanted to hear.

Shimon sat back in his chair with a smile on his lips and exhilaration in his eyes. His excitement could not be contained.

"That's not all," Michael added. "There was a box next to the table."

"And the lid?" Shimon demanded with excitement.

"The inscription on the top was correctly translated."

Shimon shot to his feet, looked up to the ceiling, and clasped his hands together in prayer. "Thank you, Lord. We have waited so long for this day. Praise be to you for this honor. Your followers have been patient for centuries." Shimon's joy shifted to immediate concern as he looked back at Michael. "Did anyone see you take the sheath and dagger?"

"No, the fire tripped the alarm and opened the doors. I was the first one into the vault, and I was able to hide the dagger and sheath inside my shirt. No one saw a thing," Michael told him assuredly.

"And what happened to the bodies of the staff?" Shimon asked.

"Burned completely to ash."

Gutstein fell back in his chair again looking toward the ceiling. "Truly the work of the Lord. And what of the bones?"

"They were returned to their drawer in the cage along with the box."

"You're sure they are still there?"

"Yes … they were still there as of last night."

"With the deaths of four people, the police will surely want to investigate everything completely. Did they respond quickly to the museum emergency?"

"Yes, within thirty minutes they arrived, but they don't suspect the fire had anything to do with the artifacts. They are attributing it to an electrical fire because all of the lights in the vault were broken and burned."

"We can't take any chances. We have to move quickly. Can you get us inside the museum vault within the next week?"

Michael nodded his head in the affirmative. "It will have to be planned carefully, but I believe I can do it."

"Good." Shimon reached for the intercom button. "Arnona, I need to set up an emergency meeting of all of the consultants."

"Yes, sir. When would you like the meeting scheduled?" Arnona asked.

"Tomorrow night at seven o'clock, here in my office.

"Very well, sir, I'll see to it."

Shimon turned and placed his hand on Michael's shoulder. "You've done well, Michael. Get a room for the night and be here at three tomorrow afternoon so we can prepare the presentation. Will they miss you at the museum?"

"No, sir. I start my regular days off tomorrow."

"Good. Get going and make the preparations you need for the presentation. We need to move quickly," Shimon said as he walked Michael to the door.

Michael smiled and exited the room. Like many of the employees and followers, he had longed to hear praise from his leader. It was something he had never received before. Michael was ecstatic at the praise that had been heaped upon him. He smiled defiantly at Arnona as he walked past the front desk, exiting the building into the afternoon sun.

Shimon walked back to the desk and placed his hands on the dagger. He had never dreamed that he would be the one to fulfill the prophecy that had been made almost three millennia ago. Prior to this day, he and the followers of Ba-al had viewed their purpose as keepers of the faith and guardians of the sacred scrolls for sometime in the distant future. The group of 150 followers had always viewed their task as static, meeting once a month for worship and to be guardians of the scrolls for the next generation, as so many of their predecessors had been. This day had changed all of that. Now, with the discovery of the remains of their queen, Shimon knew his responsibilities would be enormous. The discovery of the remains meant that soon their Lord would reveal the location of the ancient temple and, ultimately, of even greater importance, the identity and location of the *Anointed One*. Shimon beamed with pride as he stood over the dagger looking upward. "Lord, how blessed we are to fulfill this—your most honored of tasks. Reveal the Anointed One to us that we might defy your enemy." Shimon raised his open palms to the ceiling. "Give us the Anointed One, Lord, and allow your servants to fulfill your destiny and defy the God of Abraham." He fell to his knees, his eyes filling with tears. "Deliver the Anointed One to me, Lord, and your prophecy will be fulfilled—I swear it!"

* * * * *

Gary came into the house through the mudroom, kicking off his flip-flops at the door. Wearing shorts and a T-shirt, he was dripping with perspiration from the humidity of the day. He pulled a bath towel from the linen closet and wiped his hair, face, and neck. He bent over and ran the towel over his legs, removing the grass clippings. He stood silent for almost a minute, enjoying the twenty-five degree difference of the house from the outside temperature. Gary had experienced a renewed sense of enthusiasm since Clay's visit. The unexplainable interaction between Clay and their daughter had given him a sense of purpose he had not had in many years. He couldn't contain his newfound energy. He exhaled loudly as he threw the towel into the washing machine. "Whew, I'm glad that's done." He called out to Beth who was at the sink washing dishes. "You know, I finally figured out what God's punishment for the Garden of Eden is," Gary said as walked into the kitchen, "yard work!"

Beth remained silent and continued with the dishes. Gary walked to the cupboard and removed a glass and placed it under the ice dispenser in the refrigerator door, filling it to the top with ice. He removed a bottle of iced tea from the fridge and poured it into the glass. "What's the matter? Profundities not your gig today?" he asked, kissing Beth on the cheek from behind.

Beth turned to face Gary with tears in her eyes. Her face was gripped with fear as she looked at her husband. Gary immediately put his glass down and held his wife tightly, feeling awful for joking while she was obviously so upset. "I'm sorry, honey. What's the matter?"

"Oh, Gary, I just can't stop thinking that all of this is my fault," Beth was now crying uncontrollably.

"What do you mean? What's your fault?"

"I mean all of this that's happening with Allyson, and everything that's gone on from the time we discovered she was different."

Gary looked down at his wife tenderly. "Honey, none of this is your fault. You've been a wonderful mother. Allyson and I are blessed to have you in our lives." He hugged her more closely.

"That's not what I mean, Gary." Beth sobbed as the words came out. "It's my stupid bull-headed stubbornness that has put us where we are."

"What can you possibly be talking about, Beth?" Gary asked, confused.

"Israel!" Beth shouted. "If I hadn't insisted on going into that cave, none of this would have happened." As she was sobbing, her body was trembling with fear.

Gary held his wife's hands tightly as he looked into her eyes. "I thought we resolved this years ago, Beth. The doctors gave you and Allyson a clean bill of health after the incident in the cave. Scans and tests showed Allyson was okay. Nothing that happened in that cave can be attributed to this … nothing! This is not your fault," Gary said forcefully.

"There's no other possible explanation for what's going on. Especially after seeing how she reacted to Clay. Somehow, Allyson's condition is linked to what happened that day—I'm convinced of it! And if I hadn't insisted on going in there, none of this would have happened!"

"Beth, I'm not going to let two educated people be led down a path of mystic mumbo jumbo because it's the convenient answer. There's no scientific explanation for that theory."

"I understand, Gary, but right now I've run this over in my head a thousand times, and it keeps coming up as the only possible and probable explanation."

"Look, Beth, it's all I can do to keep from being emotional as well. I just had a complete stranger come into our house and have a conversation with my daughter … a conversation I would have cut off my right arm to have. It hurt. It cut me deeper than anything in my whole life, but I have to have confidence in Clay that he can help. We can't let emotion rule our lives right now. We have to trust that two PhDs know better than two master's degrees," Gary said with a smile, wiping the tears from his wife's face with his hand.

Beth clung to Gary tightly. She had blamed herself for Allyson's condition from the day they realized she was *different*. None of the people in the cave that day could have predicted what would happen when they opened that box. But that didn't stop Beth from placing the blame on herself for what had happened in the cave that day. Her maternal instincts had not yet come to light in 2000, but they had taken control her since the birth of her daughter. "You're right, of course. I guess I just let all of the emotions of the past week overwhelm me. But just the same … I think we should tell Bill and Clay about what happened in Israel."

"I don't think it is necessary right now, Beth, but if it becomes important later, we can tell them about it. We still have a lot of questions that need to be answered, and that might confound what they are doing. Let's wait a bit."

"But it may be important, Gary. Why are you avoiding it?"

"I'm not avoiding it. I'm just not ready to enter into a discussion centered on mysticism. We still don't know what happened that day and we probably never will, and it makes no sense to discuss it without facts to back it up. Everything will be okay, honey. I don't know how to explain it, but I just know this will all work out. I have a really good feeling about what's happened this week." He gently held her face between his hands.

Gary had avoided discussions of the events of that day. The terror that had gripped him when he believed he had lost his wife had haunted him over the years. Nothing could have ever prepared him for what had happened, and he certainly didn't want to be reminded of it.

His job now was to protect his wife and daughter, and the last thing he wanted was for Beth to feel responsible for what had happened. His eyes slammed shut at the memory of that day.

Beth reached up and kissed Gary on the lips. "Allyson and I are lucky to be loved so much. I love you, baby … I love you two weeks."

Gary slowly opened his eyes and looked at his wife. "And I love you twelve weeks," he whispered with a smile, as he hugged her tightly.

CHAPTER 10:

RESEARCH—RESEARCH—RESEARCH

CLAY WAS STILL NUMB from the interaction with Allyson he had the day before. He fought to clear his head and focus on what needed to be done. He and Bill had decided to bury themselves in research in the library at Northwestern University in an attempt to make sense of the revelations of the previous day.

The large tables in the library offered reading lights, electrical outlets, and Internet access. Clay was sitting at the table in the center of the large room, taking up enough space for four people. His laptop computer, journal, and pages from Allyson's art pads were spread out around him. People walking by looked at Clay with mild annoyance, moving on to try to find an empty table. With his usual less than approachable manner, Clay would look up and lower his brow, responding with that look he was famous for. Nothing further was required.

Bill approached the table with two steaming cups of coffee. He placed one of the cups in front of Clay. "Cream no sugar, right?" Clay looked up from his computer. "Yeah, thanks. You know, you drink enough coffee to kill two dozen lab rats."

"Hey, it's the only thing I have left. I gave up alcohol and cigarettes years ago. I don't use drugs and I'm too old to chase women. If coffee kills me … too bad. It's my one pleasure left in life." Bill smiled as he sat down across from Clay. He took a sip and sighed contentedly in Clay's direction.

Clay shook his head at Bill. "Man, I feel sorry for you people who don't drink, cause when you wake up in the morning, that's the best you're gonna feel all day."

Bill chuckled as he opened his notebook. He decided not to respond, mostly because Clay might realize it had been two days since he had taken a drink. Clay had completely immersed himself in this project since meeting Allyson. Even Bill didn't realize how much this special little girl had affected his friend. Bill's excitement was twofold. Not only had he seen a renewed sense of purpose in Clay's life, but the hope of progress for Allyson as well. He was finding it difficult to not become emotional. While Bill enjoyed many friendships, both at work and socially, his friendship with Clay was his most treasured. A special bond exists with someone you have been under fire with, and it only grows stronger with time.

"Have you found any new words in Allyson's writings?"

"Just one word—*bearer*."

"What could that mean?"

"It could mean to 'carry.' It could also mean 'responsible.' It could even mean in some circumstances 'authority, '" Clay explained.

"And is Jezebel still the most repeated word?" Bill wanted to know.

"Yup, easily, by four-to-one. Every page has Jezebel repeated multiple times. But then there's the bird pictures … I can't quite figure them out," Clay said, tugging at his right ear. "At this point, the only thing I can think of is that she just enjoys birds. Although Beth and Gary didn't indicate she was fascinated with them. Maybe if we get more words, they will somehow be tied to the bird pictures."

"Do the birds have any significance in terms of the language?"

"They can signify any number of things—war, peace, flight to heaven, crop failure, fertility—it depends upon how they're used."

"But they have to be tied in with the words, rather than just a chance sketch. I mean why else have them there other than what you said about her being fascinated with them, right?"

"That would follow. Again, maybe they'll make sense once we have more words to go on. Or maybe we can even get Allyson to tell us if she opens up more."

"And at the rate we're going, she just may open up more now that you're involved. You know, I agree with Beth. I just can't help but feel that Jezebel is the key to this."

"You mentioned something at Gary and Beth's when we were talking about Jezebel and Ba-al that was curious—something about God not wanting Israel to marry outside of the faith. I still don't follow the reasoning behind that." Clay was fishing for more information and insight.

"It's really simple. If you marry a nonbeliever, you have Satan for a father-in-law," Bill responded.

"You mean Ba-al for a father-in-law, don't you?" Clay asked with a puzzled look on his face.

"No, Satan. Look, Clay, the whole message of the Bible is a choice between God and Satan. There never was a Ba-al … only Satan."

"But then why all the different gods? I don't get it. Why not just call it God versus Satan?"

Bill shifted forward in his seat. "Throughout time man has looked to the heavens for answers to questions. God was too simple for them. God's message was simple—just worship me and all else will be taken care of. That was *too* simple for them, so they invented more complex deities to worship that offered solutions to their specific problems. Ba-al was the god of rain and fertility. When there was lightning, they called it his spear. Thunder was his voice, storm clouds, his chariot. If they wanted rain, they would sacrifice to him … usually their own children. Still no rain—more sacrifices. God finally got fed up trying to show them the error of their ways, so he eradicated Ba-al from the worshipers of Northern Israel by having all of Ba-al's prophets killed."

"Then why did the people still follow false gods?" Clay asked.

"Because, when Ba-al is gone, he just comes back in another form," Bill continued.

"You mean they're all Ba-al?" Clay was thoroughly confused at this point, and put his pen down, focusing completely on Bill's words.

As Bill took another sip of coffee, he tried to be more precise in his explanation. "El was one of the earliest recorded false gods. God eradicates him. Man invents Dagon, son of El. God eradicates Dagon. Man invents Ba-al, son of Dagon. God eradicates Ba-al. Man invents Ashtoreth, wife of Ba-al … and it just keeps on going and going. The Energizer Bunny would be proud," Bill said jokingly.

"So then they're all tied together?"

"In a manner of speaking—yes. In the truest sense they're all Satan. There is a lineage down through the ages. Ashtoreth, the wife of Ba-al, was the beautiful goddess of war and fertility. She was the same goddess of Babylon, worshipped as Ishtar. She was also worshipped as Aphrodite in Greece and as Venus to the Romans."

"How far does the lineage go?" Clay asked.

"It's just a theory, but many theologians believe that there is a genealogy that goes from the first false god all the way up to the false gods of today … Mother Earth being just one example."

"And that brings us back to the original question—why Allyson is tied to an Assyrian queen?" Clay asked.

"Not Assyrian—Samarian. Or I should say more correctly, Samarian/Phoenician," Bill continued.

"Okay, Samarian, but it still doesn't figure how Allyson would be tied to an ancient queen in Northern Israel some 2,800 years ago. I mean she's never studied the language or culture, and she's never been there. It just doesn't make any sense," Clay speculated.

"That's not entirely true. She has been there. At least technically it's not true. Gary and Beth were there on a job for SH&R in 2000 when Beth was pregnant with Allyson."

"Really?" Clay sat back in his chair. "It may be thin, but at least it's a connection. Did anything of consequence happen?"

"I'm really not sure. They don't talk about it much. They were doing some kind of classified work for the Israeli military. Beth was three months pregnant with Ally. They returned to the States early for some reason. They have never mentioned it, so I never asked. I did, however, place a note in my tablet about the trip. When I brought up the subject again, Beth avoided answering me, so I dropped the question completely, committing it to memory."

"Sounds like something happened that she and Gary don't particularly want to discuss."

"That's my supposition as well. I figured it wasn't anything of significance related to Allyson or they would have told me."

"Guess maybe I'm just grabbing at straws then. Biblical language—biblical figure—biblical location, it's probably nothing … just trying to make a connection to something." Clay's intelligence instincts were kicking in. Everything in the intel world has significance, either proving or disproving a theory. He jotted the information down in his journal for future reference.

As Bill finished his coffee, he couldn't help speculating a bit more. "It might still be something, Clay. I mean, it's the only thing we have so far. I think we should pursue it." As much of a long shot as it was, Bill had picked up on Clay's instincts, rethinking the incident.

"What do you have in mind?" Clay asked.

"There is a Gustave Doré exhibit at the Field Museum in downtown Chicago. The Theology Department at Northwestern is on the mailing list for new exhibits. They also have biblical artifacts from Israel along with it."

"Who's Gustave Doré and what does this have to do with Allyson?"

"He's a nineteenth century French painter that's known for his illustrations of scenes from the Bible, two of which are paintings of Jezebel. I think we should take Allyson down to see them."

"Are you mental? Has all that coffee warped your brain?" Clay cried out. "Even if Beth and Gary let us take her down there, which would be a huge stretch, she's bound to go into convulsions in a public forum. Beth would put us both into the hurt locker for even mentioning it!" He could not believe what Bill was suggesting. He was also thinking of how he would react if it were his daughter.

"Not necessarily." Bill mused, leaning forward. "Gary, Beth, and I saw tremendous progress with Allyson in the six months before your arrival, and phenomenal progress since you got here."

"Progress that could all be undone if Allyson is traumatized," Clay pointed out.

"Clay, you know better than anyone that any in-depth analysis has risks if you expect to have gains."

"I don't know, Bill. Risk damage to her based on the hope of gains … it's too dicey."

Bill held both hands out toward Clay, trying to make a point of his own. "Look, you've said it a thousand times. If intelligence is going to be accurate, you have to let the facts lead you to a conclusion, not your emotions. We've had the only facts available lead us to a possible answer. Clay, we have to take the chance."

"I'm not so sure, Bill," Clay added as he rubbed the back of his neck.

Bill sat quietly, looking directly at Clay and murmured, "What has happened between you and Allyson is nothing short of a miracle. You have to see that God's hand is involved in this somehow."

Clay sat up and pointed his finger at Bill. "You leave him out of this. He abandoned me years ago when he let Mary and Jody die. He hasn't had anything to do with me since. Don't bring him into this," Clay said angrily.

Bill responded, again saying quietly, "Clay, you accepted God into your life almost ten years ago. Once you do that, he never abandons you."

"Then why do I have to keep waking up in this toilet day after day when everything I ever loved is gone?" Clay cried out with a louder more emotional voice.

The young man sitting in the middle of the table turned toward Bill and Clay. "Shhh!" he demanded.

Clay stood up quickly looking at the man. Bill reached across the table, placing his hand on Clay's forearm, grasping him firmly. "We're sorry," Bill said to the young man as he looked pleadingly back at Clay.

Clay looked back at Bill and sat back down slowly. "And what could God possibly have in mind for a used up old drunk?" He said, shaking his head.

"I don't know. Maybe it's Allyson. Why else would you be the only one that's ever been able to communicate with her? And in case you haven't noticed, it's been awhile since you've had a drink … hardly a used up old drunk in my eyes." Bill felt bad about mentioning Clay's abstinence.

While still looking at his friend, Clay wanted to be angry, but he couldn't. He had to admit that he had been focused on something for the first time in years. He knew his outburst was wrong, but his stubborn pride wouldn't let him admit it. Bill was correct about one thing though—Allyson had touched him, touched him more than anything since his own daughter. In some inexplicable way, he had been given the opportunity to help someone—someone that he had connected with beyond his comprehension. A tenderness he had not felt since being around his daughter had fallen over him over these past months, and it had changed him for the better. The change had been so dramatic that he had not noticed his abstention. He took in a deep breath as the realization hit him. "That's because I haven't wanted a drink," he said stubbornly.

"Okay, Harker—whatever you say." Bill smiled.

"But you're selling this junket downtown to Gary and Beth," Clay warned, pointing his finger toward Bill.

"No problem—but you're gonna be the one to tell Allyson." Bill looked seriously at his friend.

Clay nodded his head in agreement. "Agreed. We've been at this for a long time today. I'm starving. Lets get some lunch—and by the way, it's on you, Monroe."

"Why me?"

"It's the price you pay for winning the cat fight," Clay said smiling.

"Okay, we'll eat at the French restaurant here on campus."

"Really?" Clay responded curiously.

"Yeah. Le Café Ptomaine," Bill responded.

"Great. Maybe I should have tried harder to win the argument," Clay was still grinning as he loaded his backpack.

* * * * *

The folding wall of Shimon Gutstein's office had been pulled back, allowing access to the full space. Chairs were set up in three-fourths of the expanded room, and the podium had been moved to the western end. Although it was in the evening, no one would have known because of the lack of windows. The lights above the chairs had been turned down lower than those above the podium, giving an air of importance to the front of the room.

Most of the people in the room were seated. The remainder were milling about involved in conversations.

Known to the employees of Gutstein's company as consultants, the group met once a month, not to discuss software, but to worship their god—Baal. Their high priest, Shimon Gutstein, moved to the podium to address his followers. He turned and looked at Michael Kazez. Michael nodded that he was ready.

"Please be seated. We're about to begin," Shimon started.

The remaining worshipers hurried to their seats as Shimon waited for the room to come to order. The people in the room locked their focus on their leader. Shimon was dressed in his full-length hooded robe, adorned with gold braiding at the sleeves and the edge of the hood, identifying him as the high priest. The hood of the robe was pulled back off his head, gathered around his neck.

"My brothers and sisters, thank you all for responding to this request on such short notice. We have all been patient in our worship, and our reward is near. Our Lord has been faithful," Shimon announced.

The group sensed the excitement in their priest's voice. They began to shift in their seats with puzzled looks on their faces. The room was abuzz with excitement as Shimon leaned forward on the podium with a determined look on his face.

"Our Lord has sent us a message—a message that can mean only one thing—his prophecy will be fulfilled soon," Shimon continued.

The crowd grew ecstatic. Some in the room began talking amongst themselves. Others were raising their open hands to the ceiling. Shimon raised his hands to quiet the room. They all became silent in obedience.

"The past generations of believers have not worshipped in vain, my children. Our Lord has spoken. He has shouted from his kingdom!"

Shimon's voice was building slowly to the climactic point. He looked at Michael and nodded. Michael dimmed the lights and depressed the switch, lowering the projector screen. The projector suspended from the ceiling turned on and illuminated the screen. Shimon clicked the button on the remote control, and the screen lit up with the picture of the dagger. The silence of the room was instantaneous; only the hum of the air-conditioning could be heard as the group took in the sight before them.

As quickly as the silence had arrived, the crowd erupted in cheers. Many of the believers fell to their knees wailing with moans of joy as they looked upward. Gutstein then removed the dagger from the podium and walked down the center aisle holding it in his hands. He moved the dagger back and forth from left to right as he walked down the aisle showing the followers the weapon. Some of the followers fell at his feet, lying prostrate as he passed. Shimon moved slowly back toward the podium, his eyes locked on the believers, working them into a frenzy. When he reached the podium, he set the dagger down and raised his hands, quieting the believers.

"Brother Kazez not only located the Lord's instrument, but has found the remains of the queen," Shimon exclaimed, raising his open hands to the ceiling.

The room exploded with cries of joy. In spite of Shimon's attempts to quiet the crowd, they continued to sob and wail. For the next ten minutes, members of the crowd walked forward to thank Michael, hugging, kissing, and congratulating him. Shimon raised his hands and finally quieted the crowd of people.

"Our queen was found in the lost temple of our Lord. Her remains are at the museum in Jerusalem." Shimon again depressed the projector remote. "This is a diagram of the vault where she is resting, and it is heavily guarded. The large cages in the back of the vault are where we believe she and the rest of the artifacts are being kept. Michael will keep us informed if there are any changes. He believes the file showing the location of the temple is also maintained in the vault. This too will be closely monitored."

Gutstein pointed to the seats in the front of the room. "I have selected a team of our followers to enter the museum. Along with Michael's help, we will bring our queen here in preparation for the ceremony."

"And what of the Anointed One?" a voice from the crowd asked.

"Our Lord will deliver her to us as the prophecy has foretold. Our day has come. Our father and queen will be avenged," he responded with worshipful excitement. The room again erupted in applause and cheers.

Two of the men in the front row walked to the west end of the room and opened the cabinet doors. The lights were turned on inside the cabinet, and a six-foot-tall statue was illuminated. The statue was that of a man standing on a bull with a crown of lightning bolts on his head. The golden statue gleamed brightly under the lights, commanding immediate reverence from the worshipers.

Gutstein knelt before the statue, kissing the base. He raised his head and shouted loudly, "Give us vengeance, Lord! Give us vengeance against your enemy! We who have remained faithful through the ages, we who have remained loyal to you, give us vengeance!"

The crowd all knelt and began chanting. "Ba-al, our Lord … Ba-al our Redeemer … Ba-al our Deliverer … Ba-al our Father."

CHAPTER 11

NOT JUST BIRDS

THE CARTER HOUSEHOLD WAS deeply involved in the morning ritual of taking care of Allyson. The washing machine droned in the mudroom just off of the kitchen as Gary wiped off the table. Gary and Beth had performed their daily tasks so many times, they had almost become robotic. After Bill and Clay's revelations about Allyson's writings, Gary had taken the week off from work in anticipation of more information. Time off had never been a problem for Gary, since he used so little of his vacation days throughout the year. Although his boss was not fully aware of Allyson's condition, he did know that their daughter was a special needs child as well as a shut-in. Always supportive, he marveled at how Gary was able to maintain a grueling work schedule and devote so much precious time to their daughter. He was always happy to see his dedicated workaholic employee take some time off.

Beth was walking up the stairs with Allyson's breakfast of fruit and toast when the doorbell rang. She called out to Gary.

"Honey, can you get that? It's probably Bill and Clay," she said.

"Got it, baby," Gary responded from the kitchen. He walked to the front door and opened it to see Bill and Clay standing there with anxious looks on their faces. "Good morning, guys—come on in," he said warmly.

Bill extended his hand in greeting and immediately asked, "How's Allyson doing today?"

"She's doing good, thanks for asking. Beth just took breakfast to her."

Beth came into the kitchen and hugged Bill. "How are my two favorite doctors doing this morning?" she asked with a smile, looking at Bill and Clay.

"Not too good. I'm not getting much sleep lately. My new roommate snores," Bill said with a smile.

"Well, if you fed me better, I might not snore so much," Clay responded.

Gary smiled at them both and commented, "It's easy to see why you guys are such good friends."

"Believe me, it's been painful over the years," Clay added.

"So, did you find anything new on the papers?" Beth asked Clay.

"Just one word, Beth ... *bearer*."

"As in carrying?"

"Precisely. It's still not enough to get a picture of what the words could mean, but we'll keep trying."

Bill then went on, looking rather apprehensively at Beth and Gary. "That brings us to the next question. Clay and I have a request—one that's going to be tough, but we would really like you to think about it."

"Anything, we owe you guys a lot," said Beth, looking at Gary for agreement.

"This might be more than a little difficult, Beth. We'd like to take Allyson to the Field Museum today to see an exhibit," Bill continued, knowing full well the effect his request might have on both parents.

Beth's eyes opened wide as she heard the request. "Wow, you're right. That is big. Bill, I know we've recently had monumental progress, but that's kinda pushing the envelope, don't you think?" she asked, showing all the concern and trepidation Bill expected.

"Clay and I feel that the gains we could make outweigh the risks."

"What gains do you think we can make?" Gary asked.

"The Field Museum has an exhibit of religious artwork and artifacts. We've been thinking for awhile now that this condition Allyson has may somehow be religiously based."

"Define religiously based, Bill?"

"Primarily *Jezebel*, although the words *behold* and *sayeth* also support it. The wording seems to be biblically based, or at minimum, a period in the Bible," Clay went on to explain.

"That's pretty thin, Clay," Beth said.

"Razor thin, Beth, but it's the strongest lead we've had so far," Bill mused.

Beth reached out and tenderly held Bill's hand. "Bill, you know we trust and love you and, more importantly, Allyson loves you, but this could do a great deal of damage."

"I know Beth, and believe me, I wouldn't even suggest it unless I thought we could benefit from it. Look, she's made incredible gains with Clay and is definitely connecting to him somehow. I'm very confident that so long as Clay is with her, nothing will happen to her. And I'll be right there as well," Bill went on. Bill's faith and trust in Clay had been forged over decades of experience, but he understood Gary and Beth's reservations. He knew they were operating solely on his word alone.

Clay leaned toward Beth trying to reassure her. "Beth, for some reason Allyson has connected with me. I don't understand why, and as such, I understand your concern. I'm new to this whole thing as well, but Bill feels strongly that this trip could be beneficial, and if there is one thing I know about him, it's that his analysis and hunches have always played out. And I can echo his stand that if anything happens, we'll bring her right back," Clay said convincingly.

"If it would make you feel better, why don't you and Gary come with us?" Bill asked.

"Believe me, I would like to go with you, but you're right—there is a connection with Clay. When he's around her, the rest of us seem to be invisible to her," Beth admitted. "It's more difficult than you could ever imagine for me to say that. For a mother to admit that a complete stranger has a deeper relationship with her daughter than she does is troubling. I'm having a very difficult time with that, but for now, Gary and I will just have to trust."

"I have a suggestion," Clay offered. "Why don't we ask Allyson and see how she feels about it? If she says no, we won't do it."

"I agree with Bill, honey. I think it's worth a try," Gary said.

Complete fear gripped Beth as her body trembled. "Gary, I can't go through another one of Ally's episodes … I just can't watch that," Beth responded in a small frightened voice.

Gary reached across the table and held Beth's hand. "Honey, either we try to resolve this now, or we live the life of a shut-in family maybe forever. Look, baby, we need to try this. Someday Allyson will be in her forties or fifties, and we'll be gone. If her condition isn't resolved, she'll wind up in an institution, in a cell, locked away from the world for the rest of her life. We need to do everything in our power now to avoid that," Gary pleaded.

Beth lowered her head and stared at the floor with tears filling her eyes. Gary's words made sense. Truth was she had thought of that very scenario many times. She took a breath and raised her head. Beth pressed her lips together tightly and sighed. "Okay, let's ask Ally."

Gary smiled at his wife. "It's going to be fine, honey. I feel good about this. It will be okay."

They all stood and walked up the stairs to Allyson's room. Beth stopped in the middle of the stairs and turned toward Bill.

"You'll bring her right back if anything happens, right?"

"Of course, Beth, I wouldn't risk anything happening to her."

They reached the top of the stairs, and Beth opened Allyson's door. The four of them entered the room. Allyson was in her usual place, at the table writing on her art pads. Gary and Beth kneeled down next to her.

"Honey, Dr. Bill and Mr. Harker are here to see you," Beth said.

Allyson stood and turned to face Bill and Clay with a smile on her face. She ran to Clay, hugging him tightly around his waist. Clay knelt down, and Allyson immediately hugged him around the neck. Tears came to Beth's eyes as she watched her daughter's interaction with Clay. It was apparent to her that she needed to trust not only her and Gary's instincts, but Allyson's as well. She was truly connected to Clay in some unexplainable way.

Clay smiled back at the little girl. "Hi, Allyson, it's good to see you again."

Allyson smiled back at Clay. "Thank you for coming to see me."

"Allyson, Dr. Bill and I have a question to ask you. We would like to take you downtown to the museum to see some artifacts. Would you like to go with us?"

Allyson had a curious look on her face. "What are arktifaxed?"

Clay smiled back at her. It had been many years since he had to speak with a young child. "They're very old things from the past. You don't have to go if you don't want to, but Dr. Bill and I would like to show them to you. Would that be okay?"

Allyson turned and looked at Beth and Gary. "Would that be okay, Mommy?"

Beth and Gary stood up and walked next to Clay and Allyson. Beth knelt down and held her hand. "Yes, honey, that would be okay with Daddy and me."

Allyson turned back toward Clay. "Yes, I can go."

Beth held Allyson's face in her hands. "Would you like Daddy and me to go with you?"

Allyson hugged Beth. "No, Mommy, it will be okay."

Beth could not contain her emotions any longer. She held her daughter unable to control the tears. What miracle had occurred to allow her to have a conversation with her daughter, a conversation she had thought for the longest time she would never have.

Clay fought back the urge to become emotional as he choked the words out. "Allyson, if you get scared or want to come back, we'll bring you home—okay?"

"Okay."

"Would it be okay if we went now, Allyson?" he asked.

"Yes." Allyson responded enthusiastically.

Bill leaned toward Beth whispering. "Does she need to change clothes or have something to eat?"

"No, she's fine now. She finished breakfast earlier, but if you're out longer than two hours, she may get hungry."

Beth reached for Allyson's right hand. They all walked from her room slowly. Beth let Allyson set the pace as they descended the stairs.

Allyson looked at the inside of the house, taking in all of the sights she had not seen in a very long time. Her hand held Beth's tightly as they entered the living room. They stopped at the foyer by the front door. Beth kneeled down and looked at her daughter.

"I love you, honey. You do what Dr. Bill and Mr. Harker say—okay?" Beth told her.

"Okay, Mommy, I love you too," Allyson responded.

Beth stood and grasped Gary's hand tightly. Bill reached for the doorknob and looked at Allyson. He slowly opened the door to reveal a sunny June day. Holding Allyson's hand, Clay moved through the doorway following Bill. They all stopped on the front porch, allowing Allyson to move at her own pace. She looked around in wonder at the sky, the houses, and the trees. She looked up at a bird chirping in the tree in the front yard. She touched her face to feel the warmth of the sun on it, a feeling she had not known in a very long time.

"Are you ready to go, Allyson?" Clay quietly asked.

"Yes." She gazed up at him with a little smile.

They walked down the steps, Clay holding her right hand and Bill holding her left. Beth and Gary watched from the front window. They had walked halfway down the front walk when Allyson stopped. Bill and Clay stopped and looked down at her. Allyson was frozen, her eyes locked on the house across the street. Clay was the first to notice the tremble in her hand. He knelt down in front of her.

"What's the matter, sweetheart?" he asked.

She didn't respond, her eyes still fixed across the street. Clay turned his head and looked across the street in the same direction, trying to see anything. The only thing he could see was the neighbor mowing his lawn. He turned back toward Allyson.

"Allyson, what's the matter?" he repeated. "Can you tell me?"

She responded to Clay with her eyes still locked on the man across the street. "Scary men chasing him."

Clay turned his head again to see the man mowing the lawn. Bill heard the front door open and turned to see Gary and Beth coming outside. He held his hand up, palm out signifying for them to wait. Gary and Beth stopped in the doorway as Bill knelt down next to Allyson.

"Can you tell me what you see, Allyson?" Bill asked.

"They're chasing him," Allyson said with a trembling voice.

"Them? Allyson, what do you see?" he asked again.

"The birdmen," she murmured.

Bill and Clay looked at each other, their brows furrowed.

"Honey, I don't know what you mean. There's only the man mowing his lawn ... do you mean him?" Bill said.

"No, Dr. Bill, the birdmen chasing him," she responded, but seemed agitated.

"Birdmen?" Clay said looking at Bill curiously. He looked across the street once again to see the man mowing the lawn. "Allyson, can you tell me what you see the man and the birdmen doing?"

She moved closer to Clay, leaning into him for comfort. "The man is walking and two birdmen are flying around him."

Bill turned and smiled at Gary and Beth, not wanting them to be worried, or come out and possibly interrupt the interaction with Allyson. He mouthed the words to them with a reassuring smile. "It's okay."

"Allyson, it's very important that you tell me exactly what you see. What do the two birdmen look like?" Clay asked.

Clay let go of her hand and reached around her with his arm, holding her close.

"They are flying around and talking to him," she slowly began to explain.

Clay continued to look at the man in disbelief. "They're flying around him ... how many?"

"Two."

"Tell me what they look like, Allyson."

"They have wings," she replied.

"You mean wings like birds' wings?"

"No."

Clay looked at Bill; he couldn't believe what he was hearing. Could she be hallucinating? Certainly she believed what she was seeing. He felt her trembling getting worse.

"Can you hear what they're saying?" he asked.

"No," she muttered.

Bill looked at Clay. "Clay, she's starting to tremble ... we should get her back in the house."

Clay didn't respond to Bill. He picked Allyson up, holding her to his chest. They walked back up the sidewalk to the house. Allyson continued to look across the street over Clay's shoulder. As they walked through the door, Allyson saw a woman jogging in front of their house with a birdman flying behind her.

Beth closed the door behind them. "What happened?" she said nervously.

"I don't know," Clay responded as he handed Allyson to her.

Beth carried Allyson through the living room and up the stairs to her room as Bill and Gary walked into the living room. Clay opened the front door and looked across the street once again to see the neighbor mowing his lawn. He closed the door and shook his head.

"What happened?" Gary insisted.

Clay answered as he entered the room, "Allyson said she saw birdmen flying around your neighbor across the street."

"What?" Gary exclaimed.

"That was my reaction," Clay said.

Beth came down from Allyson's room and walked into the conversation.

"How is she, honey?"

"She's okay. She fell asleep in my arms so I put her in bed. Please tell me what happened."

Bill spoke first. "We don't know. She said she saw birdmen flying around your neighbor. She got scared so we brought her back in."

"Birdmen … what could she be talking about?" Beth anxiously asked.

"I thought maybe hallucinations, but she's never exhibited that trait before," Bill commented.

"She's never hallucinated in the past. What could possibly be happening now?" Gary repeated.

Bill looked down at the stack of Allyson's papers on the coffee table. He listened to Clay, Gary, and Beth's comments while he focused on the papers. Chills ran up his spine as he saw the image. He turned to interrupt Clay. "We need to go back and do some more research on this, Clay," he said.

Clay stopped talking to Beth and looked at his friend. Clay had been around Bill too long to miss the telegraphed message he had just received. He knew that Bill's anxiety needed immediate attention. Gary and Beth looked at the two men curiously.

"Is everything okay, Bill?" Gary asked.

"Yes. I just want to get back and follow up with Clay on this. I'll touch bases with you guys tonight, or the first thing in the morning. Are these the latest drawings?" Bill asked, pointing to Allyson's papers.

"Yes, I set them there for you," Beth answered.

Bill picked up the papers and walked to the front door with Clay. "You'll let me know if there's any change with Allyson," Bill went on.

"Sure thing, Bill," Gary responded with a concerned look on his face.

"Talk to you soon," Bill added as they walked out the door.

Clay waited for the door to close before he asked the question. "Okay, what's up?" he asked.

Bill handed Clay the papers. "I didn't want to alarm Gary and Beth while we were there. Look at the pictures on the papers."

Clay looked at the pictures of Allyson's birds. "Yeah … and?"

Bill hurried to the driver's side of the truck as Clay stood by the passenger side door. "Clay, she's not seeing birdmen … I believe she's seeing demons."

"Demons! Have you gone completely nuts, Monroe? You dragged me out of there to tell me fairy tales."

"What we saw in the drawings as the forked tails, I believe are actually the legs, and the bird's beaks are probably the horns." Bill couldn't control his emotions. He felt an urgency pouring over him to get back to the house and get into his books and reference material. "Clay, it all makes sense to me now. Her episodes … the total fear … the screaming and trembling. It all makes perfect sense."

Bill and Clay entered the truck and buckled their seatbelts. "You expect me to believe that little girl is seeing mythical creatures?" Clay protested.

Bill started the truck and backed out of the driveway. He answered as he drove. "Not mythical, Clay, demons are real. They're just not visible to us."

"Then how would she be able to see them? Can you answer me that?" The information Clay had just received was way beyond what he was able to digest. All of his training over the years had taught him to only believe in what he could see, not what he was told, and now all of his senses were screaming at him.

"No, but I can't answer why she writes in an ancient language either," Bill reiterated as he stopped in the street, putting the truck into drive.

Clay looked at the drawings, and then turned to look at the neighbor, still shaking his head in disbelief. The man smiled and waved at Bill and Clay as they drove off down the street.

CHAPTER 12

BARING ONE'S SOUL

Shimon Gutstein knelt before the idol of Ba-al in his office. His team of disciples were behind him, also kneeling in submission to their god. The group of people all wore white linen hooded robes, and softly whispered in prayer as they clasped their hands together. Shimon kissed the base of the idol as he softly whispered his closing prayer. The big man slowly stood as he backed out of the enclosure. The disciples followed their leader and stood, bowing at the waist as Shimon closed the doors to the cabinet.

The ten people began removing their robes and sitting down at the conference table. Shimon pulled his robe over his head, revealing his dress shirt and tie. He folded his robe and placed it on the edge of his desk. He lifted the gold medallion of Ba-al from around his neck, kissing the center of the medallion, and placing it inside the wooden box on his desk. Pulling a cigarette from the container on his desk and lighting it, he then removed his suit coat from the back of the chair and put it on. He was purposely taking his time as his disciples waited at the conference table. Shimon was a master of manipulation, holding both the attention and loyalty of his employees and followers. The opposite end of the conference table was loaded with coffee, juice, and snacks for the meeting. Walking to the head of the conference table,

Shimon sat down and looked at the group of people seated in front of him. He had handpicked the nine people seated in his office not only for their skill sets, but for their unquestionable loyalty.

All of the team was either retired military or ex-military. The team leader was Douglas Weiss, a retired army sergeant, and Shimon's most trusted follower. Second was Rebecca Isaroff, who had the distinction of being "the meanest, nastiest bitch I have ever been around" according to Weiss. David Greenblatt, the forty-year-old man who could drive or fly anything with wheels or wings came next. Levi Ain, the youngest man on the team, was a weapons expert and a self-proclaimed lady's man. Twenty-nine-year-old Omer Esterson, whose only expertise was information systems, seemed to be the geeky "odd man out" on the team. Tamir Berkowitz, the only American-born person on the team, had been a counter-intelligence expert with the U.S. Army until his less-than-honorable discharge four years earlier. Paz Freedman was a cold and calculating man who killed on command, with seemingly no remorse. Joseph Mokotoff had been chosen solely because of his loyalty to Douglas Weiss. Finally, there was Michael Kazez, whose only contribution was his position with the museum security staff. Had it not been for his position, Douglas would not have him anywhere around the team. He disliked him intensely because of Michael's talent for ass kissing.

Shimon puffed on the cigarette as he fired off commands at the group. "We need to enter the museum as soon as possible. The date for the prophecy is close, and we need to be ready when the Lord reveals the Anointed One to us. I would like to enter within the next five to six days. Michael, when is the least amount of staff on duty at the museum?" Shimon asked.

"Without question, Saturday or Sunday. Although it may be more difficult to get everyone inside undetected, there will be fewer staff there," Michael answered.

"And what do we need in order to get access to the area where the artifacts and our queen are located?"

"The vault requires two proximity cards, one of which has to be from a director. The security post isn't manned on the weekends, but it could still be opened if we had the two cards," Michael went on to explain.

Shimon walked behind where Douglas Weiss was sitting and placed his hand on the big man's shoulder. "Douglas ... your thoughts about entry."

The forty-two-year-old Douglas was chosen for his loyalty and tactical abilities. At well over six feet tall and 225 pounds, his muscular and fit frame was also more than capable of performing any task given him. "Better to enter at night, but without the two cards, we may have to do this during the day." Douglas leaned back in his chair. "You know, Lord, if we went in just before closing, we could be in an excellent position to surprise them completely. That way, the visitors would be out of the building."

Shimon puffed on his smoke as he thought about the information. He looked across the table toward Michael. "How many directors are there at the museum?"

"Eight."

"Any of them work on the weekends?"

"Not on a regular basis. They will come in from time to time, but nothing that we could count on. Besides, it's rare that the vault is accessed on the weekends."

Shimon continued walking around the table puffing on his cigarette. "All right then, we go in this Friday, just before closing. Does that work for everyone?"

The team members nodded in agreement as Shimon looked on. "Can we be ready in three days?" He looked inquiringly at Douglas.

Weiss turned toward Rebecca Isroff and handed her the list of required items he had written down during the conversation. "Can these be obtained by Thursday?" he asked.

The thirty-six-year-old woman had been with the order for eight years, and had proven herself a very loyal follower. Her five-foot-eight, 180-pound manly frame commanded respect, and usually got it. Rebecca ran her index finger down the list slowly. "No problem," she said looking back at Weiss.

Douglas looked up at Shimon. "How many items do we need from the museum?"

Shimon walked back to his desk and looked at his notepad. "The ten floor lamps, the two smaller lamps, the queen's remains, and the site file," Shimon responded.

"Don't we need the box and the altar cloth?" Michael asked.

"No, it's not necessary that we have them. Besides, the box is too heavy to transport."

Douglas panned his eyes around the table as he spoke. "I only want silenced pistols. Everyone wears rubber gloves and keeps them on until we have left the building. Rebecca will have radios for us. Don't use any of the security radios. Michael, is there security at the other buildings?"

"Yes, two per building and one mobile patrol. The mobile patrol is usually at the main building for closing. You'll know if they're in, because the patrol vehicle will be parked by the loading dock."

"Good." Douglas turned back toward Shimon. "Based on that, we can be ready in three days."

"Very well then—we go in on Friday," Shimon concluded.

"Lord, even if we obtain everything, can we be ready by the seventh of July? We will be cutting it very close," Tamir Berkowitz asked.

"If the file contains all the information we need, then we can be ready." Shimon turned toward Michael. "Can you confirm the file is in the vault by tomorrow?"

"Yes, sir, I'll be in the vault first thing in the morning."

"Good. Call Douglas as soon as you've verified that it's there. What would be the best time to enter?" Shimon asked Weiss.

"We will enter the museum an hour before closing time and be ready after the doors are locked. Michael can give us the best places to hide to avoid detection until all the visitors are out of the building." Weiss turned toward David Greenblatt. "We'll need you to park the van at the service dock at precisely 6:45 p.m." David nodded his head in agreement.

Shimon panned his eyes, looking at all his disciples. "I don't want anyone at the museum harmed. There will be enough excitement made over the incident without harming anyone. Do you all understand?"

All of the disciples responded in the affirmative.

"Bring all of the items here, and we will make all the preparations for the ceremony on the seventh," Shimon said.

David Greenblatt leaned forward in his chair. "Lord, this will all mean nothing without the Anointed One. Do we have any idea where she is?"

"Not yet, but the Lord will reveal her to us when the time is ready."

"Does the prophecy tell when she will be given to us?" Rebecca asked.

"No, only that she and her mother will be delivered to us. The prophecy states that the Anointed One was identified just a few days before the ceremony in 807 BC. She was to be transported to the temple and then sacrificed," Shimon explained.

"Holiness, our forefathers failed. Does the prophecy tell us how?" Rebecca again asked.

Shimon leaned forward and took a deep breath. "The prophecy tells us that our ancestors failed to take the mother to the temple with the Anointed One. They failed to follow the Lord's commands. The Sacred Scrolls have told us what to do. We will not waver from its commandments," Shimon responded.

Recovered from the original high priest's home, the Sacred Scrolls had been the most treasured writings of the followers, and carefully handed down to each succeeding priest for almost three millennia. Over the centuries, only the priests had been allowed to see the writings. Shimon had followed the direction of his predecessors, keeping the scrolls locked away at his home.

"Then what is to say that we will not fail?" Paz Freedman asked.

"Because the time was not right for them. They acted too soon because they were in too big a hurry for the vengeance of their parents' death. Our Lord's followers were too few then. His children now number as the stars in the sky. The God of Abraham has no power here on earth in our Lord's kingdom. We will not fail. Our queen will be restored to her throne and her enemies vanquished. We need only be patient for the Anointed One to be delivered to us. And make no mistake, the Lord will deliver her, and we will be victorious," Shimon stated.

"Do we know where she will come from, Holiness?" Rebecca asked.

"She could be anywhere—anywhere at all. She could even be outside the country. Be assured, she will be given to us no matter where she is," Shimon repeated confidently.

* * * * *

Beth came down the stairs with Allyson's empty dinner tray. Gary was sitting in the living room easy chair reading the newspaper. The sun was setting on another day's chores at the Carter house. When Gary would come home from work, he enjoyed reading the evening paper before assuming his responsibilities. He would then see to Allyson's needs for the rest of the evening and into the morning before he would go off to work to begin another day's duty. At this time of the day was when Beth would usually go out for a drive or a walk around the neighborhood to relax. That routine had been interrupted since the arrival of Clay Harker. Beth wanted to be close to the house and the phone since the revelations of Clay's first visit. There was now a newfound spring to her step, and an endless amount of energy since that day. She had even started getting up with Gary in the morning, rather than sleeping in till he left for work. A new hope had entered the Carter household, a hope that had become infectious.

Gary looked up at Beth as she walked by him. "How is she, honey?"

"She's fine. I just got her out of the tub and put *The Lion King* on the TV for her," Beth answered.

Gary folded the paper and followed her into the kitchen. "I was hopeful that Ally would talk more after the interaction with Clay, but she hasn't said any more than usual."

Beth poured a cup of coffee and sat across the table from Gary. "I know. I was kind of hoping for more as well, but she is only opening up around Clay. I thought Bill would have called by now with an answer as to what happened this morning. Guess they got busy. Has Allyson said anything to you about what happened?" Beth asked.

"No … you?"

"Nope, nothing," Beth muttered.

"I still don't understand what Clay said about Walt. Something about Ally seeing someone around him while he was mowing the lawn."

"Bill hustled him out of here so fast, it's almost like something scared him," Beth replied.

"I know—but Ally didn't seem to get scared, just agitated … I think that's significant. I'd be more worried if she had started screaming or shaking."

Beth sat up in her chair as if she had been hit by a brick. "Yeah, you know you're right. I hadn't thought of it until you just mentioned it. Wow, that is significant. I guess I've been too busy worrying about what might happen to Allyson that I'm not seeing the bigger picture. Gary, just think of the progress we've made in only a few days, and all due to Clay coming into our lives. We really have a lot to be hopeful for. Honey, this is exactly why I think we should tell Bill and Clay about what happened in Israel. I still feel it's tied to Allyson somehow."

"Beth, I really don't want to relive that day again. I thought I lost you, and I can't go through that again," Gary said.

Beth hugged her husband tightly. "I know, baby, but everything worked out okay. We're all fine."

"Honey, three of the people that were there that day have since died … all of whom were in their forties."

"Gary, you can't possibly think that it was related to what happened that day?" Beth looked at him inquiringly.

"Three heart attacks within a couple of years? Come on, Beth, I'm not a superstitious man, but when three seemingly healthy men keel over so close to each other, believe me, it got my attention. And remember, Beth, they were the ones closest to the box with you."

"If your supposition is correct, then why didn't I die of a heart attack?"

"Because you were blown away from the box and almost died that day!" Gary responded emphatically.

"Look, Gary, you make my argument for me. We need to tell Bill and Clay about what happened. Maybe there is something to what you say—maybe not—but either way we won't know unless we involve them in the dialogue. We've kept this to ourselves for too long."

"Beth, we told the authorities everything that day. They didn't have a clue about the reasons for what happened, and they're the experts. Why do you think Bill and Clay would know more than them?"

Beth looked across the table at Gary. Her brow furrowed as she looked deep into her husband's eyes. "Gary, what is it that you're not telling me?"

"What do you mean?"

"Gary Carter, I can tell when you're hiding something from me—you should know that by now. Why are you trying to avoid talking about what happened that day—what are you trying to hide from me?"

Gary looked away from his wife's eyes. He ran the fingers of his right hand through his hair and cleared his throat.

Beth could read her husband's mannerisms even better than he could. "Gary, now you're scaring me. I know you're keeping something from me—now tell me what it is!" Beth pleaded.

Gary looked up from the table with a look of fear on his face. "Honey, I thought you had died that day. You weren't breathing when I got to you." Gary's elbows were on the table as he cradled his head in his hands. Beth remained silent, but reached across the table and touched his arm. He raised his head and looked into her eyes and continued.

"Before I passed out, I checked your pulse and looked at you." his voice quavered. "Then I saw writing on your forehead."

Beth sat back in her chair. "Writing—what do you mean writing?" she demanded.

"I didn't put much credence in it initially. In fact, I thought I was hallucinating. I could hardly see because of the pain from the howling, and the light was so dim. I completely discounted it. I've thought about it in passing over these past six years, but didn't give it much importance until Ally's writings."

"What do you mean, Gary?" Beth said with concern in her voice.

Gary looked into his wife's eyes. "It's the same kind of writing, Beth … it's the same writing as Ally's."

A cold chill ran down Beth's spine as she listened to Gary. "Are you sure it wasn't your imagination?"

"I wasn't at first, but after watching Clay translate Ally's words, I realized it was the same. And I've been reliving the nightmare ever since."

"Why didn't you tell me this before?"

Gary took a deep breath and exhaled slowly. "I wanted to, but when you told me how you thought the whole incident that day was your fault … well, I just couldn't do it. I certainly didn't want you hurt anymore."

Beth grasped Gary's hands tightly. "Thank you, honey. I'm so very sorry for placing that burden on you. It was wrong of me to do that to you, but I still can't help thinking we could have avoided all of this had it not been for my insistence that day. That being said, it happened, and we need to deal with it." Beth got up and walked to the other side of the table and hugged Gary.

Gary looked at her. "I'm sorry. I should have told you. It wasn't something that I gave any importance to then, but now that Ally is opening up, it has new meaning. Besides, it didn't even look like words to me then, but after seeing Clay translate those characters, I realized it was writing," he continued.

"Do you know what the words were? I guess I mean to say, would you recognize them if you saw them again?" Beth asked.

"I think I would remember, but I can't be sure."

"But you're sure you saw something on my forehead?"

"Very sure, it was plain as day."

"I mean it couldn't have been dirt or dust or anything else, could it?"

"No, it was writing of some sort, the same writing as Allyson's."

"How long did it stay there?"

"Honey, everything happened so fast after the explosion. The screaming was so loud and painful. I didn't stay conscious for long after getting to you. I saw the words for just an instant and passed out almost immediately after that. When I woke up, I carried you outside. After I got us out, I noticed the writing was gone. That's when I decided that it must have been due to hallucinations of some kind. The rest of the team came out while I was looking after you. You woke up shortly after that, and the rest you know about," he finished.

"And you think you could recognize the words if you saw them again?" Beth repeated the question for her own satisfaction.

Gary scratched the top of his head. "Yeah, I think so."

"And none of Ally's words look like what you saw?"

"No … and believe me, I've been looking."

"Gary, that's all I need to hear. We have to tell Bill and Clay about this as soon as possible."

"I suppose you're right, honey, but when they hear this, they'll call the men in the little white coats."

"Gary, what could possibly be weirder than Ally writing in a foreign language?"

"Point well taken," Gary grudgingly conceded.

CHAPTER 13

I SEE YOU

THE JOSEPH SCHAFFNER LIBRARY was almost vacant. Only an occasional student or professor milled about the area. Located on the second floor of Wieboldt Hall, on Northwestern University's Chicago Campus, the facility is the only campus library within the University Library system. It provides library and information services for the Kellogg School of Management, the School of Continuing Studies, and the Institute for Learning in Retirement. The library traces its history back to the original campus in the Tremont House on Lake Street, the home of the first School of Commerce. As a founding member of the Hart, Schaffner and Marx clothing giant, Schaffner was a trustee of Northwestern University from 1910 through his death in 1918. In his honor, the library was named after him in a ceremony in 1927. The library's extensive collection serves as a perfect start for any research project and had always been a favorite sanctuary for Bill Monroe.

Bill and Clay were at their usual place, taking up the entire end of one of the long library tables. Because of the library's requirement for a Net ID, Bill was doing research on the web in the facilities extensive history of the ancient world, while Clay poured over five books on demons. The two men had been engrossed in their project for over four hours, and it was taking its toll on Clay. His body was screaming for a cigar fix.

Clay finally raised his head. "How do these people even know what a demon looks like? I mean there must be thousands of different depictions describing them. I must have looked at two hundred different pictures, each of them pretty much the same. Each one of the pictures shows them with horns, wings, tails, and a face that would stop a clock. If no one has seen them, how do they know that they look like this?" he pondered.

"There are a few examples throughout history of sightings," Bill responded.

"But individual sightings can best be explained by fantasy, hallucinations, or even outright lying," Clay went on. "How do we know if they're accurate sightings?"

"Most are probably in the categories of hallucinations or fabrications. There are however a few sightings witnessed by multiple parties. One sighting was just a few years ago at a revival in California. It was witnessed by over a hundred people."

"Really? What happened?" Clay's interest was piqued as he tried to get in a more comfortable position.

"It was at a revival in Los Angeles about three years ago. When the pastor asked people to come forward to be saved, a woman came up to the podium and stood before him. After looking at her for quite some time, the pastor informed her that she was demon possessed. When he commanded the demon to depart the woman, everyone said that a dark gray creature, covered in fur with a tail, came out of her mouth. Everyone in the church saw it. There was another sighting at a church in Boston around the turn of the last century. It was a winged creature with horns and a tail. That one was witnessed by thirty or so people," Bill continued.

"So then it differs as to how they appear?" Clay asked.

"It gets a little sketchy as to how they may appear. I suppose a lot depends on what we expect them to look like, and the fact that they can appear to us in many forms. And of even greater importance, it depends a lot on what scares us the most," Bill replied.

"What do you mean?" Clay said curiously.

"Satan knows our greatest fears. If you're claustrophobic, then he uses that—if you fear heights, then he'll use that. I think that what would scare you the most about demons would be manifested in how they appear to you personally."

"So then Allyson's vision of what they look like may be different from what we would see," Clay mused.

"From what I understand, yes. But the only thing we have to base it on is what the angels look like," Bill said.

"Okay, Monroe, you've really lost me now," said Clay, frowning.

"There are examples in the Bible, and throughout history by the way, of what angels looked like when they appeared to people—sometimes with wings, sometimes with halos, or an aura if you will, and sometimes in all manner of clothing. During the Six Day War, the Syrians overran an Israeli position. They were shooting all the wounded Israeli soldiers. When they came upon a wounded Israeli officer named Gershon Klein, they dropped their weapons and ran back across the border. Later they all reported to the United Nations that there were thousands of angels around Klein.

During the Yom Kippur War, an Egyptian officer surrendered his tank column to a single Israeli soldier. When asked why he surrendered to one soldier, the officer said, 'What do you mean one? There were thousands of them.' Clearly the angels appeared in Israeli uniforms," Bill went on.

"But that's angels, not demons," Clay added, still skeptical.

"Okay, theological history lesson. When Satan battled God and lost, he was cast out of heaven with his followers, which numbered a third of the hosts of heaven."

"So how many were a third?" Clay asked.

"We just don't know … hundreds of thousands, millions, billions, trillions. We just don't have a clue. What we do know is that there are two different groups of fallen angels—those who can move around freely and those who are locked up by chains and held in darkness."

"So the ones that roam freely are what we are dealing with here, right?"

"Precisely," Bill responded.

"So from what I've read so far, the remaining ones are here to torment or possess us. Depending upon how many people are being tormented, it could very well be billions of them."

"Yup," Bill agreed.

"Billions of demons flying around tormenting all of humanity—the concept is frightening," Clay exclaimed, rubbing the back of his neck.

"But probably not everyone."

"Why not everyone? I thought we were all affected."

"The torment primarily goes to those who belong to Christ. Why bother tempting those you already own? Why allocate your assets on the people who deny God? Better to deploy them where they're needed. What Satan and his followers want is to pull as many souls away from God as they can. They want to drag as many into damnation as possible. They already know they're doomed to spend eternity in hell, so why not drag as many down with them as they can and deprive God of as many souls as possible. Given that, the primary focus is on those that haven't made a decision to follow God yet, and those that have committed to a life with him, versus those that deny God. And that's not all—the demons don't sleep or rest. They are available 24/7 to haunt, torment, deceive, plan, and execute all manner of iniquity to try to pull you away from God."

Clay sat back in his chair, trying to absorb what he had just heard. It was very hard to imagine millions, possibly billions, of demons roaming the earth, constantly tempting humanity—grotesque creatures, involving themselves in the everyday lives of people walking the earth. How horrific it would be to have the capability to see that. He was just now beginning to understand what Allyson might be going through.

"If that's what Allyson is seeing, what must it be like to witness that?" Clay wondered.

Bill reflected on what Clay was asking and then responded. "I remember what one of my theology professors said many years ago. He said that 'if we could see the demons that haunt us, it would drive us mad.' That should put it into perspective for all of us."

"It certainly explains a lot about Allyson's screaming and crying episodes. What must she be going through, Bill? But that begs the next question. Why doesn't she see demons around us, or Gary and Beth for that matter? I mean if your analysis is correct, at a minimum she should see them around you and me."

"The only thing I can think of, Clay, is divine protection. What I mean is that she is being watched over. I don't have an answer why she wouldn't see them around us."

"Not seeing them around me is one thing, but you're a man of God. Even her parents are church-going believers. Why not see them around Beth and Gary?" Clay interjected.

"You're missing the point Clay. The demons could even be around the nonbeliever. They can use the people they already own to their purpose. I suppose the most classic example would be Adolf Hitler. While I have no evidence to support it, I'm sure they influenced him regarding the holocaust. And by the way, don't sell yourself short; I'm the one that baptized you—remember?" After years of requests from Bill and pleading from Mary, Clay had finally agreed to be baptized. The ceremony had taken place on Labor Day in 1997 at Mary's church in Georgetown, with Bill performing the service. To Mary, Jody, and Bill's delight, Clay had reached a point in his life that he was feeling his mortality and wanted to move to the next level. During his military career, Clay had seen Mary sacrifice so very much over the thirty years, and it was time to focus on her. Four years and ten days later, Clay had his entire life turned upside down. He never went to church again after that day.

Clay smiled back. "Okay, point taken, but if she's being watched over, why allow her to be able to see them in the first place?" He needed to know for his analytical curiosity, but also for the long-ignored spiritual side of him.

"That's where the trust issue comes into play. God is allowing it for a reason. We just need to trust that it will be okay in the end," Bill reasoned.

"Bill, I've read a lot here in recent days and understand very little, but could it be that she's possessed?"

Bill shook his head quickly from side to side. "I don't believe that for a minute. God watches over all of us, but especially the little children, the infirm, and the innocent. I can't believe he would allow an innocent little girl to be possessed. Possession is such a violent act. The possibility of demons controlling our thoughts and actions is one that would be terrifying to any adult. It would drive a child mad beyond any hope of recovery. Humans inherently fear the unknown more than anything they can see. I'll give you an example, Clay. Do you know what has been voted to be the scariest movie ever made?"

"No."

"*The Exorcist*," Bill responded.

Clay sat back in his chair with a sigh.

Bill continued. "Satan and his demons should be scary. I think that *The Exorcist* should be considered more of a documentary than a work of fiction. With the exception of the fact that it occurred to an innocent little girl, it was spot on. It begins with a flirtation with the occult—a curiosity about the spirit world—which opens your mind to the darker forces in the universe. The last step needed to tip someone over the edge is that age-old hook—ego."

"What do you mean ego?" Clay asked.

"It's the same hook that Satan used on Adam and Eve. He told Eve, you don't need God—you can be God yourself. You can have all knowledge on your own without him—just follow me."

Clay was focused on Bill intently. He set his pencil down and took a sip of coffee. "I think I understand—Allyson couldn't be possessed because she can't yet make a conscious choice."

"Precisely. The Bible has countless examples of possession. Probably the most quoted is when Jesus cast a legion of demons from a man. He cast them into a herd of swine, who then ran over a cliff, killing all of the pigs."

"Wow, then multiple demons can occupy one body?" Clay asked.

"Yes, according to accounts in the Bible and some accounts that have been recorded throughout history."

"But then you'd have to ask Satan into your life for the demons to enter you, right?" Clay reasoned.

"Rather than ask, I think a better word would be 'invite.' You don't need the spoken word. Actions alone would, or could, invite them in," Bill went on.

"So then the next obvious question would be … can Allyson see the demons inside of someone?"

Bill sat back in his chair. "I hadn't thought of it that way, but if she can see them tormenting someone from the outside, it would be entirely possible she could see them on the inside." Bill took a deep breath and slowly released it. "Wow, Clay, what must she be going through?"

"I know. It's all starting to make sense now. But that raises yet another question. Where does Aramaic come into play in this?" Clay asked.

"The only things I can think of are the two strongest clues we have so far … Gary and Beth's trip to Israel, and the one word that keeps repeating itself in her writings—*Jezebel.* She seems to be the dominating force in all of this."

Clay began writing in his journal as he listened to Bill. "You gave me some background on Jezebel before, but what else made her such a key figure?"

"I suppose the two things most prominent were the vineyards of Naboth and the killing of God's prophets. Her husband, King Ahab, wanted a vineyard owned by a man named Naboth. He asked Naboth to sell him the vineyard. Naboth refused, saying that the vineyard was the only thing he had to pass on to his sons. Ahab tells Jezebel, and she crafts a devious plan to falsely accuse Naboth of heresy. Naboth is killed and Jezebel presents Ahab with the gift of the vineyard."

"What a piece of work," Clay said, while shaking his head.

"Oh, she did far worse than that. She had all of God's prophets killed. She believed God's voice would be silenced if the prophets were killed. It wasn't, of course, and the slaughter of the prophets cemented her doom. Once the prophet Elijah told Ahab about his sin against God, he repented, but Jezebel refused to repent. God stated that she would not be buried, and that her body would be ripped apart by dogs. The rest I told you about."

Clay rubbed the back of his neck. "We have to establish a connection between Jezebel and Allyson," Clay murmured.

"Tall order. We don't have enough to go on yet," Bill responded.

"It might be a bit risky, but we could possibly show Allyson the pictures of demons we have found in the books. It might be a long shot, but I think it's worth it," Clay went on.

Bill pulled one of the books across the desk and turned it around. The grotesque depiction stared back at him—a winged creature with horns on his head, pointed ears, and a long tail. Gray skin covered the demon's entire body with the exception of a black loincloth over its groin. The creature's face was half man and half beast, pointed teeth, and a snarl on its lips outlined by full facial hair. It showed claws for hands and hoofs for feet. The demon was hideous, but the true evil was punctuated by the creature's eyes. The ivory-black eyes were that of a cat. The vertical slits of the eyes stared back at Bill. Could this be what they might look like, or was this what the artist believes they look like? Either way, it made him uneasy that something like this just might be hovering over him—tormenting him, whispering any number of inequities in his ear. Cold chills ran down his spine as he quickly slid the book back toward Clay. Clay turned it around and looked at the image. He rubbed the back of his neck again and looked back at Bill.

"Scares you to think that Allyson might be seeing something like this, huh?" Clay considered.

"Yeah, it sure does," Bill said.

"But again, we're back to square one. Allyson's seeing demons—how do we approach it?" Clay asked.

"First, we show her the pictures, and then we show her the exhibit at the Field Museum," Bill responded.

"Okay, it makes sense to show her the pictures and go to the museum. I guess we need to move in that direction. Actually, I'm curious to see her responses to the pictures more than anything," added Clay.

"Me, too, but I really want to get her to the exhibit as well. I think our supposition about this being religiously based is correct," Bill said.

"And on that we both agree. Now let's get some food. We've been at this too long."

Clay and Bill began picking up their books and papers in preparation to leave. Clay picked up his journal and put the computer bag on his shoulder. Bill put the books and notes in his bag. As they turned to leave, Clay was still rubbing the back of his neck. Bill turned to Clay as they started to walk out.

"What's the matter, bud? You've been rubbing the back of your neck all morning. Are you feeling okay?"

Clay put his hand on Bill's shoulder and laughed nervously. "Just a nervous feeling like someone's watching me. I haven't had those feelings since the war," Clay commented.

Bill smiled back at his friend. "Demons, huh?"

They both laughed as they walked out of the library to Bill's truck.

The two creatures looked down at the departing men as they crouched on top of the ten-foot-tall bookshelves. They were dressed in full-length black hooded robes. The features of their humanlike faces slowly changed to a dark shade of gray as the robes disappeared, blending into their dark gray bodies. Wings of gray skin unfolded from their backs as tails slowly emerged. Horns sprouted from the top of their foreheads as facial hair slowly appeared. Their bodies had changed to resemble the picture from the book that Bill and Clay had been studying. One of the demons raised his right arm and watched as his fingers transformed into a claw. He turned his head toward his companion and gave him a sinister smile.

CHAPTER 14

HONOR AMONG THIEVES

THE STAFF OF THE Israel Museum Jerusalem was winding down from a week of business and visitors. The floor personnel unconsciously looked at their watches as guests began working their way toward the exit.

Benjamin Meyer stood up from his seat in the lobby and walked to the doors for the main entrance. The forty-one-year-old man was the lead security officer for the second shift at IMJ and responsible for the smooth and efficient closing of the facility. His blue blazer and gray slacks were the standard uniform for the museum staff. The only way to distinguish his position of Museum Security from the other employees was the nametag on his left breast. The blazer concealed his radio, can of mace, and handcuffs.

Benjamin looked at his watch and verified it was 6:00 p.m. He removed the key ring from his belt and thumbed through the keys until he found the small Allen wrench. He began releasing the locks on the crash bars until all eight of the front doors were locked.

The prerecorded female voice came over the public address system, "The museum is closing for the evening. Please depart through the main entrance at the south end of the building. We hope you enjoyed your visit with us today. We look forward to seeing you again. Have a nice evening."

Benjamin stood at the main entrance with his hands clasped in front of him as he smiled pleasantly at the departing guests. There were eight security officers and six tour guides on duty in the main building. Each one began performing their assigned duties as the business day was coming to an end. The security officers began making their rounds through the building, checking for any visitors who were lingering.

Yankel Cohen emerged from the Security Command Center to begin his rounds of the building before closing. He entered the cafe and found the seating area vacant. The four cafe employees were leaving as he walked into the kitchen. He smiled and said, "Good night," as they walked past him.

Yankel made his way to the restrooms and slightly opened the door marked "Women." "The museum is closing. Is anyone in here?" After waiting for a response, he entered the room and walked down the row of stalls, looking under each door. He walked out of the ladies' room and into the men's room. Repeating his routine, Yankel looked under each stall door. Once he reached the end of the stalls he turned and started walking out. Paz Freedman stepped off of the top of the commode seat where he had been hiding and opened the door. He raised the tranquilizer gun and fired at the guard. The dart found its mark, hitting him in the lower back. Yankel grunted in pain and fell to the floor.

Paz walked to Yankel's unconscious body and removed the dart from his back. He was dressed in the same gray slacks, white shirt, and black shoes as the rest of the staff, with the exception of a gray lightweight windbreaker. He removed his coat and replaced it with Yankel's blazer. Paz pulled the remaining five darts from a pocket of the windbreaker and reloaded his weapon. He then placed the remaining four darts into the inside pocket of the blazer. Paz placed the spent dart into the center of the windbreaker and rolled it up. Removing the clip-on necktie, access control card, and radio from Yankel, he pulled the unconscious body into the end stall and sat it up on the commode, and then placed the rolled up windbreaker on the back of the commode until he could retrieve it later. Paz walked to the mirror and straightened himself, putting on the necktie. He walked into one of the stalls and sat on the commode waiting for the team leader to contact him.

Seth Cooper walked down the east hallway toward the emergency exit door. He was in just as big a hurry as the rest of the security staff to close up for the weekend. He stopped at the door and pushed the test button. The loud screech of the alarm sounded briefly, signifying the alarm was active. The six-foot-three-inch young man turned and walked back down the hall, checking each door as he passed it. Seth reached the janitorial closet and opened the door. He stepped inside of the large dark room and turned the light on. The figure standing in front of him was clad in a ski mask and pointing a pistol at him. Seth heard the low thump of the pistol discharging and looked down to see the dart sticking out from his stomach. He groaned in pain as his body collapsed in front of his attacker.

Rebecca Isroff stepped over Seth's body and then closed and locked the door. She began removing Seth's equipment from his body. She pulled the dart from his stomach and reloaded her weapon with another one. She put on his coat and looked at the three inches of sleeve that hung over her hands. Her lips pursed with frustration as she rolled the sleeves up to her wrists.

Rebecca sat down on the floor holding the radio in her hands waiting for Douglas Weiss's instructions.

Rachel Wise walked to the receptionist's desk in the main lobby and looked at the sign-in roster. The five-foot-three-inch tall, twenty-one-year-old was one of many young people working their way through school as guides at the facility. Her beaming smile and professional demeanor made her a favorite of not only the staff, but the guests as well. Rachel walked to the front doors and stood in front of Benjamin Meyer.

"We still show twelve visitors in the building," she said.

"Has the office staff left yet?" Benjamin asked.

"Yes, everyone has left except the director."

"Have the other tour guides left as well?"

"No, not yet."

"Well, let's wait for everyone to complete their rounds."

Rachel nodded in agreement and returned to the receptionist's desk.

Michael Kazez sat at the security desk outside the vault, nervously looking at his watch. The three archeologists walked out of the vault and looked at Michael as they closed the door behind them.

"Is there anyone left in the vault?" Michael asked the three men.

"No, we're it."

"Okay, have a nice weekend," Michael responded.

The three men walked to the elevator and pressed the main floor button. The elevator doors opened on the main level, and the men exited, walking to the main entrance. They smiled at Benjamin as they exited.

Caleb Wiener and Sharon Yager met in the open area adjacent to the main stairwell. Caleb removed the radio from his belt and called in to the security console.

"Central, this is units three and four," Caleb announced.

"Go ahead three." The center responded.

"The West and North sectors are clear."

Aaron Rosenblum, the security dispatcher, responded from the command center. "Copy three and four, West and North secure."

The darts hit the two guards in the lower back almost simultaneously. Caleb and Sharon groaned in pain as their bodies crumpled to the floor. Omer Esterson and Levi Ain ran to the two downed guards, retrieved the darts, and then dragged the bodies into another one of the restrooms.

Dr. Brandon Harrison was sitting at his desk intensely writing. The newly appointed museum director had been buried in work since he assumed the position just a week ago. The six-foot-two-inch tall thin-framed man was engrossed in the monumental task of learning the inner workings of his new assignment. The knock on his door was both loud and annoying.

"Enter," Brandon said without looking up.

The second knock was louder still.

"Enter," he said much louder.

Brandon looked up and waited for the door to open. Disgusted at the nonresponse, he set his pen down and got up to answer the door. He turned the knob and opened the door to see a big man wearing a ski mask. Brandon turned quickly and ran back toward his desk. He fell to the floor as the dart hit him in the back. Douglas Weiss removed his mask and walked to the director's body, pulling the dart from his back. He turned him over and removed the access control card from around his neck, and then walked back to the door, handing the card to Tamir Berkowitz.

Tamir walked down the hallway to the Security Command Center door. With his mask on and tranquilizer gun at the ready, he passed the access card in front of the reader. The deadbolt snapped open, and Tamir entered the room. Aaron was sitting at the console with his back to the door typing entries into the security log on the computer. Aaron spun around in his swivel chair to see who had entered the room. The dart hit him hard in the chest. He tried to stand, but fell back into the chair. Tamir reloaded his weapon, pulled his mask off, and walked out of the room.

Rachel Wise looked at her watch for the third time and stood up from her seat at the receptionist's desk. She again walked toward Benjamin and asked, "Benjamin, would it be okay if I left? All the other tour guides have gone home except Asher."

"That's fine," he replied. "I'll finish up here."

"Thank you. I'll see you Monday."

"Have a nice weekend," he called as Rachel left.

Benjamin looked at his watch. Twenty minutes after 6:00 p.m. What could be keeping everyone? Why hadn't he been called to secure his post? He lifted the radio to his mouth.

"Control, this is unit two. Are we clear yet?" There was no response. "Control, this is two. Are we clear yet? Aaron, are you asleep in there—can you read me?

Benjamin rechecked the front doors to make sure they were locked and walked the seventy-five feet to the main stairwell area. He looked down the main hallways, all of which were eerily vacant.

"Control, this is two." He said with frustration in his voice. Benjamin checked the battery readout on his radio, which indicated the battery was at 50 percent. Benjamin turned and started to walk toward the Security Command Center. The thump from the tranquilizer dart echoed through the hallway as he fell to the floor. Douglas Weiss walked to Benjamin's body and removed the dart from his back. Weiss removed the radio from his waist and lifted it to his mouth. "This is X-ray. We're all clear."

Weiss walked back to the main foyer and waited for his team. The remaining seven team members met him in the foyer carrying their gear. Joseph Mokotoff stepped up, carrying in two large bags, and placed them in the center of the group. Weiss looked at Rebecca and smiled as he saw the rolled up sleeves of the coat she was wearing. Rebecca smiled back sarcastically. The team removed clothing and equipment from the large bags and began putting on the gear. They all placed their blazers, wind breakers, spent tranquilizer darts, and ski masks into the bags.

As they were changing, quite unexpectedly another one of the tour guides emerged from an office, ten yards from them. Asher Liber froze in his steps, startled to see the strangers in the building. He turned and bolted toward the main door.

Weiss pointed to Mokotoff. "Get him!" He shouted.

Asher was running toward the main door shouting at the top of his lungs. "Intruders in the building! Intruders in the building!"

Joseph raised the pistol and fired, hitting the young man in the back. Asher fell, his body sliding to a stop on the marble floor. Omer Esterson came to a halt behind Joseph.

"What do we do? He saw us!" Omer said.

The demon hovered over Joseph, his wings flapping wildly as he whispered in Joseph's ear. Joseph put the tranquilizer gun in his belt and stared at the young man on the floor.

"Joseph … he saw us!" Omer said.

"I know, I know!" Joseph shouted back at Omer.

The demon began screaming into Joseph's ear. He flew around him, and then angrily screamed at him above his head.

Joseph pulled the silenced HK-P7 from his shoulder holster and pointed it down at Asher.

"No, Joseph, you can't!" Omer yelled, trying to stop him.

The demon turned toward Omer, snarling at him. He flew at Omer with his claws open, screaming at him. Omer's eyes opened widely as he took in a deep breath, not knowing why he suddenly couldn't speak. The demon turned back toward Joseph, shouting at him.

Joseph gripped the weapon tightly as he pointed it at Asher's chest. The weapon discharged with two muffled cracks, "Clack! Clack!" Asher's body twitched and then went limp.

Douglas Weiss came to a halt next to the two men as he looked down at the dead body in front of him.

"He shot him! I can't believe he shot him!" Omer cried, dazed.

Douglas turned toward Omer and grabbed him by the throat. "Shut up, you fool, it had to be done. Now get the body into the closet before someone walks by out front and sees us."

Joseph stood frozen in place staring at the body. He couldn't believe he had just shot the man lying in front of him. This wasn't the first time he had taken a life, but it was the first time he had done it without thinking. The demon laughed as he hovered over the men.

"Move it you two … I mean now!" Douglas ordered.

Joseph rolled the body over and pulled the dart from his back. He picked up the two spent nine millimeter casings and put them in his pocket. He bent down and grabbed Asher's ankles and dragged the body away.

Douglas looked at Omer. "Wait here out of sight until we call you, and then meet us at the dock."

"Yes, sir," Omer murmured, still stunned by what had happened.

Joseph pulled Asher's body to the janitor's closet and dragged him inside, laying him on top of Seth Cooper. He closed the door and rejoined the group in the foyer.

The team members walked to the freight elevator. Douglas passed the director's badge in front of the reader, and the doors opened. He pushed the basement level button once they were all inside.

The doors opened, and the group exited, walking toward Michael Kazez. Michael held his badge in front of the right side reader as Weiss passed the director's badge in front of the left one. The bolt released, and Douglas opened the door. He handed Michael a small canvas bag. "You have ten minutes," Weiss ordered.

Michael turned and ran toward the elevator as Douglas took the three-ring binder from the security podium and wedged it under the door. The team entered the vault and walked to the cages on the north wall. Douglas walked down the row of cages until he saw number thirty-two. He turned toward Paz.

"The file will be in the Clean Room in the filing cabinets under site number 482," Weiss said, pointing to the glass enclosure at the end of the room.

Paz responded as he was running toward the room. "Yes, sir."

Michael entered the Security Command Center and walked behind the console. He put on a pair of rubber gloves and opened the inspection cover of the main security computer. He released the catches at the back and pulled the four hard drives out of the computer. The hard drives stored the access control data and camera footage for the facility. He placed the four hard drives into the canvas bag, zipped it closed, and ran out of the room. He reached the elevator and inserted his key into the door control. With the computer disabled, the doors would only work with a key. He exited the elevator at the basement level and ran all the way to the cages inside the vault.

Michael then stopped in front of the cage in time to see them pulling the wooden box down from the shelf inside the cage. Douglas placed the box on the floor and looked up at the group smiling. His excitement could hardly be contained. He slowly opened the box to see the remains inside. Kneeling in front of the box, he gently removed the skull from inside the box and held it above his head.

"Praise be to Ba-al … it is our queen." He reverently said as he looked at the followers standing above him.

Paz came into the cage holding the file. He smiled as he saw Douglas holding the skull of the queen over his head. The group was silent as they looked in awe at the remains.

Douglas looked in the box to ensure the hands and feet were among the other bones. He slowly replaced the skull back into the box and closed the lid. He looked at Paz. "Is that the file?"

"Yes, sir, site 482." Paz responded.

Douglas took the file and opened it. He verified the contents and placed it in one of the duffle bags. Michael placed the canvas bag with the hard drives into the duffle along with the rubber gloves he was wearing. Five of the team members picked up the floor lamps, carrying them from the vault.

"Okay, let's get out of here," Douglas ordered.

The team's driver, David Greenblatt, pulled the van into the service dock area of the museum. He looked at his watch before backing against the dock. The dial showed 6:45 p.m. He looked to his left and saw the mobile security vehicle parked against the dock. He eased the van back against the dock and set the parking brake.

The team members stopped at the security podium outside the vault. Michael took off his access badge and dropped it on the floor. He unclipped his key ring and handed it to Douglas.

"The keys for the back dock door and the elevator are the two smallest ones," Michael instructed.

"Okay, get to the high priest's office as soon as you can," Douglas ordered.

Weiss raised the tranquilizer pistol and pointed it at Michael's stomach. Michael tightened his muscles as Douglas fired the pistol. His body went limp and fell to the floor.

The team walked to the end of the hall and entered the freight elevator. The doors opened on the main floor, and they walked to the service dock area.

Weiss thumbed through the key ring and inserted the key into the door alarm, disabling it. Once on the dock, Weiss dropped the key ring and walked down the stairs to the waiting van. He issued his last order for the night.

"Does everyone have all their equipment?" he said looking around.

The team all responded in the affirmative.

"Good, let's go," he said.

They all entered the van from the side cargo door. Each one of the team removed the rubber gloves and placed them into the duffle bag as the van drove off.

David turned his head slightly as he drove. "Did everything go as planned?" he asked.

Douglas Weiss removed his gloves and placed them in the bag. "It could have been better," he said as he looked at Omer with a sneer.

The three human figures dressed in black robes stood on the dock and looked on as the van drove away. Wings sprouted from their backs as they laughed and flew away.

CHAPTER 15

SECRETS REVEALED

GARY WAS WATERING HIS flower bed as Bill and Clay drove into the driveway. He walked to the tap and turned the water off and wiped his hands on his gym shorts.

"Good morning. We thought you guys went on vacation for two days," Gary said, extending his hand toward Clay. Gary and Beth had fought the urge over the past two days to call Bill, but had decided to give them the time they needed.

"Every day is a vacation when you're retired," Clay responded as he shook Gary's hand.

"Come on in. Beth has the coffee on," Gary invited.

"Excellent," Bill said as he followed Gary inside.

"How can you drink so much of that stuff?" Clay asked Bill.

"Cause it's good."

"Man, I'd hate to see your stomach."

"Cast iron." Bill smiled and patted his stomach.

Gary waited for Clay and Bill to enter the house and then closed the door behind them.

"Honey, Bill and Clay are here," he announced.

Beth entered the living room and hugged Bill and Clay. "Sit down, you guys. I'll get coffee for you."

"None for me, thanks," Clay said as he placed his notebook on the coffee table.

"So, did you find anything?" Gary asked.

Bill stood up to take the coffee from Beth as she came back into the room and sat down. "We've got good news—and not so good news." He sat back down on the couch.

"Okay, shoot," Gary said as he leaned forward enthusiastically.

Clay sat back in his chair and crossed his legs. "Last time we were here, when we took Allyson outside, she said she saw something across the street by your neighbor. We believe we found what it was that she saw."

"That's the good news," Bill interjected.

Beth clasped her hands together and leaned forward toward the two men. "So then what's the not so good news?"

Clay took a deep breath and looked back and forth from Gary to Beth. "We don't know how—we don't even know why, but Bill and I are convinced that Allyson has the ability to see demons."

The room fell silent. Tears began to fall down Beth's face, as Gary dropped his head, looking at the floor. Gary began to slowly speak as he raised his head. "Demons—as in the biblical sense?" he asked.

"That's what we believe, Gary," Bill quietly responded.

"Okay, you guys, I quit being surprised by what's going on with Allyson over the past week. But this is way off base," Gary continued, angrily.

Bill leaned forward looking at him. "Gary, it all makes sense. Allyson said she saw something flying over your neighbor. When we asked her to describe it, she said it was two men with wings whispering in his ear. Don't you see, this explains why she has been so terrified around people over the years?"

Beth began sobbing loudly.

"Oh, Beth, I'm sorry for springing this on you like that," Bill said.

"It's not that, Bill. We've been keeping something from you. Something that is connected to this and it's all my fault." Beth continued to sob.

"Honey, it's not your fault." Gary went over to Beth and put his arm around her shoulders.

Looking up at him with love in her eyes, Beth stated, "Enough, Gary, this has to stop. It is my fault, and I have to make it right."

Bill and Clay looked at Beth with surprise. Neither one wanted to ask her to what she was referring. They waited for her to compose herself. Beth took the handkerchief that Bill offered and wiped her eyes. She took a sip of water and a deep breath.

"In 2000, Gary and I were part of a construction team in the mountains east of Jerusalem. The project was for the Israeli military and highly classified. Without giving up any secrets, we were cutting into the side of a mountain."

Clay interjected, "For a missile battery?"

"I forgot what you used to do for a living." Beth forced a smile. "We were just a few weeks into the project when we discovered a cave in the side of the mountain at the site. There was a carved façade around the opening, and the entrance way had clearly been man-made. The inside of the cave had clearly been used as some sort of temple, or place of worship. What we found would change our lives forever." Beth was clearly having difficulty talking about the incident. She was stopping frequently while looking down at the floor clutching Gary's hand tightly.

Bill listened intently as Clay wrote furiously in his journal. They listened for almost an hour as Beth described the inside of the cave. She was careful not to omit any detail, no matter how small. Clay only looked up from his journal when Beth would pause. He found himself now agreeing with Bill completely; this had to be religiously based. There's just no other answer. When Beth told about trying to open the bronze box, Clay was so fixated on her he dropped his pen. As she described the eerie story of hearing the woman's voice, chills ran down his spine. All of his training was telling him not to believe what he was hearing, yet he found it strangely credible based on all that had occurred so far. Once Beth had finished, Bill was the first to speak.

"Did everyone hear her voice?" Bill asked.

"No, only the four of us who were the closest to the box," Beth responded.

"And you don't know what the voice said?" Clay asked.

"No, it was in a foreign language … as far as I could tell," she answered.

"And what happened after that?" Clay asked.

"You'll have to ask Gary. The lights went out for me after the box was opened."

"You passed out?" Bill asked her.

"Not exactly," Gary interjected. "When the box was opened, an explosion of gas and dust came out, and it threw Beth against the wall and knocked her unconscious. I started toward her, but the howling and moaning was so intensely ear shattering, we were all on the ground writhing in pain. Ultimately it was so bad we all passed out," Gary continued.

"A howl—what kind of howl?" Clay asked.

"It was nothing like I've ever heard before. A deep growl like someone was in severe pain, it was ear splitting. I was in such pain that I had to crawl to Beth. As hard as I tried, I couldn't get up. I checked to see if she was okay. She had a pulse but was unconscious. The pain increased to the point that I could feel myself passing out. That's when I saw it." Gary paused to take a drink of coffee. He tried to shake off the haunting feeling that he was overcome by, after recalling the events of that day. He continued after composing himself. "I saw writing appear on Beth's forehead."

"What?" Bill said, almost shouting.

"I know what you're thinking … believe me, I've thought it myself over the years," Gary went on.

"Are you sure it was writing?" Clay asked.

"I wasn't at first. When I woke up I was so focused on getting Beth out of there, I didn't think about it. I didn't see it after I woke up. Later after I thought about it, I attributed it to hallucinations, or from just being dazed."

"Do you recall what the writing looked like?" Clay asked.

"No, but I suppose if I ever saw it again, I might recognize it. I think it was the same kind of writing that was on the wall of the cave, but I can't be sure. With the pain in my ears and head, coupled with the limited light down there … I just can't be sure, Clay," Gary said.

"And what about the box? Did anyone see what was inside?" Bill asked.

"I don't know. I carried Beth out of the cave and tended to her. One by one the other people began coming out and were helping each other. I didn't go back in."

"And you're relatively sure that no one else looked in the box?" Bill asked.

"Not that I know of; they all got out of there as quick as they could, just like me. The ones that looked at the box after they woke up said it was only open a few inches. No one could see inside. We called it in to the Israeli military and after about an hour passed, they arrived and sealed the cave off. We learned later that some people from one of the museums came in to take over," Gary said.

"And no one went back into the cave?" Bill asked.

"No, they didn't have the guts. We were all interviewed by the military and told not to discuss the incident with anyone. Two days later we were called back home by SH&R. We never saw or heard about the site again."

"And the supposition was that the cave was a temple?" Bill asked.

"Yes, but Colonel Stern also believed it was a sacrificial chamber," Beth said.

"You had a colonel there with you?" Clay asked curiously.

"Yes, Colonel Adar Stern from the Israeli Army," Gary replied.

"Well, what the colonel said makes sense. There were a lot of sacrifices in ancient Israel, by both Jews and pagans," Bill said.

"But the Jews didn't practice human sacrifice, right?" Beth wanted to know.

Bill raised the finger of his right hand pointing it toward Beth. "That's not exactly true. Jews that followed false gods performed many human sacrifices, most of which were their own children," he said.

"Ba-al, the one you told us about was the false god they sacrificed to, right?" asked Gary.

"It wasn't just Ba-al. There were several false gods that humans were sacrificed to—he was just one of the most influential," Bill went on to explain.

"There's that name again—Ba-al—which keeps tying it to Jezebel," Clay said.

"It sure does." Bill had a curious look on his face. "This just keeps coming back to a religious answer. I'm telling you, we need to get

Allyson down to the museum. I'm convinced that the exhibit will give us some answers to many of the questions we have."

"Bill, if Allyson is truly seeing demons, I don't want to put her in downtown Chicago," Beth said fearfully.

"But Beth, what is most important is that Allyson wasn't scared when she saw the demons. She was shaking, but no screams of terror that we have seen in the past," Bill reminded her.

"Beth and I talked about that after you left. We came to the same conclusion that she seemed to be strangely composed. Of course, that was before we knew the reason for her fear," Gary said. "If there's anything to your theory that this is biblically based … and it's looking more and more like there is … Bill's right. She didn't have an episode." He responded while looking toward his wife trying to reassure her.

"And it can be attributed in large part to Clay," Bill added.

Clay shifted uncomfortably in his seat. "I fought that premise at first, but it does appear she is somehow connected to me. I also agree with Bill that somehow this is religiously based and that the exhibit downtown may provide some answers. I think we should try again, especially now that we know what's happening. We can protect and prepare Allyson now," he said.

"But you said Allyson saw two men with wings. Couldn't it have been angels instead of demons?" Gary had to ask.

"I don't believe so. I asked her if the wings had feathers and she said no. Also, I can't imagine the sight of an angel bringing her to the point of hysterics. But there is one way to find out for sure if you guys agree to it." Clay looked at Beth and Gary very intently.

"What's that?" Beth asked, holding her breath.

"Bill and I brought some pictures of demons we found at the library. We'd like to show them to Allyson," Clay said.

"What do you think, honey?" Gary asked Beth.

"I agree. But before we go any further, there's something else you guys need to know. Out of the four of us that were standing next to the box that day, three have died, and all within a year of each other," she said.

"Died … from what?" Bill asked.

"Heart attacks!" Beth responded.

"This site is beginning to interest me. Screaming that causes people to pass out, words written on foreheads, heart attacks. I'd give a year's wages to find out what was in that box," Clay responded intently.

"Me, too," Bill replied, equally as intense.

"Honey, it's your call." Beth looked carefully to Gary. Still drying her eyes, she fought the urge to shut this whole thing down completely. "I suppose that if Allyson really is seeing demons, that would confirm it, but we need to move very cautiously. I don't want anything we do to damage the progress we've made."

Gary took in a deep breath and let it out loudly. "Okay, let's go for it. I think we're on a roll here. And I also think it is the right thing to let Bill and Clay take her to the museum. Let's pull out all the stops, no holds barred. We need to find out what's going on here, because life as it is now for Allyson is no life at all." He looked frightened but determined.

"Okay then, whatever you guys say ... you have complete control. I agree with Gary completely—enough is enough." Beth's reservations had taken a backseat to the logic that had been presented to her. If Allyson had any hope of a normal life, it rested with the findings of Clay and Bill.

"Excellent," Bill replied, knowing how hard the decision had been to make.

Clay gathered up the books and his journal and, along with Bill, followed them to Allyson's room. As usual, Beth and Gary entered the room first with Bill and Clay following. Allyson was at her usual place, sitting at the table writing and drawing. Clay fought back the urge to say hello to Allyson from the door. He felt a tremendous connection to the little girl, but did not want to rush anything. His whole life had been an issue of trying to control situations. He was actually pleased to see his "Type A" personality being held in check.

Beth knelt down next to Allyson. "Honey, Dr. Bill and Mr. Harker are here to see you."

Allyson turned quickly to see Clay smiling at her. She dropped her pen and slid off the chair, running to him. He knelt down and placed the books on the floor in time to receive Allyson's hug around his neck.

"It's good to see you again, Allyson," Clay said softly.

"I missed you," she said.

"I missed you too, honey." Clay replied with a beaming smile.

Bill looked down at her. "Hi, Allyson."

"Hi, Dr. Bill." She looked up to him and continued to smile.

Clay leaned back, holding Allyson's arms with his hands. "Allyson, Dr. Bill and I brought some books for you to look at. Would you like to see them?"

"Yes."

"Allyson, some of the pictures in the books may be difficult for you to see or understand … these are pictures of birdmen. Would that be okay?"

Beth walked to Allyson and knelt down. "It's okay with Daddy and me, honey. We think it would help. But if you don't want to, that's okay."

Allyson turned back toward Clay and responded, "Okay."

Clay picked up the books and his journal and walked to the table holding Allyson by the hand. Allyson sat at her chair while Bill and Clay pulled chairs up to the table and sat next to her. Gary and Beth stood behind them. Clay had placed post-it notes on the pages with pictures for quick reference. He slowly pulled the first book in front of her.

"Allyson, I'm going to turn the pages slowly. If you want to stop seeing them you tell me, all right?" Clay asked.

"Okay." She seemed only a bit nervous.

Clay slowly opened the book to the first marked page. The first picture was of a demon with wings of skin like a bat. The demon's body had a dark gray color to its skin. It had a humanlike face with an evil smile. Allyson uncomfortably sat on her hands as she stared at the picture.

"Does this look like what you saw flying around the man across the street?" Clay asked.

"Kind of like them," she murmured quietly.

"What was the same about them?"

She lifted her right hand and pointed to the wings. Clay was watching her closely as he continued taking notes.

"Did they have that color of skin?" He asked.

Allyson nodded her head yes as she put her hand back on the table.

Clay slowly turned the page to the next picture. "What about this one, Allyson? Anything like this?"

Allyson slowly pointed to the horns on the head.

"They had horns?" he asked.

She looked at Clay and again nodded her head yes.

Clay continued to show her pictures from the books, writing the similarities down in his journal. Allyson had not said a word throughout the process, only pointing her fingers or moving her head to indicate a yes or no.

They had gone through almost all of the pictures when Clay opened the final book to the picture that he and Bill had discussed in the library. As he turned the page to the picture, Allyson began shaking.

Bill noticed her trembling and placed his hand over the face of the demon. He turned his head toward her. "Is this what they look like, honey?" he asked gently.

Allyson turned her head toward Bill. "Yes, Dr. Bill," she said with a trembling voice.

Beth grasped Gary's arm as she began to silently cry. It was now obvious to her that Bill's and Clay's observations had been correct. Gary pursed his lips and knelt next to his daughter.

"Are you sure that this is what they look like, Allyson?" he asked.

"Yes, Daddy," she responded.

Clay closed the book and moved it away from her. He placed his hand on her shoulder. "Allyson, do these pictures look like the birdmen that were flying around your neighbor?"

"Yes."

"And they were talking to him as he walked?"

"Yes."

"And do you ever see them around any of us?"

"No."

"Have they ever come after you, Allyson?" Bill asked.

"No."

Bill placed his hand on Allyson's back reassuringly. "The birdmen can't hurt you, Allyson. They're just scary to look at. Do you believe me, honey?"

Allyson nodded her head yes. "Do you see them, too, Dr. Bill?"

"No, honey, no one sees them except you. You know that makes you very special, don't you?" He placed his hand on top of her head very gently.

Allyson smiled at Bill. "I guess so."

"And so long as your mother and father or Mr. Harker and I are with you, they can't hurt you. Do you understand that?"

"Yes, Dr. Bill, I think so.

Clay leaned toward Allyson. "Honey, Dr. Bill and I have a favor to ask you. We would like to try to take you to the museum again tomorrow. Would that be okay?"

Allyson looked toward Beth. "Mommy, can I go?" she asked.

"If you want to try and go again, that would be okay with Daddy and me. But remember, sweetheart, if you get scared or just want to come home, all you have to do is tell Dr. Bill or Mr. Harker, and they will bring you back home."

"Mr. Harker, are we still going to look at some arktifax?"

Clay smiled at her. "We sure will, and we'll look at some paintings too. But you know, Allyson, you don't have to call me Mr. Harker. I'm a doctor just like Dr. Bill. You can call me Dr. Clay if you would like."

Allyson smiled back. "Dr. Clay, what was your daughter's name?"

Clay smiled back at her. "Her name was Jody."

"Do you miss her, Dr. Clay?"

"Very much, Allyson. I miss her very much."

Allyson hugged Clay tightly. "It's okay, Dr. Clay. God will take care of her."

Clay hugged her tightly as tears began to fall down his face.

CHAPTER 16

THE INVESTIGATION BEGINS

YAIR KLEIN PULLED UP to the front of the Israel Museum Jerusalem in his white Volkswagen Golf. The dark of the night was illuminated by the lights from the emergency vehicles parked in front of the museum. The forty-six-year-old chief of detectives looked around the front of the building and took mental notes of the scene. At five-foot-ten, 180 pounds, the chief possessed a command presence that everyone respected. Clad in his usual sport coat and tie, he always looked the part of the most important person within the Investigations Branch of the Israeli Police Department. He walked up the stairs and smiled at the uniformed officer standing guard at the front entrance. The entire facility had been cordoned off with police tape and uniformed officers, ensuring crime scene protocol. Yair showed his badge to the officer and waited for him to enter his name on the protocol list. Yair walked up the stairs and entered through the main doors, walking to the security podium, where one of the lab personnel was taking fingerprints.

"Where's Lieutenant Steyn?" Yair asked.

"He's in the director's office down the south hall," the man responded.

"Thanks." Yair walked away.

The museum was occupied by no less than two dozen personnel, both uniformed and nonuniformed, from the Israeli Police Department. He walked by the spot where Asher Liber had been shot. Two men from the lab were gathering blood samples from inside the taped off scene. Yair walked down the hallway and stopped by the door of the conference room where employees of the museum were being interviewed. Paramedics were providing care to the remaining museum staff in the hallway. With the exception of the deceased Asher Liber, the injuries to the remaining personnel were minor, mostly from the dart-entry wounds and the effects of the sedatives and bumps and bruises from the falls. Yair took mental notes of the scene and continued down the hall to the director's office. He stepped inside the office and waited for Lieutenant Steyn to finish writing in his notebook. The thirty-four-year-old lieutenant was busy compiling all of the data he had received to this point. His slight frame and short black curly hair made him about as intimidating as a schoolboy, but Yair had complete faith in his abilities.

"What do we have, Mark?" Yair said as Steyn stopped writing.

"Hi, Chief. It's shaping up to be a robbery so far, although we haven't established yet what was taken. The director has ordered an inventory of the items, but we probably won't have the results for a couple of days," Steyn replied.

"Who was in the building when it took place?" Yair asked.

"From what we know so far, it all went down shortly after closing time. Most of the administrative staff had left for the day. The director, the security staff, and one tour guide were still here."

"What about the custodians?" Yair asked.

"They weren't due in until 8:00 p.m."

Yair grimly looked at Mark and asked, "And one dead—correct?"

"Yes. Come back to the main entrance and I'll show you." They both walked back toward the lobby.

Mark stopped in front of the blood stained floor. "The body was found here … two shots to the chest. They dragged him into the closet just around the corner," he explained as he led Yair to the custodial closet. Mark opened the door showing Yair the inside. "One of the security officers was placed here with the body. When he woke up, the body was lying on top of him."

"So then they were drugged?"

"Everyone had been shot with tranquilizer darts, even the deceased," Steyn replied.

"So then he probably surprised them," Yair deduced.

"That's my guess as well. There was a puncture wound in his back. We won't know for sure until the coroner takes a look at him, but he was probably tranquilized as well. My guess is he got a good look at his killers. Those that got a look at the intruders said they were all wearing ski masks," Steyn said.

"Do we have any of the darts?" Yair asked.

"No, they took them all. Some of the staff said they heard the low thump of the shot just before they felt something hit them. This was professionally done, Chief. There's nothing left behind. They probably wore gloves as well, so I'm betting we won't get any prints either."

Yair rubbed the back of his neck. "Were any of the display cases broken into?"

"No, it looks like the only place that they entered was the vault downstairs."

"Who called this in, Mark?"

"We got the call from one of the security officers assigned at one of the other buildings. She had been monitoring the radio traffic, and when the Security Command Center failed to respond, she decided to come to the main building to see why they weren't responding."

"Did she say how long it was between the radio going dead and when she responded?"

"She said it was no more than thirty minutes. She heard the lead officer trying to raise the center and waited for him to respond. After no one responded, she decided to leave her post and check. From the time of the radio going out to when she arrived was no more than thirty minutes."

Yair pulled at his chin with his right hand. He mentally calculated the time from when the radio went dead to the time they exited the building. *"These guys had this planned well,"* he thought. "And where is the director now?"

"He's down in the vault with some of the lab people," Steyn replied.

"Okay, let's go take a look. I'd like to talk to him anyway," Yair said.

Steyn led Yair to the freight elevator and pushed the down button. "They disabled the security system and took the hard drives from the main computer. Normally, it works off of a proximity card. The staff overrode the system for us tonight so we could use it. After they took the hard drives out, they had to use keys that they took from the security staff."

"Looks like they might have had some help from inside," Yair speculated, thinking out loud.

"It's beginning to shape up like that. At minimum they had knowledge of the site beforehand."

The elevator door opened, and the two men exited into the hallway. Yair stopped before walking to the desk to assess what he was looking at. He looked down the hall to see a police officer standing guard at the entrance to what he assumed was the vault. Mark waited for his boss to move before he said anything. Yair couldn't help but notice how eerily quiet it was in the hall. He could hear nothing, not even machinery noise. The white ceilings and walls, and the sodium lights in the thirty-foot-high ceilings made it brighter than he was used to seeing in a windowless environment. The concrete floor had been covered in gray nonskid paint. The hall was extremely wide, allowing for forklifts and equipment, Yair assumed. He looked down the hall to see the twenty-five-foot-wide double doors, with a security podium next to them. He started walking to the doors as he spoke. "What's the vault used for?" Yair asked.

"Mostly for new, unidentified, or excess items."

"And who has access?" Yair asked.

"It requires two cards to gain access, one of which has to be at the director level. There are no restrictions on who can enter the vault, so long as someone at that level is inside. The museum director told us that the security officer on duty at the podium has to pass his or her card along with a director-level employee. They also have a two-person integrity rule in the vault, so no one can be in there alone," Steyn went on to explain.

"And was someone on duty when this went down?"

Steyn thumbed through the pages of his notebook. "Yes, a security officer named Michael Kazez."

"And what does he say happened?"

Mark looked at his notes as his index finger scrolled though them. "He said two masked men approached him and shot him in the stomach with a tranquilizer dart. We found his access card on the floor in front of the vault door and his key ring on the floor of the dock area outside."

Yair turned back around to look down the hall toward the elevator. He slowly turned and looked up at the camera mounted on the ceiling by the security desk. "And I take it that the hard drives had the camera footage on them," he said.

"Yes, everything was shut down when they were pulled out. The RAM on the computer may have some video on it, but it won't be much, only about three to five minutes backup before the drives were pulled."

"Let's make that video a priority, Mark. It may be just enough to ID someone."

"Yes, sir."

Yair held his badge out toward the officer at the security podium for him to record his name and time of entry. The officer entered the names and then looked up at Yair. "Thank you, sir." The two men entered the vault and weaved around the crates and articles on the floor. They reached the rear of the vault where the lab personnel were busy collecting evidence. The director was sitting in one of the chairs from the vault speaking to one of the detectives as they stopped next to them.

"Mr. Harrison, this is Yair Klein, the Chief of Detectives," Steyn made the introduction.

"Brandon Harrison," he said as he shook Yair's hand.

"Mr. Harrison, did you see any of the intruders?" Yair asked.

"Only briefly. They knocked on my office door, and when I opened it, I saw two people in ski masks. I turned to run away and got hit in the back by something. The detective later told me it was a tranquilizer dart," Harrison replied. The normally orderly and impeccable Dr. Harrison was holding an ice pack to his head. His necktie had been loosened, and his shirttail was completely out of his trousers. He fought the effects of the tranquilizer as he looked back through half-opened eyes.

"What did they look like?" Yair asked.

"They were dressed in museum uniforms. One was about five-feet-ten inches ... the other one was over six feet, maybe six-two or three. I can't tell you much more than that. When I woke up, one of the security staff was checking on me."

"Did they say anything to you?" Yair asked.

"No, but to tell you the truth, I wouldn't have heard it anyway. My heart was pounding so hard, and the adrenaline was so high, I probably wouldn't have heard anything ... I was too scared," Harrison admitted.

"Lieutenant Steyn tells me you've ordered an inventory. How long do you think that will take?" Yair wanted to know.

"We'll put a rush on it, but it will still take a few days, maybe even a week," Harrison responded.

"If you could expedite that it would really help."

"I'll make it a priority, Chief."

"In the interim, have you noticed anything that's missing, out of place, or disturbed?"

"The only thing so far is this cage," Harrison said as he pointed to the open cage.

Yair walked into the open cage and looked at the shelves on the wall and the bronze box on the floor. "Is anything missing from here?" He asked.

"We won't know until we can get the file off the mainframe. The folder for this cage is missing from the cabinet in the Clean Room. I'm sorry I can't be more help. I've only been the director for about a week. The old director could tell you, but he died in a fire here," Harrison stated, feeling the need to expound on his answer.

"Was that the fire you had here about two weeks ago?" Yair asked.

"Yes, we lost four people—three archeologists and the director."

"What was the cause of the fire?" Yair asked.

"An electrical fire in the Clean Room," Harrison answered as he pointed to the glass-enclosed room at the rear of the vault.

"Electrocuted?" Yair asked as he looked at Mark.

"No, all four bodies were burned to ash," Steyn told him.

"Can electricity do that?" Yair said with a surprised look on his face.

"If the voltage is high enough I guess it could."

Yair tugged at his right ear as he looked around the vault. *"Nothing disturbed in the entire museum except items from one cage. Millions of dollars worth of treasure all around them, and they focus on items from this enclosure. It had to be very valuable for them to risk entry. But if it was that important, the staff would have remembered what was in there. And why would they protect something so valuable with a cheap padlock?"* He reflected to himself as he looked down at the floor where the padlock laid.

Yair then walked to the Clean Room and opened the door. He folded his arms and slowly walked around the room. He looked up to the ceiling at the light fixtures. The concrete ceiling still had smoke stains from the fire. He walked to the end of the examination table and looked down at the concrete floor. The four burn marks were still visible, about a meter apart. He knelt down and rubbed his fingers hard on one of the marks. It was permanently etched into the concrete. He lifted his fingers to his nose and made a face at the smell. "Sulfur," he whispered. "The fire would have had to have been white hot to permanently stain the floor." Yair stood back up and folded his arms. "White hot fire with the smell of sulfur … electricity alone couldn't produce that, could it? Could it be related to this crime?" His years of experience told him that there was no such thing as coincidence. He decided to file his observations in the back of his mind. *"Stick to the facts as they are presented,"* he told himself. He walked back to the entrance of the cage. "Mr. Harrison, thank you for your help. If there is anything you discover, please let Lt. Steyn know immediately."

Dr. Harrison lifted the ice pack from his head and looked up at Yair. "I will. Thank you, sir."

Yair walked back to the cage and nodded to Mark. The two men walked from the vault and stopped at the security podium. He looked at the podium and then down the hall to the elevator door. Yair stepped behind the podium and looked under the countertop to see a panic switch. The lever had not been tripped. He walked quickly toward the elevator, looking at his wristwatch and counting his steps while he walked. Twenty-five meters at twenty seconds time. He looked left and saw the stairwell door next to the elevator. He opened the door and looked at the frame at the top to see a door alarm.

Steyn walked up to him. "What are you thinking about, Chief?"

"The stairwell door has a screamer on it, so they probably used the elevator." The audible alarm was referred to as a *screamer* by the security staff because of its loud noise when activated. "Either way, it's still twenty-five meters to the podium. The guard had maybe fifteen to twenty seconds to react. I'm wondering why he didn't," Yair said.

"They were dressed in museum uniforms," Steyn stated.

"But you said he told you they had masks on," Yair answered.

"Yeah, that's right." Steyn had surprise in his voice. "But what could he have done? None of the staff is armed."

"But there's a panic button under the podium counter. And even if he wasn't surprised, he would have taken the dart in the back or in the chest, not the stomach."

Steyn rubbed his chin. "It makes sense. Maybe we need to take a second look at this guy."

"Is he still here?" Yair asked.

"He's upstairs with the rest of the staff. No one has been released yet."

"Let's go back up and make Mr. Kazez uncomfortable, shall we?" Yair said with a smile.

Steyn pushed the elevator button and the door opened. Yair rubbed the back of his neck. He hadn't been able to get rid of the tingling in his spine since he arrived at the museum. He tried not to think about it, but it still felt like someone was watching him. He dropped his hand back down at his side as the door was closing. The two demons looked at each other and smiled as the elevator door closed.

* * * * *

Gary was lying in bed watching the news as Beth came into the bedroom. She kicked off her slippers and got into the bed, leaning over and kissing him. "Did you check on Ally?" Beth asked.

"Yeah, I tucked her in. She smiled at me and said, 'Good night, Daddy.' Honey, I'm blown away at her progress. The transformation that has taken place since Clay arrived is nothing short of a miracle."

"I know. She seems to open up more and more by the day. I agree with Bill that this is somehow tied to Clay," Beth said.

"She sure is talkative when he's around."

"I still have a hard time with the whole demon thing, but it does make sense after listening to Bill and Clay's explanation."

Gary turned in the bed to face his wife. "I know. After I thought about it, I remembered so many things that had occurred over the years that now make sense. The different doctors, the trips to the mall and other places, it really made me think."

"I remember how hurt my mother was when she tried to pick her up so many years ago. I would like to be able to tell our folks about this, but it may be too soon," Beth said quietly.

"Not only too soon, the explanation may freak them out more than Allyson's rejection."

Beth rolled against her husband's side. "Yeah, if it freaked us out, it may tip them over the edge."

"That might not be a bad thing for your mother," Gary said as he hugged his wife laughing.

Beth quickly rose up and hit Gary in the side. "Be nice. One day you're going to be old and need comfort," she said laughing with him.

Gary rolled over on top of his wife kissing her. "And you'll be there to provide it," he said while looking into her eyes.

"Don't bet the farm on it, Carter," she said as she hugged him tightly.

CHAPTER 17

THE UNSEEN AMONG US

Bill Monroe's familiar red and white truck pulled into the Carters' driveway at 7:45 a.m. Clay placed his journal on the dashboard of the truck as he exited. Bill held his usual cup of Starbucks coffee as they both walked to the front door. Gary had observed them drive up and opened the door before they could ring the bell.

"Good morning, you guys, come on in. Beth is getting Allyson ready. Can I get you anything?"

"No, thanks," Clay replied.

Bill and Clay entered the living room in time to see Beth and Allyson descending the stairs together. Allyson was wearing her favorite white flower print dress, with her signature pigtails. Allyson's eyes opened wide and a huge smile appeared as she saw Bill and Clay standing in the living room. She let go of Beth's hand and ran to Clay. He knelt down in time to receive a big hug. Allyson let go of him and stood back with a smile.

"Good morning, Dr. Clay," she said. She then turned and looked at Bill. "Good morning, Dr. Bill."

"Good morning, Allyson," Bill responded with a big smile.

"Are we going to go to the museum, Dr. Clay?" she asked.

"We sure are, honey, if you still want to go," Clay said.

Allyson smiled and nodded her head yes.

Clay looked at Gary and Beth. "Then I guess we're ready."

Beth knelt down next to Allyson. "Remember, honey, if you get scared or just want to leave, tell Dr. Bill or Dr. Clay, and they'll bring you back home."

Allyson hugged Beth. "I will, Mommy." She turned toward Gary and smiled. "Bye-bye, Daddy."

Gary knelt down on one knee and hugged her. "Good-bye, baby—I love you."

"I love you too, Daddy," she responded.

"Oh, yeah? How much do you love me?" He asked with a smile.

"Two weeks," she replied, smiling back at Gary.

Not able to fully contain his emotions, a tear fell down Gary's cheek as he stood and smiled at Beth.

"All right, let's get on the road," Clay said as he held out his hand to Allyson.

Clay and Bill walked to the front door. Bill put his hand on the doorknob and looked down at Allyson.

"Are you ready, Allyson?" he asked.

Allyson nodded her head yes and turned to face Beth. "Good-bye, Mommy." A flood of emotions fell over Beth. She fought the maternal instincts to reach out and grab her daughter and protect her. Beth crossed her arms tightly around her chest as she looked on. "Good-bye, honey," she said tearfully.

The three walked out into the morning sunshine. They slowly walked to the truck, allowing Allyson the time to adapt to the surroundings. Clay was careful to look for people in the immediate area that would surprise her—thankfully, there were none. Clay opened the passenger door and lifted Allyson up and onto the middle section of the seat. He then got in and reached across her and fastened her seatbelt as Bill started the truck. Clay closed the door, watching her all the while.

"Are you ready, honey?" Clay asked.

Allyson stretched her back upward, looking out of the windows of the truck nervously with wide eyes as she nodded her head yes.

"Allyson, it's very important that you tell Dr. Bill and me if you see a birdman. And remember what we told you. They can't hurt you as long as we're with you, okay?"

"I remember, Dr. Clay," she replied.

Bill drove as slowly as he could through the neighborhood. It was now eight o'clock in the morning, and most everyone had left for work by now, so the streets were bare. Bill pulled up to an intersection and stopped at the red light. Allyson began trembling as she pointed to the woman walking across the street in front of them.

"What is it, Allyson?" Bill asked.

"A birdman is flying behind the lady, Dr. Bill."

Bill and Clay looked to see an attractive woman in her thirties crossing the street in front of them.

"What is the birdman doing, honey?" Clay asked.

"He's talking to her," Allyson said with a trembling voice.

When the woman reached the middle of the crosswalk, the demon suddenly turned and looked at the truck. The demon's teeth bared as its wings flared wide and its claws reached out in front. The demon flew toward the truck as it howled loudly.

"He's flying at us, Dr. Clay!" Allyson said loudly and fearfully.

Clay placed his arm around Allyson as he looked toward the front of the truck. He felt paralyzed as he sat motionless looking on.

"He's coming!" she screamed.

The demons wings flared as he saw Allyson sitting in the front seat. He screamed and covered his eyes as he turned and flew away.

"Where is he, Allyson?" Clay asked, nervously.

Still trembling as she watched the demon fly away, she whispered, "He flew away, Dr. Clay."

Bill didn't wait for the light to turn green. He hit the accelerator and turned right, parking next to the curb. Clay turned in his seat and looked at Allyson.

"He flew away?" Clay asked.

"Yes, Dr. Clay, he got scared and flew away."

"How close did he get, Allyson?" Bill asked.

As she pointed to the front of the truck, she answered, "He was right there."

"You mean above the hood?" Bill asked as he pointed to the front of the truck.

Allyson nodded her head yes. "Who was he looking at when he got scared?" Clay went on.

"At me, Dr. Clay."

Bill and Clay looked at each other not knowing what to say next. Could they really be afraid of her, Clay thought. He had told her they were afraid of her to ensure her it would be okay, but he had no idea his words would prove to be correct. How could something so terrifying be afraid of an innocent six-year-old little girl, and for what reason? Clay looked at Bill with wide eyes.

Clay was the first to speak. "I told you they wouldn't hurt you, Allyson … they are more afraid of you than you are of them." Even if it wasn't true, Clay felt it necessary to reassure her. "You believe me, don't you, Allyson?"

Still trembling, Allyson nodded her head in agreement.

"Honey, do you want us to take you home?" Bill asked.

"No, Dr. Bill, I want to go with you and Dr. Clay to the museum." She said it with a shaky voice.

"It's okay if you want to go home, honey. There will probably be more birdmen."

"No, Dr. Clay, I want to go to the museum," she replied.

Bill nervously put the truck into gear and pulled away from the curb. They continued down the road as Bill and Clay looked for people on the street. Allyson peered over the dashboard as they entered traffic. Bill pulled up next to a car at a stoplight, as Allyson looked inside the vehicle. She pointed toward the car without saying a word. The man in the car next to them was looking ahead at the streetlight smoking a cigarette. The demon was on his knees in the passenger seat whispering in his right ear.

"Is that another one, Allyson?" Bill asked.

She nodded her head yes.

Bill pulled away from the light and accelerated to get ahead of the vehicle. "Was he talking to the man?" he asked.

"Yes," she answered.

As they continued to drive, Allyson pointed to people walking and driving who had the entities with them. Clay kept his left arm solidly around her as she looked around nervously. Not everyone had a demon with them, some had multiple demons, and others had one. Children, for the most part, were unmolested by the demons, unlike the adults around them. A traffic officer was surrounded by demons, and a businessman had none. Street vendors, delivery people, commuters, there seemed to be no common thread for who was being attacked. By the time they reached the heart of the city, Allyson had stopped trembling. Even the demons that flew at her seemed to no longer bother her. Clay's reassurances had proven to be true—they really were afraid of her. Clay noticed that after a while, she had stopped pointing them out, and sat still in the seat.

"Are you still seeing the birdmen?" Clay asked Allyson.

"Yes."

"Where are they?" he wanted to know.

"Everywhere," she said quietly as she sat still in the seat.

Allyson was watching thousands of the creatures flying everywhere, darting back and forth between the people. They were in the heart of the city now, and the scene was frightening. Thousands of people going about the business of the day with demons flying around them—whispering, sometimes shouting, but tormenting them all. Bill pulled into the parking garage three blocks away from the museum. As he approached the parking booth, Allyson saw a demon inside with the attendant. She pointed her finger toward the man. The demon looked up to see her and shrieked with fear. He covered his face and flew away.

"Is there a birdman with him, honey?" Bill asked.

"No, Dr. Bill, he flew away."

"See Allyson, they really are afraid of you," Clay said, trying to reassure her.

Bill took the ticket from the attendant and drove to the nearest empty stall. Clay retrieved his journal from the dashboard as he opened the door. He released Allyson's seatbelt and placed his hand on her shoulder. "Do you still want to do this, Allyson?" he asked.

"Yes, Dr. Clay," she said, smiling back at him.

"The museum is seven blocks away. Would you like me or Dr. Clay to carry you, or do you want to walk with us?" Bill asked.

"I want to walk." She seemed to be fine and more than willing to go with them.

"Okay, honey … just remember, they're all afraid of you. Just keep a tight grip on our hands and they won't hurt you," Clay assured her.

Both men held her hands as they walked up the ramp to the street level. The sounds of the city were all new to Allyson as they exited the parking garage. Honking horns, vehicle engines, and the smell of exhaust fumes filled her nostrils. Her head turned back and forth as she took in the sights. Her head tipped back as she looked at the tall buildings around her. Clay looked down at her as they walked. "The buildings are pretty tall, huh?"

"Yes," she said as they walked through the busy sidewalk traffic. Allyson looked around with her mouth open as she saw thousands of demons flying around the city. As they walked, demons were tormenting approaching people, but they screamed and flew away when they saw her. She winced every time they got close, but continued to walk. By the time they had walked two blocks, she was no longer closing her eyes when they approached. What Dr. Clay had told her was correct; they were all afraid of her. As they approached the intersection three blocks from the museum, Allyson saw a homeless man sitting on the sidewalk against the building on the corner. A demon was crouched next to him screaming in his ear. The demon turned his head and saw Allyson staring at him. The creature shrieked and covered its face while jerking his head back and forth, screaming in fear. Its wings fluttered as he tried to get airborne and away from the little girl. He fell to the ground, crawling away with his eyes still covered. He finally got to his feet and staggered away from them. As he moved away, his body passed through people that were walking toward him, disappearing then reappearing as the demon walked through them. Each of the people he passed through stopped and took in a deep breath as they tried to shake off the effects, not knowing why they had such sudden feelings of terror.

As the three stopped at the streetlight, Allyson turned her head and looked at the homeless man. The man looked back at her with a smile as he waved to her. Allyson's face lit up with a beaming smile as she looked back at him. The light turned green, and they stepped out into the crosswalk. Allyson continued to look at the man until they had crossed the street.

Allyson looked at the front of the Field Museum as they approached. Her eyes were open wide as she gazed at the building. How beautiful the museum looked to her. The brightly colored banners that hung from the front of the building glittered as they fluttered in the breeze between the stone columns.

"Are you still okay, honey?" Clay asked as they stopped at the bottom of the stairs.

She looked up at Clay with a big smile as she nodded her head yes.

They walked up the stairs and entered the building, Allyson looking on in wonder the whole time. They stopped in front of the directory as Bill looked for the exhibit.

Allyson watched as hundreds of demons flew around inside the museum focused on their prey. As a man and his son were leaving the building, the demon that was with him saw Allyson and screamed. He flew to the ceiling and howled. Suddenly, all of the demons in the museum flew to the ceiling above the foyer. Allyson looked on as they all shrieked at the sight of her, vanishing as they passed through the roof of the building.

"Come on, it's this way," Bill said as he pointed to the hallway to their left.

Allyson's focus shifted back and forth from one display to another as they walked down the huge hallway. The curiosity and excitement could be seen on her face. She was beginning to enjoy the first of her many adventures and experiences that had been stolen from her since the beginning of her young life.

The museum staffer smiled at them as they entered the room of the Doré exhibit. He handed Bill and Clay pamphlets as they entered. They fell in behind the line of people who were working their way through the exhibit.

Bill bent over and spoke to Allyson quietly. "Honey, a long time ago, a man painted these pictures. They are all scenes from the Bible that happened thousands of years ago. Your mother and father have read the Bible to you, haven't they?"

"Yes, Dr. Bill."

"Well, these are pictures of what happened in the Bible," Bill explained to her.

Allyson was focused intently on the paintings, almost appearing to analyze each one. When they reached the painting of King Solomon, Allyson let go of Bill's hand and tugged on his shirtsleeve.

"Yes, honey." Bill looked down at her.

"Dr. Bill, he didn't look like that."

Both Bill and Clay looked down at her in surprise. "What do you mean, Allyson?"

"The king didn't look like that," she responded.

"Do you know who that is?" Clay asked.

"Yes, Dr. Clay, it's King Solomon."

"Did your mother and father tell you about him?" Clay asked.

Allyson nodded her head yes.

"And did they show you a picture of King Solomon?"

She shook her head no.

"When did you see a picture of him, Allyson?" Bill asked.

"I didn't see a picture of him, Dr. Bill. I saw him," she answered.

"You're saying you saw the real King Solomon?" Bill was truly perplexed.

She nodded her head yes.

Completely baffled, Bill looked at her and said, "Allyson, that's not possible. He lived thousands of years ago. Maybe you just saw someone who looked like him."

"No, Dr. Bill, I saw him," she firmly repeated while pointing to the painting.

"When did you see him, Allyson?" Clay asked.

Allyson shrugged her shoulders. "I don't know, Dr. Clay."

"How was he different, honey?" Clay asked.

"He was bigger and his face was different."

Bill and Clay looked at each other curiously, not believing what they had just heard. As they continued walking, Allyson stopped and pointed to the painting of King Herod.

"He looked different too, Dr. Clay," she remarked.

"How so, Allyson?" Clay asked.

"His hair was different," she said.

Bill and Clay were not ready to believe what they were being told. She just thinks she saw them, Bill thought. Childhood fantasies, dreams, anything could explain this away.

"How was his hair different, Allyson?" Bill asked.

"It was a different color, and it was straight, not curly. He was a very mean man, Dr. Bill," Allyson said with her lips pursed.

Clay let go of her hand and began taking notes furiously in his journal as they continued to walk. When they reached Doré's depiction of the death of Jezebel, Allyson suddenly froze in place. The painting showed the palace guards standing over the remains of Jezebel. Dogs had ripped her body apart, leaving only her hands, skull, and feet. Tears began falling down Allyson's cheeks. Clay knelt down next to her as visitors passed them by, looking down to see a little girl crying.

"What is it, Allyson?" Clay spoke to her very quietly.

"The picture makes me sad," she answered him.

"Why, honey? It's just a painting."

"They killed our queen," she murmured, still crying softly.

Clay's head jerked up to look at Bill, his brow furrowed. Bill knelt down next to Allyson.

"She's not your queen, honey," Bill whispered, softly.

"Yes, she is, Dr. Bill. She's everyone's queen." Allyson's voice started getting louder, and her tears were suddenly drying up. "She's everyone's queen and they killed her!" She almost shouted.

Clay quickly gathered Allyson up in his arms and moved away from the painting. One of the museum staff walked up next to them. The young man leaned in close to Clay and asked softly, "Is everything all right, sir, or can I be of help?"

Bill turned to the man. "We're okay. She's just tired. I think we just tried to see too much today," he said with a smile, hoping the man would just leave them alone.

"Okay, if you need anything, please let us know."

Clay let Allyson down as he and Bill knelt in front of her.

"It's okay, Allyson. You don't have to be sad anymore. We'll leave now, okay?" Bill asked.

Allyson wiped away the tears left on her cheeks. "Okay, Dr. Bill."

"Are you hungry, Allyson? We can get you something to eat if you like." Clay wanted to change the direction of her thoughts.

Allyson didn't respond; her gaze was focused between them at one of the display cases.

"Honey, are you hungry?" Bill asked.

Allyson started to tremble as she continued to stare. Bill turned around to see what had caught her attention. His eyes locked onto a ten-inch dagger lying inside the display case. The weapon was resting on a sheet of red satin. Bill turned back to see the fear on her face.

"What is it, honey? What's the matter?" He asked.

Allyson's trembling was getting worse as her eyes remained locked on the case. Clay turned to look at the display. He stood and walked over to it. He read the card lying next to the dagger, which described it as a "Sacrificial Dagger," probably from the fourth century BC. As he turned back to look toward Allyson, he could see her trembling, her skin turning pale, and her breathing becoming labored.

"Come on, Bill, let's go!" he said as he scooped her up in his arms.

They walked at a pace just short of running until they reached the lobby. Clay held Allyson as Bill looked at her.

"Is she breathing?" Clay asked.

"She is now!" Bill responded.

"Allyson—Allyson!" Clay said intensely to the little girl in his arms. Her eyes slowly opened as she looked at Clay. "Are you okay, honey? Can you talk to me?" he said.

"Yes, Dr. Clay—I'm really tired. Can we go home now?" She said.

Clay let out a long slow breath of relief. "You bet, honey, we'll leave right now."

Clay cradled her in his arms as they walked out of the museum. He looked down at Allyson in time to see her eyes close as she fell into a deep sleep.

CHAPTER 18

THE EMISSARY RETURNS

BETH STOOD NEXT TO the living room window with her arms folded as she waited to see Bill's truck pull into the driveway. Gary walked up behind her and whispered in her ear.

"You can sit down now, honey. You've been standing for an hour," he said.

"It's just that I'm so worried and, I'll admit, scared too," Beth said, trying to remain composed.

"Look, honey, they both have cell phones ... if there was a problem we'd have gotten a call. Everything's fine. I'm sure of it."

Beth couldn't help herself. Too many emotions had come to the surface these past weeks, too many revelations about Allyson's condition or, for that matter, her possible fate. Beth was trying to hold back the emotional tidal wave that resided just beneath the surface. As she stared out the window, she saw the red and white truck turn the corner and pull into the driveway.

"Honey, they're here!" she said with excitement. Beth had only moved from the kitchen to the living room since Bill, Clay, and Allyson had left three hours earlier. She could hardly contain her worry. When she opened the front door, she saw Clay carrying Allyson in his arms. Before she could speak, Bill saw the concern on her face.

"She's okay, Beth. She's just asleep," he said with his hand held out toward her. Beth nodded her head in relief.

Clay's voice was soft as he approached her. "She fell asleep at the museum and hasn't woken up yet. I'll carry her up to her room."

Beth followed Clay up the stairs and opened the bedroom door. Clay laid Allyson on the bed gently as Beth pulled the sheet up over her. She softly stroked Allyson's forehead as she kissed her. Allyson stirred, curling into a ball as Beth caressed her. Beth closed the door behind them as they left the room.

"What happened?" Beth said nervously as they descended the stairs.

"She got tired after seeing the exhibits and asked to come home," Clay responded.

He was already formulating his explanation of what happened, not wanting to worry Beth, but he put his emotions in check, deciding to tell the events to both Beth and Gary together after they were calmer. Beth led the way to the kitchen where Bill and Gary were seated at the table.

"Was everything okay?" Beth asked as she sat next to Bill.

Bill was clearly attempting to choose his words as he leaned forward. "We believe we confirmed two things. One is that Allyson is in all probability truly seeing demons. The second is that for whatever unexplained reason, it appears they are afraid of her."

Gary and Beth were locked onto Bill's every word. Both of them remained speechless as he continued to speak.

"On one occasion, shortly after we left here, Allyson said a demon started to fly toward us but got scared and flew away. The times she saw other demons, they were also surprised and frightened by her and flew away," Bill continued.

"But, Bill, was she terrified or screaming?" Gary asked.

"That's the surprising thing—she was incredibly calm after the first couple of incidents. Once she found that they were afraid of her, she became almost accepting of them," Clay stated.

"But did she become hysterical when the first one appeared?" Beth asked.

"No. She trembled at first, but after she said it flew away, she became unusually composed. The first incident was only about six blocks away from here. We asked her if she wanted to come back home, but she said no. She said she wanted to go to the museum."

"It was almost spooky how composed she became," Bill said.

"Spooky!" Beth fired back. Her protective maternal instincts were operating at full speed.

"Okay okay, poor choice of words—uncanny. She even walked with us for seven blocks from the parking garage to the museum." Gary and Beth both smiled at the concept of Allyson walking through downtown Chicago. They couldn't help but be envious of these two people enjoying something they had wanted to do for so long.

"We also had some unexplained moments in the museum," Clay interjected, clearly indicating that more had taken place.

"What do you mean?" Beth asked with a worried tone to her voice.

Clay opened his journal to the last page of entries and paused before continuing. "Allyson thinks ... no that's not entirely true given the events of the past weeks ... let me rephrase that ... Allyson knows what certain biblical characters actually looked like," Clay ventured.

"What?" Gary and Beth said in unison, not believing what they had heard.

"I know. Bill and I had the same reaction. She proceeded to inform us that Gustaf Doré's depictions were incorrect." Clay continued to talk as he looked at his notes. "King Solomon didn't look like that. He was bigger. And King Herod's hair was a different color, and it was straight, not curly. And, oh yeah—he was a very mean man," Clay said, half smiling.

Beth and Gary sat motionless with their mouths open. Was there no end to these revelations from Allyson? Beth finally forced the words out.

"And she seemed sincere?"

Very! Almost matter-of-factly. And that's not the most fascinating thing—when we got to Doré's depiction of the death of Jezebel, Allyson began crying and said that it was 'sad what they did to our queen.' And, when we tried to explain to her that Jezebel wasn't our queen, Allyson became almost defiant, saying she is everyone's queen. Not *was* everyone's queen, mind you, but *is* everyone's queen," Bill said. Gary and Beth seemed dumbstruck at what they were hearing. There was just no response to the information they were receiving about their daughter.

"Wow!" Gary said with a sigh leaning back in his chair. "We've read the Children's Bible to her, but certainly no specifics as to what any of the characters looked like."

"Well, Bill, it seems as though your supposition is correct. For whatever reason, Allyson's condition is somehow biblically based. The evidence is certainly supporting that," Beth added, looking confused and worried.

"And today's trip also supports that somehow Jezebel is at the center of it." Frowning, Gary looked at Bill and spoke again. "You were right, Bill. The trip to the museum did bear fruit. I wish Beth and I could have been there to see all of this." He fought the urge to be jealous that he hadn't been with them. Someone else was enjoying the interaction he should have. He took a deep breath and reminded himself that Bill and Clay had given them hope. That was definitely something he needed to remember.

"There's still a lot of missing pieces though. We still don't know the origin of where this is all coming from," Bill speculated.

He turned toward Beth. "I know it's a great source of pain for you, Beth, but it just may be connected to that site in Israel."

Beth's hands began to tremble. "I know, Bill," she said, "I've been trying to avoid that conclusion, but everything continues to point there."

"So even if this is all tied to the site, how do we confirm that?" Gary asked.

"Simple, we have to go there," Bill replied.

Clay barked back at Bill. "Go there? Are you completely mental, Monroe? Unless you've been living in a pickle jar or on drugs for the past thirty-five years, you'd know that the site just happens to be in the West Bank."

"I know that, Clay. I didn't say it would be easy."

"And since they just had a major conflict there last year, it's not exactly safe either," Clay went on.

"Clay, why are you getting so excited?" Bill asked.

"Because if you're correct that we need to go to the site—and you just may be—no one has taken this to the next logical step. Allyson would have to go with us," Clay continued.

The realization hit them all like a freight train. No one other than Clay had made the connection. Of course she would have to go with them.

"We can't do that!" Beth said, her body trembling with fear. Her experience with the site had been horrific, and the last thing she wanted to do was put her daughter in that place.

Gary seriously looked at Beth and said, "Honey, Clay's right. Without Allyson there, the trip would be pointless. She would have to go. It's either we face the potential danger there, or live with the possibility of never resolving this and accepting her condition permanently." He had come to the realization that if they were ever going to resolve this, risks had to be taken. He wasn't happy about taking Allyson there either, but the chance for a normal life for Allyson made the risk worth it.

As much as she wanted to disagree with the premise, Beth couldn't argue with its logic. "Okay, assuming we go, how difficult would it be to get to the site?"

Clay ran his fingers through his hair as he took a deep breath. "Not impossible, but difficult and dangerous. I have an old friend there who's retired from the Israeli Army. I worked in intelligence with him. If it can be done, Amir is the one to help us. But even if he can, it's still a huge safety issue." Clay knew Bill had not been to Israel, and didn't fully understand the complications and protocol.

Bill turned toward Gary and Beth. "The decision is yours."

More frightened than she'd ever been in her life, Beth looked at Gary with tears in her eyes. "What do you think, honey?"

Gary rubbed the back of his neck. "It's the next logical step, Beth. Believe me, I'm no fan of going back into that cave again, but I agree with Bill. It has to be done. We need to give Allyson every chance at a normal life, if possible. I think we should go. I think we *have* to go!"

Beth took a deep breath as she looked at Clay and Bill after carefully assessing the risks. "Okay, you guys, we're in."

Clay looked across at Beth and placed his hand on her arm. "Before you make that decision, there's something else you and Gary need to know."

"What?" Beth said with a great deal of worry in her voice.

"It's the reason we brought Allyson home."

"Why? What happened?" she said, starting to panic.

"When Allyson got upset over the painting of Jezebel, I picked her up and walked to where we were out of its view. Bill and I were trying to calm her down when she began to tremble. Her eyes were locked on a display case behind us. The look on her face was one of total fear. She was so scared she turned pale and held her breath. Once we took her out of the exhibit hall, she started breathing again. She slowly opened her eyes and said she was tired and wanted to go home. It was then that she fell asleep in my arms as we were leaving."

With a shaky voice, Gary asked the question. "What was in the case?"

"A dagger," Clay said.

"Why would the sight of a dagger scare her?" Beth whispered.

"It wasn't just a knife, Beth. It was a sacrificial dagger," Clay explained further.

"But surely you can't make a connection between Allyson and a sacrificial dagger, can you?" Gary asked, not believing what he was hearing.

"Look, it may be nothing, or it may be something. Maybe she just has a fear of blades. I know I did when I was a kid," Clay said.

Beth turned toward Bill. "What would a dagger like that be used for?"

Bill responded, knowing he had to tell them the truth no matter how difficult it was. "Sacrifices were common in the Old Testament. Sacrifices to God were made on a regular basis. An unblemished lamb was usually the norm. There were also child sacrifices that were made to the pagan gods."

Gary leaned forward in his chair, his mind reeling. "But if Allyson's earlier statements were correct about seeing biblical figures accurately, would it not stand to reason that she would be afraid of seeing what the dagger was used for? I mean any child would be horrified at seeing an animal sacrificed."

"Or a child being sacrificed?" Clay pondered.

"That would stand to reason. If Allyson could see people or articles and what they truly are, or what they were used for, she would most definitely be terrified," Bill said.

Clay stopped short of opening his mouth and saying what his deductive brain was telling him. Maybe Bill was correct. Perhaps it was only what Allyson thought it was used for. He decided not to pursue the conversation any further. "If you still want to go, I'll contact my friend in Jerusalem and see what he can do for us. But the final decision to take Allyson needs to be yours totally."

Beth looked across at Clay. "I know you're apprehensive, Clay, and your concerns for Allyson are appreciated ... they truly are. Gary and I will think on it and let you know. It's a big decision, and one that requires a lot of prayer and thought."

"But I still think *we* need to go, Clay, even if Gary, Beth, and Allyson don't join us," said Bill.

"Agreed," Clay responded.

"Clay, you and Bill have already done so much. We can't possibly ask you to go halfway around the world for us," Gary said.

"No, Bill's right. We need to go. The evidence is leading us in that direction."

"Besides, the Middle East has the best coffee in the whole world," Bill said with a smile.

"I might have known that coffee would be a deciding factor in this for you," Clay was glad to let some of the anxiety out of the situation.

The tension of the afternoon was broken by the laughter.

* * * * *

Shimon Gutstein and Douglas Weiss pored over the museum files that were spread out on Shimon's conference table. They had removed all of the photographs from the clear plastic holders in the binder. The photos were spread out in front of them in neat rows above the hundred plus pages of documents. The two men sat next to each other on one side of the table. Both were taking notes as they reviewed the file.

"I can't believe that the temple is so close to Jerusalem ... just an hour's drive. All these centuries it's been right under our noses," Shimon solemnly observed.

"Yes, Lord, but may I remind you that the temple is in the West Bank? Getting everyone in there will pose as more of a problem than we may believe," Douglas said.

"I don't think so, Douglas. We can have Sharon look into getting any permits we may need. It would be better to have written permission from the army, and her position in the Israeli Defense Forces could help us with that."

"We better hurry then. What we're talking about is less than two weeks away. And that's not the only problem we have. We have to get the queen and all the other items to the temple as well," Douglas reminded him.

"That shouldn't be too much of a problem. We have five or six disciples that are in the military. Let's see what they can do," Shimon said.

"Okay, I'll get on it. We're also going to need a lot of provisions for the followers ... tents, food, and transportation."

"Pack as light as you can. We only need provisions for three days at the site. We also need to take care of anyone who lives close to the site. There has to be someone living near the area," Shimon said.

"I can take a small team up there a few days before you arrive and deal with any of the locals."

"Good, the last thing we need is someone interrupting us or alerting the authorities."

"I'll take care of it," Douglas replied.

"Now, on to the problem at the museum. I'm worried about the death that occurred."

"There shouldn't be a problem," Douglas answered. "We removed all the camera footage, so no one got a shot of us before or after the incident. We all wore gloves, so there won't be fingerprints anywhere close to the vault or the offices. The only thing that could be a problem is Michael. He's the weakest link in the operation."

"Speaking of Michael, he should be here any minute. He called from the hotel to say he was on his way here," Shimon informed him.

"Good. Short of him, there's no way they can tie us to the museum. We need to ask him what the investigators said," Douglas replied.

"We'll know when he gets here. Are you sure you retrieved everything from the museum?" Shimon asked again, indicating he was still worried.

"Yes, everything down to the last dart. We even picked up the two spent cartridges," Douglas explained patiently.

"Good. Absolutely nothing must interrupt us this time. I don't want to leave anything to chance. We will not fail as our ancestors did," Shimon said.

Douglas turned his head toward Shimon. "Lord, I will not fail you."

"I know, Douglas. I have every faith in you. If it weren't so, you would not be in charge."

"Thank you, Lord," Douglas responded gratefully.

The tone of the telephone intercom interrupted the conversation. "Sir, Michael Kazez is here to see you," Arnona announced.

"Good, send him in," Shimon responded.

Shimon walked to the door to meet Michael. He opened the door and greeted him with a smile and an extended hand.

"Michael, it's good to see you. Can I get you anything?"

"No, thank you, Lord, I'm fine." Michael took a seat and smiled at Douglas.

Shimon sat back down at the table. "So, Michael, tell us about what happened at the museum."

Michael leaned back and took a deep breath. "Well, I guess I was the last one to wake up from the tranquilizer. The others called the police, and they arrived before I woke up."

"Did they interview you?" Douglas asked.

"Yes, twice," he responded.

Shimon's eyes opened wide. "Twice—what did they ask you?"

"The first time they asked pretty routine questions like what did the intruders look like, just general descriptions, if anyone spoke or had any other identifying features … stuff like that," Michael responded.

"And what about the second interview?" Douglas asked with more apprehension. Michael looked at him and answered, "They asked me why I didn't trigger the duress alarm when I saw you coming down the hall toward me."

"And what did you tell them?"

"I told them I was too scared to react, and that I didn't have time because you ran toward me."

"Good, that was the best thing you could have told them. What else did they ask?"

"One thing I didn't fully understand. The lead detective asked why I was shot in the stomach. He asked me that three times. I didn't understand why he kept focusing on that particular aspect. Then he asked where I was actually located when I got shot."

"And what did you tell him, Michael?" Douglas went on.

"I told him I was at the podium," Michael explained further.

"Why would he ask about that?" Shimon asked, looking at Douglas.

"The detective is focusing on the fact that Michael could have triggered the duress alarm and didn't. Also, if he's standing behind the podium, it's higher than the entry wound. This guy's no dummy ... it may be a problem for us," Douglas speculated.

Shimon rubbed his chin with his right hand. "Okay, Michael, let's stick with your statement that you were too scared to respond. If they ask again, keep telling them you were terrified and couldn't move."

"Yes, Lord."

"Do you think that will work, Douglas?" Shimon said.

"Yes, so long as he remains consistent, that should work," Douglas answered.

Shimon stood up from the table. "Thank you for the report, Michael. You should probably get back to Jerusalem as soon as possible. We don't want to raise suspicions. Get back home quickly, and we'll let you know when we're ready for you to meet us at the site."

Michael and Douglas stood and followed Shimon to the door. Shimon had his right hand on Michael's shoulder as they walked to the door.

"You've done a good job, Michael, and we're all very proud of you. This could not have happened had it not been for your efforts," Shimon assured him.

"Thank you, Lord, it was an honor to serve you," Michael responded.

Shimon opened the door for Michael and, as he let him out, spoke to him again. "See you soon."

"Good-bye, Lord." Michael left the office feeling pretty proud of himself.

Shimon closed the door and turned toward Douglas. He nodded his head as he placed his right hand on Douglas's shoulder. Douglas bowed his head in return as he left the office.

CHAPTER 19

THE ANOINTED ONE

Bill and Clay sat at the dinner table in the townhouse enjoying an evening meal of Bill's tuna casserole. The two men pored over their notes as they took occasional bites of food from their plates. Clay had a stack of Allyson's papers that he had finished looking over at his right foot and was reviewing his findings. The only sound that was being made was the rhythmic ticking of the grandfather clock.

Bill stood up from the table holding his plate. "More casserole, bud?" he asked.

"You bet," Clay said, handing his plate to Bill.

"Have you found anything new in Allyson's writings?" Bill asked.

Clay stood up with his hands on his hips and bent backward stretching. "Only one thing so far … *Anointed One.*"

Bill answered back from the kitchen. "Anointed one … I wonder what that could mean."

Clay sat back down at the table. "I don't know. If I were to guess, I'd say Jezebel, only because she is the one that's referred to so much in the writings."

Bill came back into the dining room and placed the plate in front of Clay. "That would make sense, but we still don't have a clue what

Allyson is really writing about. Is there a sequence to her writings, or do they appear to be random?" Bill asked.

"So far, they still appear to be random. That may change however if we get any more words from her."

"From what I can see, she is still drawing the pictures of demons." Bill asked.

"Yes, but with more frequency. It could be tied to our trip to the museum or just the fact that someone is talking to her about it."

"It was strange how she became almost accepting of the whole thing. By the time we reached the museum, she was eerily calm about it," Bill observed.

"But, Bill, we can't get a false sense of security about this. From what we can gather, the demons fear her so far. We don't know why yet, but all it's gonna take is for one of them to show no fear, and we're back to square one." Clay was more pessimistic about Allyson's sightings than Bill.

"I don't worry about that, Clay. My take on it is that the Lord is watching over her. I mean it makes sense because she sees the demons, but the Lord keeps them from hurting her."

"Bill, I wake up in this toilet of a world every morning and see the filth in the streets of D.C. I read the paper at night and it makes me want to puke. Drugs, filthy predators molesting little children, murders, robbery, rape, and that's just here. It happens across the world on a scale that makes the holocaust look like child's play. Do you expect me to swallow the theory that he watches out for one little girl, and lets the rest of the population fend for themselves?" Clay's attachment to Allyson was growing with every day he became more involved with her.

"Clay, I don't speak for the Lord. He does a good job of that on his own. I can't say why some suffer more than others. I can only surmise that their reward will be greater in the kingdom because of their suffering. The bottom line is that we live in a sin-scarred world, a world that is destined to be destroyed because of that sin. And the only solace we have is that the Lord takes care of those that belong to him. As for Allyson, it is crystal clear to me that he is watching over her." Every fiber of Bill's existence would have it no other way.

"Even if what you say is true, I still hearken back to my original question: why bother letting her see them in the first place? Why would a loving God—to borrow one of your phrases—allow an innocent child to see them at all? Maybe I'm just thick, but that seems pretty cruel," Clay went on, still very skeptical.

"Clay, the Lord is using her for some purpose. It's up to him how and why he does that."

"Using her," Clay shook his head slowly, "that sounds even worse. Why would God use her in the first place? It makes it sound like we're property. I'm having a really hard time with this whole thing."

"We don't have the right to ask that Clay. It's up to him. We're the created. We have no business questioning the Creator as to how he uses his creations.

"Even if he kills them off?" Clay shot back.

"Oh, Clay, get over it!" Bill said with a stern voice.

Clay was stunned by Bill's sharp response. It took him completely by surprise. He had rarely seen his friend angry, and had only seen Bill vent toward him once before, many years ago.

"And what the hell is that supposed to mean, Monroe?" Clay barked back.

"What it means is that I'm tired of listening to you blame God for your loss. Beat me up all you want, but stop putting this on God. He took Mary and Jody for a reason, just like he took Carrie. I was devastated, but I understood that it was for a reason—his reason, and we have no right to question the omnipotent, omniscient God of the universe why he did it. Maybe Mary and Jody would have suffered a painful agonizing death from cancer, and he took them quickly before they had to suffer. Maybe they had completed the tasks that he had for them here, or maybe he just wanted to reward them early for their obedience. Whatever the reason, we're not worthy to ask why. So maybe it's time for you to quit being bitter, shut your mouth, and get on with what he has for you to do."

"What, watching a little girl suffer?"

"Maybe—or maybe to see you finally let some reason enter that rock you call a heart." Bill leaned forward toward his friend. "Look, Clay, you're like a brother to me, and I love you with all my heart, but you've got to get rid of the bitterness that has kept you from allowing God's love to touch you. Open your eyes and your heart for just a minute and try to see what he's doing with and for you. When you accepted him into your life years ago, that meant you have an obligation to trust his judgment. You're putting too much stock into this world, and not enough into his kingdom. It's clear to me that he has given you the task of helping Allyson to focus on—maybe that's your calling. Maybe that's how he's *using* both you and Allyson."

"And what happens after that? Does he just kill me off too?"

"Maybe," Bill responded.

"Oh, that's reassuring."

"Clay, will you quit focusing on what you want and think about what he wants? Maybe he will take you home to be with him. I hope not. I enjoy having you here with me. But in the final analysis, it doesn't matter what we want, only what he wants. It's all about acceptance."

For the second time since Clay had arrived in Chicago, Bill had put him in his place. Clay had held onto the pain of losing Mary and Jody and had not wanted to let go. He had dreamt of growing old with his wife and looked forward to bouncing his grandchildren on his knee. Now, everything he had worked so hard for during his life held no meaning. Somewhere deep down in his heart, he had wanted to move on, but he just couldn't muster the courage to do so. Clay sat silent, spinning his fork in the food on his plate.

"Look, Clay, I'm sorry for jumping on you like that. I truly am, but it hurts me to see my friend suffering like this. Let it go, bud—get rid of it. We need all of your focus and a clear head to help that little girl."

"You know you're the only one I would ever let talk to me that way. Anyone else would be taking their meals through a straw for a year after a tirade like that."

"I know. I've seen you in action before," Bill said with a smile. "How about I get you a glass of wine?"

Clay looked up at his lifelong friend. "No, thanks, water's fine, or are you testing me?" Clay said with a grin.

"Well, maybe just a little," Bill answered with a smile.

Clay looked down at his plate and began talking. "Bill, you're my best friend, and I couldn't have made it through Mary and Jody's deaths without you. You mean more to me than you will ever know.

But maybe I just need a little longer to grieve than you did. Your point is well taken. I have been a little over the top lately." Clay looked up at his friend. "I apologize. It won't happen again."

"Wow, maybe *I* need a drink. Clay Harker apologizing, this is a first." Bill smiled.

"Well, I have to apologize at least once every decade." Clay grinned.

The doorbell rang as the two men were laughing.

"Who in the world could that be?" Bill said as he stood up.

He walked to the front door and opened it up to see Gary smiling back at him. "Come on in, Gary. What a nice surprise. To what do we owe the pleasure?"

"I brought Allyson's latest writings, and I wanted to bring this over to you guys before you made reservations," Gary explained, as he held up the two envelopes in his hand.

Clay stood up to shake Gary's hand. "What's up, Gary?"

"Beth and I talked about it, and we both agree that we need to go with you to Israel."

"Excellent," Bill said, as he sat back down at the table.

"We talked a lot about it and decided that it really makes no sense for us to not go because we have been at the site before, and you will probably need our insight."

"Well, I guess we can go ahead and make reservations then," Bill said, looking at Clay.

"No need. Beth and I took the liberty of making all the arrangements," Gary said, as he handed the envelopes to Bill and Clay.

"What's this?" Bill asked.

"Airline tickets and reservations at the King David Hotel are in there," Gary continued as he placed the stack of Allyson's papers on the table.

"Gary, you didn't need to do that. Clay and I are fine getting our own tickets," Bill said, overcome with their generosity.

"Yes, we did. It's the least we could do for all your kindness. The flight leaves tomorrow night—I hope that's okay with you."

"Of course. Clay and I planned to leave as soon as you and Beth gave us your decision anyway," Bill said.

"Is Allyson going to be okay going with us?" Clay asked.

"Yes, Beth talked to her and she said she would like to go so long as Dr. Clay was going," Gary said with a smile.

"Well, if the boss says we go, then I guess we better do so."

"Gary, can I get you some dinner or something to drink?" Bill asked.

"No, thanks, I'm fine. I apologize again for interrupting you, but I wanted to get Allyson's papers and the tickets over to you."

"Good. By the way, Clay got two more words today," Bill told him.

"Oh really, what did you find?"

"*Anointed One*," Clay said, as he pointed to the words in his journal.

Gary's face turned white as he stared at the words in the book. He slowly moved his head closer to the page, his eyes opening wider the closer he got.

"What's the matter, Gary?" Bill asked.

Gary didn't respond to Bill, his eyes still locked hypnotically on the two words. Clay placed his right hand on Gary's shoulder and gently nudged him. "Gary, what is it?"

"That's it," he said, turning toward Clay with a look of astonishment on his face.

"That's what?" Clay wanted to know.

"These are the words that appeared on Beth's forehead."

Bill's head snapped to the right, looking at the words. "You mean *Anointed One?*"

"Are you sure?" Clay inquired very carefully.

"Unmistakable—now that I see them written in Aramaic," Gary responded.

Bill looked at Clay, his brow furrowed. "Clay, what can that mean?"

"I haven't the foggiest idea. I'm as lost as you guys. Aside from the classic definition of being 'chosen,' I don't have a clue," he responded.

"What in the world could Beth be chosen for?" Gary asked.

"I suppose the better question would be chosen by whom?" Clay said.

"I think it's probably by God, based on what we have so far," Bill ventured an explanation.

"And what do you base that on, Sherlock?" Clay asked with a smirk.

"So far, we have determined this to be religiously based, and since he is controlling the process at this stage, that's a fair assumption. Without further data, or additional words from Allyson, I think it's a fair analysis."

Clay's eyes opened wide. He stood up from the table and began rifling through Allyson's papers. He frantically circled repeated words with his red felt pen.

"What's up?" Bill said curiously.

Clay spoke as he thumbed through the pages. "I just had a thought from years ago. What if Allyson's words are a code?"

Bill's eyes opened wide as the theory hit him. "Yeah!"

"What's going on?" Gary said as he looked at Bill.

Bill stood beside Clay, looking at his journal. "It's the oldest form of code, Gary. If you scramble the words, and withhold key words, it can't be translated unless they are placed in the right order," Bill answered.

"God writes code?" Gary asked.

"No, but his followers might if they feared detection. That would explain why the site you guys found was so remote."

"Precisely," said Clay.

"That makes sense—but why would Beth be the Anointed One?" Gary desperately needed to know.

"Maybe for a position—or a task," Bill mused.

"Here's another one!" Clay exclaimed, as he scribbled in his journal. "*God*."

Bill smiled excitedly as he watched Clay. "See, I knew this was from God."

"*True*," Clay said, as he circled and underlined the word.

Bill could hardly contain his excitement. He put both his fists in the air. "Yes, Lord, thank you!" he said.

Clay was throwing the papers on the floor as he finished, not bothering to stack them. "*Abraham*," he said, as he wrote the name in the journal. He reached the last paper and turned it over, writing the words on the back. He turned his journal to the first page and added the three words to the others. "*Behold*, *buried*, *defiance*, *joined*, *bearer*, *sayeth*, *God*, *true*, *Abraham*, *light*, and *Jezebel*. That's what we have to work with. Does this mean anything to you, Bill?"

Bill stared at the words as he twisted the pen in his hand. He began jotting the words down in different order, flipping them in his mind. "Back then, God was more commonly referred to as the God of Abraham, the one true God. We know Jezebel was not to be buried, so we can assume it's her he's speaking about regarding the word defiance. His light shines forth. That's probably what that means." Bill rubbed his chin as he stared at the words. "Got it!" He said as he wrote and spoke the words. *"Behold, the true God of Abraham. His light shines in defiance of Jezebel, who shall not be buried."*

"How in the world did you come up with that?" Gary said.

"I just borrowed some common phrases from the Bible, and took a little literary license," he explained, smiling.

"But you forgot *bearer* and *Anointed One*," Clay reminded him, looking at the paper.

"That could mean Beth is the bearer of something, or it could mean God is bearing the Anointed One for something. I think if we get some more words from Allyson, it may fall into place. Man, I'm excited about this," Bill said, slapping Clay on the back.

"Well, it certainly makes more sense than anything else so far. After all, you're the theology professor."

Bill was beaming with excitement. "You do know what this especially means, you guys—our trip to Israel absolutely has to happen now."

For the first time in years, Gary felt a peace fall over him. For the first time since Allyson's condition had surfaced, he felt as though closure was within their grasp. He could hardly wait to share the news with Beth.

"And it will. I've got to get home and share this with Beth. We have a lot of preparation and packing to do." Gary walked toward the door.

"Okay, Gary. Clay and I will meet you all at the airport."

"Will you and Beth be okay taking Allyson?" Clay asked.

"We'll be fine, Clay. I'll just tell her Dr. Clay will meet us there." Gary was smiling as he left.

Bill closed the door and turned back looking at Clay. "Man, that was really nice of them to get tickets for us."

"Yeah, wasn't expecting that."

"They're good people, Clay, and I'm sure they are very appreciative of the progress that has been made. They've been more patient than I would have been."

"I have to admit it, Bill, I feel pretty good about this as well," Clay said, yawning. He walked to the table and closed his journal for the night. "I'm tuckered. Hope you don't mind if I call it a night?"

"Not at all—I'm pretty tired as well. Let's get some rest," Bill responded.

Clay picked up Allyson's papers and placed them on the table, straightening them into one neat stack. The drawing of the demon looked back at him. Clay placed his right middle and index fingers on the figure. The tingling in his spine gave him a cold chill causing him to shudder.

What is it, bud?" Bill asked.

"Nothing. Just happy to have such phenomenal progress on this. I'm just tired, too much emotion."

"Me, too," Bill said as the two men walked to the stairs to go up to bed for the night.

The two figures clothed in black robes watched as Bill and Clay walked up the stairs. One of the demons walked to the table and stared with contempt in his eyes at the stack of Allyson's papers. A snarl came across his lips as he raised his right hand and swung at the papers, scattering them on the floor. Both figures ran across the room and leapt into the air, passing through the wall, and into the night.

CHAPTER 20

TYING UP LOOSE ENDS

Chief of Detectives Yair Klein exited the rear door of the Ministry of Police building on Clermont-Ganneau. As usual, the business of the day had kept him late at work. He nodded politely at the two officers entering the building as they passed. It was late and Yair was looking forward to his nightly ritual of a glass of wine when he arrived at his house.

He stopped at his car and unlocked the driver's door and groaned with fatigue as his body fell into the seat. He backed out of his parking stall and drove to the exit. Yair negotiated the concrete posts of the exit and waived at the guard as he drove over the tire shredders that protected the enclosure. As he turned onto Clermont-Ganneau, his radio barked out commandingly.

"Charlie One, this is 221."

"Oh great!" he said as he pulled his radio from the belt holster. "Go ahead 221."

Police Lieutenant Mark Steyn's voice answered from the other end. "Chief, we need you at 519 Paran."

"What do you have, Mark?"

"It's a homicide, sir. You're going to want to see this."

"Copy. I'll be there in five."

Yair put the radio back in its holster and turned his car north. He knew that it had to be important in order to warrant a call for a response. Usually a telephone call would suffice, as his presence was rarely required. No police supervisor ever wanted to arrive at work in the morning and be asked a question by a superior without having an answer.

The drive to the call location was a very quick one, less than three miles from the station. Yair pulled up to the ten-story apartment complex and parked his car in front of the control point entrance. The building wasn't that different from any other modern apartment building in the city—reinforced concrete with heavily tinted glass windows, an abundance of exterior lighting, and the complete absence of any kind of foliage. Over the years, Yair had learned to accept the differences between the place of his birth and his beloved Jerusalem. He had lived in Jerusalem for almost forty years, but did on occasion miss the character of the buildings in London and the green of the parks and streets in the city. He pulled his badge and credentials out of his suit coat and placed the back of the bifold badge holder in his front suit pocket. He exited the car and looked at the front of the building. He lifted the radio to his mouth and depressed the button. "Two twenty-one, this is Charlie One. What is your location?"

The voice on the other end responded. "Around back, Chief, just come through the passageway in the center of the building."

The entire building had been cordoned off as Yair approached the makeshift entry on the main sidewalk. He stopped and showed his badge to the officer as the man wrote the name and time of entry on the log. Yair walked to the center of the building and through the open passageway, exiting into the alley behind the apartments. He looked to his right and saw Lieutenant Steyn with two uniformed officers standing by the row of large trash bins. Another protocol and barricade had been placed around the crime scene at one of the trash bins. He approached the officers, stopping in front of Steyn.

"What do you have, Mark?"

Steyn pointed to the bins. "One of the tenants found him when they were dumping their trash."

Yair looked at Mark. "Have you processed the trash bin yet?"

"Yes, Chief, you can look inside."

Yair grabbed the top of one of the bins and stepped on top of the ledge, lifting himself up to look inside. He saw the medical examiner examining a body. The M.E. was kneeling on the floor of the almost empty trash bin gathering evidence. The body was lying on its back, with both legs straight but separated by twelve inches at the feet. The left arm was straight alongside the body, and the right arm was at a forty-five-degree angle to the chest. The head was turned to the right and offered an eerie scene as his eyes were open wide, making it appear as though he was surprised. Yair could see blood on the floor of the bin around the head. He breathed out a long sigh as he looked at the face. He stepped down from the bin and turned toward Mark.

"That's the guard from the museum, isn't it? What was his name?"

"Michael Kazez," Mark responded.

"How long has he been there?"

"About twenty-four hours according to the M.E."

"And what was the cause of death?"

"A puncture wound at the base of the skull. It's an elongated entry wound to the right side of the spine … looks like a knife wound. The knife goes into the base of the skull next to the spine and scrambles the brains. Kazez was dead instantly. This looks like the work of a professional, Chief."

Yair placed his hands on his hips as his head tilted backward. "Guess this answers the question as to who was the inside man." Yair knew that there was little chance of finding a connection to the killer or the perpetrators at the museum now. The only hope was for them to make a mistake. Everyone makes a mistake sooner or later, Yair thought, but the odds were not in his favor. "Do we know where he lived, Mark?"

Steyn pointed straight up toward the top of the building. "Eight floors up."

"Do we have people up there?"

"Yes, two people from the lab are going through his apartment."

"Let's take a look. We really need a break."

The two men walked back through the passageway to the lobby entrance and into the elevator. Yair looked at Mark as the elevator door closed. "Well, there goes our link to the robbery."

Mark turned toward Yair as they ascended. "Maybe we can find something in his apartment. Short of that, however, you may be right.

Those responsible for the museum heist are no dummies. They took out the only connection we had."

"Have you discovered anything about the site where the artifacts were located?"

"The only thing we know so far is that the items taken were from a site somewhere in the Mountains of Eastern Israel. It may be a while before we find out where the site is because all the files were taken along with the artifacts."

"And do you know what was taken yet?"

"A dagger, some bones, and twelve oil lamps. The only thing we really know for sure at this point is the number of the site, number 482."

"And nothing else was taken from the museum? No artwork, precious metals or gems, anything else of value?"

"No, only the lamps, the dagger, and the bones."

The two men exited the elevator on the eighth floor and walked to the apartment. They waited for the officer guarding the entrance to enter their names on the log and then entered the apartment.

The one-bedroom apartment had a small kitchen, open to the living area, and one bathroom. It was sparsely decorated with very few amenities, and the walls were free of any pictures. One reclining chair in the living room was placed in front of a large bookshelf against the wall, with a small twelve-inch television in the center. A folding tray sat next to the recliner with a half-eaten microwave dinner resting on it. The kitchen had a small round table with two chairs next to it, with a salt and pepper shaker in the center. Even the kitchen counter tops were clear of clutter. Only a microwave oven and an electric can opener were on the counter. The entire apartment was painted flat white, with a light tan colored carpet throughout.

"Looks like he was single," Yair observed, as he stood in the center of the living area.

"So far it looks that way. We haven't found any signs of a wife or girlfriend yet," Mark replied.

Steyn handed Yair a pair of latex gloves. The chief put the gloves on and removed a pen from his suit coat pocket. He looked at the papers and books on the shelves, moving them with the pen. He meticulously examined the contents of the shelves, taking notes on the contents.

Most of the papers were training materials from the museum security department and gave little indication as to who the man was.

The chief walked to the bedroom, where he saw one of the men from the Forensics Lab, Joseph Malka dusting for fingerprints at the nightstand. The bedroom was as empty as the rest of the apartment. A bed, a nightstand, and a dresser were the only contents. Yair looked into the open closet and saw two pair of shoes on the floor, four security uniforms, and an assortment of street clothes hanging from the rod. Joseph looked up and nodded to Yair and then went back to his work. Yair then walked to the dresser and looked at the figurine that rested on the top. It appeared to be made of bronze. A man standing on top of a bull, with what appeared to be lightning bolts in his hand.

"Joseph, have you ever seen anything like this before?"

Joseph looked over the top of his glasses at the figure. "No, Chief, I sure haven't."

Yair made an entry in his note pad regarding the statue and walked to the bathroom, where Marta Liebowitz, also from the lab, was dusting for prints. "Hello, Marta."

"Hi, Chief, what brings you out tonight?"

"Oh, I just got bored and needed some excitement," Yair said with a chuckle. "You find anything of interest in here?"

"Just some medications." She pointed to the two bottles in the medicine cabinet.

Yair looked at the bottles: Wellbutrin and Effexor. "It looks like our guy was depressed."

"Not anymore," Marta replied.

Frowning, Yair looked very seriously at her and commented, "Marta, take extra care with this one. He's shaping up to be high profile."

"Will do, Chief."

Yair walked back into the living area. He stood in the center of the room and slowly turned in a circle as he mentally took notes. *This was looking pretty grim*, Yair thought. Even his apartment wasn't giving any clues about Michael. "This guy lived an almost Bohemian lifestyle," he commented to Mark.

"Yeah, it's easy to see why there wasn't a woman in his life."

Yair put the pen back in his pocket. "Okay, Mark, do all the follow-up work—family, friends, coworkers, and neighbors. Someone is bound to know something about this guy that can help us. I saw some prescriptions in the bathroom. Contact the doctor and get a complete rundown on him."

Mark was jotting down notes on his pad as Yair spoke. Both men walked out of the apartment and down the hall. Yair entered the elevator and turned around looking at Steyn.

"See if we can locate his family first. That's going to be the best chance at getting an idea of who his friends were. Put all your other cases on hold, Mark. This takes priority for now."

"Yes, sir."

Yair quickly reached his hand out and stopped the door from closing, and leaned out into the hall. "And take some pictures of the statue on his dresser. It just might mean something."

"Yes, sir."

Yair pulled his hand back into the car allowing the elevator door to close. He took a deep breath as he looked up at the ceiling of the elevator. Deep in thought, he spoke out loud, "We'll be very lucky if anyone knows this guy."

* * * * *

The knock on Shimon Gutstein's door was both loud and commanding. "Enter!" he shouted.

Douglas entered the room and closed the door behind him. Shimon took off his reading glasses and placed them on the desk.

"Well?" he asked, as Douglas sat on the chair in front of him.

"It is done."

"Good … any problems?"

"No, sir. I called him and asked that he meet me behind his building. It was clean."

"Was there anything in the house that would connect Michael to us?"

"No, Lord. Even if there was, we will be done long before they could tie it to us. There is nothing to worry about. Michael was an only child, his parents are dead, and he had no friends outside of the temple that we know of. I asked him if he had spoken to the police since the first night, and he said no, so they didn't get anything additional out of him."

"Very well. What have you found out about the site?"

Douglas was beaming with a smile. "Rebecca drove to it yesterday. It is perfect for us. There is about twenty to twenty-five acres of nice flat land on the western slope of the mountain. It's high enough so no one can see us, and at least fifteen miles from any settlements or populated areas … it's perfect, Lord."

"And what about the temple?" Shimon said with excitement in his voice.

Douglas leaned forward in his chair. "The entrance is blocked by a plywood door and a chain link fence."

"Rebecca didn't enter the temple, did she?" Shimon fired back.

"No, sir, we will wait for you to enter first."

"Very good. Is anyone working at the site?"

"No, Lord, there is no evidence of anyone having been there in quite a long time. And according to the file we reviewed, work at the site was suspended until further research could be conducted. I don't see any problems."

"Just the same, Douglas, I want a team ready in case anyone shows up there. Security must be controlled tightly."

"Yes, Lord, it will be done."

"What about services while we're there?"

"Everything has been collected. We have tents, transportation, and food all set aside. It took a large portion of the temple's funds, but it is all assembled and ready to go."

"Don't worry about what it costs, Douglas. Whatever it takes—buy it."

"The only thing we haven't addressed, Lord, is what is to be done after the ceremony."

"That's why we have explosives. After the ceremony, we need to totally destroy the temple. I want the whole mountain brought down."

"Why must that be done, Lord?" Douglas asked with a surprised look on his face.

"As soon after the ceremony as possible, the queen will be buried, and I don't want anything to lead to her grave site. Blow the place to pieces, Douglas."

"Yes, Lord. Where will the queen be buried?"

Shimon smiled at Douglas. "I have a burial plot purchased and approved near where the old palace was in the ancient city of Samaria. No one will have any idea that it is the queen who will be buried there. She will rest with the other people in the cemetery forever. Once the Anointed One is revealed to us, I'll have a headstone cut with a common name on it. No one will ever be the wiser."

Douglas could hardly contain his excitement. "Perfect, Lord—it is absolutely brilliant."

"We'll have the ceremony as soon after the sacrifice as we can. I don't want to wait more than a couple of days," Shimon continued.

"We have to be ready for the Anointed One, Lord."

"We will be, Douglas. Is your team ready to intercept her once she is identified?"

"Yes Lord, myself and five others. We will be ready."

"Good. Once she is revealed to us, we will need to move swiftly."

"Lord, what do the Sacred Scrolls tell us about the ceremony?"

"Only that the Anointed One will give us guidance. She will speak the holy words for the ceremony. We are to trust our Father to deliver her to us, and guidance will be provided."

"We are getting very close to the date, Lord. I hope she will be revealed soon."

"Have faith, Douglas, he *will* deliver her to us. The prophecy will be fulfilled."

"I wish I had your strength and faith."

"Don't be troubled, Douglas, the Father will defeat the God of Abraham this time. We have been very patient and careful in our preparations, and have seen to everything. Our predecessors kept the Sacred Scrolls at their homes for safekeeping. This time they will be taken to the temple with us and destroyed after the ceremony. We here are now prepared. Our forefathers were not. We will succeed this time, Douglas. But even though they were defeated the last time, the Lord still delivered the Anointed One to them, and he will deliver her to us this time as well. The Anointed One will be in our hands very soon. Nothing can stop her from being delivered to us."

* * * * *

Beth pulled the covers back and climbed into the bed with Gary. She leaned over and kissed him on the cheek. Gary pressed the power button of the remote and turned off the television. She leaned into Gary's body. "Honey, I feel really good about what Bill and Clay discovered. This is all coming together. I have to admit that for the first time in years, I have a peace about Allyson's condition."

"Me, too, honey, I'm really looking forward to going back to Israel. I didn't think I'd ever say that, but I'm excited about this."

Beth smiled back. "I know, babe. I think it's going to all come together."

"Do you think you'll be able to go back into that cave?"

"For Allyson's sake, yes … I'd live in that stinking cave if I thought it would help her."

Gary kissed Beth. "I would, too, honey."

Gary and Beth both turned toward the bedroom door as they heard the doorknob turn. The door opened slowly and Allyson walked in.

"Are you okay, honey?" Beth asked.

"Yes, Mommy. Can I sleep with you and Daddy?"

Gary and Beth sat up in bed with smiles on their faces. "Of course, honey."

Allyson crawled up on the bed and lay down in between Gary and Beth. Beth looked at Gary with a smile on her lips and tears in her eyes. For the first time, Allyson had left the safety of her room on her own. And for the first time ever, she was lying down in bed with her parents.

Allyson pulled the covers up to her chin and smiled at Beth. "I love you, Mommy."

"I love you too, baby."

Allyson turned her head toward Gary and smiled. "I love you, Daddy."

Gary beamed with a smile. "I love you too, Ally."

"How much do you love me, Daddy?" Allyson sweetly asked.

Gary leaned over and hugged his daughter tightly. "I love you a million weeks, baby."

CHAPTER 21

THE LONG-AWAITED ARRIVAL

At Police Headquarters, Mark Steyn stopped in the doorway of the chief's office and lightly knocked on the door jam.

Yair looked up from his desk. "Yes, Mark, what do you need?"

"Sorry to interrupt you, sir, but I wanted to bring you up to date on Kazez."

Yair put his pen on the desk and took off his glasses. "You're not disturbing me. Come on in."

Mark sat in the chair across from Yair and opened his notepad. "Not a lot to tell so far. This guy was a total recluse. No friends in the area that we've found so far. His co-workers didn't even hang around with him. I checked on the prescriptions, and the doctor said he was being treated for depression. He didn't have much to say about his private life, other than that he was a loner as far as he knew. The doctor said his file showed he was an orphan, so finding family is probably out. His credit cards didn't reflect anything out of the norm, with the exception of hotel and restaurant charges every month in Haifa."

"Haifa! Maybe a girlfriend, or social contacts."

"I've asked the department in Haifa to talk with the hotel. So maybe we can get lucky."

"What about his bank accounts?" Yair asked.

"That's the funny thing—the guy lived like a pauper, and had 180,000 shekels in his savings account. This guy was a mystery."

"I think the link to this guy will be in Haifa. Keep on it, Mark. So far it's the only lead we have right now."

"I will. Oh, by the way, the statue you wanted a picture of ..."

"Yes?" Yair said curiously.

"It's a statue of the god Ba-al."

"Ba-al? What in the world is he doing with a statue of Ba-al? I didn't know anyone had an interest in him anymore beyond history."

"I'm doing a search to see if there are other followers. Kazez didn't have an interest in history that we know of, so he just may have been a follower."

"Check with the museum. He may have taken it from there. Maybe the director can shed some light on it. When is the autopsy scheduled for?"

"This afternoon at three."

"Good. Let me know what the results are as soon as you get them."

"Will do," Mark said while scribbling in his notepad.

As Steyn turned to leave, Yair looked up from his desk and called him back. "Mark, go back to the museum. I know this may be a stretch, but my gut is telling me that the fire they had may be connected. Use the proverbial fine tooth comb, and see if there is anything we missed."

"Yes, sir," Steyn said as he walked from the office.

Yair stroked his chin hard. *Ba-al,* he thought, *now there's a name I haven't heard for a long time, not since I was in Yeshiva. Oh, well. Nobody follows Ba-al anymore. Right? Probably a trinket or an ornament of some kind.*

* * * * *

Bill and Clay followed behind Beth and Gary as they walked to the Israel Railway train. Gary was carrying their baggage as Beth carried a very tired Allyson. Her head was over Beth's shoulder as she looked behind them.

The trip had proven to be a challenge for the little girl. It was the longest period she had ever been away from the house. The demon sightings during the trip had been intense. She held onto Gary and Beth tightly throughout the journey. The only relief had come during the flights, and the only solace had been in the fact that they were still flying away at the sight of her. With sleepy eyes, she looked at Clay walking behind them. Clay smiled and winked at her from behind. Allyson smiled back with half-open eyes.

The five of them entered the train car and located adjoining seats. Gary raised the armrests, allowing Allyson to sit closer to them. Allyson curled up next to Beth and laid her head on Beth's lap. The four adults relaxed in their seats and watched as the train left the station for the forty-five minute ride to Jerusalem. Jet lag had taken its toll on the group, and they all wanted to get to the hotel to relax and have dinner.

Beth stroked her daughter's hair as she looked out the window. The reality of returning to Israel after almost seven-and-a-half years was finally hitting her. The flood of emotions poured over her. Had she done the right thing by bringing Allyson here? It had to be done, she told herself; they all needed to face their demons. *"Boy, Carter, what a choice of words,"* she said to herself.

The last thing Allyson saw as she closed her eyes were more demons, thankfully flying away from her.

* * * * *

Shimon Gutstein sat in his home in the comfort of his reclining chair. The late afternoon sun was shining into his living room. A devoted workaholic, he spent very little time at home. His wife of ten years had left him two years prior for the comfort of another man's arms. The grueling schedule of running a software business and performing the duties of the high priest had proven too much for her. She enjoyed a life of anonymity with her new husband in Jerusalem, as far away from Shimon as she could get.

The home was sparsely decorated and had few personal items adorning the walls or shelves. He lived according to the precepts of his church, "*Be a riddle to everyone. Let no one know who you are.*"

His shoes were off as he smoked a cigarette and pored over the details of the upcoming ceremony. The smoke from the cigarette in his left hand curled upward in a plume as he looked at his notes and the file from the museum. He took a drag from the smoke and placed it in the ashtray. Shimon took in a deep breath and looked up at the ceiling, exhaling slowly. As he began to write, his body jerked violently in the chair. The pen and notepad fell to the floor as he grabbed at his chest, taking in a deep breath. He vaulted out of the chair, his eyes wide with fear.

His hands were pressed tightly to his chest, as his heart pounded. There were no chest pains. *"Am I having a heart attack?"* he thought. Fear gripped him throughout his entire body as he fell to his knees.

A voice began to scream at him as he moved his hands to his ears. The pain was intense as he fought to remain conscious. Every muscle in his body weakened as he fell over on his side, curling up in the fetal position. Sweat poured from him as he lay trembling on the floor. "Yes, Lord! Yes, Lord!" he screamed.

The voice in his ears slowly subsided until gone. Shimon remained silent and motionless on the floor. He waited for what seemed like an eternity before finally opening his eyes. "Am I dead?" he cried out.

Shimon rolled up and onto his knees, breathing rapidly. He slowly rose to his feet, supporting himself on the arm of the chair. He ran his hands over his face, sliding up and over his bald head. He was dripping with sweat, his shirt completely soaked. He staggered to the kitchen, retrieving a glass from the cupboard. After filling it from the tap, he drank the water intensely, spilling a third of the contents of the glass on his chest. He refilled the glass, pouring the contents down his throat, holding the glass with both hands. Shimon deposited the glass in the sink and placed his hands on the edge of the counter, leaning over the sink.

After his breathing slowed, Shimon walked with shaky legs to the desk back in the living room and removed the telephone handset from its cradle. He punched in the numbers and collapsed into his recliner.

Douglas Weiss responded on the other end of the phone. "Hello."

Shimon breathed heavily into the phone. "Douglas, she is here!"

"Is everything all right, Lord?"

"Yes. The Lord has spoken to me—she is here. The Anointed One is here in Jerusalem, Douglas." Shimon was solemn, but definitely excited.

"Praise be to him!" Douglas exclaimed.

"I will meet you at the office first thing in the morning. Call your team and get them ready."

"No problem. I will have them there." Douglas paused, and then added, "Lord, I am sorry for ever doubting you. This is truly a joyous occasion."

"Yes, it is Douglas. The Father has been faithful. I will see you in the morning," Shimon replied with awe in his voice. He placed the handset in the cradle and fell back into the chair, completely exhausted. "Thank you, Lord," he said out loud as his body went limp in the chair.

The demon, clad in a black hooded robe, stood before Shimon. His mouth opened with a wide smile showing brilliantly white pointed teeth. He folded his arms and slowly ascended, disappearing through the ceiling.

* * * * *

Bill, Clay, and the Carters emerged from the train station into the heat of the afternoon. Beth was holding Allyson's hand as they walked from the station. Allyson's eyes were open wide as she looked at the landscape. The birdmen were greater in numbers here but still seemed to be afraid of her. Allyson seemed to be, in a strange way, accepting the creatures. What Clay had told her had proven to be correct; they were, in fact, more afraid of her than she was of them. She held tightly onto Beth's hand as they approached the curb at the front of the station.

Bill was the only one of the adults that had not been to Israel. The look on his face had "first timer" written all over it. "Man, I had no idea it would be so beautiful here."

"I know. I had forgotten how beautiful it was," Beth replied remembering her first impression of Israel so many years ago.

The white Ford nine-passenger van screeched to a halt at the curb in front of them. Amir Kurtzman exited the driver's door and ran to the other side, grabbing Clay in a bear hug. The five-foot-ten-inch tall Israeli was built like a wrestler. His hair and closely cropped beard were streaked with gray. The golden color of his suntan did little to hide the scars on his face—scars that came from a dozen battles over the decades, and which he wore as a badge of honor. It was difficult to tell by looking at him that Amir had reached his sixtieth year of life. His English was very good but retained the classic hint of a Hebrew accent.

"Clay, you old warrior, it is good to see you my friend," his face beaming with a huge smile.

Clay shook his friend's hand firmly as he smiled back. "It's good to see you, too. I swear, Amir, you haven't gotten any older."

Amir slapped his stomach with both of his open hands. "I've gotten fat, old, and useless since I retired."

Clay turned to the side toward his friends. "Everyone—I would like you to meet an old colleague and a dear friend, Amir Kurtzman. This is Bill Monroe, Beth and Gary Carter, and this is Allyson," Clay said pointing to Ally.

Amir shook the three people's hands with a huge smile on his face. "I'm so very glad to meet you all." He knelt down in front of Allyson. "And I'm so very happy to meet you, Allyson. I've heard a lot of good things about you."

Allyson smiled back at Amir and extended her hand toward him as she had seen everyone else do. Amir gently cradled her hand in his and winked at her.

"I have a welcoming gift in the van for you, Allyson. Would you like to see it?"

Allyson nodded her head at Amir with a huge smile.

"Come on, let's get you all to the hotel," Amir said as he opened the side door of the van. Bill, Gary, Beth, and Allyson entered the back of the van as Clay and Amir loaded the luggage into the back.

"You were right, Clay. She's an adorable little girl," Amir spoke quietly.

"Yeah, she's captured my heart for sure," Clay answered, just as quietly, as he closed the door.

"It is really good to see you, my old friend," Amir said, slapping Clay on the back.

"And you as well." Clay then asked with a smile, "And how is Moira?"

"She's fine. She sends her love and hopes that we can all get together while you're here. Can you believe we have been married for thirty-eight years, Clay?"

"Wow, you really are old," Clay went on, chiding his friend. Clay already knew that he probably would not be seeing Amir's wife while they were in Jerusalem. Amir and Moira had lost their son to a Palestinian bomber twelve years earlier. Aaron had joined the army, following in his father's footsteps, and was killed while on patrol in Gaza. The loss had been painful to Amir, but Moira had fallen into deep depression over the loss. Had it not been for their only remaining child, Theresa, Amir feared his wife would have taken her own life. He and his daughter dedicated every free minute to caring for her.

Amir laughed loudly at his friend as they entered the front seats and buckled their seatbelts. He lifted the beautifully gift-wrapped box from the floor in front of his seat and turned to hand it to Allyson.

"This is for you, Allyson. Welcome to Jerusalem."

Allyson's face lit up as she accepted the gift. She tore at the paper with excitement and lifted the lid from the box. She gently pulled the handmade doll from the box and immediately pulled it to her chest.

"My daughter made that just for you, Allyson." The handmade porcelain doll had long wavy black hair and was dressed in a bright blue long dress. Theresa's doll-making hobby had turned into a home-based business and fit in well with the duties of looking after her mother. She had jumped at the chance to make a special little girl happy with one of her creations once her father had told her about Allyson.

"Thank you, sir." Allyson realized the gift was special.

"Allyson, you can call me Amir if you would like."

"Thank you, Uncle Amir," she said with a smile.

Amir choked back his emotions. "You're welcome, sweetheart. Now, where are you staying?" he asked Clay.

"We're at the King David Hotel."

Amir pulled the van from the curb and entered the traffic. "Okay, King David Hotel it is."

Beth leaned forward in her seat. "Thank you for the gift, Amir, you didn't have to do that."

"You're most welcome. I felt it was important to make sure she feels at home here," Amir answered, looking at Allyson in the rearview mirror.

"Where do you know Clay from?" Beth asked.

"We met in the late seventies. Clay was the U.S. Army Liaison Officer here, and I was in the IDF."

"IDF?" Beth asked.

"Israeli Defense Forces. Clay and I worked next to each other for three years."

"I can't believe it's been almost thirty years since I was here last," Clay stated.

"You guys haven't seen each other since then?" Bill asked.

"We got together in Europe a few times, but I never got back here," Clay explained.

"Always Shana Ha'ba-ah b' Yerushalayim," Amir said.

"Yes, my friend. Always 'next year in Jerusalem,'" Clay responded.

The van pulled into the front entrance of the hotel. Amir exited the vehicle and gave the van keys to the attendant and requested a luggage carrier. They all walked into the lobby and stopped at the front desk. Gary, Bill, and Clay all provided their credit cards to the desk clerk.

Built in 1931, the King David Hotel had become as much of a landmark as the Dome of the Rock on temple mount. The beautiful tan stone exterior shone brightly in the sun. The structure had weathered many years of conflict and, with the exception of a terrorist bombing on June 29th, 1946, had remained unscathed. A group of Jews dressed as Arab construction workers placed explosives in the basement of one of the hotel's wings. The bombing was in response to the occupation of the British and the Palestinians. At the time, the hotel housed the headquarters of the British Forces in Palestine and Transjordan as well as the Secretariat of the Government of Palestine. The deaths of the ninety-one people remain a black mark on the country as well as a reminder of Israel's past and present dangers.

The lobby of the hotel was finished in shades of blue and white, with deep blue couches and chairs, accented by the tan and blue tile floors. Beth took in the sights and sounds as she waited for Gary to check in.

"Your keys, Gentlemen. Welcome to Jerusalem. Enjoy your stay." The clerk smiled his welcome.

"How about some dinner?" Amir said to the group.

"Boy, that sounds good to me." Not having had much on the plane or train, Clay, as usual, was starving.

Being aware of how all of this was affecting Allyson, Beth replied, "If you don't mind, I'm going to take Allyson up to the room. Gary, would you bring us something when you come up? Some chicken for me, if they have any, and a hamburger for Ally."

"Sure thing, babe, I'll see you in a bit."

Before moving toward the elevators, Beth stepped toward Amir with her hand outstretched. "Amir, it was so nice to meet you, and thanks again for the gift."

"You're welcome, Beth. I'll see you tomorrow." He knelt down next to Allyson. "And I'll see you tomorrow too, Allyson."

Allyson smiled back at Amir, holding the doll tightly in her arms. Gary handed a tip to the bellman and waved at Beth and Allyson.

The four men entered the dining room and sat at one of the larger tables.

"Amir, thank you for making Allyson's day. She's had a bit of a rough trip," Gary said.

"You're more than welcome, Gary. Clay told me all about what has happened to her. I'm really sorry."

"If it wasn't for Bill and Clay, we'd still be in Chicago, with Allyson as a complete shut-in. The progress has been nothing short of a miracle."

Bill spoke up. "Believe me, I didn't have anything to do with it. Clay here is the miracle worker. Allyson took to him immediately."

"You mentioned that her writings are in Aramaic. Is this correct?" Amir questioned.

"Yes, but the amazing thing is that she doesn't have a clue what the words mean," Clay answered.

The waiter interrupted the conversation. "Gentlemen, can I get you something to drink?"

"Iced tea for me," said Amir.

"That sounds good, make that the same for me," Clay added.

"And me as well," Gary told the waiter.

Bill's eyes opened wide. "I'm going to have some of your famous coffee, please."

Clay smiled at Amir as he placed his journal on the table. "Bill has been waiting to have some good coffee from the Middle East. I've had to hear about it now for weeks."

"Hey, if I have to have a sin, then coffee is it." Bill smiled back.

Clay opened his journal, thumbing through the pages. "Bill thinks this anomaly with Allyson is biblically based. From what I've seen so far, I agree with him."

"Because of the incident at the construction site?" Amir asked.

"Yes, we think that the site holds the key to this, and also because of the sightings she's experiencing. Did you have a chance to find anything out about the site?" Clay asked.

"I've been in touch with some of my friends in the army and asked about it. All they said was that your site turned out to be unsuitable. They moved about five miles to the south for the missile battery."

"Can you get us in there?" Clay asked.

"Yes. I think I can do that. When do you want to go?"

"As soon as possible. Some time in the next few days. Can you make the necessary arrangements?"

"Sure thing. I'll be ready when you are. I also spoke with a rabbi friend of mine, Chaim Bronstein. He's a historian, and I thought he might be able to help us."

"Excellent. I think it would be a good idea if we speak with him first, and then go to the site. It makes sense to get as much information as we can beforehand. Are we all agreed?" Clay inquired of the group.

Bill and Gary nodded their heads in agreement.

Clay looked at Amir. "Can we see the rabbi tomorrow?"

"I'll call him tonight. I'm sure it will be okay."

"Amir, do you know where the artifacts from the cave were taken?" Bill asked. "Probably to the Israel Museum Jerusalem. There is a repository for most all of the artifacts found in Israel. I'll see what I can find out."

"It would probably be better to go there before going to the site," Gary stated.

"If we can, Gary. If not, we'll have to go there after we see the site. Let's play it by ear," Clay advised.

The waiter came to the table with the drinks and placed them in front of the men. They all raised their glasses in a toast.

"Here's to good fortune," Amir offered.

They all clanked their glasses together. Bill took a sip of the coffee and looked at the waiter. "Wow, this is really good. What blend is it?"

"Sir," the waiter answered quietly, "we proudly serve a Columbian blend coffee."

Clay, Amir, and Gary all laughed loudly as Bill set the cup on the table with a scowl on his face.

CHAPTER 22

THE PLAN

BILL WOKE UP WITH a start and looked around the hotel room. He hadn't slept soundly—probably due in part to jet lag, different bed, hotel sounds—but mostly because of his apprehension and anxiety over what might happen today. His main concern, of course, was for Allyson. He thought of how brave Gary and Beth were being. They had to be sharing the same anxieties he was having, but on a much larger scale. This was their precious daughter. This was definitely a "giant leap" for a little girl who had never left the confines of her bedroom in six years! What must she be going through?

Looking at the clock, Bill saw that he needed to get up and get ready. He was meeting Clay and Gary for breakfast in thirty minutes down in the hotel dining room. All the while he was showering, shaving, and finally getting dressed, he couldn't shake this feeling of uneasiness. He was the one who had basically started the investigation into Allyson's problems. Let's face it, he thought, he didn't have a clue what they might be getting into today. He didn't want anyone to get hurt, but he knew they had to move forward. He worried that more harm than good could be done. And he was also the one who believed the situation was religiously based. Where might that lead them? But he decided to be positive, especially around Gary and Beth.

With these thoughts is mind, Bill quickly finished dressing and took his usual time to say his morning prayers. He grabbed his wallet and briefcase and left to go to the dining room to meet Gary and Clay. After his morning prayer, he always felt much better, and today he felt more at peace with what they were going to try to do to help Allyson. Prayer had a way of doing that for him, and he had a feeling that they would all be praying a lot more before this was all over.

Bill entered the dining room and approached the table as he saw Gary and Clay pouring over Clay's notes. "Good morning, Gentlemen. It's a beautiful day, and I'm ready to attack it."

Clay looked up to greet his friend. "Wow, somebody took a happy pill this morning."

"I'm fired up. We're finally here, and I'm ready to get this resolved for Allyson," Bill responded.

"Well, let's get on with it." Clay smiled at his friend's enthusiasm. Clay, however, was more reserved and proceeding at a very cautious pace. He had spent most of the first night in Israel poring over his notes. While excited about helping the Carters, he couldn't help but feel there was something very sinister about this. He had finally dropped off to sleep at midnight after searching his notes for something that would help him quell the tingling in his spine. This whole experience surrounding Allyson had forced him to rethink his lifelong mantra—never believe anything you hear—and only half of what you see.

Gary and Beth had decided to keep Allyson in the room as much as possible, taking turns being with her. In spite of the incredible progress that had occurred with Allyson, they both agreed that she should stay in the room as much as possible to avoid seeing the apparitions, especially considering that the unknown of taking her to the cave was still in the mix. Allyson had been talking to Gary and Beth more often since their arrival, but still spoke less to them than she did to Clay. She had been surprisingly relaxed since arriving in Israel, a condition they both wished to maintain.

"How's Allyson holding up, Gary?" Bill asked.

Gary couldn't help looking a bit skeptical, but happily replied, "She's doing surprisingly well. Who would have ever guessed that we could have done this? A month ago I'd have called you crazy if you suggested we even take her out of her own bedroom. Now we have her halfway around the world. It's more than we could have ever expected. There is no way I can ever thank you for this."

Clay smiled at Gary. "Happy to do it. Have you and Beth thought anymore about taking her to the site?"

"Well, Beth and I have reservations naturally, but we think it's the next logical step. Let's see how everything goes. But I must tell you that after Bill's revelations about the words she's writing, it makes sense to take her."

"I agree. I think God is directing this whole scenario, but ultimately the decision belongs to you and Beth," Bill added.

Amir entered the dining room, walked to the table with excitement in his voice, and addressed the group. "Good morning. I hope you all slept well."

A waiter approached the table. "Good morning, sir, what can I get for you?"

"I'll have coffee and the fruit plate, please."

"Very good, sir." The waiter turned and made his way back to the kitchen.

Amir turned toward Bill. "So, how's the Columbian coffee this morning?" he asked with a smile.

"Just as good as it is in Chicago," Bill answered with a smirk.

Getting down to business, Clay asked, "Did you find out anything about the site?"

"A little," Amir began. "Just as I suspected, the artifacts from the site were taken to the Israel Museum Jerusalem. I couldn't find out about the items that were taken. I should have that sometime today. I'll let you know as soon as I get it."

"Well," Clay mused, "that means we have to make a trip to the museum to find out what they know. We also have to have the writings from the wall that Gary and Beth spoke about."

"That may prove to be more difficult than you think. They're under no obligation to talk to us," Bill stated.

Clay opened the back flap of his journal and pulled out his Smithsonian ID badge. He smiled as he held it up. "I knew I brought this for a reason. All I need is the name of the director. I can buffalo my way through the rest of the conversation when we meet him."

"You mean you're gonna pull a snow job on him?" Bill queried, looking very doubtful.

"No, *we're* gonna pull a snow job on him. You're the theology expert from Northwestern University that has come to look at the artifacts from the site."

"Perfect," Bill said with a smirk.

"Amir, can you find out the director's name?" Clay asked.

"Sure, but he's only been the director for two weeks. The last one died in a fire at the museum."

"Fire!" Clay said sitting up.

"Yes, it was all over the papers. The previous director and three archeologists were killed in some sort of electrical fire that occurred at the museum two weeks ago."

"That may work to our advantage. We'll tell him that the old director wanted us to examine these particular artifacts for religious connotations." Clay turned toward Gary. "Do you remember exactly what was in the cave, Gary?"

"Yeah, I wish I could forget it."

"Excellent. All we need is the name or designator for the site and we're in. Can you get that, Amir?"

"I'll see what I can do."

"But there can't be that many sites, can there? It should be easy to get this information," Bill queried.

Amir put down his coffee cup and smiled at Bill. "Bill, this whole country is one big archeological site. You can't dig a ditch without finding an artifact."

Clay interjected. "Well, see what you can do."

Amir nodded back at Clay.

Clay leaned forward in his seat. "Okay then, here's the plan. We meet with Amir's friend the rabbi first and then go to the museum. After we've gathered as much information as we can, we'll go to the site."

They all nodded their heads in agreement.

Gary took a deep breath. "I gotta be honest, Clay. Even though I know we have to go in there, I'm still very uneasy and more than a little scared. We still aren't sure what exactly we're dealing with here."

"I understand, Gary. The call is entirely yours. Even if you decide not to go in when we get there, it will be all right. It's up to you and Beth."

Amir was listening to this exchange and curiously asked, "Why? What happened at the site? Clay only mentioned the cave. He didn't say anything about something happening."

Looking at Amir very intently, Gary leaned forward in his chair. "Once we discovered the cave, the whole team went in. We walked into the cave through a tunnel that led to a stairway cut into the side of the cave. When we got down to the ground level, we saw a stone table with a cloth on it, along with a dagger. There were ten oil lamps around the table and two smaller ones on top of it. The real trouble started when we saw that stupid bronze box."

"Bronze box!" Amir exclaimed.

"Yeah, it was about three feet tall, three feet wide, and three feet deep. One of the guys said they wanted to open it, so Beth and three others started to push the lid aside. Beth said that she heard a woman's voice as they started to open the box. She got scared and decided to stop, but by that time the rest of the guys had pushed the lid off. That's when the lights went out for everyone."

"Lights went out?" Amir asked with an inquisitive look on his face.

Clay responded to him. "It's an American phrase—it means they all passed out."

"Oh. So what was in the box?"

Gary took a sip from his coffee before answering. "Don't know—we never found out. When we woke up, we all hightailed it out of there. We waited in the construction trailer for the military to show up, and then we left. Two days later, SH&R brought us home."

Bill rather reluctantly brought it up, but knew it was necessary as he said, "Gary, you need to tell Amir about the words on Beth's forehead."

Gary's gaze went from Bill back at Amir. "Just before I passed out," he went on, "I was hovered over Beth's unconscious body and saw some words appear on her forehead. While Clay was translating some of Allyson's writings a few days ago, I looked at the words in Aramaic and recognized them ... *The Anointed One*. I'm not sure what these words mean, but it's pretty scary."

Amir sat dumbfounded. He was completely at a loss for words. He spun the fork in his food, contemplating what he had just heard. Looking over to Bill, he asked, "*Anointed One.* Do you have any ideas as to what that could mean, Bill?"

"No, we haven't been able to place any special meaning to it so far," Bill answered, quietly.

"You mentioned a woman's voice?" Amir asked of Gary again.

"Beth has said that she'll never forget that voice. She said it was a whisper when they first started to open the box. Once the box was opened, the voice screamed at them."

Amir laced his fingers together. "Words on foreheads, unknown woman's voice—this gets more interesting by the minute." He turned back toward Gary. "What about the other people in the cave, did they see what was in the box?" Amir asked.

"No. The three men that were standing next to Beth by the box all passed out. And, as of today, she's the only one of the four that's still alive."

"You mean they died when the box was opened?"

"No, they passed away a couple of years later ... heart attacks I think."

"Were the deaths related in any way to the incident in the cave?"

"I don't think they were. Beth and I have talked about it, but there isn't anything to tie the deaths to the incident at the cave."

"Has anyone gone back there since that day?"

"No, at least no one from SH&R went back there. The company shut the operation down—or I should say more correctly, the Israeli Government shut it down. There was an Israeli army colonel with us that day. Maybe he went back. His name was Adar Stern. Maybe we can find him and talk to him."

"Adar Stern. Are you sure of this name?" Amir asked.

"Yes, he was the liaison officer assigned to us, why?"

"I knew him," Amir responded.

"What do you mean you *knew* him?" Clay asked.

"He died about five years ago," Amir answered, reflectively.

"Don't tell me ... heart attack, right?"

"Yes." Amir responded in almost a whisper.

Everyone at the table sat in silence, reflecting on what they had just heard. So many relatively young people had died—people that had been connected to the events of that day in the cave. For the first time, the specter of death had been brought into this. Clay felt an air of urgency come over him.

"Gary, has anyone else died from the construction team?" Clay asked.

"Not that I know of. None of the team lived in Chicago other than Beth and me. Most of them left the company for other jobs." Urgency gripped Gary as he thought about the conversation. "I can make a call to the human resources director at SH&R and find out." Gary stood up and walked from the table.

"Clay, this is turning bad right in front of us!" Bill announced.

"I know. This is getting spooky. Amir, maybe I got you into something you'll regret."

Amir waived his right hand in the air. "Oh, please, if I can survive the Palestinians, I can certainly survive this."

Clay smiled at his friend. "You're right—Arafat was scarier than this." Amir laughed loudly.

Bill turned to Amir and said, "Amir, we need to see your friend the rabbi as soon as possible."

"We can see him today. He said to stop by anytime during the day."

Clay agreed. "We need to talk to him before we go to the museum or the site."

Gary returned to the table and sat back down. "I called the human resources office and left a message. I forgot about the time zone difference, so maybe not an answer back until late tonight, or first thing in the morning when they get into the office."

"We can see the rabbi and then hopefully have that information before we go to the site," Clay replied.

Gary looked at Clay and admitted, "This is getting spooky, and I'm starting to feel uncomfortable with going into that cave again."

Bill pointed at Clay. "You know, Clay, if the museum has any of the data about the site, we may not have to go into the cave at all."

"Why not?"

"You wouldn't need to go in there if they have pictures of the writings, would you?"

"I suppose not. A photo of them, or even if they were written down somewhere, would suffice. But I would however like to see the artifacts, especially that dagger."

"Dagger? Clay, I just remembered the incident you had with Allyson at the Field Museum … remember?"

Clay's eyes opened wide as it struck him. "Yeah, I do. Why didn't I put that together until now?"

"Tell me what happened," asked Amir.

"Bill and I took Allyson to the museum in Chicago," Clay began. "She had what could be considered revelations regarding some of Gustaf Doré's paintings of biblical characters. She *thought* … no, that isn't entirely accurate—she *said* that the characters didn't look like how Doré painted them. She even got upset over his painting of the death of Jezebel, so we moved her away from the painting to calm her down. We were standing next to a display case when she freaked over the sight of a ceremonial dagger."

"What did it look like?"

"Double edged, about ten inches long, just like pretty much any other dagger."

"We thought that if in fact she could see through the paintings, maybe she could see what the dagger was used for," Bill managed to say as he realized how unnerved he was becoming.

"Gary, do you recall what the dagger that was sitting on the altar looked like?" Amir asked.

"It was about ten inches long with a hilt, and jewels on the end of the handle."

"That doesn't sound much different from any other dagger used back then, or even today for that matter. They were used for either military or sacrificial purposes. I can see how Allyson could have been scared if she saw their proposed use. If this site is a place of worship, there would have been sacrifices performed there. But it would have been a long time ago."

"About 2,500 years ago, right?" Bill asked.

"Yes, as I understand it." Amir sat back in his chair. He was very hesitant to broach the subject, but felt he had to point something out to the others. "You know, it sounds more like Beth is the one that's tied to the site rather than Allyson. From what you have said, your trip here was to resolve the issue for Allyson, but if Beth is the Anointed One, then maybe the focus should be on her. What we don't know is why the anomalies are occurring to Allyson."

Clay folded his napkin and placed it on his plate. "Well, we can sit here and speculate all day long. I think we need to get to the rabbi's house. He's the one that can shed the most light on this."

"Agreed. At this point he's going to have a lot more answers than questions. I'll get the van and meet all of you at the front entrance," Amir said while standing up.

"I'll let Beth know where we're going and meet you there," Gary announced.

Clay gestured toward Bill and said, "We'll see you there, too."

* * * * *

Shimon sat at the conference table in his office with the team members he had chosen for the museum break-in, going over the itinerary for the upcoming events. His encounter from the previous day had given him a renewed sense of urgency, not to mention a higher opinion of himself. He presided over the meeting with a firmer hand than usual.

"Is everyone on your team ready, Douglas?"

"Yes, Lord, I believe we have everything in place."

Shimon pointed his finger toward Douglas. "I didn't ask what you believed, Douglas. I want to be absolutely sure we're ready. This is too important. There can be no mistakes!"

Douglas Weiss arched his back and responded with confidence. "Yes, Lord, we are ready."

"Who is watching the site?"

"Joseph is there now and will be relieved by Tamir tomorrow. Everyone who goes there knows they are to contact me immediately if anyone shows up at the site," Douglas reiterated.

Shimon turned toward Rebecca. "Are all the supplies in place for the worshipers?"

"Yes, Lord. We have transportation, food, portable showers, and water closets. Everything including the trash goes into four trucks when we're done. No one will ever know we've been there," she assured him.

"Also make sure we have extra garments. No one gets inside the temple without one."

"Yes, Lord," Rebecca responded.

"What about security, Paz?"

Paz Friedman opened his notebook. "We plan to stage all of the needed equipment in the small town of 'Aqraba, about fifteen miles from the site. As Douglas said, there will always be someone at the site from now until the ceremony is over. We plan to have someone at the base of the mountain on the road after the site is occupied. They will both have satellite phones to call in with. That will give us ample warning in case someone gets through."

Douglas leaned forward. "Lord, I think it would be better to wait to stage in 'Aqraba until we have the Anointed One in case the locals get curious."

"I agree, Douglas. We'll wait until we have her and then get everyone to the site." He panned his head back and forth looking at the team members. "If any outsiders get to the site, I want them eliminated. Is that understood?"

Each of the followers nodded their heads in response to Shimon.

"Lastly, we need to have everyone on alert for the Anointed One. We don't know when the Lord will deliver her to us. If she is not revealed to us until the last minute, we may not need all of the supplies, but I still want enough for three days just in case. Douglas, it may be the last minute when she is delivered to us, so you need to be ready."

"Yes, I understand. With the satellite phones, we can reach each other in seconds. Where do you want her taken when we retrieve her?" Douglas asked.

"Rebecca will have the honor of being in charge of her and her mother. Rebecca and her assistants will prepare her." Shimon looked intently at Rebecca. "It is imperative that you understand that the mother is not to be left behind. We will not make the mistake that our ancestors did."

"Yes, Lord, but what of the father?" Rebecca asked.

"He is to be killed as soon as you have secured the Anointed One and her mother. He is insignificant as far as the prophecy is concerned, but the Sacred Scrolls tell us that he is not to live."

"Did the Lord tell you where she came from?" Paz asked.

"No, only that she has arrived in Jerusalem."

Paz beamed with joy. "Lord, it is exciting to know that the prophecy will finally be fulfilled. The Anointed One is finally here."

Shimon smiled as he stood from the table. "Yes, she is among us."

* * * * *

Allyson stood next to the window of the Carters' fourth-floor room. Her eyes were fixed on the skyline above the city. Beth walked to the window and stood next to her daughter. She gently stroked Allyson's hair with her right hand. For the first time in her young life, Allyson had wanted to look out of a window.

Beth had not taken her eyes off of Allyson since she had opened the drapes. Allyson had not moved from in front of the window since it had been opened—almost an hour now.

Beth placed the breakfast meals that Gary had brought up to the room on the table. "Ally, breakfast is here. Are you hungry?"

"No, thank you, Mommy."

Beth knelt down next to her. "Sweetie, you need to eat something. Will you do that for me?"

Allyson's eyes remained locked on the skyline. "No, thank you, Mommy."

"What's the matter, Ally? What are you looking at?"

Allyson pointed to the sky above the city.

"What is it, honey?"

"Birdmen, Mommy."

"How many birdmen do you see?"

"I don't know."

"Can't you count them?"

Allyson shook her head no.

"Why not?"

"There are too many to count, Mommy."

Beth hugged her daughter tightly as tears began to pour down her face.

CHAPTER 23

A RABBI'S KNOWLEDGE

GARY WALKED OUT OF the main entrance of the hotel to meet the group as the valet driver pulled up with the van. The four men entered the vehicle and buckled their seatbelts. Amir pulled out of the driveway and pointed the van north.

"Is it very far to the rabbi's house?" Clay asked.

"No, it's really close, only about fifteen minutes."

"Where do you know him from?"

"Oh, I've known Chaim for about fifty years now. His family and mine were friends when we were growing up."

"Can he keep what we're going to tell him to himself?"

"Of course, he would take anything you tell him to the grave. I trust him completely." Bill's eyes hadn't blinked since they left the hotel. How beautiful this city was, he thought. This trip had always been on his list of things to do, although the reason for the trip could have been different; he was awestruck nonetheless. As he looked to his right, he could see the most recognizable landmark in Jerusalem: the shiny golden roof of the Dome of the Rock, a site that was visible from anywhere in the city. The Dome of the Rock is the crowning glory of the Haram es-Sharif ("Noble Sanctuary"), or Temple Mount. A common mistake is that the Dome is a mosque. It is not, however;

rather it is a Muslim shrine. Like the Ka'ba in Mecca, it is built over a sacred stone. This stone is believed to be the place from which the Prophet Muhammad ascended into heaven during his Night Journey to Jerusalem.

The Dome of the Rock is the third most important pilgrimage site in Islam, after Mecca and Medina. It is the oldest Islamic monument that stands today and certainly one of the most beautiful. The sacred rock over which the Dome of the Rock is built was considered holy before the arrival of Islam. Jews believed, and still believe, the rock to be the very place where Abraham prepared to sacrifice Isaac (an event which Muslims place in Mecca). In addition, the Dome of the Rock (or the adjacent Dome of the Chain) is believed by many to stand directly over the site of the Holy of Holies of both Solomon's Temple and Herod's Temple. Even though Islam ran completely afoul of his faith, Bill was nonetheless captivated by the history and beauty of their holiest of shrines. This was, after all, the cradle of civilization; it had all begun here.

The city was densely populated and diverse in its inhabitants. Every country it seemed was represented here. No wonder it had been the site of so much conflict over the centuries; everyone had wanted to occupy it. Bill brought his attention back to the task at hand as the van pulled up in front of the rabbi's house.

The house was a light brown stucco home with a tile roof. The small and humble two-bedroom house was not that different from the rest of the houses in the area. With land at a premium, the lots of all the houses were small and devoid of foliage. Parked under the carport was a Volkswagen bus that had faded blue paint and a surplus of mileage on it. The men exited the vehicle and walked to the front door of the house. Before they could knock on the door, it opened and Rabbi Chaim Bronstein exited to greet them. Chaim had a huge smile on his face as he embraced Amir. His attention turned toward Clay as his arms were held out palms up.

"You must be Clay Harker. I have waited so very long to finally meet the hero that Amir has told me so much about. I am so very glad to meet you," Chaim said as he hugged Clay tightly. Clay was surprised at the rabbi's comments. Always desirous of being an enigma, Clay felt uncomfortable at the recognition of his accomplishments.

"Chaim, this is Bill Monroe and Gary Carter," Amir went on with the introductions.

Chaim reached out to shake each man's hands with both of his. "Welcome to my home. Please come in."

Rabbi Chaim Bronstein was anything but threatening with his five-foot-six, 175-pound frame. The sixty-year-old rabbi had a close cut, neatly trimmed beard and wore simple clothing with his signature tennis shoes. For the first twenty years of his career, he had been an Orthodox Rabbi, but chose the less rigid Conservative sect to pursue his love of teaching. He had recently taken a less demanding schedule of teaching for three days a week at the Hebrew University. He and his wife Sarah were enjoying the fruits of their labor after forty years of work.

The men entered the home to the greetings of Sarah. The five-foot-three grandmother smiled at the men as she greeted them. The older woman was dressed in a flower print dress, with her completely gray hair bound close to her head. Bill offered his hand in greeting, but withdrew it sharply when he noticed that she kept her hands clasped together at the waist. For Sarah, the old orthodox traditions of not touching another man's hands other than her husband's had been hard to shed.

"Please have a seat," Chaim indicated several chairs around the comfortable living room.

"Can I get you something to drink?" Sarah asked.

"Water would be fine, please," Clay said.

The others responded the same.

"Your English is very good, Chaim," Bill commented.

"Thank you. It is the product of many years of teaching."

"Really. What do you teach?" Bill asked.

"Comparative religious studies at the Hebrew University."

"Bill here is a theology professor at Northwestern University," Clay added.

Chaim smiled widely looking at Bill. "My friend, there are several questions I should like to ask you."

Bill smiled back. "And me as well. If we have time, I would like to spend a day with you." He was always on the search for any information of a theological nature he could obtain, and to speak with Chaim would certainly be a coup.

"I would like to do that, too … but for now, I know you have something of grave importance to discuss. How may I help you?"

"I don't know how much Amir has told you, so I'll give you a rundown from the start," Bill took the lead.

"Very good," Chaim said as he sat back in his chair.

Chaim listened as Bill gave him a complete history of Allyson. He sat with disbelief on his face as Bill told the story leading up to Clay's involvement. The details unfolded like a novel. It was the most unbelievable story he had ever heard. If it wasn't being told by two doctors, he could have easily discounted it as fiction. After almost thirty minutes, Bill finished, almost totally exhausted. He could only wonder what this religious man must think of all he had revealed.

Clay saw the astonished look on Chaim's face and went on, "Rabbi, I know this is a lot to take in. Believe me, I wouldn't have believed it myself if I hadn't witnessed it firsthand."

Chaim leaned forward in his chair, with his elbows on his knees and hands clasped together, and directed his question to Bill. "And you're confident about her ability to see demons?" Chaim asked.

"Yes, completely. I don't know why, but I'm convinced it is, for whatever reason, divinely ordained."

"If it is occurring, and from what you tell me the evidence supports it, I would have to agree with your supposition. This site you discovered, Gary, what was inside the cave?"

"There were ten floor lamps, two smaller ones on the altar, a three-by-three-by-three-foot bronze box, and a dagger with a leather sheath that were also sitting on the altar. And there was a ten-pointed star on the eastern wall."

Chaim turned around in his seat and retrieved a notepad and pen from the table next to him. "Could you draw a picture of what they looked like?"

Gary drew a depiction of the dagger, the bronze box, and the floor lamps. His engineering skills came into play as he sketched out the items. He turned the pad sideways as he continued to draw the items, showing it to Chaim. Gary explained the dimensions and descriptions of the items. "Chaim, the leather sheath was about fifteen or sixteen inches long, with a pocket at one end where the dagger fit. It could be rolled up and tied off when closed. The handle of the dagger had both clear and blue stones imbedded in it, and was about ten inches long. The box looked to be made of bronze. It was probably solid metal, because of the difficulty they had in trying to remove the lid ... it appeared to be very heavy. It was about three-by-three-by-three feet in size. The lamps looked to be made of bronze as well, and were about six feet tall. They were probably fueled by oil, because there were stains around the base of them." Gary sat back as he completed his explanations of the items.

Chaim rubbed his chin whiskers as he responded. "Are you quite sure the floor lamps looked like this?"

"Yes, why?"

"Because this is what the lamps in the temple looked like."

"In King Solomon's Temple?" Bill asked.

"Yes, the very ones," Chaim responded.

"Could they be the ones from that particular temple?" Bill asked.

"Not likely. I believe all of the original ones from the temple have been recovered. These are probably copies."

"But if it's a temple, wouldn't it have the same kind of lamps as the ones in King Solomon's temple? I mean wouldn't all temples have the same kind of lamps?" Bill asked.

"The place you are talking about may have been a place of worship to make sacrifices to God, but not necessarily a temple," Chaim went on to explain.

"And why not?" Gary asked.

"Because it would have been recorded somewhere. The only true temple was the one that was on Temple Mount. Besides, the bronze box and the ten-pointed star on the wall make no sense. I would however like to see the writings on the wall after you go there."

"But from what Bill has told us, the sacrifices would have been made to God, would they not?" Gary still wondered.

"Maybe to *a* god, but probably not *the* God," Chaim responded.

"To a god like Ba-al, for instance?" Bill asked.

"It could be. It could also be to El or Dagon, depending upon how old the site is."

"But Colonel Stern said the writings on the wall were Aramaic," Gary said.

"If that's true, then in all probability, it is to Ba-al because of its location in Northern Israel. That's where his influence was the greatest."

"So then this all goes back to what we originally discussed. Jezebel dragging her husband the king … what was his name?" Gary asked, pointing to Bill.

"Ahab," Bill replied.

"Yes, Ahab. And the queen, dragging him toward the worship of Ba-al, and dooming the Northern Kingdom. I guess I'm trying to get a handle on why all of this happened." Gary shook his head in frustration.

Chaim leaned forward in his chair. "The people of ancient Northern Israel had a history of defiance. I hesitate to use the word rebellion, although it may be more fitting. Almost without exception the northern kings defied God and married outside their faith. It led to many of them worshipping false gods."

"I'm surprised the people tolerated it from Ahab," Clay stated.

"They had no choice, Clay. All of the kings had absolute authority, and Ahab was no exception. Although I think initially his intention was not to worship Ba-al, because he named his two sons, Joram and Ahaziah, in honor of the one true God."

"In Hebrew they mean 'the Lord is exalted' and 'the Lord grasps,' don't they?" Bill offered. "Correct," answered Chaim. "So there is the feeling that it was not his intention initially to follow his wife's beliefs. But as always happened, after years of her influence and deception, I think he probably just gave in to her wishes."

"But Bill said he repented later, right?" Clay said.

"Yes, but Jezebel never did. Ultimately, because of all the crimes against God and Israel, God destroyed her."

"That's where you said that the only thing left of her was her head, hands, and feet, and that God said she would never be buried, right?" Clay asked Bill.

Bill nodded his head yes.

"Rabbi, the practice of taking hands, feet, and heads was for body count, wasn't it?" Clay asked.

"Yes, it was a sign that the enemy had been conquered. Usually the victorious army would bring back a hand or a head as proof of body count and, even in some cases, ears. In fact, when the Philistines captured the Ark of the Covenant, they placed it in the Temple of Dagon as a showing of authority and dominance over the God of the Hebrews. The next morning, when they went into the temple, the statue of Dagon had fallen to the ground with the head and hands broken off, signifying victory over the false god. I'm not sure that that's what God did with Jezebel, but it would make sense."

Bill smiled at Chaim. "That's right. I had forgotten that. Besides, you can't bury a person that isn't whole."

"Correct, again, and God said she would never be buried. After that, he had all of Ba-al's prophets killed, and then he had King Jehu destroy the temple of Ba-al," Chaim continued.

"Man, no messing around with God, huh?" Clay smiled.

"Clay, the people of Israel have suffered immeasurably throughout history because they did not listen to God. Ba-al was the chief reason at that particular time. While there have been others, Ba-al was probably the most influential."

"Okay, I keep coming back to my original question. Why would Allyson be tied to Jezebel?" Gary asked.

"I don't know Gary. Without seeing the artifacts, or being able to read the writings on the wall, we can't make a determination." Chaim rubbed his whiskers. "Are you sure we can rule out possession?"

"I'd stake my life on it, Chaim," Bill replied. "There is just no evidence to support it."

"Even in light of the fact that she claimed to know what certain biblical figures looked like?"

"Chaim, you would have to have been there to understand," Clay stated. "No, I agree with Bill—possession is not an option."

"I only say that because I can't imagine how or why a child would be given the ability to see demons. There would be, after all, a reason for that. I know that in the Christian Bible, there is a greater propensity for that anomaly. Perhaps in her schooling?" Chaim said as he turned to Gary.

"Not possible, Chaim. Beth and I never spoke of it to her. In fact, she refers to them as 'birdmen,' hardly the same verbiage."

"That makes sense. Again then, assuming this is all accurate, we need more data," Chaim replied.

"Then we need to make those two trips we talked about—one trip to the museum and then one to the site," Amir confirmed.

"Are you going to the museum first, Clay?" Chaim asked.

"Yes, that's what we decided."

"Could you get me a copy of the writings? If you can do that, I'll do the necessary research while you are all at the site."

"Sure, if they have them. I'll get it to you tomorrow," Clay responded.

"The words Allyson has written, what were they again?"

Clay thumbed through his journal. "*Light*, *behold*, *Anointed One*, *joined*, *Jezebel*, *true*, *defiance*, *sayeth*, *buried*, *God*, *bearer*, and *Abraham*."

"Not a lot to go on but, of course, I'll try." Chaim wrote more notes on his notepad.

Clay went on to say to Chaim, "Bill put the words together in a possible sentence. We don't know if it's accurate, but it made more sense than anything we could come up with so far."

Chaim leaned forward with his notepad as Clay read from the journal. "'Behold, *the true God of Abraham, His light shines in defiance of Jezebel, who shall not be buried*.' Bill thinks that the missing words of *bearer*, *joined*, and *Anointed One* could refer to God's plan for Beth … joined with, or bearing something. It may have been a code of some kind to avoid detection, which would explain why the site was so remote," Clay went on.

Chaim rubbed his whiskers while looking at the words he had written. "It makes sense. There are a few variations to it that are possible, but basically the same meaning. Yes, I would say that makes sense. Bill, after hearing your story, I agree with you that God's hand is probably on this. To what purpose I don't know yet, but it is clear he is involved in this little girl's ordeal. Please get me all the information you can from the museum and the site."

"We will, Chaim. Thanks for your help with this. We probably need to get going to get back to the hotel. We'll let you know as soon as we find anything."

"Is there anything else I can do for you in the meantime?" Chaim asked.

"There is one thing," Bill said with a smile. "Can you tell me where to get a good traditional cup of coffee?"

Clay rolled his eyes. "I might have known."

"There is a sidewalk café just down from the hotel called the Blue Parrot. It's owned by a Turkish man that serves traditional Turkish coffee. Amir can show you where it is." Smiling, Chaim responded and chuckled.

"Thank you." Bill gratefully smiled back.

Clay stood and shook Chaim's hand. "Thank you, Rabbi, we'll be in touch."

They all stood and walked to the front door.

"It was a real pleasure to finally meet you, Clay," Chaim said as he opened the front door.

"And you as well, Chaim. We'll see you soon."

Amir waived to his friend as the men walked to the van.

Bill turned toward Clay as he reached for the door handle. "Hey, Clay, when we first arrived, what did Chaim mean by 'hero'?"

"I helped the Israeli Defense Forces when I was here years ago. It was really nothing."

Bill got in the rear seat and buckled his seatbelt. "Oh, I get it ... all very hush-hush, huh?"

"Apparently not too hush-hush," Clay said, looking at Amir with a frown.

Amir responded with a big smile as he started the van. The satellite photographs provided by the U.S. Air Force that Clay had given to the IDF had proven to be invaluable for the 1981 Iraqi reactor raid. While Clay was only the courier, he had garnered great favor in the eyes of many of the IDF, chief among them, Amir.

* * * * *

Yair entered Mark Steyn's office holding a cup of coffee in his left hand, a sandwich wrapped in cellophane in his right hand, and a folder held to his chest by his right arm. Mark looked up and acknowledged him as he sat down.

"What did the autopsy turn up, Mark?" Yair asked.

Mark reached into the basket on his desk and retrieved the report folder, opening it in front of him. "An entry wound six centimeters wide and twenty centimeters deep at the base of the skull. We were correct. It was professionally done. The blade goes up and into the brain, then the victim goes limp immediately and loses consciousness. He died within seconds."

"Well, that answers that, Mark. Anything with the Haifa connection?"

"The hotel manager said he came in late on Friday nights once a month, almost always on the first weekend of the month. He stayed for two nights and would leave on Sunday afternoons. He was gone the whole day on Saturdays and half a day on Sundays. He never went in or left with anyone."

"And no other charges on the credit card in Haifa?"

"No, sir. This guy had a lot of money in his bank account and very few charges on his card … he lived like a pauper. It doesn't make any sense."

"Well, then, we can probably rule out a girlfriend in Haifa."

"But I still think Haifa is the key, sir. He didn't do anything in Jerusalem but eat, work, and sleep, and no one responded to the article in the paper. It's like he didn't exist."

"And what about the articles that were taken from the museum? Anything on them?"

"Nothing, yet. The museum is still in the dark about their origins."

"You didn't tell them about the statue in his bedroom, did you?"

"No, sir. Do you think we should tell them?"

"Not yet, Mark, let's wait for a while. It may be tied in if this guy was truly a worshiper of Ba-al, although, I can't imagine him being a worshiper. The only mention of Ba-al around here anymore is in the history books. If we find out where the site is, it may be beneficial to make a trip there."

"The museum doesn't even know where it is. All the records were taken, but if they find it, I'll let you know."

"Okay, and let's talk to his co-workers again. There may be something they remembered since the last time we talked to them."

"Will do, sir."

"And let's get a list of prior Special Forces people in the area of Jerusalem and Haifa. Our killer might have had army training."

Mark's eyes opened wide in response to the size of the task he had just been given. "That will take some time, Chief."

Yair stood and walked to the door. "Keep your search to the age of twenty to forty years old. At this point, I'm willing to try anything," Yair said as he walked from the room.

CHAPTER 24

THE DOCTORS' MEETING

THE TAXICAB PULLED UP to the front of the Israel Museum Jerusalem, and Bill and Clay got out of the rear of the vehicle. Clay paid the driver and walked with Bill to the curb.

"Are you sure we can pull this off, Clay?" Bill asked with concern in his voice.

"You bet. Just put on your game face, Monroe—we'll be fine."

"Just remember, be ready to pull my foot out when I stuff it into my mouth."

Clay smiled at his friend as they walked to the main entrance. He opened his journal and read the name of the former museum director. Bill opened the door, allowing Clay to enter first. The two men walked to the information desk, smiling at the receptionist.

"May I help you?" Rachel Baruch asked, returning the smile.

Clay placed a business card on the counter. "We have an appointment with the director."

"One moment, please," Rachel replied, while picking up the telephone receiver and punching in the numbers. "Ms. Rhoades, I have Dr. Harker from the Smithsonian here to see the director. Yes, I'll tell him. Doctor Harker, the director's assistant will be out to see you momentarily."

Clay smiled back. "Thank you."

Clay and Bill stepped back from the podium and walked to the center of the foyer.

"This better work, Clay."

"Relax, Bill, everything will be fine. Just pretend you're talking to your students."

"But my students can't throw me out of class if I screw up. I'm nervous about this."

"Then just pretend your audience is naked. That should relax you," Clay said smiling.

"Oh that's cute," Bill answered sarcastically.

Anna Rhoades appeared from the hallway to their right and walked toward them. She extended her hand toward them with a smile.

"Hello, I'm Anna Rhoades. May I help you?"

Clay shook Anna's hand. "Hello, I'm Dr. Clayton Harker and this is Dr. William Monroe. Mr. Curwin had contacted the Smithsonian and requested assistance with one of your archeological sites. I informed him that we were coming to Israel on other business, but while here, we would stop by the museum to meet with him and discuss the site. He agreed it would be all right if we came by sometime this week to look at the artifacts."

Anna's eyes opened wide with surprise. "Oh, Dr. Harker, I'm so very sorry. Dr. Curwin died tragically in an accident here at the museum two weeks ago."

Clay looked back with feigned surprise on his face. "I'm so very sorry. What happened?"

"We had an electrical fire here at the museum, and Dr. Curwin and three archeologists perished."

"I'm sorry for your loss. I'll make sure the management at the Smithsonian is notified," Clay replied.

"Thank you, that's very kind."

"Ms. Rhoades, have you appointed a new director?"

"Yes, we have. The new director is Dr. Brandon Harrison."

"I realize this is very short notice, but would it be possible to see him? Dr. Monroe and I will only be here for a few more days, and today is one of the only days we can see him," Clay continued.

"I don't know, Dr. Harker. As you might imagine, he has been very busy. I'll have to ask him if he can see you."

"If he can, it would be greatly appreciated," Clay said, smiling at her.

"I'll see if he can speak with you. Could you and Dr. Monroe please sign our visitor log, and then I'll take you to the conference room."

"Of course. I really appreciate this, Ms. Rhoades." Clay proceeded to sign the log. Not prone to being overly nice, he found himself being very cordial, not wanting to give Anna any reason to deny their request to see the director.

Bill also signed the log and took the visitors badge and clipped it on his collar. They walked with Anna to the hallway door. Anna passed her identification card in front of the reader, and the bolt clicked open. They entered the hallway and walked to the conference room doorway.

"Gentlemen, please have a seat inside, and I'll see if Dr. Harrison can meet with you."

"Thank you very much," Clay said as he and Bill walked into the conference room.

"I never knew someone could spread it so thick," Bill whispered in Clay's ear.

"Hey, it's a gift," Clay murmured with a smirk on his face.

Clay slowly walked around the conference room looking at the photographs displayed on the walls. The photos showed the changes that had occurred to the museum over the years. Clay held his hands clasped together behind his back while he leaned closer looking at the oversized diagram of the main building. He turned as he heard the voice from behind him.

"Dr. Harker, I'm Dr. Brandon Harrison."

Clay turned to see a six-foot-two-inch-tall man in a light tan cotton suit. Clay estimated his age to be somewhere in his early fifties, with closely cut salt-and-pepper hair. Bill joined Clay as they both walked to the entrance to greet him.

"Dr. Harrison," Clay said, extending his hand. "It's very nice to meet you. This is Dr. Bill Monroe from Northwestern University."

Dr. Harrison then shook Bill's hand and smiled at the two men. "How may I be of service to you?"

"I spoke with Dr. Curwin quite some time ago, and he had asked if the Smithsonian could assist him with some artifacts. I mentioned that coincidentally Dr. Monroe and I were going to be in Jerusalem, and he asked if I could stop by and look at them. Your assistant told us that he had unfortunately died in a fire here at the museum. I'm very sorry."

"Yes, the fire took him and three archeologists. It was a very sad day for the people here at the museum. Dr. Harker, I don't know how much help I can be, but I have about an hour that I can devote to you."

"I appreciate you making time. Would it be possible to see the artifacts he mentioned?"

"Did he say which artifacts he wanted you to look at?"

"He said something about some lamps, a dagger, and a bronze box." Clay struggled to remember the site number that Amir had given him. "As I recall, they were from site number 482," he responded.

"We can go to the vault where we store unfounded artifacts to see if they are there. Unfortunately, in the confusion of the fire, the museum has misplaced most of the items. What did Dr. Curwin tell you about them?"

"He only mentioned what the items were."

"I can take you to the vault and show you what we have."

"That would be very much appreciated," Clay said as they walked from the room.

Bill and Clay followed Harrison as they walked down the hall toward the freight elevator.

"Do I detect an American accent?" Bill asked Dr. Harrison.

"Yes, you do, Doctor. I'm from New York."

"Really, what brought you here?" Clay asked.

"I've been trying to get a post here for years. I was at the American Museum of Natural History in New York and was finally able to obtain a position here."

"I've been to your museum in Central Park several times, Dr. Harrison—it's an excellent facility," Bill said.

"Thank you. It was small, but we were very proud of it. Are you an archeologist, Dr. Monroe?"

"No, a theologian," Bill responded.

"Don't let him kid you. Bill here is an expert on religious artifacts," Clay interjected.

"Really … and you, Dr. Harker?"

"I'm a linguist for the Smithsonian."

"Wow, I'm a little out of my league here." Harrison went forward and passed his ID badge in front of the elevator reader.

Clay smiled as he entered the elevator behind Harrison and Bill. It had been a long time since he had been interrogated, but certainly knew Harrison had been sizing up both him and Bill from the time he had met them. Clay couldn't blame him; he would have done the same thing had the roles been reversed.

The three men exited the elevator and walked down the hall toward the vault entrance. Harrison stopped at the security podium.

"Good morning, Caleb, is there anyone in the vault?" Harrison asked.

"Yes, sir, Ezra Hawkins and Paul Cox are in there," Caleb answered.

"Caleb, this is Dr. Harker and Dr. Monroe. They will be going in with me."

"Very good, sir." Caleb entered the two men's names in the visitor log.

Caleb and Harrison passed their ID cards in front of the door readers, and the bolt clicked open. Caleb returned to the Security Desk, and the other three men entered the vault and stopped to take in the sight.

"Man, if the Smithsonian was set up like this, we wouldn't have to use so much off-site storage. This is incredible, Dr. Harrison." Clay looked on in wonder at the immense size of the facility. He was immediately struck by the familiar musty odor that could only come from storing ancient artifacts. He was impressed with the large painted grids on the floor that held items within the borders and the wide passageways allowing a forklift easy passage. This was truly a state-of-the-art operation.

"Thank you, we're very proud of this facility."

Harrison slowly worked his way through the vault, pointing out the various methods of storage, including the large chain-link fence storage against the walls. The three men stopped in front of the Clean Room.

"This is where artifacts and exhibits are examined. It is climatically controlled and independent of the rest of the building," he stated in explanation.

Harrison handed Clay and Bill gloves and caps before they entered. He knocked on the glass door of the Clean Room and waved to the two men inside. Ezra Hawkins walked to the door and opened it.

"Ezra, can we come in?"

"Yes, sir, we're just finishing up," Ezra answered.

"Dr. Harker, Dr. Monroe, this is Ezra Hawkins and Paul Cox, two of our archeologists," Harrison said as he made the introductions.

Ezra and Paul exchanged smiles with the men, not wanting to shake hands for sanitary reasons. They were examining various pieces of pottery that were laid out on the table. Two plates, a cup, and an urn were placed carefully in the center of the table, with the broken pieces of each arranged to form the whole piece.

"This is where the bulk of the artifacts are brought for initial analysis before being catalogued and recorded," Ezra started to explain as they moved over to the table.

Clay bent over and looked at the pottery. "So everything that is discovered in Israel is ultimately brought here?"

"Yes, sir, for the most part. The museum is the central repository for the bulk of the items. These pieces came from a construction site right here in Jerusalem. The items were found while they were digging a foundation for a new building," Ezra responded.

Clay lowered his eyes to the floor as he noticed the four burn marks in the concrete. He turned and looked at the equipment in the large room. He noticed that the four computers in the room looked new. He observed that the chairs and desks were new as well. *This must be where the fire took place*, he thought.

"Wow, you guys must have a good budget. You sure have a lot of new equipment here," Clay said innocently.

Harrison walked to where the four burn marks were and stood over them, attempting to cover them from sight. "Yes, this facility has top priority. Ezra, where are the items from site 482?" Harrison said in an attempt to move them out of the Clean Room.

"They are in the cage just outside the Clean Room, sir." Ezra pointed to one of the cages outside the room.

"Well, let's go take a look, shall we?" Harrison said as he quickly led Bill and Clay out of the room.

As they walked out of the room, Clay looked up to see burn marks in the ceiling around the new light fixtures. He quickly picked up on Harrison's efforts to cover the burn marks on the floor. The three men walked to the chain-link cage against the north wall. Dr. Harrison opened the double chain-link doors and entered the storage area. The twenty-by-thirty-foot cage was identical to all the other cages against the outside walls and had a single halogen light in the ceiling thirty feet above them. They stepped to the rear of the cage where the bronze box was sitting on a wooden pallet.

"This is one of the items that were recovered," Harrison pointed out.

Clay knelt down and looked at the lid of the box. "The Anointed One shall return," he read aloud.

Bill knelt down next to Clay. "What?" He asked excitedly.

"You are very well informed, Dr. Harker," Harrison said with surprise.

"Clay, it says *The Anointed One*," Bill remarked loudly, eagerly looking at Clay.

"Does this have significance to you, Dr. Harker?" Harrison said.

Clay placed his hand on Bill's shoulder, signifying for him to be silent. "Bill and I did some research on Northern Israel some years back, and these words were discovered in the writings," he told Harrison, trying to down play Bill's excitement.

"It referred to the prophet Elijah," Bill said as he tried to recover from his outburst.

"I thought for a minute that you might be able to help us with its origin," Harrison said.

"No, it is nonrelated. What was in the box, Doctor?" Bill asked.

"Nothing, that I know of. The records for the site were in the computers that were destroyed in the fire. We continue to look for backup files, but haven't been successful so far," Harrison replied. His eyes looked away from Clay as he responded. He decided not to reveal the information about the site folder that had been stolen when the break-in occurred.

"You mentioned that you had other items from the site," Clay casually commented.

Harrison walked to the side of the cage and opened one of the four-foot-wide three-inch-deep drawers. "Just this cloth."

Bill and Clay looked at the large clear plastic bag that held the remnants of a large white linen cloth. Clay presumed that this was the cloth that covered the altar that Gary and Beth had spoken about. He decided not to share the information with Dr. Harrison.

"Is this all that you have?" Bill asked.

"Yes, this is all that remains. Did Dr. Curwin mention any other items?" Harrison asked.

"Just the lamps and the dagger I mentioned earlier. He also mentioned there were some writings at the site, would you have them recorded somewhere?" Clay asked.

"No, I'm afraid that would have been in the computer files. I'm sorry."

"If you find the items, I would like to take a look at them if possible," Clay inquired.

"Of course, how can I get in touch with you?"

"We are staying at the King David Hotel." Clay jotted down his room number on his Smithsonian business card and handed it to Dr. Harrison.

Dr. Harrison looked at his watch. "Well, I have a meeting to get to, so, unfortunately, we have to cut this short."

"We understand," Clay acknowledged.

The men walked out of the cage and toward the entrance of the vault. Harrison thanked Caleb as they walked past the podium and toward the elevator.

"Dr. Harrison, if you're ever in Washington, please let me know and I'll get you a back-room tour of the Smithsonian," Clay offered.

"I will. Thank you," Harrison said as they all entered the elevator. "I'm sorry I have to go to this meeting, but you are welcome to stay and go on one of our tours if you'd like."

"No, that's okay. We want to get to the Dome of the Rock today. But thank you for the offer," Clay said as they walked from the elevator.

The three men stopped at the main entrance podium. Bill and Clay handed Rachel their visitor badges and turned toward Dr. Harrison.

"Thanks again, Dr. Harrison, you've been very helpful," Clay said as the three men shook hands.

"I'm sorry I couldn't be more help, but if we locate the items, I'll give you a call," Harrison stated.

Bill and Clay walked out of the building into the noonday sun as Harrison watched them from the foyer. He removed a business card from his wallet and punched in the numbers on his cell phone.

"Hello, Lt. Steyn, this is Brandon Harrison from the museum. I just had two visitors asking questions about the items that were stolen. No, they haven't left yet. They're in the front of the museum waiting for a taxi. Yes, I'll wait right here for you." Harrison closed his phone as he watched Bill and Clay get into a taxi.

Bill closed the rear door of the taxi. "I'm sorry, Clay. I guess I just got excited when I saw the box. And then when you translated the words, I just lost it."

Clay spoke softly as he placed his index finger in front of his lips, not wanting the driver to hear what they were saying. "That's okay, bud. We salvaged it. Not to worry."

Bill looked at the driver and responded as Clay had requested. "What do you think about Dr. Harrison?"

"He's lying."

"Why do you say that?"

"Mostly his body language, but he didn't follow up when I mentioned the other items in the cave. Besides, how can you not find ten floor lamps?" Clay asked quietly.

"Yeah, that's right."

"Did you notice anything unusual about the Clean Room?" Clay asked.

"No, what about it?"

"The four burn marks on the floor and the scorch marks on the ceiling around the lights. It's probably where the former director and his men died."

"Do you really think so?" Bill said curiously.

"Well, it would sure make sense. Everything in the room is new. There were Halon nozzles in the ceiling, so there wouldn't have been any water damage from sprinklers. I'd say they had one really hot fire that took everything out before the Halon could discharge."

"Clay, what in the world is going on with that site? Everyone associated with it winds up dead."

"I don't know, Bill. I hope Amir found out something. Since the museum didn't have the writings, we're going to have to go to the site tomorrow."

"Do you think Amir will be able to take us there by then?" Bill asked.

"I hope so. If not, we'll have to go by ourselves. The key to all of this is in that cave … I'm convinced of it," Clay said as the taxi completed its short ride from the museum, pulling up in front of the café that Chaim had told Bill about—the Blue Parrot.

CHAPTER 25

THAT UNEASY FEELING

Clay and Bill exited the taxi after Clay paid the driver. They walked toward the entrance of the Blue Parrot café, when they heard a whistle from the sidewalk tables to their right. Clay turned to see Amir and Gary waving at them from one of the tables. They weaved in and out of the tables until they reached their friends. Clay flopped his journal down on the table as the two men sat down.

The name of the café, the stucco exterior, and the large blue parrot painted on the front was a close copy from the movie Casablanca, right down to the Turkish owner. The sidewalk portion of the café was like any other in the district, tables crowded together and patrons engaged in conversation. The large tan-colored umbrellas offered refuge from the noonday sun but little protection from the searing heat. Everyone at the small round table talked low to avoid curious ears. Always the intelligence officer, Clay repeatedly pressed his hand down, telling the others to keep their voices low.

"Well, what did you find out?" Amir asked.

Clay opened his journal and began jotting down the findings from the museum. "Not much; they're clueless about the site. They don't have any more details than we do. We did meet the new director though. Amir, do you know anything about him?"

"Yes, he came from a museum in New York. The IMJ hired him about a month before Dr. Curwin was killed. He was going to take the assistant director position, but when Curwin died, they just moved him into the director's position instead."

"What did he say, Clay?" Gary asked.

"Very little. His name is Dr. Brandon Harrison. He said that the museum had misplaced most of the artifacts because of the confusion after the fire. He was lying, of course, but I don't know why. And maybe I'm just being hypercritical, but the guy strikes me as an uptight dweeb, to borrow a phrase my daughter used to use. He seems a little too caught up with himself for my taste … too much like a high school English teacher," Clay mused.

"He is lying because they had a break-in two weeks ago," Amir interrupted.

"A break-in … do I need to ask what was taken?" Clay said with a smirk and some exasperation.

Amir pulled the notepad from his pocket and opened it. "My source tells me that ten floor lamps, two table lamps, and human remains were taken."

"Human remains!" Clay said, sitting up erect in his chair.

"Yes, from what I can gather, a complete skeleton was taken," Amir answered.

Clay looked at Gary. "Did you guys see any remains when you were in the cave?"

"No, we didn't, but it was so dark there we could have missed it."

"Could they have been in the box?" Amir asked.

"Not likely. The box is too small to have been a coffin or sarcophagus," Bill added

"Well, since Gary and Beth said there wasn't any blood on the cloth, it was probably someone that got caught in the cave when the landslide occurred. I knew Harrison was lying," Clay went on.

"That would make sense," Bill replied.

"Did they have the words from the wall written down?" Gary asked.

"No, we're going to have to go to the site, Gary. Harrison said that the fire destroyed the files," Bill explained.

The men stopped talking as the waiter approached the table. "Can I get you gentlemen something?"

"Iced tea for me please," Clay ordered.

Bill smiled. "I would like a Turkish coffee, please." Amir and Gary still had their unfinished tea.

"Very well, sir," the waiter replied and walked away.

"Well, the statement that the director made is probably another lie. Nobody keeps information in one place only. There would have had to have been a backup hard copy somewhere," Clay stated emphatically.

"Or stolen with the artifacts," Amir interjected.

"That would make sense," Clay agreed.

"Was the box there?" Gary asked.

"Yes, the cloth and the box were the only things they had. There was an inscription on the lid ... *The Anointed One shall return.*"

"*The Anointed One*—those are the same words that appeared on Beth's forehead," Gary said in a very solemn tone.

"What could that mean, Bill?" Amir asked.

"I don't know, and without the writings, we could only guess. If Beth is the Anointed One, the box would somehow be tied to her."

Clay agreed with Bill, too. "Bill's right. Without the writings, we're shooting in the dark here. But the robbery tells us that someone else is most certainly interested in the site. We have to assume they have the file, or that they know where the site is located. We have to go there as soon as possible, Amir. Can we possibly go in the morning?"

"Yes, not a problem. What time do you want to leave?"

Clay looked at the others at the table. "Does six in the morning work for everyone?"

Bill and Gary nodded in the affirmative.

"Okay then, six it is. Why don't you pick us up then?" Clay said.

"I'll be out in front of the hotel at six. What do we need?"

"A lot of lights for a start, and maybe some ropes. We'll also need a digital camera." Clay was thinking as fast as he could. He knew their time was going to be limited, and he wanted to prepare as much as possible ahead of time.

"I've got my Nikon," Bill replied.

"Good, can anyone think of anything else?"

"I'll bring some water and food," Amir said.

"I'll let Beth know we have to go. With four deaths now surrounding the site, it'll be a tough sell though," Gary replied grudgingly.

"Six deaths, Gary," Amir interjected gravely.

"Who else?" Clay asked.

"Two museum guards were killed—one at the museum during the robbery and the other at his house a few days later."

"How were they killed?" Clay asked.

"The one at the museum was shot. The one at his house was found in a dumpster with a stab wound," Amir responded.

Clay pulled at his right ear. "Well, it was probably an inside job, then. I'd bet my pension that the one in the dumpster was in on it. Do we know anything about him?"

"No, just that he was a long-term employee."

Clay smiled at Amir. "It appears that you are just as well connected as you were when I was here years ago. How are you getting such good information about the museum?" Clay asked.

Amir smiled back at Clay winking. "The director's assistant is my cousin."

"Anna, I might have known."

"What could be so important about that place that someone is willing to kill for it?" Gary asked.

"I don't know, Gary, but something *is* important enough to kill for it. We need to get there and get out as soon as we can, that's for sure," Clay warned. The gnawing feeling in Clay's stomach was getting worse. He fought the urge to throw cold water on the mood because Gary and Beth had placed so much faith in the trip, but he couldn't shake the feeling of dread that had fallen over him.

Gary snapped his fingers. "Oh, I almost forgot. The human resources manager called me back. She didn't have information on all the people that were at the site, but said that five of them that had taken other jobs had passed away."

"From heart attacks?" Bill asked.

"Don't know, but every one of them died within two years of being at the site."

Clay rubbed the back of his neck. "Man, we need to get to that site. Without the writings available, we definitely have to make the trip. Is everyone up for that?" Clay asked.

They all nodded their heads in agreement.

Amir looked across the street and saw two men looking intently at the café. "Clay, did anyone follow you here?"

"Not that I know of, why?" Clay wanted to know.

"Don't turn around, Clay, but there are two men watching us from across the street. They look like police," Amir noted.

"If they're cops, then the museum director dropped a dime on us," Clay responded.

"What should we do?" Bill asked.

Amir took over and started issuing orders. "We need to get out of here. The van is parked around the corner. Let's get you to the hotel. We'll go to the site first thing in the morning and then follow up with Chaim in the afternoon. By then we should have what you need, and we can talk to the police then if needed."

"I agree. We can talk to the cops later after we visit the site. That way, at least we'll hopefully have what we need," Clay said.

The four men stood as the waiter was bringing the drinks. Bill hesitated as he approached. Clay placed money on the table and nodded at the waiter.

"Come on, Bill, let's go. You can have some coffee later," Clay said as they followed Amir toward the entrance.

Bill looked back at the coffee as he walked away. "Ooh rats!" he said with a frown. The two men across the street watched as the four men left the café and walked around the corner to the van. They entered their car and waited to follow the van.

* * * * *

Lt. Steyn stopped at the doorway of Yair's office. "Chief, we may have a break in the museum case."

Yair sat back from his desk. "What do you have, Mark?"

"The director just called and said that there were two Americans that visited him earlier who were asking questions about the artifacts from the break-in."

"Americans! What in the world is going on? Now this has turned international? Where are they now?"

"They left the museum in a taxi. I was able to get two officers on them shortly after they left. They stopped at a café and met up with two other men. I'm leaving now to get the details from the director."

"Make sure you don't lose them, Mark. This is the only lead we've had."

"We don't have to worry about that. The director said they were staying at the King David. He got a business card from one of them."

"Excellent. Keep me posted."

"I will. I'll get to the hotel as soon as I talk with the director," Mark said as he walked from the office."

Yair grunted as he put his glasses back on. *Americans? What possible reason could the Americans have for being involved in this? Things were getting crazier by the minute*, he thought.

* * * * *

Shimon sat at his desk as he addressed the eight remaining members of his team. "It appears that we won't have time to occupy the site before the day of the ceremony. Douglas, we'll be staging at 'Aqraba. Can you make sure everything we need will be there?"

"Yes, Lord, I'll leave as soon as we're done here and take care of it," Douglas replied. "Everything will be ready and loaded.

"And do you have the explosives?"

"The explosives and detonators are in the truck."

"Make sure we keep the curious away, Douglas. I don't want to be discovered before the ceremony," Shimon warned.

"We have military trucks, and every person that will be in view will be in army uniforms," Douglas stated.

"Good. It appears we are ready then. I'll be leaving for Jerusalem tonight. If anyone needs me for anything, call me on the cell phone after this evening. Is there anything else?" Shimon knew the importance of precise preparation.

"Lord, we don't have the sacred words spoken by the Anointed One yet. You said the prophecy revealed that she will speak the holy words for us. What will we do if we don't have them?" Rebecca asked.

"I don't know, Rebecca. We have to have faith that they will be revealed," Shimon responded.

"But our ancestors had the words *before* the ceremony, didn't they?" Paz asked.

"The first Anointed One was from Samaria, and we were able to be close to her from her birth. The Lord's shepherds were with her from birth, kept constant watch over her, and revealed her to the followers. All we know of this girl is that she came from outside the country. We have to assume that the shepherds have been with this Anointed One as well."

"But do we need the words for the ceremony?" Douglas inquired.

"Yes. I must speak the words over her before the ceremony. But you all need to be more faithful. The Lord revealed to me that she was in Jerusalem, and we must have faith that he will give us the sacred words before the ceremony so we can combine them with the words at the temple. What we need to do is be ready for his revelations," Shimon responded.

"And we will be, Lord," Douglas said looking at the others.

The other team members looked at their leader and nodded their heads at him. The team members were true believers of Ba-al, and never questioned their high priest. Each one of them knew the importance of this mission, and would die to protect it. They were getting ready for something that all believers and worshipers had been waiting on for centuries. They threw themselves on their knees saying over and over again, "Praise be! Praise be!" Shimon's pride welled up as he looked on at his devoted followers.

* * * * *

Allyson sat silently in the bedroom of the hotel suite and watched television. She had required very little attention since their arrival. Gary and Beth had purchased movies and art pads for her, knowing she would have little time outside of the room until their trip to the site. She had slept in Gary and Beth's bed since arriving at the hotel, and had been significantly more affectionate. Beth was happy to see that the doll Amir had given her never left her side, even during bedtime. Nothing would have pleased Beth more than to be able to take her daughter out into the city to see the sights, but for now that was not an option. Beth got up from the chair in the living room and set her book on the table. She walked into the bedroom to check on Allyson. She stopped after entering the room and smiled as she saw Allyson sitting quietly on the bed watching the movie.

"Honey, do you want anything?"

Allyson turned toward her mother. "No, thank you, Mommy."

"Aren't you hungry, baby?"

"No, Mommy."

Beth looked over at the top of the dresser to see the writing pads. "Allyson, you haven't used your writing pads since you got here. Don't you want to write?"

"No, I'm done writing now."

"You mean that you're done for the day?"

"No, Mommy, I'm not allowed to write anymore."

Beth's brow furrowed as she sat down on the bed next to her daughter. "Honey, who told you that you can't write anymore? Did Daddy tell you that?"

"No, Mommy."

"Then who told you, honey?"

"A lady told me."

"Which lady told you that, Allyson?" Beth asked with concern in her voice.

Allyson shrugged her shoulders at Beth. "I don't know, Mommy."

"Allyson, it is very important that you tell me where this lady is."

"I don't know—she just told me."

"I don't understand, Allyson. If you didn't see her, when did she speak to you?"

"She spoke to me in my head, Mommy."

Beth clutched her daughter in her arms as tears started to form in her eyes. She began to cry softly, not truly understanding why, as she rocked back and forth not wanting to frighten Allyson. She couldn't help whispering a prayer, "God, if you can hear me, please help us. Please help us, God. I beg you, please help us!" Allyson remained unemotional and detached as Beth left her sitting on the bed watching television. Her blank stare only added to Beth's grief and fear.

CHAPTER 26

THE RETURN

THE WHITE FORD VAN moved through the desert of Northern Israel with its cargo of six. Amir was driving while he made small talk with Clay sitting in the passenger's seat. Gary, Beth, and Allyson sat behind them and took in the sights. Bill rode alone in the third-row seat with a grin on his face as he finally got to enjoy being in Israel.

The temperature was already eighty degrees at six thirty in the morning. The van was negotiating the rural route of Highway 458, just sixty miles north of Jerusalem. Gary sat behind Amir with a map, ready to give directions to Amir. It had been seven years since he had traveled the route, and he was looking intensely for familiar landmarks.

"Where is it that we turn, Gary?" Amir asked.

"I think we have a while yet, Amir. It's a right turn about three or four miles after the town of 'Aqraba, if I remember correctly."

"Is it marked?"

"No, at least it wasn't at the time. In fact, you need to slow down when we get close, because it doesn't even look like a road, more like a trail."

Allyson sat between Gary and Beth in the backseat. Since leaving the hotel, Allyson's focus had been on the doll that Amir had given her.

She sat silently in her seat, only responding to the smiles from Beth and Clay when they would look at her.

Beth looked out the right side of the van with a smile. "You know, as much as I hated it here before, I have to admit it really is beautiful."

"I know. I've been awestruck since we arrived," Bill commented, "and there's so much history here." Bill couldn't turn away from the view he was taking in. The beautiful arid countryside dotted with the occasional green fields of farms was surrounded by hills and the bluest sky that Bill had ever seen.

"It wasn't that many years ago that bombs were dropping in this area," Amir said.

"Going back as far as recorded history, this area has always had some kind of conflict. Seems like someone always wanted to conquer this land," Clay interjected. "We used to say that Moses traveled for forty years in the desert and settled in the only place that didn't have any oil," he joked.

"That is true. Nobody wanted it until the Jews settled here," Amir laughed.

Amir slowed down as they entered the small town of 'Aqraba. "Here's the town, Gary—you said the turnoff is about three or four miles further?"

"Yeah, it should be just up the road a bit now," Gary responded.

Amir accelerated after driving through the town's main road. All eyes were focused on the right side of the van as they looked for the trail. Beth was beginning to feel the anxiety of returning to the site slowly building in her chest. She looked down to see her clenched fist resting on her knee. She quickly opened her hand and wiped the sweat from her palm. She looked to the left to see Gary observing her actions. She smiled at him through pursed lips.

"Slow down, Amir, we're really close," Gary instructed.

"There it is, honey," Beth cried out excitedly, seeing the road.

"Yes, there it is, Amir," Gary said leaning forward and pointing to the right.

The road was barely visible and would have easily been missed had Gary not pointed it out. Amir turned onto the narrow overgrown road and pointed the van east toward the mountain. His focus was intense as he concentrated on the path in front of him that disappeared and reappeared randomly.

* * * * *

The unmarked white BMW slowed as it drove past the access road. Lt. Steyn pulled the cell phone from his belt holster and punched in the numbers for Yair Klein, his superior officer. “Hello, Chief, it's Mark. They turned east off Highway 458 about twenty kilometers north of 'Aqraba. I don't want to follow them any further. They might see me. All right, I'll wait by the road at 'Aqraba for them to come back down. Yes, sir, I'll let you know when they return. Good-bye.”

Mark turned the BMW around for the drive back to 'Aqraba.

* * * * *

“Amir, in just a few miles, you'll see the road cut into the mountain—it'll be on your left,” Gary explained.

“Man, how did you guys ever find this place?” Clay asked.

“It was mapped out for us by the Israeli Army. We went out looking for the easiest access and stumbled onto an old road. Most of the original road had deteriorated, or was too steep for the equipment, but it provided us with a starting point. We just had the Caterpillars cut it wider to get the equipment up the hill.”

Amir glanced left and right, trying to see the access road as he approached the mountain. The road came into view on the left as they passed a large rock formation to the left of the vehicle.

“Wow, whoever did this sure didn't want to be discovered, did they?” Clay commented as the van turned left behind the formation. The automatic transmission shifted down into second gear as they started the climb up the mountain.

Amir was intensely focused on the road as he negotiated the steep grade of the mountain. A flood of emotions poured over Gary as the van drove up the mountain road. None of the anxiety of that day seven years ago had dissipated after all these years. His stomach tightened as they drove up the road toward the site that had altered their lives.

Clay watched as the original road disappeared above them and then reappeared below. The Cats had cut a more gradual and even grade than the original road.

The van began a wide and gradual right-hand turn as it approached the summit. The occupants of the vehicle remained silent as the twenty-five acre summit came into view. Beth took in a deep breath. As she looked to the right, she saw the entrance to the cave. She exhaled slowly as she stared at the entrance. Beth tried desperately to avoid voicing her feelings. Every fiber of her being wanted to scream out to turn back and return to Jerusalem, but her desire to resolve the question of Allyson's condition stopped her. She fought to control the trembling that had come over her. Could this trip answer the question of what the Anointed One meant? She hoped so. For Allyson's sake, she gathered her courage.

Gary heard Beth inhale, and as he turned around to look at her, he asked, "Are you okay, honey?" His own survival instincts were kicking in. The thought of returning to the place that had started all of this evil was burning a hole in his stomach. Just like Beth, the hope of resolving Allyson's condition was the only thing that kept him moving forward. *What evil would be wrought upon this family this time?* he thought.

"Yeah, it's just spooky to see it again," she replied nervously.

Amir stopped the van twenty yards from the cave entrance and turned the engine off. The cave entrance had been blocked off by a gated chain-link fence that extended in a semicircle around the front and attaching to the flat face of the mountain, three feet from the opening on each side. The entrance was blocked by a locked plywood door that displayed warning signs in Hebrew, Arabic, and English, stating emphatically "No Trespassing."

Amir opened the driver's door and stepped from the vehicle, arching his back to stretch away the discomfort. "Well, we're here."

Clay opened the side sliding door and stepped out. "I can see why the Israeli Defense Forces chose this place. It's perfect for a missile battery."

"This was the premier location," Gary explained as he exited the vehicle. "We were all excited about this site, because it was going to be the Central Command Center for the missile defense battery, and the last site to work on for Beth and me. That, of course, went away with the discovery."

Amir walked to the rear of the van and opened the cargo doors. He began unloading the generator, lights, and other equipment as Bill, Beth, and Allyson stepped from the van. The men carried some of the equipment to the entrance as Beth held Allyson's hand tightly.

Amir came back from the van a second time with a pair of bolt cutters. He raised the cutters and opened the jaws. He grunted slightly as the jaws snipped the shank of the lock on the chain-link fence. Clay came up beside him, removed the lock, and opened the gate. Everyone walked into the enclosure and waited for Amir to cut the second lock. As the second shank was cut, Clay slid the plywood door open. The bottom of the door produced an eerie grinding noise on the ground as it opened.

It had been seven long years since the cave had been explored. The Israel Museum Jerusalem had been the last occupier of the site and sealed it off after leaving for the last time, taking everything they deemed important from the temple. The museum management had made the decision to leave the site unguarded—or so they thought. The three demons inside the cave slowly opened their eyes as they turned their heads toward the entrance. Their teeth bared as they flew to the landing at the top of the stairs. The three creatures were on all fours as they readied themselves for the intruders.

Gary entered the passageway first followed by Beth and Allyson. Beth and Gary held a floodlight as they walked through the tunnel. Beth could feel her heart rate increase as they worked their way through the corridor. The musty smell she had experienced seven years earlier filled her nostrils. Beth held Allyson's hand tightly as they approached the landing. Bill, Clay, and Amir followed close behind, carrying the equipment. As the group approached the landing, the demons prepared themselves to attack the intruders. They slowly stood as Gary and Beth approached, raising their arms, ready to pounce. Then suddenly they recoiled as they saw Allyson between Gary and Beth. They covered their eyes in fear as they flew to the top of the cave, taking refuge behind the rock formations. Because of the darkness of the tunnel, Allyson had not seen the intruders.

Gary stopped at the landing where the stairs began to descend. "Okay guys, put the generator and lights here." Amir set the generator down and took the cords of the halogen lights from Clay and Bill. Gary moved the handheld floodlight back and forth on the east wall until he located the ten-pointed star.

"Point the lights in the direction of that star," he directed them in a very quiet voice, as if he didn't want to disturb anything or anyone.

Clay and Bill set the lights on the ground and pointed them at the star. Amir primed the carburetor and depressed the start button. The generator came to life supplying power to the lights. Bill and Clay turned the halogen spotlights on and pointed them toward the concave star. The beams from the lights searched out the target and slowly came to rest in the center of the star. The light bounced off the jewels and illuminated the entire cave as if it were daylight.

"Unbelievable!" Bill exclaimed with excitement and awe.

The group stood motionless as they looked at the floor of the cave seventy-five feet below them. A wide-eyed Bill was eager to get things started, and spoke to Gary with anticipation, "Let's get down there."

"That's how it started last time," Gary whispered as he moved his left hand in front of Bill's chest.

Bill took the hint and stepped back on the landing. Gary moved to the right and began slowly descending the steps with Clay and Bill following behind. Beth picked Allyson up in her arms and followed with Amir behind her. Allyson looked around the cave with half-opened eyes that were attempting to adjust to the brightness as Beth carried her down the stairs. She held on tightly, not quite understanding why she didn't want to be in this place.

The droning of the generator's engine sounded above them as they inched their way to the bottom of the cave. Gary stepped to the side as he reached the bottom. He depressed the off switch on his light, realizing he no longer needed it.

Clay looked at the floor as he walked off the last step. "It's all uniform," he noted. "They must have hauled a boat load of dirt and stone in here to make it so level."

"Someone with engineering skills had to set this up," Bill observed as he looked above him at the concave star.

"Based on what we could figure out, the sunlight coming through the tunnel hits the star sometime between 6:00 and 8:00 p.m.," Gary went on to explain.

Clay walked toward the stone altar just off the western wall. "Was this where the cloth was?"

Gary walked to his side pointing to the top. "Yes, the cloth was draped over the altar, hanging down to the ground. The two lamps were at each end, and the dagger and sheath were here in the center."

The remainder of the group gathered around the altar. "And where were the floor lamps?" Bill asked.

Gary turned his right hand in a wide circle. "They were arranged on the floor around the altar."

Clay knelt down and looked at one of the stains on the floor. "About here, Gary?"

"Yes, that's exactly where they were."

From 150 feet above the cave floor, the three demons peered around the rock formations. They looked at the humans as they stood next to the altar.

Beth set Allyson back down on the floor of the cave. Allyson watched as her father described the events of January 2000. Still holding tightly onto Beth's hand, she slowly raised her head and looked toward the ceiling above her. The demons quickly jerked their heads back behind the rocks, trembling with fear. Allyson turned back toward the group.

Gary continued explaining the events of 2000 to Bill and Amir, as Clay walked around the altar identifying all ten of the spots where the lamps had been. He looked for evidence of blood on the floor, but could find no additional stains, other than those of the oil lamps. "I can't see any blood, so our supposition about sacrifices is out."

Bill looked back at Clay. "Then I think it's safe to assume the remains the museum found are from someone who got trapped in here."

Clay lifted the Nikon from around Bill's neck and opened the lens cover. He began taking pictures of the cave. The light generated from the concave star was so bright, the camera's flash didn't activate. He walked to the western wall and began taking close-up shots of the writings. He hung the camera strap around his neck and removed the journal from the belt behind his back. He wrote the words in his journal, first in Aramaic, and then below, he slowly translated them into English.

Clay walked to the altar and set the journal on top of the stone surface. The words didn't make sense; they were incomplete thoughts at best. Why put random ... "*The Code,*" he said to himself, remembering the conversation he had with Bill about Allyson's words being part of a code. Clay tore a blank sheet of paper from the back of the journal and wrote Allyson's words on the paper.

"Bill, come over here."

"What do you need?" Bill asked as he looked over to Clay. "Monroe, get your butt over here," Clay said somewhat sternly.

Bill walked quickly to the altar followed by the rest of the group. He stopped next to Clay as the others gathered around the two men. They were all on the eastern side of the altar facing the western wall.

Clay pointed toward the writing on the wall and then back to his journal. "That's what it says."

Bill read the words out loud. "*The sacrifice of the to the one shall be made in the seventh year, and on the date of the Queen's death. On the seventh hour the shall be with queen on her seventh year and in of the God of thus the Lord, the of the.* Clay, it makes no sense."

"That's because it's the code we've been looking for."

"Could it be?" Bill responded excitedly.

"What are you guys talking about?" Amir asked.

Clay responded while he tore two more blank pages out of his journal. "The words Allyson has been writing are part of a code. The words on the wall complete it."

The revelation struck Gary and Beth as they moved in closer to Clay and Bill. "You mean the words that Allyson has been writing fit into what's on that wall?" Beth asked.

"We'll see ... if we're able to put them in the right order," Bill answered her.

Bill and Clay inserted and removed words into the phrase trying to form complete sentences. In then out—the words slowly began to fit. Bill looked at the last word, *Jezebel.* He slowly wrote the word and began reading the phrase to himself.

"Beth, when did you say Allyson's birthday is?" Bill asked.

"Tomorrow, why?"

"Dear God, Clay," Bill said as he took in a deep breath.

"What is it?" Clay asked.

Bill stood back from the altar and ran his right hand through his hair and down the back of his neck. "We've delivered her to them on a silver platter." His statement was met with disbelieving eyes from the others.

Clay read the words out loud to the group. *"Behold, the sacrifice of the Anointed One to the one true god shall be made in the seventh year and on the date of the Queen's death. On the seventh hour, the Anointed One shall be joined with Queen Jezebel on her seventh year, and buried in defiance of the God of Abraham. Thus sayeth the lord, the bearer of the light."*

Bill turned toward Beth and looked deeply into her eyes. "You're not the *Anointed One*, Beth—Allyson is."

"I don't understand, Bill. What's going on?" Beth said with a confused look on her face and fear in her eyes.

Clay placed his hand on Beth's shoulder. "It means that the box you guys opened held the remains of Jezebel, and her followers now want to join them with her and bury them," Clay said tilting his head down toward Allyson.

Beth's face turned white with fear as she tried to catch her breath. She immediately picked Allyson up and held her close. "Oh my God, we have to get out of here!" she shouted, frantically looking around the cave for any dangers to keep them from escaping.

The rest of the group looked into each other's eyes as the urgency hit them. Clay quickly gathered up his journal and the papers. Amir ran across the cave and up the stairs, followed by Beth and Gary. He waited at the landing until Gary and Beth exited through the tunnel, and then turned the generator off. Bill, Clay, and Amir stopped at the landing and gathered up the remaining equipment and exited the cave.

The men then ran to the rear of the van, throwing the lights, extension cords, and generator into the rear. Amir ran to the driver's side and opened the door, sliding into the driver's seat with one fluid motion as he made sure everyone was inside. He placed the gear lever into drive and spun the tires as he sped off toward the road.

Levi Ain stepped from behind the large rock as the van sped off the plateau and onto the road. He pulled the cell phone from his pocket and called Douglas Weiss in 'Aqraba.

Tears were streaming down Beth's face as she held Allyson tightly in her lap. Allyson sat silent as tears began falling down her cheeks as well. Bill pounded his fist into the seat as his teeth ground together. "I can't believe I was so arrogant. I was so caught up in the excitement of it all. I've now jeopardized Allyson."

"It all makes so much sense. Why couldn't we see it before?" Clay said, clearly feeling the urgency of the situation.

Amir negotiated the curves just short of going out of control. He knew he had to get as far from this place as possible, and as quickly as he could. No one said anything further as the van sped down the mountain. He reached the bottom of the mountain and out to the main road in record time. The van's tires squealed on the pavement as Amir turned back onto Highway 458.

Amir turned toward Clay. "Clay, in order for this to work, there would have to be someone to perform the task."

"Or some *thing*," Bill said from the rear.

"What do you mean?" Amir asked.

In explanation, Bill answered him very seriously, "Allyson has the ability to see demons."

"No!" Clay exclaimed. "There would have to be some people involved … followers maybe?"

"Ba-al worshipers, you think?" Amir replied.

"Stop it, all of you!" Beth shouted. "You're scaring her!"

Clay immediately turned to see tears falling down Allyson's cheeks. He smiled reassuringly, trying not to let her see his anxiety and fear, and then turned back toward the front. *"What sick demented bastard would harm this innocent little girl?"* he thought.

* * * * *

Lt. Mark Steyn was parked by the side of the road just outside of the town of 'Aqraba, and watched from his car as the van approached. As it drove by him, a tan Citroen pulled up next to the driver's side of his car with four occupants inside. The man sitting on the front passenger side leaned out of the window.

"Excuse me, sir, could you help me?" Douglas Weiss asked.

Mark turned to his left toward the car next to him. His blood ran cold as he saw the HK P-7 pointed at him. Before he could react, the silenced weapon discharged. The two rounds found their target as Steyn's body fell to the right.

Douglas removed the cell phone from his pocket and punched in the numbers for Shimon. "Lord, we've gotten rid of the police tail. No, sir, no one else was following them that we have observed. Very well, Lord, we're following them back to Jerusalem. Yes, sir, they'll be eliminated. We'll see you at the site." Douglas closed the cell phone as the Citroen pulled away from the BMW and turned south onto the highway. Douglas separated the suppressor from the pistol and placed them in the bag at his feet as David Greenblatt drove back toward Jerusalem, following the white van.

CHAPTER 27

A CHANGE IN THE PLAN

GARY OPENED THE SIDE door of the van as it slid to a stop in front of the King David Hotel. Still holding onto Allyson, Beth slid across the seat and exited the van.

Gary hesitated before getting out. "Clay, don't take too long at the rabbi's house."

"We won't. I need to follow up with him though. I promise we won't be long."

"I'll get us the first flight out that I can," Gary said as he closed the door.

"We'll be right back!" Clay assured him as the van pulled away.

Gary and Beth entered the lobby, stopping in front of the main desk. "Honey, take Ally up to the room. I'll make the airline reservations and get us something to eat," Gary told her.

"Just don't be long, Gary. I don't want to be here any longer than we have to," an anxious Beth ordered.

"Don't worry, honey. I won't," Gary said kissing his wife. He fought intensely to ward off the panic that was consuming him. How could all of this have gone so wrong? Unbelievable hope and promise had been the order of the day as early as this morning. Now, that hope and promise had shifted to survival. Gary walked quickly and with purpose toward the concierge's desk.

Amir drove as fast as he possibly could without bringing attention to the vehicle. The three men remained silent, their eyes locked onto the road ahead. Clay was unconsciously gritting his teeth as Bill stared blankly out the side of the van. Amir concentrated on the task of driving. So much so that he had failed to notice the tan Citroen following him thirty yards behind. The four men in the Citroen watched intently as the van drove through traffic. David Greenblatt was in his element, driving under pressure. He expertly positioned his vehicle as close to the van as he could without detection, awaiting his superior's orders.

Sitting in the front passenger seat, Douglas Weiss reached down between his legs and unzipped the duffle bag, revealing the four Uzi submachine guns. David depressed the accelerator and closed the distance on the van as the two men in the rear took their weapons from Douglas.

Just as David passed by an alley entrance, a cargo truck pulled out blocking the Citroen's path. He hit the brakes and slid to a stop on the truck's left side as he shouted, "Damn!"

"Don't lose them!" Douglas yelled at David.

The driver of the truck turned his head toward the Citroen and waved apologetically. He stopped the truck and placed it in reverse, backing up into the alley. David revved the engine as he released the clutch and sped around the front of the truck. He looked ahead of him but was unable to see the van.

"You've lost him!" Douglas said, hitting the dash with his fist.

* * * * *

Rabbi Bronstein opened the front door to see Amir, Bill, and Clay waiting to enter. From the looks on their faces, he knew something was terribly wrong. "Come in, come in, can I get you something to drink?" Chaim offered.

"No, Rabbi, we're okay and we haven't much time. We really need your help," Clay said as they all entered the house.

"Please, sit down." Chaim could see the urgency on the men's faces.

Clay opened his journal and presented the translations to Chaim. "We found the cave and translated the writings on the wall. Bill and I inserted Allyson's writings into the phrase, and this is what we came up with."

Chaim read the words intently. When he was done, he pulled his glasses off and set the journal in his lap. "And you're certain this is the correct translation?"

"Without a doubt," Clay answered.

"And the little girl's birthday?"

"Tomorrow," Bill interjected.

Chaim took in a deep breath and let it out slowly. "Then we have to assume that the box you described held the remains of Jezebel."

"That's our supposition as well," Clay responded.

"But, Chaim, there would have to be followers of some sort, correct?" Bill asked.

Chaim rubbed his whiskers. "There has always been a following of people who have held onto the worship of false gods, particularly in the north. Northern Israel has always held factions that were rebellious to God. Look what I'm saying … for that matter the whole country has as well. As a people, we have from time to time down through the ages looked to other forces for help and guidance. At times, we just weren't content to allow God to take care of us. The worship of Ba-al was such a time for us. Neither the Torah nor the Bible said what happened to Jezebel's bones, only that God did not want her buried. He had all of Ba-al's prophets killed to destroy any ties to the false god, but it appears as though Jezebel's remains were somehow retrieved and, based on what you have discovered, placed in the box at the site. Given the fact that someone had to save her remains, yes—I suppose it is possible to have followers in this time."

Amir leaned forward. "Chaim, the artifacts from the cave were stolen from the museum. The lamps, the dagger, and the bones were all taken."

"Then however preposterous it may sound, we must assume that followers exist, and that they mean to join the little girl with the remains of Jezebel for the purpose of burying her."

"But why? It makes no sense. They can't possibly achieve anything from it, can they?" Clay wanted to know.

"To defy God, that is their motive. The answer lies in the end of the phrase. *Thus sayeth the lord, the bearer of the light.* The 'Light Bearer' is one of the names for Satan," Chaim went on to explain.

Bill and Clay sat with stunned looks on their faces. Bill exhaled and dropped his head into his hands. "Why didn't I see it?" He turned toward Clay. "I blew it, Clay. My arrogance pushed us into the museum in Chicago, and now it has brought us here. I have jeopardized that little girl through my stupid arrogance."

"No, you didn't. Your logic was sound. Hell, I'm just as guilty. We both just wanted to help a little girl." Clay turned back toward Chaim. "Rabbi, we are leaving as soon as we can get a flight out. We cannot risk Allyson coming to any harm. I'll send a copy of my journal to Amir. If you could follow through with this, we would greatly appreciate it."

Chaim grasped Clay's right hand with both of his. "Of course, Clay, anything I can do." He stood up and walked to the door with the men. "Now, you need to leave so you can get that little girl back home where, hopefully, she will be safe."

"I can't thank you enough, Rabbi," Bill said also shaking Chaim's hand as he walked outside.

Amir waived to his friend as they entered the van. He started the vehicle and backed out of the driveway. Looking at Clay, he said, "Well, my friend, I wish we could have spent more time together." Clay was sitting in the front passenger's seat looking out of the front window. "Well, then, next year in Jerusalem," he said in a low voice.

Amir reached across toward Clay and put his hand on his shoulder. "Yes. Besides, you have to bring our friend Bill back so he can get that cup of coffee he keeps missing out on," he said smiling.

"Don't remind me," Bill remarked as he sat in the back, staring out the side window. He had a lot to think about.

* * * * *

The tan Citroen was parked on the side of the road, one hundred yards from Chaim's house. As the white Ford van drove by, Joseph Mokotoff placed the pistol in his belt behind his back and opened the right rear door of the car.

Douglas leaned out of the front passenger's window. "As soon as we're done, Joseph, we'll be back to get you."

The Citroen pulled away from the curb as Joseph walked toward Chaim's house. Sitting in the center of the backseat of the car, Paz Freedman inserted a magazine into the Uzi. Douglas turned his head around and looked at Paz to see if he was ready. Paz nodded back at him. Douglas turned toward David. "Okay, take him."

David depressed the accelerator pedal as he tightened his seatbelt. The Citroen lurched forward as he weaved back and forth in traffic, closing the distance on the van.

Amir prepared to change lanes as he looked into the left side rearview mirror. The erratic driving of the Citroen caught his attention. He started to move into the left lane, but stopped when the Citroen moved up to the left rear corner of the van. As Amir lifted his foot off the accelerator to allow the Citroen to pass, he turned his head to look into the car. He looked down at Douglas and saw the Uzi sitting in his lap.

Amir shouted as he jammed on the brakes and instinctively turned right to avoid the Citroen. "Gun!" he shouted to Clay and Bill.

Clay's body was thrown to the left as the van slid sideways. Amir looked back toward the left in time to see the two men on the right side of the vehicle pointing weapons at them.

"Get down!" he shouted to Clay and Bill.

Bill threw his body to the right in the rear seat, getting as low as he could. The 9 mm rounds exploded into the van, blowing out all of the windows on the left side of the vehicle. As Amir completed the right-hand turn, he stomped down on the accelerator, lurching the vehicle forward. The Citroen completed the right-hand turn too, cutting off cars in the outside lane. The other vehicles screeched as they tried to stop, honking their horns as the Citroen sped off, following the van.

Clay shot back upright in his seat, looking around, assessing the damage. "Anybody hit?" he shouted as he looked at Amir.

"I'm okay," Bill responded from the backseat, clearly shaken by the gunshots.

Clay looked at Amir. "You're hit.

Amir lifted his left hand from the wheel and rubbed it across the left side of his head. He pulled his hand back in front of his eyes, seeing blood on his hand.

"I'm all right. It's just a cut from the glass." He put his hand back on the wheel.

Clay turned around in his seat to see the Citroen still following them, dodging traffic as they sped toward them. "Do you have a gun?"

"Yes, in the glove box," Amir said as he darted in and out of traffic.

Clay opened the glove compartment and removed the 9mm Beretta. He jerked the slide back and chambered a round. He reached back into the glove box and pulled out the leather pouch containing two additional fifteen round magazines.

"What's going on?" Bill yelled from the rear seat.

"I'm guessing someone didn't appreciate our trip to the cave," Amir answered him.

"Yeah, guess this answers our question about Ba-al worshipers, huh?" Clay stated sarcastically. "We're better off to stay in traffic, Amir, we have a better chance in the city."

Amir nodded as he tapped on the brakes and turned the van left. Halfway through the turn, he hit the accelerator, and the van powered through the turn. All around them, other cars were swerving and honking their horns trying to avoid a collision with the two speeding vehicles.

Amir turned the van left onto Yekhezkel Street, directly into the oncoming traffic of a one-way street. He frantically dodged oncoming traffic as they honked and flashed their headlights at him.

"How far back is he?" Amir barked at Clay.

"Thirty yards and closing!"

Amir moved the van to the right as he looked up the street to see an IPD traffic officer parked on the right side of the street facing them. The right front of the van scraped down the right side of the patrol car as Amir sped past. The IPD officer yelled out as the collision took him by surprise. He turned on the overheads of the BMW patrol car and turned right, affecting a u-turn, and accelerating into the oncoming traffic behind the Citroen. The police officer turned on the siren as he sped toward the van. His focus was locked onto the van as he lifted the microphone of the radio to his mouth. Before he could call the chase into headquarters, he looked to see the man in the rear of the Citroen raise the upper half of his body out of the right rear of the vehicle.

The thirty rounds from the Uzi found their mark, laying siege to the hood and windshield of the patrol car. The BMW police car swerved to the right, hitting the sidewalk and launching the car into the air and through the front window of a restaurant. Paz slid back into the vehicle and reloaded his Uzi with a fresh magazine.

"They took out the police car, Amir," Clay shouted as he leaned around the side of his seat, not believing what he was seeing.

Amir moved the van to the left side of the street as he approached Me'a Shearim Street. He pulled the van up and onto the curb as he negotiated the left turn.

Paz leaned out of the left side and fired at the van as the Citroen turned left. The rounds struck the van's rear doors, blowing out the rear windows. Bill ducked down behind the seat as the rounds rattled against the vehicle.

The engine whined as Amir hit the accelerator. Clay leaned to the right, waiting for an opportunity to return fire.

Amir slid the van to the left, turning onto Zonenfeld Street. "What are you doing? You're going back out of the city!" Clay yelled in question.

"I'm going to see if I can get to Police Headquarters," Amir told him without taking his eyes off the rearview mirror.

The van's tires howled as Amir turned right onto a dead end street. Clay leaned out of the window and aimed the pistol at the Citroen with his left hand. The weapon discharged twice, hitting the car in the hood. David instinctively jerked the car to the left as the rounds impacted.

"Brace yourself!" Amir shouted, as the van approached the end of the cul-de-sac. Clay looked to see the approaching curb and vacant land beyond the street. He put his right hand on the ceiling, bracing himself as the van left the roadway, launching into the air. The engine screamed as all four of the tires left the pavement. Clay groaned loudly as the vehicle slammed back down on the dirt. He looked back quickly to see the Citroen airborne as it followed them. The van slid back and forth as Amir tried to keep it upright on the dirt surface.

Amir mashed down on the accelerator as he approached an embankment ahead to climb the incline. The van shot up the embankment and became airborne again, slamming down onto the roadway. Amir knew where he was going as he turned the wheel right and hit the accelerator, squealing the tires. He honked his horn repeatedly, warning the cars ahead of him as he sped down the busy road. With his hand held down on the horn as he approached the forty-five degree left turn onto Derekh Sh Khem, the right side of the van slid toward an oncoming car, slamming into it hard. The Volkswagen Jetta rolled onto its left side, sliding into the oncoming traffic. Amir looked behind him in time to see the carnage of his actions. The approaching Citroen darted around the incapacitated vehicles as it continued the chase closely behind.

Amir readied himself as he approached the 180-degree turn to the left. He tapped the brakes slightly as the van entered the turn. He had unknowingly committed a fatal error by exposing the entire left side of the van. Paz and Douglas both emptied full magazines into the side of the Ford.

Amir overcompensated by further turning the van to the left. The "G" forces of the turn took over, and the van lurched to the right. Without the protection of their seatbelts, Bill and Clay's bodies flailed as the van rolled over three times before coming to rest on its left side.

Clay's unconscious body fell on top of Amir. Bill had been folded into a ball in the rear of the van, his unconscious body lying on the exposed ground of the glassless window. Barely conscious, Amir found himself unable to move because of the weight of Clay's body. Blood poured down his forehead and into his eyes as he fought to see out of the glassless windshield cavity.

Amir could see the Berretta, resting on the ground in front of him. The pistol was lying next to Clay's journal, both of which were just beyond his reach. He watched as two men ran toward him from the Citroen, their weapons at the ready. He strained to reach the pistol with his left hand, clawing at the pavement with his fingers as Douglas and Paz reached the van.

Douglas slid his right foot on the ground, sliding the Berretta away from Amir's hand. Paz bent over and picked up Clay's journal from among the glass of the windshield and placed it in his belt. Both men raised their weapons toward Clay and Amir. Amir took in a deep breath and held it, awaiting the explosion that would end his life. He had faced death before, but never so imminent as now. As the two men held out their Uzis, they heard shouting from the approaching crowd who had run from the nearby British School. Douglas and Paz quickly turned away and ran back toward the Citroen.

Amir could hear the sirens from the approaching emergency vehicles as he watched the Citroen speed off. As he began to lose consciousness, he heard the voices of his rescuers kneeling down in front of him.

CHAPTER 28

THE PROPHECY'S CHILD

Gary sat at the desk in the lobby of the hotel while the concierge worked on the computer making flight arrangements. He held on to the two plastic bags of food for himself, Beth, and Allyson, swinging them between his legs nervously.

"All right, Mr. Carter, I have reservations for five people, tomorrow morning at 10:00 a.m. on El Al out of Tel Aviv."

"Isn't there anything out sooner?" Gary asked anxiously.

"No, sir, that's the earliest I can get you reservations."

"Very well, I guess that will have to do," Gary responded with a sigh as he stood up from the desk. "Can you bill my credit card?"

"Yes, sir, I'll take care of it. The tickets will be at the front desk when you're ready."

"Thank you."

Gary walked slowly from the lobby, his head hung down looking at the floor as he assessed the events of the day. His whole world had been turned upside down and the life of his daughter placed in jeopardy by that one foolish moment of deciding to enter that damn cave. All the money on the planet, nor the best job in the world could be worth the price that had been paid. He fought the urge to blame Bill and Clay for bringing them to Israel. The blame, he thought, should be laid at his feet alone. How could they have ever known what the trip today would have revealed? Trying to put the events of the day behind him, Gary took in a deep breath and exhaled slowly as he pushed the elevator button. He entered the elevator and pushed the fourth floor button, and then leaned against the railing of the car. The tone of the elevator bell sounded, and Gary moved toward the door. The door rolled open, and Gary stepped out into the hall. As he turned right to walk to his room, he saw three figures about fifteen yards away. They were dressed in uniforms of the Jerusalem Laundry Service. The two men and one woman were walking toward him, their eyes locked onto him. They spread out and took up the entire width of the hall. The man in the center reached into his coat and pulled out a pistol. Gary froze in his tracks as Nuri Liber pointed the pistol at him. Gary dropped the bags and turned to run away.

The silenced Walther PPK discharged twice, striking Gary in the back. He cried out as his knees buckled and he fell to the floor. Nuri put the pistol back in his coat and dragged Gary's body into the maids' closet and closed the door.

Rebecca Isroff and Tamir Berkowitz turned and knocked on the door of Room 418. "Who is it?" The voice on the other side asked.

"Maid service," Rebecca replied.

Beth turned the deadbolt and pressed down on the door handle. As the latch released, the door burst open, striking Beth in the forehead, knocking her to the ground. Dazed and panicked, Beth rolled over on her back to see Rebecca and Tamir standing over her. Tamir placed his knee on Beth's chest and held a gauze pad over her nose and mouth. Beth's arms flailed at her attacker, but the effect of the chloroform was too fast. Her body went limp, as her last thoughts were that of her daughter.

Rebecca walked into the bedroom and looked to see Allyson sitting with her back to the door watching television. She hesitated as she looked reverently upon the Anointed One. Allyson turned slowly toward Rebecca. Her eyes opened wide as she saw the two demons standing behind the woman. Allyson trembled as the realization struck her that the demons were no longer afraid of her. Tears began to fall down her cheeks as she cried out for her mother.

Allyson screamed loudly as Rebecca lurched forward, grabbing her and placing the chloroform-laced gauze bandage over her mouth. Allyson struggled, but the little girl had no hope of overcoming the woman's grip. Rebecca carried the unconscious little girl out into the main room and waited for Nuri to signal that the hallway was clear.

Nuri pulled the two laundry carts up next to the door. "Hurry, let's go," he ordered. Rebecca placed Allyson into the first cart and then helped Tamir load an unconscious Beth into the second one. Tamir and Nuri pushed the carts toward the elevator as Rebecca closed the door to the Carters' room. As they made their way down the hall, the two demons dressed in black robes followed behind them.

* * * * *

The silver 750 BMW negotiated the traffic on Highway 458 as Shimon hurried to meet his worshipers in 'Aqraba. He pored through the details of the ceremony as he rehearsed his sermon. The cell phone on the console rang, interrupting him. He reached down and opened the phone.

"Hello."

"Lord, this is Douglas."

"Yes, Douglas, what do you have for me?"

"Lord, Rebecca has secured the Anointed One and her mother."

"Excellent—and what of the father?"

"He was eliminated at the hotel."

"Very good, Douglas." Shimon smiled. "Did you take care of the rest of the Americans?"

"We believe so, Lord. Their vehicle crashed during a chase. I saw them inside, and to the best of my knowledge, they didn't survive the crash. The police were coming, so we couldn't verify it, but I believe they died at the scene."

"Very good, Douglas, we'll just have to hope they didn't make it. How long will it take you to get to the temple?"

"We should be there in three hours at the most."

"Good, I'll see you there," he said as he closed his phone. Shimon raised his left hand and smiled. "Thank you, Lord. We will not fail you. We will be victorious."

* * * * *

Yair Klein's cell phone rang as he pulled up in front of the St. Johns Hospital. "Chief Klein," he answered.

"Chief, this is Joshua Cassel. I have some bad news. They found Lt. Steyn dead from a gunshot wound inside his car."

Yair hesitated before responding; he couldn't believe what he was hearing. He had sent Mark on what was supposed to have been a routine surveillance. Mark was only supposed to follow the Americans and report their activities. How could he be dead? Yair choked the words out, "Where and how was he found?"

"He followed the Americans to a road just outside of 'Aqraba. Last contact we had with him was when he said he was waiting for them to come back down the mountain. One of the locals found him and called it in."

Yair bowed his head. "That would have been shortly after he contacted me. Okay, Joshua, I'm at the hospital to talk to the victims of the crash. Call me as soon as you get more information."

"I will. I'm very sorry, Chief. Mark was a good man. We'll get to the bottom of whatever is going on and find the ones responsible for his death."

"I know. Thank you, Joshua." Yair closed his phone and exhaled slowly.

* * * * *

Beth slowly opened her eyes. Her head pounded from the effects of the chloroform. She couldn't get her bearings, but thought she was in a large cargo van because of the movement and the noise from the diesel engine. The translucent fiberglass rollup door in the rear allowed enough light to enter so that she could make out the interior details of the compartment.

She tried to raise her hands to rub her eyes, but the restraining straps held them tightly to her side. She instinctively tried to move her legs, but found them strapped down as well. The events of the abduction came to the forefront as she slowly came into consciousness. Her thoughts immediately went to Allyson. She rolled her head to the side to look at the interior of the van. Beth could see racks against the opposing wall, five high. Each rack had bags and boxes on them, except for the third rack up from the bottom. Beth was lying on the bottom rack on the right side of the van. She could hear the humming of the diesel engine and the methodical thumps from the seams in the road. She rolled her head back, trying to see what was in front of her, but couldn't see because of the boxes and bags stacked on the floor.

Rebecca was sitting on a large bag at the front of the van compartment and saw Beth struggling in the rack. She stood and walked to the rack where Beth was lying. She held onto the rail of the third rack on the left side as she looked down at Beth. Beth looked closely at Rebecca and recognized her as one of the attackers from the hotel.

"Where's my daughter?" Beth demanded.

Rebecca turned her head and looked across into the third rack. "She's right here."

"Is she okay?" Beth asked.

"She is alive—for now."

Tears filled Beth's eyes. "Can I talk to her?" Beth asked with a trembling voice.

"She is asleep and will not be disturbed until the ceremony."

Allyson lay in the rack in a drug-induced state. Her entire body, with the exception of her face, was bound in thick tan colored bandages, reminiscent of a mummy.

Tears poured down Beth's face as she lay helpless in the rack. "Why are you doing this to us? We've done nothing to you."

"Because she is the Anointed One. The Lord has delivered her to us. Her fate was prophesied centuries ago."

Rebecca clearly had no need to talk with Beth. The smile on her face indicated that she was only talking with Beth to taunt her.

"When my husband finds you, he'll kill every one of you filthy bastards."

"That, I think you will find, would be an impossible task for him," Rebecca said with a smirk on her face. The curious look on Beth's face prompted a response from Rebecca. "He is dead. We deprived him of his insignificant life at the hotel."

Pain shot through Beth's chest as she heard the words. She fought the urge to sob uncontrollably in front of her captor. She winced in pain, closing her eyes tightly. She searched for the words that could possibly save her daughter from the same fate that Gary had suffered. She opened her eyes and looked at the gloating face of Rebecca. "Take me in her place. I would serve the same purpose. You don't need to sacrifice my daughter … let me go instead of her."

Rebecca held onto the rack with her left hand and leaned out toward Beth. "She was chosen by the Lord. She will be joined with our queen and buried. Your God won't be able to help you this time. The queen will finally be buried! And don't think that your other friends will be able to help you either. By now, they are dead as well. So you should accept your fate and rejoice that it is your daughter that was chosen for this honor."

Beth strained at the straps and cried out angrily and hysterically, "You filthy bitch, I hope you rot in hell! I'll kill you if you harm her!"

Rebecca lunged at Beth, slapping her hard on the face. She pulled the knife from the scabbard on her belt and rested the blade on Beth's neck. "You pathetic woman, it is you who will die before me. Before the sun sets, I will watch your beating black heart cut from your chest and fed to the jackals. I was told to deliver you to the temple alive, but if you don't show some respect, I will torture you to the point that you will beg me to take your miserable life." Rebecca stood and spat on Beth as she sheathed her knife and returned to the bags at the front of the compartment.

Tears flooded down Beth's cheeks as she thought of the deaths of Gary and her friends. She strained to get a look at Allyson, but could only see the railing. The horror of her and Allyson's fate poured over her. Beth silently prayed as the vehicle continued toward the cave.

* * * * *

Clay's eyes opened slowly as he tried to focus on the figure looking down at him. The bright light of the hospital room flooded into his eyes. His speech was labored as he slowly regained consciousness.

"He's awake," the voice announced.

His eyes came into focus as he recognized the nurse's uniform. The doctor entered the room and leaned over Clay, looking into his eyes.

"Mr. Harker, can you hear me?" the doctor asked.

"Yes," Clay whispered through parched lips.

"You have sustained a concussion, Mr. Harker," the doctor continued.

"That would explain this killer headache," Clay said as he slowly touched the gauze bandage around his head. "My friends, are they all right?"

"Yes, Mr. Monroe was treated for a broken arm."

"And Amir?"

"He is fine as well. They're out in the hall, waiting for word on you."

"And where am I?"

"You're in the Intensive Care Unit of St. Johns Hospital."

Clay tried to sit up, but his head fell back down on the pillow, throbbing like a herd of horses were galloping through it.

"Please, Mr. Harker, you need to rest," the doctor ordered.

"Can I see my friends?" Clay asked.

"Yes, but for just a short time. You were hurt very badly. You are lucky you're not blind. We removed several glass shards from your face and head."

"I'm really thirsty, Doc. Can I have something to drink?"

The doctor placed his thumb on Clay's eyelid and shined a light into his eye. "Yes, I'll have them bring you something." The doctor placed the pen light back in his pocket. "I'll let you see your friends now, but remember, keep it short."

"Thanks, Doctor."

The doctor stepped from the room and stopped in front of the three men. "He's awake now. You can go in, but not for long—he needs rest badly."

Amir stepped in front of the doctor. "Doctor, this is Chief Klein from the Israel Police Department. He would like to ask Clay some questions if that's possible."

"That would be fine, but again, don't take too long," the doctor said as he walked away.

The three men entered the room and walked to the side of the bed. Clay turned his head to see them.

"How you doing, bud?" A concerned Bill asked.

"I feel like I was hit by a truck. How long have I been out?"

Amir rolled his wrist over and looked at his watch. "Almost twelve hours."

"What happened? All I remember was watching the horizon rolling."

Amir answered, "I tried to avoid the weapons fire from the Citroen and overcorrected in the curve. The vehicle rolled over a few times, and you and Bill passed out."

Clay looked at Chief Klein with a curious look on his face. "Clay, this is Chief Klein from the Israel Police Department," Amir offered.

Clay very slowly extended his right hand. "Nice to meet you, I think."

"Mr. Harker, I'll try to be brief. The three of us have been putting the pieces of this whole situation together. After talking to Amir and Bill, it's clear that the incident at the museum and your attack are tied in together."

"Even the fire?" Clay asked.

"You're unusually well informed, Mr. Harker." Yair frowned with surprise in his eyes. "Somehow, although it remains a mystery as to why, we feel the artifacts are directly related to the fire and also the incident at the rabbi's house."

"What incident?" Clay fired back trying desperately not to move his head.

Amir put his hand on Clay's shoulder. "Take it slow and easy, Clay. Chaim and his wife were killed shortly after we left their house."

Clay closed his eyes as he gritted his teeth. "God, why these people … why them?"

Bill took in a deep breath. "That's not all, Clay. Beth and Allyson were abducted from the hotel."

Clay clenched his fist and struck the bed. "Where's Gary?"

Bill's voice cracked as he spoke the words. "He was shot at the hotel. He's here in the hospital … he's not expected to make it, Clay."

Clay set his jaw firmly as he pressed the button on the hospital bed to slowly raise his head so he could sit. Looking directly into the eyes of the chief, he stated very clearly, "We've got to stop them before they kill her!"

"Mr. Harker, we have every available officer looking for them," Yair responded.

"Chief, with all due respect, this isn't your fight. We got that little girl into this, and we'll get her out," Clay fired back.

"Mr. Harker, I beg to differ with you. This has become my fight, too. One of my best men, Lieutenant Mark Steyn, was killed as a result of this incident. I'm not going to have any more casualties. This is a matter for the police. Now, Mr. Monroe here tells me that you translated writings that could help us find out where Mrs. Carter and her daughter are being held. We need that information."

Clay looked at Amir, who was standing behind Yair. Amir slowly moved his head side to side.

"Mr. Harker, I need that information … now!"

Clay looked at the chief and exhaled slowly. "Based on what I can determine, there will be some kind of religious ceremony that will occur on the ninth of July at 7:00 p.m."

"And do you know where it will take place?" Yair went on.

"No, only that it will be day after tomorrow."

"Up in the mountains where the cave is located?" Yair asked.

"No. There were writings in the cave up there, but it said the ceremony will be at another location, probably near the old city of Samaria." Clay dodged a more definite response.

"Okay, then, we will need you to stay in Jerusalem until further notice. I will be in touch." Yair walked to the door and stopped before he walked out. He turned his head back toward the men, and looked intently at Bill and Amir. "I'm very sorry for the loss of Rabbi Bronstein and his wife, as well as the injury of your friend. But please remember, as I said before, this is now a police matter. If you have any other information to help us find these murderers, you need to call me immediately."

"Thank you, Chief," Bill said as Yair left the room.

Amir turned back toward Clay as the door closed. "All right, how do we want to handle this?"

"I don't know how good we'll be with Bill having a broken wing and me with a concussion, but we definitely need to get back up to the cave before the ceremony."

"I'll be fine, Clay," Bill returned, "but don't you think it would be better to have the police with us?"

"If the police bust in there, those bastards will kill her. They want to join her with Jezebel's remains, and they won't care if she dies before the prescribed time," Clay stated.

"They got your journal, Clay, so they have all the translations," Bill commented.

Clay shook his head very slowly and painfully. "First we're dumb enough to bring her here, and then I'm dumb enough to write down what they need. That just means we need to get there as soon as we can."

"All right, but are you sure you're going to be okay to go?" Bill knew they needed Clay, but not if he couldn't help them without furthering his injuries.

"I'll be fine. Amir, we'll need some things before we go up there. We need as many weapons as you can lay your hands on."

"Just tell me what you need and I'll have it," Amir assured him.

"Three pistols, a shotgun, knives, and some Uzis if you can lay your hands on them. And we'll need another car."

"You got it. Are you going to be able to get out of this hospital without a problem?" Amir asked.

Clay thought about it for a minute and then said, "Just leave me your cell phone and call me at four o'clock. Let me know where you are, and tell me where to meet you outside the hospital. We'll need to go directly to the site, so have everything that we need with you."

"What about the police chief?" Bill asked.

"By the time he figures out I'm gone, we'll be at the site."

Amir handed Clay his cell phone. "Just make sure you're downstairs at four," he said with a smile.

"Don't worry—I'll be there."

CHAPTER 29

THE COALITION

THE NURSE CAME INTO Clay's room with a tray of medications. She walked to the side of the bed and placed the tray on the bed stand.

"What are these for?" Clay asked.

"The doctor ordered antibiotics for you, Mr. Harker. They're for the wounds on your face and head."

Clay took the pills and washed them down with the juice. "Nurse, I'm really tired. I would just like to rest, if that's okay?"

"That would be fine. No one will bother you, Mr. Harker," the nurse replied with a smile. She checked his IV drip and left the room, closing the door behind her.

Clay slid his legs out of the bed and placed his feet on the cold tile floor. He slowly stood up, balancing himself by holding onto the bed railing. Slowly pulling the IV from the back of his left hand and stretching the tape over the puncture, he felt confident he wouldn't be detected because they hadn't put him on an EKG monitor. He jammed the IV drip needle into the foam pillow on his bed and stepped carefully to the tall portable closet. Still recovering from the effects of the concussion, he was unsteady on his feet as he got into his clothes and slid on his shoes. Clay turned to look at himself in the mirror.

There was swelling in his face and eight cuts with stitches in them. *"I'll worry about the stitches later,"* he thought. He pulled the gauze bandaging from his head and threw it on the bed and then placed Amir's cell phone in his pocket and quietly stepped to the door.

Clay slowly opened the door and looked down the hall both ways. The nurse who had just left his room was standing at the nurses' station with her back to him. He quickly turned to the right and walked down the hall and saw the sign for the exit elevator. Continuing down the hall, he stopped in front of the elevator and pushed the down button several times while looking back and forth for hospital staff. He was too close to getting out of this place to be discovered now. The elevator door opened, and Clay quickly stepped inside the car. Quickly, he pushed the main floor button and then the button to close the door. As the door closed, he leaned back against the railing, trying to hold off the nausea that was gripping him as his head started to throb again.

As the door opened on the main floor, he exited and looked to find signage that would identify his location. The admitting desk was to his left, so he decided to turn right to try to find the rear of the hospital. As he was walking down the hall, the cell phone in his pocket rang. He depressed the talk button and lifted it to his ear.

"Where are you?" Clay asked.

Amir responded on the other end, "We're in the rear by the loading dock."

"I'll be there as soon as I can find out where the hell I am." Clay put the phone back in his pocket. Thankfully, as he kept walking, he looked up ahead of him and saw the sign for the loading dock. He turned left and walked through the cargo doors and out onto the dock. The sunlight hit him directly in the face causing him to wince in pain. He held his hand up to his forehead to shade the light as he looked for Amir and Bill. He heard a car horn honk to his right and turned to see a red Ford Taurus with Amir waving his hand from the driver's window.

Clay stepped from the dock and walked toward the car with still shaky legs. He opened the right rear door and slid into the seat. "Let's get out of here," he wearily announced. The nausea had subsided somewhat, but his head still hurt as he leaned on the back of the seat and closed his eyes.

Amir put the car in gear and sped off. "Any trouble?" He asked.

"No, clean getaway," Clay answered. "Did you get everything we need?"

"Yes, it's in the bag on the floor next to you, and the shotgun's in the trunk." Turning around from the front seat, Bill asked his friend, "How are you feeling, bud?" Clay reached forward with his right hand and patted Bill on the shoulder. "Not too bad. Still a little queasy, but good enough for what we have to do."

Clay reached down, unzipped the duffle bag, and took inventory of its contents. He pulled one of the knives from the bag and cut off the ID bracelet from his wrist. He rolled his wrist over and looked at his watch. *"Plenty of time,"* he said to himself. Clay leaned back again, closed his eyes tightly, trying to fight off the pain in his head, and slowly fell off to sleep as his thoughts went to Beth and Allyson.

* * * * *

Beth could feel the cargo van climbing the grade, by the incline of the litter she was on. She heard the engine whining in the front of her as it labored against the grade. She felt the gravity forces trying to pull her to the center of the cargo box as the truck made the long slow right-hand turn. The van leveled off and came to a halt. After the engine was turned off, she could hear conversations around the outside of the van.

Rebecca stood up and walked to the rear of the van. She released the lever and raised the roll-up door. Beth heard the clatter as the ramp was pulled from under the cargo bay. Footsteps rang out as the two figures walked up the ramp and entered the van. Beth looked up to see two people in white robes in front of her. The full sleeves and hoods offered little as to their identity. The two people were chanting something. She couldn't hear what they were saying. It was almost in a whisper, but definitely in a foreign language. Beth felt her heart begin to pound from fear.

The two men picked up the litter from the third rack and lowered it to their waist. Beth could see Allyson lying on it. Tears came to her eyes and began to fall down her cheeks as she saw her daughter completely bound from head to toe in gauze wraps.

Still chanting, the two men walked from the van and down the ramp. Beth heard footsteps coming back up the ramp and looked to see two more people wearing robes enter the van. They bent down and lifted the litter she was on from the bottom rack. The two men softly chanted as they carried Beth from the van. Once outside in the evening sun, Beth could see the activity at the site. There were large tents spread out on the site across from the entrance to the temple. From what she could see, there were at least a hundred people walking around the site.

Several people were carrying equipment into the cave. Most of the people were in street clothes, but a few had donned the white linen robes. She couldn't see her watch to tell what time it was, but believed it to be somewhere around 6:00 p.m. from where the sun was positioned in the sky.

The two men carried Beth into the largest of the tents and placed her on a table on the far side, away from Allyson. Beth turned her head to look at her daughter. She watched as the four women removed the burlap wraps from her body. They carefully removed all of Allyson's clothes until she was completely naked on the table. One of the women pulled a white linen robe from the box next to the table and pulled it down over Allyson's body. Gold stitching accented the dark blue trim on the robe, which covered Allyson's body completely. One of the women was putting her hair into dark long curls that fell around her head, while a third woman was putting makeup on her face. The transformation was grotesque, turning Allyson into something even Beth couldn't recognize.

Beth could see Allyson's chest moving up and down as she breathed. At least she was alive, Beth thought. She looked around the tent in the hopes of seeing something she could use to get free or defend herself. Complete terror engulfed Beth as she realized that any hope of getting out of this nightmare was dwindling fast. Her body trembled as she watched the grotesque scene unfold.

Shimon Gutstein entered the tent wearing his high priest robe. The hood was off his head, gathered around his neck. Beth could see that the blue trim and gold stitching matched the robe that Allyson was wearing. She assumed that he was someone of authority, as everyone bowed toward him when he entered the tent. Shimon walked to the table and leaned over Allyson, kissing her on the forehead.

He raised his hands, palms up as he looked above him. "Thank you, Lord. Thank you for delivering the Anointed One to us."

Shimon turned and walked toward Beth. His face changed to a scowl as he approached her. Beth remained silent as he stopped next to her.

"Your offspring has been chosen for this honor. You, however, will not witness the ceremony, but have peace in the knowledge that her sacrifice will fulfill the Lord's prophecy."

Beth was unable to respond to him. She remained fixated on his face, unable to turn away from his black, cold eyes. Complete terror fell over her as she saw the evil in his eyes. Shimon turned and walked back toward the opening of the tent. He turned his head toward Rebecca as he was leaving.

"Make sure the mother is bound tightly and gagged before you bring them to the temple. I'll call for them when I'm ready."

"Yes, Lord," Rebecca said, bowing toward him.

Thinking of Gary, Beth felt helpless and so alone as she watched Shimon leave the tent. "Hope. I must not lose hope," she said to herself as the tears streamed down her cheeks.

* * * * *

The red Ford Taurus slowed as it approached 'Aqraba. Amir applied the brakes as he closed on the car in front of him. The white BMW came to a stop in front of him, allowing two pedestrians to cross the road. Amir looked in his rearview mirror watching a Mercedes Benz cargo van pull up to his rear bumper. Unable to move the car, Amir watched as the driver of the BMW opened the door and walk toward them. "This guy looks like a policeman," Amir murmured. Moshe Wasserstein stopped next to the driver's door and tapped on the window with the knuckles of his left hand. Amir rolled the window down a few inches as Clay reached into the duffle bag and placed his hand on the Uzi.

"Can I help you?" Amir asked.

"There is someone who would like to speak with you," Moshe replied.

"Who might that be?"

The man pointed to the parked car across the road from them. Amir, Clay, and Bill turned their heads to the right to see Joshua Cassel with his arms folded, leaning against a silver Volkswagen Golf talking on a cell phone. Moshe nodded to Tovi Farache, the driver of the Mercedes. The van backed up, allowing Amir to move. He turned the wheel and drove toward the Volkswagen.

Joshua spoke into the phone. "They just arrived here, Chief."

Yair Klein spoke with determination in his voice. "Get them back here, Joshua, and find out where the ceremony is being held."

Joshua responded as the Ford pulled up next to them. "Do you want them arrested?"

"No. Not unless they refuse to return." Yair responded.

"Very well, sir—we'll return immediately." Joshua stated as he closed the cell phone. He turned toward the three men exiting the red Ford. "Mr. Harker, I'm Detective Joshua Cassel from the Israeli Police Department. That was Chief Klein on the phone, and it is an understatement to say that you men are in a lot of trouble. Mr. Harker, you should be in the hospital. I take it this is a rescue mission."

"I'm okay, Mr. Cassel, but if you don't let us go, a little girl and her mother will die in less than an hour." Clay decided to be truthful as there wasn't any point now in keeping the police out of this, so he pointed to the mountain range up ahead on their left.

"They're up there now?" Joshua wanted to know.

"Yes, and if we don't get up there fast, those religious zealots will kill them … the mother may already be dead," Clay said anxiously, his voice breaking as he thought of Beth and Allyson.

Joshua angrily shot back at him, "If you had told Chief Klein this in the hospital, we could already have stopped it."

"No, you couldn't have stopped it. They ultimately need to kill the girl! If they had seen you coming, they would have killed her on the spot. Detective, we need each other now. I have the translations. I know how and when they plan to sacrifice her, and most important, we know the layout of the cave. With the help of you and your men, we can stop them. We're Beth and Allyson's only hope," Clay explained.

Joshua looked at the three men, analyzing what he had just heard. "Mr. Harker, you should be in the hospital. You have one man with a broken arm, and a retired old army officer. What good are you?"

Amir's back straightened as he commented to the policeman, "By the way, in case you're wondering, no offense taken," he said with a smirk directed at Joshua.

Clay stepped up and without trying to sound as frantic as he felt said, "Look, Detective, we have surprise on our side. They think we're dead. They're not expecting any interference and, with your help, we can pull it off."

Joshua knew he had no choice. There wasn't time to get a team in from Jerusalem, and they were just minutes away. He found himself boxed into a corner. "Do you have weapons?"

"Of course," Amir responded.

"I might have known." Joshua just shook his head as he looked at Amir. "All right, get in the back of the van. Mr. Harker, I want you in the front with me. The rest of you get in the back." Joshua turned toward Moshe. "Call this into headquarters and get the SORT Team out here as quick as possible, and contact the chief and tell him we're going in." He wasn't sure how soon the Special Operations and Response Team would take, but he knew he had to try to get them here as soon as possible. Looking at the other three, he resignedly spoke, "Well, what are you waiting for? Let's get going!" He was not happy with his decision, but knew there wasn't another option.

Clay smiled as he turned toward the Taurus to retrieve the duffle bag. Amir opened the trunk and pulled out the shotgun and bag of ammunition. Joshua entered the driver's side of the Mercedes and looked across at Clay. "You had better be right," he said as he put the van in gear and pulled away.

* * * * *

Beth was unable to move, as the wraps were wound tightly around her body. A roll of gauze had been placed in her mouth to keep her from speaking. Her arms were bound tightly to her side and her legs were wrapped together. The only opening in the wrap was around her nose and eyes. She strained to see the men that entered the tent. From her right eye, she was able to see the women lifting Allyson from the table and placing her on the litter. She cried as she looked and saw Allyson's face heavily made up. Her lips were bright red, and her eyes were painted with heavy eyeliner and thick black eyelashes. On her head was a gold crown with jewels around the band. Beth gagged as she looked upon the sight.

The two women gently laid her on the litter, arranging her hair after she was laid down. Two men lifted the litter and carried her out of the tent. Two more men entered the tent and walked toward Beth. They lifted the litter and carried her out and into the evening sun. The sun was much lower in the sky, and Beth knew the time was close when the sun would hit the concave star on the cave wall.

The site was almost vacant now with the exception of the two men who stood guard at the entrance to the temple. The two guards remained motionless as Beth's litter passed by them. She could hear chanting coming from inside the cave as the litter reached the landing at the top of the stairs. Her head elevated as they carried her down the stairs. The cave had taken on a macabre atmosphere with the candles placed all around the perimeter of the floor. She couldn't make out what the people were saying, but did recognize two of the words, *Ba-al* and *Jezebel.* She had never been more frightened in her life.

The two men carrying Beth's litter worked their way through the crowd of worshipers. All of them were dressed in white linen robes with the hoods pulled up, hiding their faces. As the litter stopped by the altar, Beth looked to her left to see Allyson. Her eyes appeared to be lifeless, staring blankly upward toward the ceiling of the cave. It was obvious they had given her some kind of drug. Beth looked at her chest to see the slow up and down movement. *"At least she is still alive,"* Beth thought. The three men lowered Beth's litter to the floor, next to the altar. She looked up to see Shimon standing behind the altar. In his right hand he held Clay's journal, his fat, stubby index finger placed between the pages, marking the spot where the translations were located.

Shimon pulled the journal up in front of him and opened it. He began to read the complete phrase in Aramaic to the crowd of worshipers. When he was done, he held his hands high in the air and looked down at Allyson. His rhythmic chant was repeated several times.

"Jezebel, our queen, come forth! Jezebel, our queen, come forth!"

Beth heard a female voice coming from the top of the altar. She didn't understand how, but knew it had to be coming from Allyson. The deep sultry female voice repeated the words Shimon had uttered. "Jezebel, our queen, come forth … Jezebel, our queen, come forth."

Beth looked up to the ceiling of the cave. She thought she was hallucinating at first. She strained her eyes to focus on the movement in the shadows. Something was up there in the darkness. It appeared as if the figures were flying, descending slowly into the light below. Fear gripped her as they came closer, their wings flapping as they dropped lower and lower into the light. Unable to scream, her body began trembling with fear as the six demons came into her view. No one else appeared to be able to see them as they flew low around the cave floor. *"Could this be what Allyson had been seeing all this time?"* Beth thought. The full horror of Allyson's condition slammed into her consciousness as the demons flew around the cave. Her body was racked with fear as she looked upon the sight. She instinctively tried to move her arms and legs, but the straps were too tight. She desperately tried to think of something to do, but felt helpless. All she could do was pray silently for help.

* * * * *

The van quickly approached the base of the mountain, and made the left turn behind the rock formations to begin the ascent to the top. Joshua slammed on the brakes as he saw a man standing on the right side of the road, dressed in an Israeli Army uniform. The army sergeant stepped to the right of the vehicle as it came to a halt.

Clay rolled his window down and looked at the man. "What's going on?" he asked in Hebrew.

"I'm sorry, sir. You can't go any further. This area has been blocked off for security reasons."

Joshua removed the badge from his pocket and held it out across the seat toward the sergeant. "This is a police matter, Sergeant. We need to pass."

"I'm sorry, sir, but I have my orders."

Clay slid the Uzi up the side of the door and stopped just before it came into the man's view.

"What are you doing?" Joshua frantically whispered.

Ignoring the detective's question, Clay stared into the man's eyes. "I'm curious," he stated, "do you remember me from yesterday?"

Paz Freedman's jaw set firmly as he swung the carbine up to his side. Clay lifted the Uzi up and over the windowsill and fired a burst of five rounds into Paz's chest.

Joshua jerked his pistol out of the belt holster and pointed it at Clay. "What the hell are you doing?" he demanded.

Clay opened the van door and responded without looking at Joshua. "He's one of the men that shot up our van yesterday." He stepped out of the vehicle and looked down at Paz's body. Everyone jumped out of the rear of the van with their weapons at the ready. Amir reached Clay first. "What happened?"

"Do you recognize him?" Clay asked.

"Hey, that's the guy in the back of the Citroen."

Joshua looked at Clay as they stood on the right side of the Mercedes. "You're lucky I didn't shoot you!"

"Sorry, I didn't have time to tell you. He's one of the three guys in the car that shot at us."

Bill looked at his watch. "Clay, we're running out of time."

"Amir, get rid of the body," Clay ordered.

Amir reached down and grabbed Paz's body at the collar and dragged it behind the rock formations. Joshua entered the driver's side and looked at Clay as he started the van again. He couldn't help muttering to himself, "Americans ... all of you watched too many western movies as children."

CHAPTER 30

SAMARIA'S REVENGE

THE EVENING SUN WAS shining directly into the left-side window of the Mercedes as it approached the summit. Clay nervously looked at his watch as he held the Uzi in his lap. His body was screaming out for a cigar, and for the first time in weeks, he would have killed for a drink. He tried in vain to ignore the pounding in his head as he stared out the window of the van. He could have used a very long vacation to heal his wounds, but that was not possible now. He had to focus on the job at hand, rescuing a frightened little girl and her mother. His stomach tightened as he thought of Allyson and what she must be going through. Clay had been blaming himself for agreeing to bring the Carters to Israel ever since the discovery in the cave. It could not have gone worse for them, and even cost the lives of two wonderful people, Chaim and his wife, as well as a young police lieutenant. He took in a deep breath as he tried to empty the feelings of guilt from his head. As he turned toward Joshua, he said, "Detective, we better stop here or we may run the risk of being seen or heard. The summit is just up the grade about a mile."

Joshua pulled the van as close to the side of the hill as he could and set the brake. Both men exited the cab of the van and walked around to the left side. Clay tapped lightly on the side of the van box. Amir,

Moshe, Tovi, and Bill exited from the rear. The men all checked their weapons and spare magazines.

"We can't approach on the road without being detected. The original road is down below us and will provide cover up to the site." They all walked to the side of the embankment and looked down. The original road was fifty feet below them. Clay led the way as he slid down the embankment. Once at the bottom, the men all checked their weapons again.

"From here on, no talking," Clay instructed them.

They all began the walk to the summit, their weapons at the ready. After a fifteen-minute walk, the road began the long slow right-hand turn, and Clay knew they were close. He held his index finger to his lips, signaling for them to be quiet. As they rounded the curve, Clay could see the plateau about thirty yards in front of them. He held his hand up, stopping the team.

Clay slowly crawled up the side of the fifteen-foot-high embankment and carefully peeked out over the site. They had stopped immediately behind the main tent. Clay moved to the left slowly and was able to see the entrance to the cave, along with two guards restricting entry. He lowered himself back down the embankment and addressed the team in a low whisper. "We're right behind a large tent. It looks like everyone is inside the cave, with the exception of two guards at the entrance."

"Can we take them out from here?" Moshe asked.

"Too risky. They're about fifty yards from us. Maybe if we can get inside the tent we could get a shot off."

"Is anyone in the tent?" Joshua asked.

"I can't tell," Clay responded.

Amir pulled a suppressor out of his pants pocket and screwed it onto his Berretta. He handed the weapon to Clay. "Here, use this."

"We'll talk about the silencer later, Amir," Joshua said with a scowl on his face.

Clay pulled the slide of the Berretta back slightly and checked to see if a round was in the chamber. Satisfied the weapon was loaded, he pushed the slide closed quietly and crawled back up the embankment. Once at the top, he belly crawled to the back of the tent, and then rose to his knees and motioned for the rest of the team to follow. He pulled the knife from the back of his belt and slowly inserted it into the canvas at the bottom of the tent. He quietly sawed it back and forth slowly until he had a twelve-inch slit in the material. Separating the canvas, he peered inside. He panned his eyes right and left and found it to be empty. Reinserting the blade, he pulled it upward, opening a six-foot slit in the canvas. The six men entered the tent. Clay walked to the entrance of the tent and peered between the flaps. He assessed the distance to the guards to be about forty yards. He turned around and looked at the team. "If we rush them," he whispered, "we might close the distance to thirty yards before they react."

"Maybe we can get closer than that," Bill said standing behind the men, holding up a white linen robe.

Clay smiled at his friend. "Excellent! Okay, here's the plan. Detective, give Bill the keys to the van. Bill, once we've taken care of the guards, you go back down the hill and bring the van back up here. Then put on one of the robes and go inside to the landing above the cave."

Clay then grabbed the pistol from Joshua and handed it to Bill. "Take this and cover us from the landing. If you hear gunfire, come in blazing." He looked carefully at Joshua, Moshe, and Tovi and spoke seriously to them. "Just inside the cave, there will be a set of winding stairs to your right, about seventy-five feet from the bottom of the cave. I don't know how many people will be in there, so be prepared for the worst."

They all nodded at Clay in agreement. Bill clutched the pistol and the keys tightly in his hand. "Okay, I'll see you inside."

Bill stood watch at the door as the rest of them put on the robes and checked their weapons. Clay pulled the hood up over his head and looked at the team. "Okay, let's go."

The five men walked from the tent and slowly made their way to the entrance with their heads held low and reverently. Joshua had the shotgun held behind his back, while Clay held the pistol up under the full sleeve of his right arm with his left hand. When they were thirty feet from the entrance, one of the guards spoke to them.

"You better hurry—the ceremony has already started."

Clay let the pistol slide down his arm to his right hand and extended it, pointing the pistol toward the men. Neither one of them had time to react. Clack! Clack! Clack! Clack! The four rounds found their target, striking each man twice in the chest. The two men fell to the ground in front of them. Clay turned around, pointing to the tent, and then down the hill, signaling for Bill to make his move to the van. He waited for Bill to exit the tent as he turned back toward the entrance.

* * * * *

Beth watched in horror as the six laughing demons flew above the crowd of people. The demons stopped from time to time and whispered in the worshipers' ears. None of the people in the cave seemed to be able to see the demons except her; their focus was totally on Shimon.

Shimon reverently bent over and kissed the Sacred Scrolls at the head of the altar and then reached down and pulled the skull from the box at his feet. He placed it on the altar just above Allyson's head. He bent back down and removed the skeletal hands and placed them next to Allyson's hands. Reaching back into the box for a third time, he placed the bones of the feet below Allyson's feet. He lifted the dagger from the top of the altar and held it high above his head. As the dagger was raised, the crowd began chanting louder and louder, "Jezebel, our queen … Ba-al, our Lord."

Beth looked up to see five worshipers descending the stairs above her. Tears of joy fell down her cheeks as she saw Clay's face under the hood of the robe-clad man in the front. Clay looked back down at her and held his left hand out low to his body, palm down. Beth quickly turned her eyes away and looked back at Shimon.

Shimon looked up at the east wall and took note of the position of the sunlight, just below the star. He stepped to the right of the altar and stood above Beth, grasping the dagger with both of his hands.

The rescue team reached the bottom of the stairs and slowly started working their way toward the altar along the southern wall. Clay held both his hands together inside the opposing sleeves, with the pistol held tightly in his right hand. He looked down on the floor of the cave and saw boxes of plastic explosives against the wall. Next to the boxes was a canvas bag containing the detonators. He stopped next to the boxes, ensuring the rest of the team would see them.

Looking back toward Beth, Clay saw Shimon kneeling over her, holding the dagger against his chest. He couldn't see the demon that knelt down next to Beth's head snarling at her. The demon bared its teeth as it came within inches of her face, holding its right hand over her chest and slowly lowering it toward her. Its hand disappeared into her chest as it laughed. Beth was trembling with the horror at what she was seeing. She took in a deep breath as she felt her heart tightening from the grip. Her body shook violently with fear as she looked at the snarling apparition just inches from her face glaring down at her. Beth's back arched as the demon tightened the grip further, waiting for the plunge of the dagger.

Amir moved to the right of Clay, as he raised the Uzi under his robe. Shimon shouted loudly, "Ba-al!" as he raised the dagger high over Beth.

Amir pushed the worshipers standing next to him away as he raised the weapon and released a hail of bullets into the air just above Shimon's head. The demon jerked its hand out of Beth's chest and snarled at Amir as it flew to the ceiling, with the other demons following it. The four remaining men produced their weapons and pointed them toward the worshipers as Amir leveled the Uzi toward Shimon.

The enraged crowd slowly started walking toward the five men, testing their resolve. Joshua held the shotgun out toward them. Blam! Blam! The two rounds discharged, sending pellets whizzing above the crowd's heads. The shotgun noise inside an enclosed area had the desired effect, as the crowd slowly moved back.

The six demons flew frantically around the top of the cave, flapping their wings wildly, hissing and snarling. Clay bent down next to Beth as Amir kept the weapon steadily trained on Shimon. He took out the knife from behind his back and ran the blade down between the straps holding her legs bound together and then again between her arms and chest to release them. Beth frantically dug at the wraps with her hands trying to free herself. Joshua handed the shotgun to Moshe and helped Beth to her feet. She stood and pulled the gauze from her mouth, looking toward Allyson. Joshua grabbed her arm and pulled her back between him and Moshe as he pulled a pistol from his belt. Moshe jerked Beth around in front of his face. "Can you cover them?" he shouted. A trembling Beth looked blankly back at him. Moshe shook her violently. "Can you cover them?" he shouted louder. Beth's eyes opened widely as she was forced back into full consciousness. "Yes!"

she responded as she grabbed the pistol from him. Moshe turned his focus back toward the crowd of worshipers as he pointed the shotgun at them.

Clay raised his pistol toward Shimon and sneered as he looked at the man. Shimon slowly backed away to the rear of the altar. He then glanced frantically back and forth from the star on the wall to the altar where Allyson lay. He clutched the dagger tightly in his hands as he held it to his chest.

Clay moved toward the altar and watched as Shimon looked down at Allyson. Douglas and Rebecca stood to the north of the altar and watched Clay as he moved slowly toward Allyson. Douglas cautiously inched his way closer to the altar, trying to get close to Allyson.

"Don't even think about it!" Clay ordered in Hebrew.

Douglas moved back next to Rebecca. Shimon slowly moved the dagger higher. Clay snapped the pistol back toward him. "You're a dead man if you do!" Clay shouted as he moved toward Allyson.

Shimon continued backing as Clay reached the altar. Clay quickly looked back and checked to see if Amir had Shimon covered, and then placed the pistol in his belt. He pulled the robe from his body and gathered Allyson up in his arms. The sunlight reached the star just as Clay turned to walk away. The piercing light flashed into the cave, disorienting everyone. A desperate Shimon lunged at Clay, driving the dagger deep into his back. Amir cried out, "No!" as he watched his friend fall to the floor of the cave. Amir raised the Uzi and emptied the weapons clip into Shimon's chest. His body danced backward as the rounds tore through his robe. Clay cried out in pain and fell forward onto the ground, causing Allyson to tumble to the ground in front of him. Beth reacted first and jumped forward, grabbing her daughter and holding her tight to her chest as she frantically shouted, "Help him—somebody please help him!"

The crowd of worshipers lunged forward as they watched their leader fall. Moshe and Tovi fired into the crowd, spraying bullets into the bodies of the people closest to them. Amir quickly reloaded his weapon and bent down to Clay. He withdrew the dagger from his friend's back as carefully as he could and lifted him to his feet, supporting him with his left arm. He kept his weapon pointed at the crowd as he moved back toward the steps with his friends.

The demons flew down to Douglas and Rebecca, screaming in their ears. The two people walked toward the team, their faces racked with rage at the loss of their leader but with eyes that showed no emotions. Douglas and Rebecca pulled knives from their belts and lunged at them. Moshe raised the shotgun and fired at Douglas. All of the 00 Buck pellets hit him square in the chest, sending his body flying backward. Before he could swing the weapon toward Rebecca, he heard the pistol next to him discharge. He looked to see Beth pointing the Berretta toward Rebecca. The woman's body crumpled to the ground in front of her. As she rolled over onto her back, the last thing she saw was Beth looking down at her with tears of triumph streaming down her cheeks.

Outside the cave, ominous black clouds boiled over the top of the mountain, growing in intensity as lightning began striking the top of the mountain. The team began moving back toward the stairs, pointing their weapons toward the crowd. As they reached the stairs, the bolts of lightning outside the cave struck the mountaintop hard, causing explosions to ring out from the ceiling inside the cave. Everyone clutched their ears in pain and tried to cover themselves from the falling rocks as the ground shook. Before they could recover, a second explosion came from the ceiling. Rocks fell on the crowd as the floor moved beneath their feet. A large rock fell onto the altar, crushing the bones of the queen and breaking the altar into several pieces.

Bill started to move down the stairs to help his friends, when a huge boulder over six feet tall crashed on the steps in front of him, halting his advance. A third explosion from the ceiling rocked the cave, dropping huge boulders on the people below. The worshipers' focus shifted from salvaging the ceremony to saving their lives. The team fought to stay upright as they made their way up the stairs. Joshua led the group, with Amir behind him supporting Clay. Moshe supported Beth as she clutched Allyson close to her chest, with Tovi covering the rear. Joshua reached the boulder that blocked their path. He climbed up on the top of the boulder, placing his back against the wall and bracing his feet against the rock, preparing to pull the others up and over the obstruction. Bill moved down the stairs to Moshe's left side and prepared to help the team from the upper side of the boulder.

Amir dropped the Uzi on the steps and gathered Clay in his arms, preparing to pass him to Joshua.

The ground continued to shake as rocks fell from the ceiling. Amir lifted Clay and passed him to Joshua. Joshua groaned as he dragged Clay over the rock. Bill dropped his pistol and reached out to pull Clay over the rock. Clay struggled to keep his footing as he grew weaker and weaker. He fell to the steps on the other side as Bill gave a final tug at his arm. Bill reached down and picked him up with his good arm. "Come on, Harker, move your ass!" Bill shouted to his friend.

Barely conscious, Clay looked sideways to Bill with blood dripping from his mouth. Bill helped Clay up the remaining twelve steps to the landing and out of the cave to safety.

Still inside the cave on the stairs, Tovi turned toward Moshe. "I'll go next and help with the woman and the girl. You cover the rear."

Tovi reached up towards Joshua. His hand had just touched Joshua's when the steps beneath the boulder gave way. Tovi screamed as he fell to the cavern floor, seventy feet below.

Joshua lunged to his left, grabbing hold of the step above him. He hung from the step by one hand as his feet flailed to find a foothold. Amir stood back as he grunted and jumped the six feet to the far side of the steps. Once he was above Joshua, he reached down and pulled him up to safety. Amir looked down to the cavern floor to see Tovi lying in a pool of blood as rocks from the ceiling fell down on him.

Amir turned back toward Beth. "Beth," he shouted, "you have to throw Allyson to me! Hurry!"

Beth leaned against the wall and lowered Allyson to her waist, preparing to swing her to Amir. She stopped as she looked to see the six demons flying toward Amir and Joshua. The demons flew directly toward Joshua as he stood up behind Amir. She watched in horror as the six demons entered Joshua's body. Unaware of what was happening behind him, Amir shouted at Beth, "Go ahead, throw her to me, Beth. I'll catch her!"

Joshua grabbed Amir from behind and tossed him in the air as if he weighed nothing. Such was the force that Amir's body crumbled on the upper landing behind him like a rag doll. Joshua then turned back toward Beth and Moshe. His eyes were black as coal as he glared at Beth. In a deep and bellowing voice, he growled at her, "The sow stays with us!"

Beth clutched Allyson to her chest as she backed down the stairs. She was horrified to see the faces of the six demons in Joshua's body. Their faces were a ghostly image from inside his chest as they snarled at her. The horrible, unrecognizable voice from Joshua demanded. "Release her at once! Give us the Anointed One!"

Joshua then did the unthinkable. He stretched his hands out to his side as his body slowly rose above the steps and levitated toward Beth.

"No!" Beth screamed as Joshua's body slowly came down on the steps in front of her.

Moshe raised the shotgun toward Joshua. Blam! Blam! Blam! The three blasts from the shotgun rang out from behind Beth. Joshua looked down at his chest as he stood in front of them. Beth looked on in horror as the six demons flew out of his body. He slowly tipped to his side, falling over the edge and down to the cavern floor.

Three explosions rang out from the ceiling in rapid succession, sending enormous amounts of rock falling to the floor below. The remaining worshipers cried out their fears as debris and boulders rained down, crushing most of them. The demons looked up to see a whirlwind forming at the top of the cave. They all looked back at Beth, snarling as they flew into the darkness of the ceiling.

Moshe threw the shotgun to the floor and grabbed Allyson from Beth's arms. He got a running start and jumped across the void. He set Allyson down on the steps above him and turned back toward Beth.

"Hurry!" he shouted at her.

Beth did as Moshe said and also got a running start as she leapt to the safety of his arms. She reached down and grabbed Allyson, pulling her close up to her chest and heading for the cave entrance. Moshe helped a semiconscious Amir to his feet. As Moshe looked down at the cave floor, he saw the whirlwind sweeping through the cavern, gathering the pieces of Jezebel's bones and carrying them up and out of the cave through the now open ceiling. The screams of the worshipers fell silent as they all died from the falling debris. The explosions inside the cave continued as Moshe and Amir reached the outside. The rear of the Mercedes van was open. Moshe lifted Amir up and into the back compartment, where the remainder of the team was waiting. He climbed inside and shouted to Bill, "Go!" The van sped off toward the road as Beth looked back at the camp. She watched as lightning bolts struck the tents, burning them to ash. The whirlwind tore through the camp, blowing the ashes of the structures into the evening sky. A huge lightning bolt above the mountain shot down through the opening at the top of the cavern and struck the explosives on the floor. The detonation rocked the van as it lifted the top of the mountain, sending it crashing back down around the site, covering the site and cavern completely. Bill mashed down on the brakes, sliding the van to a halt. He looked down the road to see the two police SORT vehicles approaching. He exited the van waving his arm and shouted to the men in the first vehicle. "We have badly injured inside the vehicle! We need a paramedic immediately!" He ordered as he ran back to the rear of the van.

Bill climbed into the compartment and knelt down next to Clay. "The medics are coming, Clay—hold on a little longer, bud."

Clay was sitting on the floor with his back against side of the van. He spoke through blood-stained lips. "Too late—for that," he said, coughing between the words. He looked up at Bill, his face and eyes racked with pain, and asked in a weak voice, "Is she safe?"

"Yes, we got her out," Bill said shakily.

Clay looked at Bill and smiled. He whispered toward his friend, but Bill couldn't hear what he was saying, so he leaned down close to Clay's lips as he heard the last words from his friend.

Bill sat back on his heels with tears streaming from his eyes. He placed his hand on Clay's eyelids and closed them. Amir sitting across from him, cried loudly as he looked at Clay, pulling at the hair on his head. Beth sobbed as she rocked back and forth with Allyson in her lap.

The paramedic jumped into the van and looked at Bill. Bill looked back, slowly moving his head side to side. Wiping the tears from his eyes on the sleeve of his good arm, Bill could only stare at the body of his long-time friend. Then he turned toward Beth who was sobbing uncontrollably at his side trying to comprehend what she was saying to him. "They killed Gary, Bill—and now Clay is gone too!"

Bill placed his hand on her shoulder and looked deep into her eyes. "No, sweetie, Gary's in the hospital. He's hurt badly, but it looks like he's going to pull through."

Beth rolled her head back, afraid to believe what she was hearing and now sobbing tears of joy for her husband as well as sorrow for her friend. Moshe stood inside the rear of the van looking back at the clouds of dust and smoke coming from the mountain, as he thought of his two colleagues. As they all grieved at the loss of their friends, the soft voice came up from Beth's lap.

"Mommy, why are you crying?"

Bill and Beth looked down at Allyson to see her awake in front of them. Beth smiled down at her little girl. "I'm crying because you're okay, honey."

"Can we go home now, Mommy?" Allyson asked in a slightly dazed voice.

"Yes, we can, baby. We can finally go home."

The cost of this day had been horrific, and the pain of their losses would be felt for a long time. This was now the time for mourning. But as always, life for the living eventually goes on.

CHAPTER 31

A HERO'S FAREWELL

THE NOONDAY SUN SHONE brightly down through a cloudless sky and onto the grounds of the Oak Hill Cemetery in Georgetown. First opened in 1865, the historic burial grounds are home to many of Washington's past political and military elite from the eighteen hundreds. Burial plots at the cemetery have long been taken, with the only ones remaining from old family plots that had been purchased decades earlier. Clay's family had passed the remaining four of the family plots down to him through his great grandfather. Burial plots were something Clay and Mary had not wanted to deal with for many years, but held onto them for that one inevitable day they knew would eventually come. Neither of them could have known they would be occupied so soon. The beautifully groomed and historic grounds had captivated Mary from the moment she saw them, some twenty-five years earlier. She had made her request that she and Clay be buried beside each other in two of the plots, and leave the other two open for their children, if and when they were born. The four plots were located by a granite walkway, under one of the many beautiful trees on the grounds, and protected by a three-foot hedge behind them.

The small group of people in the cemetery stood silent as Reverend Martin Ward addressed them. The fifty-two-year-old African American pastor spoke softly as his eyes panned through the small gathering of people, making contact with each of them. Clay's grave resided just inches from the graves of his wife and daughter. Although the two caskets were empty, Clay had always wanted to have something that reminded him of his family resting next to him when his time ultimately came.

Gary sat in his wheelchair next to Beth and Allyson as he listened to the eulogy. They had only returned to the states a week earlier, after his release from the hospital. Still weak from his wounds, he demanded to fly to Washington for the funeral of the man who had helped them so much. Allyson sat in Beth's lap as she stared blankly at the casket, with Amir and Bill behind them.

Allyson had remembered nothing of the ordeal in Northern Israel, and spoke only of being with her parents, Dr. Clay, and Dr. Bill at the hotel in Jerusalem. The sightings of "birdmen" had stopped immediately after she left the cave. Although she remembered seeing the demons, she had little recognition of what they looked like. Her conversations and interactions with Beth and Gary since she had returned home had become those of the normal seven-year-old little girl they had hoped and prayed for. Gary and Beth were looking forward to seeing their daughter enroll in school and play with friends in the neighborhood. Normalcy had returned to the Carter house, to the joy of all its occupants.

The U.S. Army Honor Guard stood at the ready by the foot of the casket as Reverend Ward addressed the mourners. "There is only one way in which we enter this world, and yet literally thousands by which we may depart. Clay departed this world giving the ultimate sacrifice. May we always honor and remember that selfless gift he so freely gave. Each of us is cradled in the Lord's loving arms as we leave to reside with him in his kingdom. His perfect love heals all our pain and suffering as he wipes the tears from our eyes. Clay lived so very long with the pain of losing his wife and daughter tragically. Their young lives were struck down many years before their time, but we should take solace in the knowledge that he is now with them and has peace as he holds them in his arms."

Reverend Ward closed his Bible and stepped back, his hands clasped in front of him. The three volleys of shots rang out and echoed through the cemetery, honoring the fallen soldier. The Honor Guard moved down each side of the casket and lifted the flag, folding it slowly and reverently. The captain walked to Bill and bent down offering the folded flag to him. "On behalf of the President of the United States, a grateful nation, and a proud army, accept this flag in recognition of your friend's honorable and faithful service to his country." Bill tried in vain to hold back the tears as he reached out to accept the flag.

The attendees watched as the casket was lowered into the grave. Amir stood and walked to the grave after the casket reached the bottom. He bent down and gathered a handful of dirt, slowly sprinkling it on the casket.

Bill stepped to the casket and choked the words out. "Good-bye, bud. I'll see you on the other side."

They all walked toward the reverend. "Martin, thank you so very much for speaking here today," Bill said gratefully.

"You're more than welcome, Bill. I was always sorry that he didn't come to any of the services after Mary and Jody died, but I certainly understood why he didn't. Their deaths hit him very hard."

"Yes, they did. No one loved his family more than Clay."

Martin looked down at Allyson. "I'm so very glad I had a chance to meet you, Allyson. Mister Monroe has told me so much about you." He gently placed his hand on her head.

Allyson smiled back at him. "Thank you, sir."

Martin held his hand out toward Gary and Beth. "Thank you for attending, Mr. and Mrs. Carter."

"You're very welcome. We would never have missed this service, Reverend. Clay gave us our daughter back. We could never repay such a gift," Gary replied solemnly.

Martin shook their hands. "If there is anything I can ever do, please don't hesitate to contact me," he said as he turned and walked from the gravesite.

Beth looked toward the casket and spoke softly to Bill. "It's so very sad to see so few people here to say good-bye to him."

"That's the way he would have wanted it, Beth. Clay's whole life was centered on Mary and Jody. They were all he cared about. I always felt honored to be included in his life; so few outside of Mary and Jody were."

Beth then moved next to Bill and wrapped both her arms around his left arm. "Bill, I've been meaning to ask you, what was it that Clay whispered to you in the truck before he died?" she asked.

"It was Latin. *Nunc dimittus. Mei opus perfectus.*"

"What does it mean?"

"They were the words that Thomas Jefferson was reputed to have said just before he died. 'Now you may dismiss me. My work is done.'"

Beth cried as she heard the words. "What a good man he was."

Allyson looked up at Beth. "Mommy, don't cry. Dr. Clay is happy now."

Surprised at Allyson's words, Beth knelt down next to her daughter. "Why do you say that, honey?"

"Because he's with his family."

"That's right, baby," Beth answered her daughter with a smile.

As Bill pushed Gary's wheelchair, the group slowly moved down the path from the gravesite toward the car. As Beth looked toward Bill, she spoke very earnestly, "Bill, I can't tell you how relieved I am that Allyson no longer sees the demons. It was literally the most horrifying thing I had ever experienced—and I only saw them for a very short time. It terrorizes me to think that Allyson had to live with that every day of her life. Gary was right. We have our daughter back from that nightmare, and we have you and Clay to thank for it."

"You're most welcome, Beth, but Clay was the one that the Lord used, not me. But you're right. It's over now, and the healing can begin."

Gary raised his hand toward Bill inquiringly. "But there is still one question that we never answered. We never found out why the demons were afraid of Allyson."

"From what we could surmise, it wasn't because she was the Anointed One, because Beth saw them briefly as well. I suspect that it was because the Lord was protecting her. Perhaps we will never know, only that the Lord's will was accomplished," Bill responded.

As they walked to the car, Allyson turned around to look back toward the grave. She smiled as she saw the angel standing next to the grave smiling back at her.

Acknowledgments

No author writes a book alone, and such was the case with this one. From the bottom of my heart, I would like to thank the following friends and colleagues, who helped me to get my dream onto paper. Ginger Blythe for her incredible editing skills. Eileen Cornwell and Bill Omnes, for countless hours of technical assistance. The Stanley Pappas family, Brent Eisen, Ann Maher, Sherrie Yellico, Stella Falconer and Douglas Riesman for your skills, friendship and tolerance throughout the process. To the people throughout my life that provided me with positive role models through their heroic accomplishments in the face of adversity. And lastly, to the lovely and gracious Claire, without whose belief in me, this project could never have gotten off the ground. I love you two weeks.